Other Novels By Carol Craig

From The Tapestry Fantasy Series:

Dancing the Loom
Threading the Loom
Restoring the Loom

Southern Historical Novels:

The Vast In Between
The Great Unraveling

The Mending Warrior Series:

A Thousand Bits of Wonderful
A Walk in the Dark

The Tapestry Series:

Restoring the Loom, the third installment in the Tapestry Series, starts with a bang and, like a windstorm of starlings, keeps the reader madly flipping pages all the way to the end. Carol Craig has done a masterful job, her imagery and world-building first rate. Whether it's a Malaysian Frogmouth who wears the expression of a "taciturn old man," or a character named Tempestous whose "dress simmers hot coals of distress," I loved each and every one of these wild and wooly beings! I would love to see this become a movie.

- Laine Stambaugh, Author of Raven Wakes the Dawn and Raven in the Runes. Watch for her upcoming novel, The Sea Raven

In an age when we feel besieged by crises on every hand, we turn to fantasy novels with increasing regularity. These novels provide a welcome means of escape. They also allow us to win victories over injustices and suffering through the grit, integrity, and cleverness of their heroes. Restoring the Loom by Carol L. Craig is this kind of unforgettable story. You will love the magic of the loom. It will restore your faith that all things are possible for those whose hearts are pure and whose loyalty and perseverance in pursuing their dreams never waver.

- Evan Howard, Author of The Galilean Secret

"Restoring the Loom," the third installment in Carol Craig's enthralling series, is a riveting fantasy adventure that keeps readers on the edge of their seats. This time, Brigid and Henry find themselves in deep trouble when a magical thread woven into Brigid's loom plunges the world into darkness.

From the very first page, Craig's storytelling prowess shines through. The plot is both intricate and compelling, filled with unexpected twists and turns that make it hard to put the book down. The palpable tension between Brigid and Henry adds depth to their characters, making their journey not just a quest to save the world, but also a personal struggle for redemption and trust.

The kingdom, now suspicious of Brigid's actions, adds a layer of political intrigue and urgency to their mission. As Brigid, Henry, and their loyal companions embark on their perilous journey, they face the menacing threat of shape-shifting magical animals from the underworld, who are determined to maintain the shroud of darkness. These villains are cunning and formidable, creating a sense of imminent danger that heightens the stakes.

One of the standout features of "Restoring the Loom" is its richly developed characters. Brigid, with her inner strength and vulnerability, and Henry, with his steadfast loyalty and bravery, are characters that readers will root for. The supporting cast, too, is vibrant and adds depth to the narrative, each bringing their unique strengths and quirks to the fore.

Craig's world-building is exceptional, painting vivid landscapes and crafting a magical realm that feels both wondrous and perilous. The action scenes are described with such precision that readers can almost feel the clash of swords and the pulse of magic in the air. The balance between action and quieter, character-driven moments is masterfully handled, allowing for a well-paced and engaging read.

"Restoring the Loom" is a testament to Carol Craig's ability to weave a spellbinding tale that captures the imagination. It's a story of courage, friendship, and the enduring fight between light and darkness. Fans of the series will not be disappointed, and new readers will find themselves quickly drawn into this magical world. This book is a page-turner in the truest sense, filled with suspense, heart, and an unrelenting sense of adventure.

- Julie Demos, Author of Blood Moon

Restoring the Loom

A Novel by

Carol Craig

For those of you who constantly strive
to make the world a better place, I salute you.
For all the rest, let's bring back joy to our world,
and care for nature and all that we have been blessed with.

1

It is said that great men never die. Did the same go for great women, or was that an honor bestowed only upon men? I wondered, as I stood at my bedroom window, staring out at the darkness like I had every morning since the gloom had taken hold.

All around me I could see lanterns. Lanterns moving to and fro amid the orchard. Lanterns in the kitchen to work by. Even the liverymen had lanterns. It was as if the lanterns had taken on a life of their own. I had come to expect them. But despite all the havoc the darkness caused, I found peace in the darkness too, as it sheltered me from prying eyes.

Even the traditions, those most odious of punishments bestowed on anyone who stepped out of line, seemed less harsh, as though they couldn't find me in the darkness. People talked less, interacted less. Perhaps that's why the traditions had seen fit to relax their quarter because we were all sufficiently divided and conquered.

Alone.

Though my standing at the window each morning might be seen as penitence for what I had so unwittingly wrought, it was none of that. Instead, it was my one time of the day to see Henry, who had been strictly forbidden from seeing me since I had so unceremoniously threaded the loom, which had then thrust the entire kingdom into darkness. I closed my eyes, ruing that day, that decision. That stupid, stupid mistake. If only I could take it back, I thought, my heart hammering in my chest as it did everytime I recalled it.

I was so lost in self-pity that I almost missed Henry, but fortunately I opened my eyes just as he was about to depart without waving as he did most days. We had even begun to develop hand signals to denote "I love you." (Two hands over our hearts.) "I miss you." (Head cocked to one side.)

This time the hand signal seemed more urgent, as though he were trying to convey something. Something awful. I placed my hands against the cold panes of the window and rested my forehead against the glass, willing myself to understand. Then I saw what he was trying to convey as he used his hands to describe a big explosion, but did he mean a physical explosion, or that someone had finally lost it and was ready to tear me to shreds? At that precise moment, I wished I was a mind reader.

I peered over at the loom, which foretold the future. Or at least it *had* until that awful day when I had weaved threads into it, given to me by Beatrice. Had she known what would happen when she'd gifted them to me? Or would it come as much of a surprise to her as it had to me, Brigid, former scullery maid? Greatest fool of all time!

Enough wallowing. I needed to find out what Henry had up his sleeve. I made hand signals for him to wait. If we were caught together, I would surely take a beating, but right now I didn't care. I just wanted to see him, touch his face, his hands, kiss his lips, his forehead. But I would have to be careful.

I flew down the stairs, bypassing Lady Bookbinder who was headed down the hallway, then flung myself into the study and hid behind the damask drapes until she passed. When I felt certain she was gone, I rushed once again into the hallway and into an alcove that led to a side door where I slowly twisted the knob so that the noise wouldn't give me away. I crept outside, careful not to draw attention to myself amid the predawn gloom. After that, I felt my way along the brick siding until I reached the corner of the building. Henry, who had been looking up at the window, searched either side of the manor to see if he had missed me somehow.

"Over here!" I hissed.

I threw my arms around him and we kissed as though we hadn't seen each other in years, though truthfully, it had been less than a week since we'd last ferreted ourselves away for some private time together where we whispered, so as not to be overheard in the darkness. We had found a spot down by the river, an old snag, divided in two at the base with just enough space for two enterprising young people to find refuge against the storms of our lives. We fled there now, eager to seek each other out, to speak like two human beings, unrepressed by the evil traditions.

I stopped to kiss him once more, then finally came up for air. "What's happened, Henry, tell me?"

"It's bad, Brigid," he said. "Really bad."

Though my heart sank, I listened with relish, for his was the only news I heard these days. Most days were spent trapped inside my room as though under house arrest.

"Alaric is back."

"Back? But how? I thought he was dead, that Birsha and Beatrice were to rule the kingdom."

"We all did," Henry said with something akin to dread. "But somehow he was released from the curse and is no longer locked inside the globe. Agnold and Pietra, Birsha's half-brothers, have fled the kingdom, but Birsha has stayed, though he no longer is in control. His father is, and now that he has freedom to move, he's planning an attack on our kingdom."

Alaric, preparing an attack?

"What will we do?" I cried as we made our way through the darkness to the oak snag and our secret hideaway.

"I don't know, especially with this darkness. It's a distinct disadvantage." The waning moon that was about to set on the western horizon lit one side of his face.

"I'm so sorry, Henry," I said for perhaps the thousandth time. "I wish I could fix it, if only I knew how."

"You can't keep letting it eat at you, Brigid. This wasn't your fault."

"But everyone *thinks* it is," I said, bitterly.

Henry stopped walking and turned to face me. "Listen to me, Brigid." He peered into my odd colored eyes, said to look like the compressed blue gas from an iceberg. He had long since quit thinking of them as remarkable, despite the fact that they sent shards of blue light flashing amid the inky void that we all reluctantly accepted. "You are *not* responsible for this. You didn't know what the outcome would be. You didn't do this out of malice."

I nodded because he was right. Never would I have sewn those beautiful threads into my magic loom had I known that it would thrust our kingdom into darkness. I had meant to do good. But as the old saw went, "No good deed goes unpunished." And I had been punished in spades. Madame Bookbinder was barely speaking to me. My good friend Emma, and Thomas, Henry's brother, avoided me at all costs, but when we did come in contact, I read the pity in their eyes which was worse than any punishment. And everyone else spoke my name like a curse and shunned me so that I had escaped to my chambers, where I sat like a prisoner doing penance. Even my rare blue falcon, Phinney, seemed to avoid me, though truthfully, I had no doubt pushed her away with my sullenness.

At last, we reached the snag where we wedged our way into its heart-shaped trunk, made so by a particularly harsh lightning storm near the turn of the previous century, according to legend.

Once there, Henry cradled me in his arms, making me feel whole again. As if I weren't the "foreign devil" that some were calling me, though I was just as much a part of the Bookbinder Kingdom as any of them, maybe more so. My parents had once been upstanding members of the community, both well respected and well loved. That's before they had invested a fortune in mills only to see their fortunes disappear overnight, swindled out of their money by those in power intent on lining their own pockets. As a result, my family had floated away like so much cottonwood, all in different directions.

Now, I was on my own again, except for Henry. He was all I had, and as such, I couldn't get enough of the feel of him, of the very smell of him. I squeezed in tighter, wishing he would never let me go, that he would keep his promise to me before this whole fiasco had started . . . to be by my side forever.

"I love you, Henry Bookbinder."

"I love you too, Brigid Anne Dunsmore." He kissed the top of my head as I rested it against his shoulder.

For several delicious moments, we sat like that, reveling in the feel of each other, of *being* together, but I knew it couldn't last. If Alaric was on the move, my women warriors would need to be ready. But how? And did they feel about me as some did? Believe that I had purposely thrust us into chaos? How could they? Surely they knew me better than that.

"The women love you," Henry said, as though reading my heart, which he knew so well. "They know you would never do anything to hurt them or the kingdom. You, of all people, should know that by now."

He lifted my chin to force me to look into his eyes. Though I had tried to be stoic, had tried to pretend that the words I'd heard spoken while in the kitchen, gathering my meals each day, hadn't hurt me. But they had. For weeks now, I'd had a knot in the back of my throat that ached with raw emotion. How I longed to cry, to scream, to stamp my feet like a small child. To beg their forgiveness, but there was none to be had. And I knew it. For now, I was *persona non grata*.

"Brigid, we have to find a way out of this—to bring back

the light. To call the women together and come up with a plan. It could become ugly and it could happen soon. Our spies have warned us for days now that Alaric is on the move."

I had only to recall the giant Chessmen he'd set against our people, or the many plagues including the jewel beetle, those most insidious of pests that had reigned terror on Egyptians, causing disease and famine. Or the storm that had stomped in with feet too large for our poor villages, picking up houses and thrusting them aside as if they were mere pebbles to be tossed by some petulant child.

"But how? How do we bring back the light?"

For days I had thought of nothing else. I had plowed through the library, torch in hand, searching out any book that might help. But none provided aid, our experience unique.

I slumped back against the bowed trunk, my head resting on an overly large knot in the tree. A leaf had fallen and landed on my arm. Absent-mindedly, I twisted it around and around in my hand. Then I saw it. Somehow, the stem of the leaf had bent in on itself as though the stem had been sewn into the leaf.

"How very odd," I said, pulling the stem out of the leaf as though sewing in reverse.

As a child, I tried my hand at knitting more than once, but I had been a poor learner indeed. Until finally my mother, exasperated at how I kept dropping stitches and asking her to redo them, simply pulled the stitches out and said, "Maybe I should teach you another skill."

I laughed now, at the memory. How dull she must have thought me.

"What are you laughing about?" Henry rubbed the back of

my hand with his thumb.

I recounted my poor workmanship and how my mother had tired of repairing my many flops. "She constantly had to remove the stitches and redo them."

"What did you say?" Henry sat up.

"I said she had to remove the stitches." A tingling began in my scalp, ran down my back and finished in my toes. "That's it, Henry! Why did I never think of it before? Of course."

I jumped to my feet and began running as Henry struggled to keep up. No sooner had I made it halfway across the wide lawn than I heard a sharp retort. "Brigid! What are you doing here, and with Henry?"

Lady Bookbinder!

In the light of her lantern, I could see by the scowl on her face that she was none too happy, but I couldn't be stopped. Not now, not when I was within reach of a possible solution to my dilemma.

"Later, Lady Bookbinder." I sidestepped her when she ran to meet me. "I'm on a mission, aren't I Henry?"

"That you are, Brigid," Henry said with a laugh. Then to his mother he added, "I'll explain it to you soon, but for now I want to be with Brigid. She's going to bring back the light!"

Then he raced to catch up with me, and together we entered the manor, through the front door this time. I said a quick prayer beneath my breath as we took the stairs two at a time. Now to see if our plan would work.

Birsha felt a rising panic. Two days. That's all it had taken to wreak havoc on his nation. From where he sat perched upon the parapet, as he gazed below to where Alaric stood commanding the troops to ready for battle, Birsha felt his gorge rise. Yet again, he had been tossed aside, none of his opinions or ideas mattering in the least. He pulled at his black goatee that he had braided and oiled, his eyes never leaving his father, who was even now strutting back and forth among the front lines of men, each in battle gear. They wore black chitinous, crenelated exoskeletons with burgundy shoulder, elbow, and knee pads, their helmets sporting both colors. The skin on Birsha's back and neck prickled at the sight. He had been so intent on watching the spectacle below that he hadn't realized someone had come up behind him until he felt a tap on his shoulder.

He pivoted around, and exhaled in relief to see that it was

only Beatrice. "Announce yourself, next time you surprise me like that," he said, his heart racing like a thoroughbred just out of the gate.

"So sorry." Beatrice reached an arm around his waist and held him tight. "This is hard for you, isn't it?" She motioned with her chin toward the now freed ruler. "To give up what you just started."

"You can't possibly imagine." He leaned down to kiss her forehead, regretting how crass that sounded.

Though not in her finery, as she had been when he'd met her at the New Year's gala in a diaphanous gown with butterflies fluttering about her, Beatrice was still as lovely as the day he'd met her. *Silky black hair done in light curls. Skin the color of porcelain.* The two of them matched, as though sewn together, he with his black hair and widow's peak, not to mention pale skin, despite his years spent outdoors. Even their clothing complemented each other. Today she wore a plain burgundy dress, as all nobles must wear, now that Alaric was once again in charge. Birsha wore a black tail coat and burgundy leggings with black brigand boots. He peered down at them with a moue of disgust. He was beginning to hate the colors burgundy and black.

"What will you do?" Beatrice turned to him and laid a hand on his chest.

He bent her way. "What do you mean?"

"Your father is to attack the Bookbinders and all they hold dear. He has usurped your place as ruler. Don't you feel the least bit—"

"Frightened?" Birsha hadn't meant for the word to come

popping out of his mouth, but there it was and he could no more take it back than eat his words.

Beatrice hesitated, then nodded her head, for he could see that she, too, was as frightened as he. Now that Alaric had returned, Birsha was not only no longer needed, he was no longer *wanted*. A mere obstacle to Alaric's ever growing power. Soon, Alaric would find a way to rid the kingdom of the heir, Birsha felt certain. But how? Would he simply send him away until needed, or . . .

Birsha stiffened. Beatrice must have felt it because she clasped his hand and gave it a squeeze. He had been right to marry her. Right to believe that she truly loved him, even though she was from the Bookbinder clan. He wondered why his father hated them so. Nothing he could recall from childhood, when his nanny had taken him to stay with them for a summer, should have caused such enmity. They were good people. He could see that now.

Just then he heard a rustle and turned, his heart leaping in his throat, for it was the Kazakh, the falconer said to set his birds upon unsuspecting victims, or at least that was the legend that had been fostered throughout the kingdom.

He came to stand beside Birsha. Though a man of few words, he stared down at the growing military campaign and said, "So it begins, eh?"

All Birsha could do was nod.

I set my hand to work at untying the threads of my precious loom that I had so ignominiously woven into the fabric, thinking it a gift of Beatrice's rather than the curse it had come to be. Again, I wondered if Beatrice had known what she was giving me. Yet despite my reservations about her, I couldn't believe she would do something so vile as to give me thread that would help destroy our kingdom. After all, without daylight, we couldn't grow crops, couldn't eat, couldn't survive. That thought, more than any other, set up a fierce anger growing inside me, and yet I knew hatred had led to the destruction that I witnessed at the hands of Alaric. I closed my eyes and took a cleansing breath before continuing.

"You can do this," Henry said, his beautiful brown eyes taking me in. He gave a nod of encouragement.

I squeezed his hand, then continued the task, uncertain how the loom would react to said removal of the beautiful silk threads. I could only hope that it was as eager as I to be rid of the hideous threads.

Slowly, carefully, I began to pull, as Henry held up his lantern so that I might choose the correct threads to remove. At the first tug, I heard a twang, like the strings of a lyre being tested for sound. I pulled a little more, but each time I pulled, the sound grew louder, more harried, as though the loom or the threads were protesting their departure. But I couldn't stop now. I had to rid the kingdom of this terrible curse.

"Take your time," Henry urged.

Still, I could see that he was in just as big a hurry as I to cast the thread and the evil it represented aside. Burn it, bury it, whatever it took to be free of the curse that was destroying our kingdom.

My hands shook, as I didn't know what would happen.

I only knew I must continue. But as I did, the loom began to shudder. The sparks reappeared against the blackened loom, as it had when I'd first woven the thread into the loom. Soon, I felt it singe the backs of my hands, but still I pressed on.

As I prepared to remove the final thread, the sparks began swirling throughout the room and I heard the stage lights come on, bringing about a faint glimmer of light that had everyone around the kingdom gasping, or at least those downstairs.

I prayed silently. *God be with me.*

As if the final threads had heard my prayer, they began to fight back, to surge inward toward my loom, but I pulled with all my might, Henry helping too. I had them nearly out when I heard another "Thwump" as the second set of stage lights turned back on, or at least it sounded that way to me.

"You can do it, Brigid." Henry moved my raven-colored hair aside so that he could see the loom better.

"This is it," I said. "Be ready."

"One, two, three, pull!" we said in unison.

It took the two of us tugging and sweating, but at last the final thread popped out with an explosion of fury that rocked me back on my feet and sent me flying through the air, only to skid across the room and into a wall, my hands blackened from the effort. The room lit up in sparks that flew in a circle twice before exiting the room through the open window.

The final "Thwump" resounded and I could see the sun rising out the window. Henry and I turned to each other and let out a cry of both joy and relief. We had done it. We had saved the kingdom from a slow death. Tears came unheeded, and I felt certain this time there would be no repercussions, or at least I hoped not.

Cries rang out throughout the kingdom. In the distance, I heard cannon fire announcing the joy of all those who had lived under the tyranny of darkness and corruption.

"You did it!" Henry cried.

"*We* did it," I amended. "Thank you, Henry. For sticking with me these past several months."

Few had been so gracious. Only my army of women had stood by me, or at least that's what Emma had told me, she who had enjoyed the freedoms of travel that I had not during these trying times.

I peered at the door, hesitant to go downstairs and face everyone. At least in the darkness, I could only hear the backhanded comments, but now I would see by people's expressions what they thought of me. Some, I knew, would forgive me, realize that I hadn't known such a horrible fate would occur by sewing in the beautiful thread that Beatrice had given me as a parting gift when I had left her behind at the fortress. Some would find me suspect. But I had done everything in my power to help, not hurt our kingdom, and though others might not be so merciful, at least *I* knew the truth of who I was. As such, I held my head high.

"Are you ready to go downstairs?" Henry said, though I knew the trepidation he must see written on my face.

"As ready as ever," I said, my shoulders slumping.

"But first," Henry said, turning me to face him once more, "know that I love you. And Brigid?"

"Yes?"

"You are perhaps the bravest person I know."

My throat constricted and hot tears flowed down my cheeks. I quickly swiped at them, hoping that none would be the wiser, and especially those of the onerous "traditions" that allowed for no weakness of any kind. None. And certainly not tears of compassion, loss, or sadness. Those brought down the greatest wrath of all. Survival of the fittest and all.

"So? Ready to face the Bookbinder clan?"

I paused for only a moment, then nodded. I took one last swipe at my tears, then opened the door to my future.

"We can't be complacent."

"What do you propose we do? Alaric is loose again and not nearly as easy to control as Birsha," Tempestous said, her fiery moire dress giving the underground chamber a decidedly red glow.

Queen of the Mammals sat at the head of the floating table, her place card a fiction that she had designed so that if any were to find the chamber, she would not be implicated. Tempestous had always wondered how such a simple looking girl could harbor such strength and cunning. She was the perfect foil, with her mousey brown hair and her human-like manners. No one would have ever guessed that she was a mutant, half human, half monster, her exterior appearing the former, her interior, definitely the latter. If Birsha would have looked more closely, he would have seen how she treated her animals. Word had scattered around that she was kind to her animals, but anyone in the know would have seen it for the fantasy it was.

"We *must* be proactive," The Queen of Mammals hissed.

"We have to seize control of the helm from Alaric, while still attacking the Bookbinder Kingdom, the easternmost outpost of Castle Kreg. There can be no other way if we are to rule, and we all agree that this is what we want, yes?"

A murmur arose among the members of what were known as the Diamōns, an ancient word for demons. Tempestous held tight to her emotions, not daring to contradict the Queen of Mammals. She peered around the table at all the other miscreants. Most were not from the Council, all except Chame Leon and Liz Herd. They were the lone exceptions. No, these monsters, or Vidunders as the elves preferred to call them, were the elite forces of the aglæca. These five were much larger than the rest, so easily visible above ground. That's why they only moved at night, and usually with an invisibility cloak.

Tempestous ticked them off one by one. Samael, the Angel of Death, looked like no other angel Tempestous had ever seen. He was cloaked in a crenelated black suit of armor that reminded one of a crustacean, only his head was like that of a rhino with a sleek black tusk. Next to him, sat Raksha, a shapeshifting monster who could move more easily among those in the upper world, as she could change into virtually anything of her choosing. At this moment, she chose to be a frilled lizard and continually fanned out her blue throat to make herself appear more ominous and to intimidate those around her. Tempestous was thankful that she hadn't been forced to sit by her.

Jinn was a shapeshifter of a different sort, because although he couldn't change his appearance and he looked quite large and masculine, he floated between good and evil. One never knew what one was getting with him, in his long, flowing white gowns like that of a Bedouin. Yet he could readily change clothes, thus making it easy for him to move above ground as well.

The last two were Belial and Astaroth, the first a personification of The Devil himself, and in fact Belial did look quite devilish, with a round red face and pointy ears, and a large snout like that of a mole rat. She, of all the monsters, had a hard time moving above ground. Whereas Astaroth was the Great Duke of Hell who appeared as a hologram that showed him amid burning flames. The two seemed always to be together. For the first time since Tempestous had joined the Council, she felt out of her league, as though her gift was nothing but poor man's fare. She would do well to keep a low profile. And yet it was too late to back out. They would perceive her as a traitor if so. Her dress simmered hot coals of distress, but the best she could do was to contain her true feelings for now.

"So, it is agreed. We must find a way to eliminate Alaric . . . again. And Birsha."

A murmur of excitement arose like so many cinnabar moths. But Tempestous only cringed. What lengths would the Queen of Mammals go to eliminate her opponents? And who among them would perish next?

Back in Battersbog, Winnifred gasped as she both heard and saw the light of the sun switch on. She jumped up from her work table in the space where the new barn would be in the coming year. In the meantime, she had managed no more than a lean-to to keep her covered from the weather so that she could still work on her many inventions she had planned. She wished her fingers were as nimble as her mind, as she had any number of inventions rolling around in her head. And Lofgren, her half-elf, half human companion hadn't helped. Instead, he'd offered multiple ideas of his own.

She peered over at her green-tinged friend with his pointy ears, dressed in brown corduroy pants and a green vest over a loose white linen shirt. He let out a whoop of joy when the sun emerged from the curse-induced darkness. As if one, the two ran together and he lifted her up in his arms and spun her around before setting her down. For a moment afterward, her heart beat in her chest and she wondered if it was love she was feeling or something else. She had never been in love . . . until now.

"Brigid did it!" Winnifred cried. "She saved us from the curse!"

"How do you know it was her?" Lofgren pushed her short brown hair past her ear and gazed into green eyes that matched his own.

"It has to be," she gushed. "I just knew she would find a way." Then on an impulse she added, "Can we go see her? I miss her. I miss all the women, the excitement of being on the road. I love to invent, don't get me wrong," she added, "but—"

"But?"

Lofgren cocked his head to one side. When he did that, it always reminded Winnifred of a Corgi she'd once seen in a painting by a Welsh artist, where one ear went up, the other drooped down. Winnifred had been immensely pleased when Lofgren had asked to come live with her. Not as husband and wife, at least not yet, but as her friend and companion. Yet in the days prior, he had become so much more than that and she felt herself melding into him just as they had mind melded in their campaign at the fortress, a campaign that had spared countless lives of both his people and hers.

"We can go to the manor," he said, "on one condition."

"Oh?" She frowned, not sure she liked this. He had never given her stipulations before, always allowing her independence, which she fought so hard to maintain.

"A kiss." His green eyes pierced hers, and they held a promise. A promise of so much more.

She swallowed hard, then licked her lips to moisten them and to buy herself time. She had been wanting him to kiss her since the day she'd met him, but knew it would be entirely inappropriate to even think it, much less ask. And yet here he was, asking *her*.

"I think I could manage that," she said, hoping she didn't sound coy.

But she needn't have worried, for if he had thought her coy, he didn't let on. Instead he bent down and kissed her full on the mouth. She savored the taste of him, the sheer manliness. Her heart stuttered in her chest until she was forced to come up for air. She gulped it in like a drowning woman, only to see the glint in his eye, the hint of mirth on the thin set of his lips.

She tapped him playfully on the shoulder. "Oh you! Well, we had better saddle up Jeter—" But before she could finish her sentence, Lofgren moved at warp speed, returning only moments later with a completely saddled horse. All Winnifred could do was laugh.

"I'll have to be careful what I say in the future. Alright

then," she said, reaching in for one last kiss. "All I have to do is pack," But she needn't have mentioned it because he opened the side saddles and showed her everything he had crammed together for their journey. Winnifred shook her head. "You're amazing, Lofgren."

If I had hoped that everything would be forgiven, I was horribly mistaken because when I entered the grand room at the base of the stairs everyone was rejoicing. Until they saw me. Then a silence ensued that found me sweating despite the early hour.

It was Madame Bookbinder who broke the silence. "Good morning, Brigid . . . Henry. Did you have anything to do with this?" She peered around as though the light were a thing that she could grasp with her hands.

Before I could speak, Henry came forward, palming my hand in his in support. "Brigid untied the threads from the loom."

He held up my arm to show the lengths at which I had gone to restore order to the kingdom. A collective gasp rippled throughout the room. And indeed, my entire arm was black where what felt like a jolt of lightning had shot through me, singing me a deep onyx. Even now, my head spun from the jolt, which had tossed me across the room like a rag doll.

"Oh my," Madame Bookbinder said. "We'd best put a potion on that."

At that moment, Chaunce, one of the downstairs maids entered and curtseyed.

"Just the person we were looking for. Could you please go have Sally put a salve on Brigid's wounds?"

With that, I was released into the downstairs chambers where I soon found a seat next to Sally, a tall woman with a long face all dressed in white. Her eyes seemed perennially sad, despite her cheery demeanor.

"So, they're calling you a hero now," she said as she poured hydrogen peroxide over the wound, then covered it in a thick salve.

"Me?" I squeaked, shocked at the turnaround.

"Well, some are. Others are . . ." She allowed the words to trail off as though fearful that she'd said too much.

"Others think me less than heroic?"

"That would be putting it mildly," Chaunce said, having stood by to eye Sally's ministrations.

"Hush!" Sally admonished. "You're always running off at the mouth." Then to me, she said, "Chaunce is young. Ignore her."

But how could I? I flinched as Sally wrapped me like a mummy. Well, at least my arm, that is. I had heard what I had heard. Besides, the whispers and rumors of a manor house eventually found their target, and since I'd had a bullseye on my back from the day I arrived, I had become accustomed to it, if not inured to all the infighting.

Just then, I heard a commotion upstairs that seemed to be making its way in my direction. What a surprise when five minutes later I heard the words "knock knock" and Winnifred and Lofgren popped in. Despite their obvious differences—Winnifred with her short brown hair and studious face, and Lofgren with his slight green tinge and elfin ears—something about them gelled. It was as if they were two sides of a half-penny and I couldn't help but smile to see them here.

"What happened to you?" Winnifred cried, rushing over to inspect my arm.

I held it up, to which Sally admonished me with the words, "Sit still until I'm finished!"

I dutifully obeyed, though it was hard for me. For months now, I had been trapped inside the dark, dungeon-like walls, or at least that's how it had seemed to me once I'd lost my freedom of movement. I missed it, the ability to go wherever I wanted, to see the mountains, the rivers. To convene with nature, the troops of women.

"Oh, Brigid. I have so much to tell you. Alaric is alive and on the move again. He has vowed to take over the Bookbinder kingdom once and for all."

Winnifred was not normally given to histrionics, so I knew what she said *must* be true. That's what I liked about her. She was always so calm, so stable. Unflappable. I reached out to hug her but received a stern warning from Nurse Sally.

"Sit still! Don't make me say it again," she said, shaking a finger at me.

Though I acquiesced, I rolled my eyes when she wasn't looking, which sent both Winnifred and Lofgren into a round of giggles, to which Nurse Sally merely frowned at the rather juvenile behavior of her charges. But I didn't care. I had been cooped up for so long in darkness that it felt good to laugh again. To smile. I had done so little of it lately.

When Nurse Sally turned to gather her scissors and clasp, Winnifred leaned toward me. "The women are preparing to gather," she whispered.

I nodded, not wanting big ears to set the manor "gossip mill" in motion as it did when anyone spoke. Often the translation went through so many iterations, that by the time I heard through the grapevine what I was supposed to have said or done, it had been blown up all out of proportion or was simply a fabrication, or more often than not a rather skewered interpretation of what I had said that wasn't what I meant at all. It left me in equal parts puzzled and mad.

"When will they arrive?" I whispered back, glancing to be sure Nurse Sally hadn't overheard.

"In two days time," she said. "Be ready."

I paused, my heart rate quickening inside my chest.

"And Brigid?"

"Yes," I said, not sure I wanted to know what more she had to say about the matter. "We're ready to fight the traditions, if we have to."

I scarcely breathed, knowing the consequences of our actions. We would be in a vise of our own making—Alaric and his dreaded Jackals on one side, our people and the traditions that brought pain to each and every one of us in equal measure on the other. Though perhaps as both the outsider and the leader, I had received more than my fair share of it. But it couldn't continue. Not as it had. We would all be dead, eventually, if we allowed the traditions to grow and flourish unchecked. We had no choice but to fight back. And yet what of the repercussions? I worried my hands together even as I feared the answer. It would be a hard fight, indeed. But I was ready.

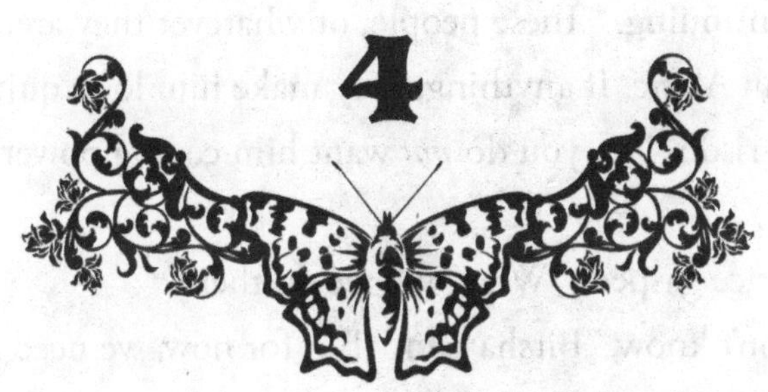

4

Birsha had been hearing rumblings for days now. "Come, Beatrice."

He clasped her hand as he hurried out of their chambers, fairly dragging her down the wide hall of the palace, that set smack dab in the middle of the fortress. "Father will be livid if we're late."

"What now?" she demanded, even as she followed him. But halfway down the hallway, she grabbed hold of his shoulder to stop him. "You know we can't keep on like this. We have to do something about Alaric. He will destroy the Bookbinder Kingdom and my family with it if we don't prevent it!"

"I know," Birsha said in a rush, "but it's not that simple."

"What do you mean?"

He waited until one of the Jackals had passed then leaned in close so that if big ears were listening, he wouldn't be overheard. "I have it on good authority that an underground has formed to thwart Alaric."

Beatrice threw a hand to her O-shaped mouth, excitement showing in the glistening of her eyes. "We will be saved."

"You don't understand," Birsha said, her excitement trying his patience. He paused again as one of the parlor maids passed before continuing. "These people, or whatever they are, are far worse than Alaric. If anything, they make him look quite docile by comparison. No, you do *not* want him ceding power to them."

Beatrice gasped. "What will we do then?"

"I don't know," Birsha said. "But for now, we need Alaric."

Beatrice peered around to make sure no one was coming. "Is he aware of the underground?"

"Again, I don't know."

Birsha rubbed his eyes. He hadn't slept well in days, ever since Alaric had resumed the throne. His father had been belligerent, stamping and nearly foaming at the mouth over his temporary confinement in the giant globe that had once stood in the library before it had gone barreling through the stained-glass domed ceiling. Birsha was unclear about what sorcery had brought Alaric back to life, but whatever it was, and whoever had helped Alaric, had yet to show his face. Birsha hoped that it wasn't Siegfried, his one true friend in the kingdom. Alaric had demanded the adjutant's return. Each time Birsha had crossed paths with Siegfried, the man had merely shrugged and offered up a forlorn expression that cut Birsha to the core.

Well, whoever had done the deed by returning Alaric to the throne was now firmly tucked away, his . . . or *her* identity safe, for now.

The day we had dreaded had finally arrived. Women had
flocked in from all corners of the kingdom, dressed in battle
gear. Lady Bookbinder had been beside herself, shouting orders:
"Keep those horses out of my garden, Brigid; Get those women
off the lawn; Who's going to feed this many women?"

I tried to calm her fears, telling her that the women had
brought provisions. Later that day, I met with Winnifred and
the others to decide where to place the encampment. But first
I spoke with Conestra, the Master Birder, since it would be
her land on which we hoped to place our encampment. When
I arrived at her grouping of aviaries, I found her feeding a
Malaysian Frogmouth and her baby, possibly the grumpiest
looking bird I had ever seen, the deep-set eyes and overcast
brows giving it the decidedly ill-tempered look of a taciturn old
man.

Conestra, on the other hand, reminded me of a peacock,
her plumage so grand and colorful that I covered my eyes to
protect them from the bright glare of the sun that glinted off
her beautifully feathered dress. Her blonde hair hung in ringlets,
two narrow braids meeting at the back and tied with what
looked like the twine taken from a bird's nest. Quite simply,
she was radiant and I found myself, as I always did in her
presence, at once both amazed and in awe of her grace and self-
confidence.

"So, you want to use my birding grounds?" she asked when
I explained why I was there.

"I know it would be an imposition, but quite frankly, if I don't find somewhere to keep my women warriors soon, Lady Bookbinder is going to be apoplectic with rage."

"My, my!" Conestra tossed the bird she held on her finger into the air to return it to its perch in the aviary. "That doesn't sound like Lady Bookbinder at all. She's normally so . . . placid."

"Yes, I know," I said, peering at another bird, this one, a Peruvian Inca Tern, according to the signage. It looked as if it was sporting a giant mustache, turned up at the ends as though waxed. I couldn't help but giggle at the sight of it.

"This is dire indeed, if you've earned Lady Bookbinder's wrath." Conestra tsked as she closed the door to the aviary and set the latch. "We must do something about that, mustn't we?"

"So the women can camp out in your field?"

"I didn't say that." Conestra turned to take stock of me as one would a particularly unusual bird.

"I don't understand."

"I need that field," she explained, "to work my birds. But I could make a trade."

"A trade?" I swallowed down my worry. If I didn't find a place to put over a thousand women, and soon, Lady Bookbinder would have my hide . . . Sir Bookbinder as well. "What sort of trade?"

"Come, see for yourself."

She marched past me without another word. With hesitance, I followed, not at all certain what she had in mind. She ushered me to a portion of her bird houses nestled farther in among the copse of pines. She pointed to one particularly towering aviary filled with birds of prey, each with its own section, the center hollowed out so that she could walk among them while she held the many keys to the enclosures, which she kept on a keyring that encircled her waist.

"I'll make you a deal." She turned to me so suddenly that I nearly tripped backwards. "Your women take turns feeding and caring for my birds, and you can use the clearing for their camp."

"Oh, thank you!" I cried.

But before I could go any further, she held up her hand. "*However,*" she said, staring at me with those intense blue eyes, "for one month only. Agreed?"

I breathed a sigh of relief, because now I had a plan. For a month, at least.

Winnifred had been fortunate to meet with the stable manager who offered her a room in the back to both sleep and work on her many projects. She'd brought her time travel machine with her, which had developed a bit of a hiccup when they'd landed, after escaping the Jackals at the fortress. One of the wheels had fallen off and hit the spoke at the rear of the machine, which had left it shackled, for now. Until she got it fixed, there would be no time travel in her future.

Lofgren watched her as she hammered the wheel, goggles down, pounding away, each ring of the hammer bringing her one step closer to success. She hoped. At last, her arms were so sore and her hands blistered by all the non-stop pounding that she finally lifted her goggles and laid down the hammer. She threw her head back and sighed, sweat dripping into her eyes and making them sting.

"Why are you doing this now, Winnifred? We should be preparing for the siege." Lofgren's light green skin grew more sallow anytime he was disturbed.

"I know," she said on a sigh. "It's just that as long as I work at something, I feel as if the future is safely tucked away for later. That maybe it won't come if I stay busy."

Lofgren captured her hand in his. "You know that's not how it works."

Winnifred couldn't help but laugh at his simple logic. Of course she knew. But in the past, it had kept her from having to deal with her father's death. Or her step-father's. Keeping busy had always been her means of escape, and she preferred it that way. No use dwelling, becoming melancholy. It did no one any good, least of all herself.

"What do you think about us doing away with the traditions?" he asked, taking a seat beside her on the workbench.

"I say good riddance!" she said, then quickly looked around, her eyes wide.

Lofgren hunkered down as though he too felt the presence of the omniscient traditions that terrorized everyone in these parts. Winnifred had learned that in his treetop village, none were subjected to such horrible penance for the slightest infraction. And for almost a year, she had been far enough away from the Bookbinder Kingdom to avoid most of it. But here, the punishments were severe, and once again poor Brigid looked like a pincushion most days. Whoever was behind the traditions hadn't liked the fact that Brigid was mounting an army full of women, right here in the central part of the kingdom. As such, the backlash had been swift and unyielding.

"Lofgren." She leaned in close, hoping to avoid any unwanted ears.

"Hmm . . . ?"

He was playing with the quantum computer she kept on her desk, the one she'd taken with her when she'd left the future. It had been in the prototype phase, and she was no further along with it, having never grown up with computers. They were still a mystery to her, but one that she hoped to crack one day.

"Who do you suppose is behind the traditions?"

"Huh?" he said.

She could tell he wasn't really listening to her. "Oh, for heaven's sake, Lofgren, put that down and look at me."

With a sheepish grin, he set it down, and yet she could see him eyeing it longingly. Still, she couldn't be mad at him because his child-like curiosity matched her own.

"Well, think about it, Lofgren. Why would our own people be behind such evil, when it affects the very people who run the kingdom?"

Lofgren crossed one leg over the other as he pondered what she'd said. Whenever he concentrated on a problem, his eyes moved in such a way that it made her think of a computer. Perhaps this is what a computer did, computed facts and figures, pondered big questions then provided answers.

Lofgren's eyes stopped moving as he alighted upon an answer. "Maybe it's a way to weaken the people, the kingdom. From within."

His words left a dry spot in her mouth. Who would want to weaken them from within except . . .

"*The Jackals*," they said in unison.

Could it be that Alaric was behind the odious traditions? That he had sympathizers within the kingdom who were doing Alaric's work to defeat her people from the inside out? Her spine tingled as the suspicion took root and began to grow.

"Do you suppose there could be people from our kingdom who secretly support their cause?" I asked.

"It stands to reason." Lofgren's expression sobered.

For several moments, neither of them moved, each lost in their own thoughts. Finally, Winnifred said, "Well, the only way we're ever going to truly know who is behind them, is to pull back the curtain, Right-O?"

"The curtain," Lofgren repeated.

But what curtain and where would they ever find it? "C'mon, Lofgren. We've got work to do."

And with that, she stood and made her way to the open doorway.

5

I had serious misgivings as I watched the women make camp. Never before had the women set foot this close to the Bookbinders. All their toil had been at a distance. I knew I had upset Lady Bookbinder by bringing them here. And yet, if the Jackals were to attack the kingdom, as Alaric had avowed, then it stood to reason that he would begin here, at the manor.

"Do you really think they'll attack here again?" Lady Bookbinder furrowed her brow, hands on her hips as if to make her appear larger and more intimidating.

"I'm afraid so," I said, as I counted down the many supplies we would need.

Already, Emma had set up an extra large tent with a giant cross on the side from which to tend the casualties. Gertrude and Jocelyn divided the women into two groups, Jocelyn beginning archery practice, while Gertrude had the women work on their marksmanship. Some practiced with a carbine rifle, for more long-range fighting, while others used the Colt Dragoon, for those fighting at closer quarters. Some women used the Sharps breech-loading rifle to run forward, fall on bended knee, and then shoot at their targets. Then they would jump to their feet, step out of the way, and another wave of women would shoot at the target. I whistled at the sight. They were so much better markswomen than they had been when they first began and I had to say, I was impressed.

Just then, Winnifred and Lofgren appeared from the nearby copse. Somewhere along the way, they had picked up Ma'am, the woman who had whisked me away to the manor when she'd discovered I owned a magic loom that foretold the future. A loom that apparently many wanted for their own, if the offers of marriage, purchase of the loom, or outright attempts at theft were any indicator.

Ma'am jumped down from her horse, and to my surprise came loping across the clearing to greet me. She hugged me tight, as though a long-lost daughter.

"Quick! Can we go somewhere to speak, alone?" She bowed slightly in apology, her eyes on Madame Bookbinder. "I'm so sorry, Lady Bookbinder. I will speak with you soon, but first I need to talk to Brigid about something of great urgency."

Lady Bookbinder licked her lips. "Of course. You can find me in the study when you're done."

With that, she turned and strode away, but I could tell by Ma'am's expression that she feared she might have offended Lady Bookbinder, a dear friend of both Ma'am and her husband.

"Come, Winnifred, Lofgren. You should hear this, too."

I nodded toward my tent, which Henry had just finished setting up. His brown eyes brightened as he saw Ma'am and the others, but the flame was quickly doused once he read Ma'am's grim expression.

"You should hear this too, Henry," Ma'am said.

I wondered why she felt safe to talk to us, but not to Lady Bookbinder who she loved and trusted.

Once inside the tent, she turned to us with a gleam in her eye and a shrill tone to her voice that bordered on frantic. "The reason I'm here is two-fold. One, to help you, of course, but the other a matter of intelligence that cannot be revealed. To anyone," she added, lest we mistake the importance of what she was about to say.

The wind whipped at the tent, as though it too understood the importance of the moment. But it died just as quickly to give Ma'am her due.

Ma'am closed her eyes, as though struggling back tears, the news so dire. Finally, she opened them and sniffed. "As you know, I have informants inside the fortress, one especially critical member who has spent years behind enemy lines."

She paused, the tension thick from inside the tent. I bit my lip to keep from urging her to tell us all she knew before I snapped.

Fortunately, Henry wasn't as circumspect because he said, "If it's something that affects us all, we need to know. Your secrets are safe with us, right Brigid, Winnifred, Lofgren?"

"Of course," we said in unison, Winnifred nodding her head.

"Okay then."

Ma'am held my hand as if to steady herself, and I dutifully obliged, both as a warrior and a friend.

"Alaric isn't running the kingdom." She paused as we all took stock of each other's reactions. "Oh, he thinks he is." She held up her hands to avoid outbursts or questions from any of us. "But I've learned through my sources that an underground has formed within his own kingdom."

I immediately brightened at the thought. "That's good, isn't it?" I said, hoping to find a positive spin on what might otherwise be a dire situation indeed.

"No, no, *no*! It's not good. Not at all."

"I don't understand." Henry urged her to continue.

"This group is a hundred times worse than Alaric."

I gasped, shocked that there could be anything worse than a dictator such as he.

"They are, quite literally, monsters."

"*Vidunders*!" Lofgren said beneath his breath. His eyes became huge saucers and his green skin paled so that he looked almost . . . ordinary.

I had learned, on our last campaign, that Vidunders were what the elves called monsters, in their language. I shook my head in confusion. "Wait, I thought the men and women from the Council were the Vidunders. They certainly *look* like monsters."

"They do, and they are, but these monsters are much more vile, much more vicious. They are from the very underworld itself." Ma'am appeared stricken, lips quivering in fear, which I had never before witnessed in a woman as strong as Ma'am. "They want nothing more than total domination, to see each and every one of us subjugated, if not dead. We simply cannot allow that to happen."

"I agree," I said. Those around me nodded, no one wanting such a dire consequence to occur. "So what can we do?"

Ma'am froze and licked her lips, as though striving to remain calm. "We have to stop them before they can strike."

"How?" I asked, jaw set in determination.

She squeezed my hand, her eyes filled with sympathy.

"We give them what they want," she said, her words ominous. "Only with one very important adaptation."

"Adaptation?" I asked.

All she said was, "You'll see."

I looked at Henry and my two friends, each and every one of them as baffled as me.

The Diamōns traversed the underground chambers in a secret wall hidden within the conference room that they used for meetings. After each meeting, those who couldn't shapeshift retired to rooms that looked like monks' cells. For those who could move freely above ground, they continued on to a fork in the musty smelling underground chamber and turned to the left, where they entered the backroom of a shop that just happened to be owned by a family who supported their cause.

Tempestous entered the shop, along with Liz Herd and Chame Leon, eager to be free of the Queen of the Mammals, who was bent on turning their world upside down. Tempestous was careful not to speak until they were well out of earshot. Spies could be anywhere. She, of all people, understood that.

Tempestous ushered them down a back alleyway that would lead to the gardens and the rear of the palace walls. When she came close to the giant Chessmen, she peered up, feeling like a dwarf in their presence. And even though she knew they were inanimate, she couldn't help but feel that they were listening, and when released would reveal her secrets. She looked toward the greenhouse.

"Let's talk. In there," she said, nodding toward the side entrance.

Liz Herd and Chame Leon kept their counsel until they reached the door, gravel crunching beneath their feet. Tempestous opened the door. Immediately, the humidity wilted her hair and moistened her brow. In light of all the greenery in the hothouse, her red dress grew muted, no longer the vibrant red it had been just moments before.

Tempestous pointed to a bench seat with cupids dancing at the base. Could she trust the pair not to repeat what she was about to say? In the end, she nodded toward a ledge, free of cupids, that sat along the rim of the koi pond filled with plate-sized lilly pads, small green frogs strewn here or there, or staring up from the water next to the edge of the pad.

Once they were all seated, she said, "So what do you think of the Queen of Mammals' plans to overthrow the kingdom?"

Even to say it out loud set her heart racing and her eyes darting to make sure that no one was within earshot.

Chame Leon held back, instead looking to Liz Herd to answer. She tested the air with her tongue. "Quite frankly, the Queen of Mammalsss ss-scares me. Alaric wass one thing, but thiss iss altogether too much."

Tempestous was surprised when Chame Leon blew out a lengthy breath, as though he had been holding it the entire way here.

"You feel the same?" she asked Chame Leon.

He turned to Liz Herd, as if to gauge her reaction, then nodded his head in agreement. "This has gone way too far. The Queen of Mammals is a madman . . . I mean woman. She will put the entire kingdom in danger, us included."

"We have to ssstop her," Liz Herd added. "Alaric iss difficult enough, as it iss. But *her* . . . She shook her head.

Chame Leon took Liz Herd's hand. Tempestous couldn't help but notice Liz Herd's surprise at the kind gesture. For months now, Tempestous was beginning to wonder if what they were doing was right. If they weren't making a huge mistake. The truth is, after Alaric's supposed demise, she had been relieved when Birsha took the throne. True, he sought power. But there was something about him. Something more humane that spoke to her gentler nature, when she wasn't spewing hot lava, but then it had always been like that. Her nature had gotten in the way of her true self. She was actually quite mild-mannered if only those in power would let her be. But she had been the daughter of a well-respected lieutenant general. Had been challenged in ways that others hadn't. Perhaps that's why she had identified with Birsha more than the dreaded leader of the Jackals, Alaric, who had one objective in mind. To control the free world. That put her in a possible position of great power. And yet she knew only too well that putting one's fate into the hands of a dictator meant that one could be railed against or outright killed at any time. Used as a scapegoat.

Tempestous turned to the pair. "So, what do you propose we do?"

Liz Herd looked at Chame Leon and nodded, as though they had spoken about this very subject in private.

Chame Leon changed colors to reflect the muted green tones of the greenhouse so all that was visible were his eyes. "I believe our best bet is Birsha. He's married to a woman from the Bookbinder Kingdom. If we stand any chance to stop this, it's with him."

Tempestous couldn't have put it any better. "I agree. So which one of us approaches him?"

Chame Leon looked her square in the eye. "We all speak to him together, but we talk to Beatrice first. She will know how to approach him."

"Then it's settled," Tempestous agreed. They put their hands together and pressed down to show that they were in alignment. They would approach Beatrice. Hopefully, she would know what to do.

6

"No! I simply won't have it!" I recoiled as if Ma'am had struck me. How could she even suggest that I give my loom to the enemy, the loom the only link, except for my locket, to my childhood and the past?

"Don't you see?" Sweat dripped down Ma'am's brow as we stood inside my bedchamber, all eyes on the loom. "We'll get it back, someday."

Her words lingered on that last word. *Someday.* It had an onerous sound. Would I *someday* get my heritage back, my family, my friends? No, I couldn't give away the loom, and especially not to Alaric and the like. Besides, how would that save us or the Bookbinder Kingdom? I threw my hand over my face as if to dispel any such image.

Henry came to me and lovingly withdrew my hands. He bent down so that he stood eye level to me. "I know this is hard for you, Brigid. But hear Ma'am out. She wouldn't have proposed it if she didn't have a plan."

I choked back the anger and frustration, but eventually nodded, hot tears hovering on my lashes. As if the traditions had discovered it, I felt claw marks run down my back and let out a mewl of pain. *What evil magic would allow such a thing?* Once again, hatred burned within me and I fought it with every ounce of my being. Love . . . *only love* could save the day. We must fight hatred. I knew that now.

"Alright, Ma'am. I will listen." But even as I said it, my chest ached with the weight of the burden it cost to never show emotion, to never be allowed to be *human*.

"Thank you, Brigid," Ma'am said, knowing how much it had cost me. "My plan is that we command the loom to listen in on all conversations so that the spies I have placed among the Jackals will learn who is planning to attack and how."

I understood her objective, but how would that stop Alaric, and now the Evil Underground, as I had come to think of them, from overrunning our kingdom if indeed they had the magic to do so?

"The loom's prophecy," I reminded her, "is that *whoever owns the loom, owns the kingdom*, isn't that right? So as long as it is in our possession, we can't lose, not entirely, at any rate."

Ma'am could see my frustration. Just then, Emma and Thomas popped in.

"Is everyone having a party without us?" But Emma must have seen our serious expressions because she frowned and pursed her lips. "Is something wrong?"

"*Very* wrong!" I spat the words out with such force that

Henry squeezed my hand to keep me in check.

Ma'am sighed, clearly determined to have the last word about the subject of the loom. "Brigid and I were discussing the loom. I want to give it to Alaric–"

Emma gasped and Thomas threw his arm around her as if to protect her from any such notion.

"–to listen in on conversations. And quite possibly a timed device to explode at just the right moment, when we have captured the culprits who plan to destroy our kingdom."

My entire body shook, and if not for Henry's quick thinking, I might have fallen to the earthen floor inside my tent. How could she? To even consider destroying one of the few things that connected me to my childhood. The ties would be severed completely, and I would be adrift, floating skyward like a silk balloon.

Henry turned to me and took my hands in his. "You'll still have your locket." He looked directly into my eyes with an intensity that burned. "And you will have me."

"And me," Emma said.

"And me," Thomas agreed, as did Winnifred and Lofgren.

"And I will always be there for you," Ma'am added, her eyes moist.

As if to prove it, they all gathered around me in a circle. It was the closest I had felt to being loved in a very long time.

"What are you doing?" Lofgren said, later that same day.

Winnifred sat in her new workshop behind the stables composing a note on her drafting table. She dared not go through normal channels lest someone from the Jackal camp find it and recognize the ruse.

When Winnifred didn't answer, Lofgren came to peer over her shoulder, only to let loose a low whistle. He placed a hand on her shoulder.

"Out with it, Winnie. What do you have up your sleeve, may I be so bold as to ask?"

"You may," she said with a chortle.

She folded the note and put it inside an envelope then sealed it, taking a moment to heat a candle. Then she poured a circle of honey-colored melted wax onto the two ends and pressed her seal into it, a half moon with stars circling it.

"Well?" He nudged her.

She peered around, then leaned in and whispered. "I plan to find a loom just like Brigid's loom."

"Why?"

Lofgren's brows pinched together, his head cocked, which never failed to make her smile.

"Because, silly, we can't let Alaric and his kind have the real loom, and especially if Ma'am plans to booby trap it. Brigid would be devastated to lose her loom, just as I would be devastated to lose you."

The words popped out of her mouth before she could retrieve them. She put her hands up to her quickly warming face, her mouth forming a wide "O." "I . . .I . . . didn't. I mean—"

Lofgren gently removed her hands from her face and stroked her cheek, his eyes hooded with a look she had never seen before. He bent in close and kissed her eyes, her nose, her lips. For several minutes, she dared not breathe, until at last they came up for air.

"I would be devastated to lose you, too," he said, his voice husky with emotion.

She collapsed in relief. "I don't know what I would do without you."

Before she knew what he was doing, he lifted her into his arms and carried her to the nearby stream. Gently, he sat her down on a large boulder where she had seen him seated, on occasion, thinking. He began to circle her, first one way, then the next, all the while incanting something in elvish.

She used the boulder as ballast to turn and watch him.

What is he doing?

Her heart skipped a beat at the seriousness by which he intoned the words, his eyes never straying from hers. Though she fretted, she dared not break his concentration, as whatever he was doing, it seemed of great significance.

This went on for what seemed like a half hour or more. Finally, he finished by dancing faster and faster in circles until it was as if the time/space continuum opened up and a heavenly being called out from above in a voice both magical and deep. Light danced on the rays that shot down from the sky, centering both her and Lofgren in the circle of its gloaming.

"What is it?" I whispered.

"I have called upon the Maker to unite us as one."

I gasped, then twisted toward Lofgren. "What do you mean?"

"Winnifred, I want to be with you until the end of time."

"Whose time?" she demanded.

But she instantly rued her choice of words, as they were on different timetables, she and Lofgren. He was 800 years old and stood to live a much longer life, whereas her lifetime was quantifiably finite.

"*Our* time," he said, his words floating across a gentle breeze. The smell of lavender and roses floated in with it.

"*Our* time?"

"You see, if you and I unite as one, you will live in my time. You will be part elvin, like me."

Her hands began to shake at the idea that she could marry this man and become like him. Did she want this? It was a commitment for not just one lifetime, but many lifetimes. She wished Brigid were here to talk to, but she and Lofgren were alone, the decision hers and no one else's.

For once in her short time here on earth, she spoke from her heart and not her head. "Yes, Lofgren. Yes. I will marry you, or unite, whatever you call it in your language."

Lofgren jumped up and spun a circle, all the joy in the world displayed on his beautiful, narrow green face. Winnifred laughed through a burble of tears. How she wished that Brigid and all the other women could share in this moment with her.

As if they had heard her plea, hundreds of women began piling into the clearing until there was no room for another person in the small glen.

"How?" she asked Lofgren in wonder.

"I mind-melded with them, only they don't know it." He smiled down at her, his green eyes filled with love.

Just then, Brigid and Henry, Emma and Thomas, and even Ma'am and Lady Bookbinder appeared.

"To give their blessings," Lofgren explained.

From above Winnifred heard the thunder from the voice of an ancient elf that she could only see as a silhouette of light. "You, fair lady, are to unite with Lofgren on this day in the year of our Lord, 1863. Be you forever united as one. May you seek comfort and joy in each other's arms for the rest of your days."

"I will," she and Lofgren said in unison.

"From this day forward, your lives are one branch of the same tree. Shall you forever live in peace and harmony. Do you agree?"

"We do," they both said. Lofgren's eyes held Winnifred in their thrall.

"So be it," said the voice.

The light flickered. Then with an odd thrum like that of a dwarf minke whale, a beam shot down that filled Winnifred with a warmth that felt almost liquid. For several moments, she could only stare in wonder as it transformed her from within.

Then the rays of light began to recede into the sky and the joyous cries of all those around cried out. Brigid hugged her, as did Henry and the others. Last of all, Lofgren swooped her up in his arms and kissed her long and lovingly. When at last he released her, all those around her gasped.

"What is it?" she cried with a frown.

"Winnifred," Brigid said, pointing at her. "Your ears . . . and you're turning—"

"Green," everyone said in unison.

Winnifred felt her ears. *They're pointed!* She looked at her arms, and indeed they were turning green. "I am a—"

"Half-elf," Lofgren said, looking at her hopefully.

For a moment, no one spoke, then it was as if the dam had broken and everyone laughed, and Winnifred hugged Lofgren so tight that he squealed with equal parts pleasure and pain.

"I'll never let you go, Lofgren," she whispered. And she meant it.

7

Now that the celebrations for Winnifred and Lofgren
had settled down, the women warriors returned to the tasks at
hand while my thoughts went to my loom and its impending
departure. Before Ma'am had the ability to set things in motion
on that score, I started the day like any other day, rising early
for breakfast, then meeting with the women to prepare for the
inevitable. As the women warriors practiced their maneuvers,
Yesimeh and I set about making plans around the campfire.

"The problem," Yesimeh said, her round glasses making her
appear owlish, "is that we don't know what magic the Jackals
will unleash on us, so it's difficult to prepare."

I concurred. "What do we do then?"

At that moment, a gust of wind blew smoke into my eyes,
reminding me of another excursion from the Jackals, one in
which half the village was set on fire. We had met the challenge

head on. But like all the other challenges we had faced, there was no preparing for it. Just responding like the well-oiled machine we had become. As a unit.

"Why don't we keep a list of all those who can help us, like birders, gardeners, entomologists, warriors."

"Don't forget those of us with magical skills."

Yesimeh paused, her smile at once child-like and that of a wizened old sage. "I doubt that sturgeon bladders will be of much use this time around, but we do have Emma and the others in standby should we need their skills."

That sobered me, because her skills would only be needed should the women require triage of some sort, never a happy prospect. "Then what do you suggest?"

Yesimeh tapped a pencil to her chin as she prepared a mental list of any and all plans before jotting them down on a yellow lined tablet that she kept on her lap.

"We contact everyone on our list. We make sure that they're ready and know what to do should they be called upon to help. Can Phinney deliver messages to the people on the list?"

Though I dare not speak for Phinney, I knew without a doubt he would ferry the messages if I asked. As if he'd overheard our discussion from overhead, my blue falcon came swooping down and let out a high "chee-chee-chee-chee" call to let me know he was in on our plans and wholeheartedly agreed.

"Good boy, Phinney," I said, as he balanced on the log beside me.

He peered up at me, one-eyed, as if asking if he might be dismissed. "Very well," I said. "Go play, for now. But Phinney," I said, pausing for effect, "stay close, okay? We may need you."

Phinney let out a little chirp then danced on two legs before dashing off, his blue wings soaring wide as he headed into the sky to hunt, his favorite pastime when not aiding us in some way.

Beside me, Yesimeh peered up, her straight brown hair lying flat on her head. She sat like that for some time, watching Phinney intently. Then she frowned. "Have you ever thought of finding Phinney a mate? He looks so lonely up there."

The suggestion gave me pause because it had never occurred to me that Phinney might be lonely. "But falcons are solitary birds," I reminded her.

"Hmm." She turned back to scribbling down names in some order known only to her, occasionally crossing out a name only to put it higher or lower on the list of importance.

"What do you suppose it will be this time?" I said rather absent-mindedly.

"Dunno." She flicked her hair over her ear. "But whatever it is, we best be ready."

I had to laugh. Leave it to Yesimeh—studious, lovable Yesimeh—to be so practical. For the first time in days, I relaxed, relieved to be spared whatever plans Alaric or the Evil Underground had for us.

That's when I heard it. A rumbling so loud that it sounded as though an army of Huns was barreling toward us in a wave so wide and ferocious that it sent us all clamoring to our feet in search of an escape hatch until we could mount a counteroffensive. But before I could run, the rumbling knocked me off my feet. All around me, people were screaming and searching for something to grab hold of to keep from being blown away by the thunderous clouds that brought in wind so ferocious that the moment our words left our mouth they were whisked away and gone.

It was useless to try to speak, so I held up hand gestures for any who could see them. *We need to find shelter.* Conestra, who had been close by waved a hand to a large aviary protected within a copse. Though it would house only a few hundred of us, I encouraged any that could, to take heed of her suggestion. Soon, a rush of women pressed against the torrential wind toward shelter.

Henry, bless him, saw me and grabbed onto my clothing, pulling me toward the stream below. It's then I realized where he was taking me. Though I tried to grab hold of Yesimeh, she was too light and blew out of my grasp, her body tumbling over and over until I could see her no more.

"We can't help her," Henry shouted. "We have to save ourselves."

Inexorably, he pulled me onward, not that I could have fought it, at any rate, because the wind had changed directions and was now pushing me forward. We had barely reached the heart-shaped tree with its underground cavern, when the next wave of foul weather rained down on us, this time hail the size of my fist. Again I heard screams as everywhere, people ducked beneath the canopy of trees to receive relief from the hail.

Within moments, I found myself shivering, as those around me did likewise, for the air had cooled a good twenty degrees in a matter of minutes. Henry held me tight.

"We have to go out there, Henry. I can't leave the women to suffer alone."

But Henry held me tight. "Wait until the storm passes. You can't do anything now. You would only risk your life as well as theirs. Trust that they will seek shelter."

I knew my women were smart, capable. I had seen them in action before. And yet I couldn't help but feel responsible. After all, I had been the one to call them together, to prepare for the next onslaught. But how could I have known it would be this, of all things? And that was the rub of it. The Jackals' magic so outmatched our own that I had no way to counter it.

By this time, my teeth were chattering and my clothes were soaked, for with the hail had come rain. Before long, my hair lay plastered to the side of my face and wet rivulets ran down my cheeks. And then, as quickly as the storm came, it was gone, leaving us all wet, cold and bruised.

As soon as the melee stopped, I jumped from my place inside the gnarl of the old tree and raced through the meadow, searching for the injured. Emma was already there with her medical bag and supplies. Her team of doctors and nurses scanned the field, setting up stations throughout the open glen. All around were head traumas, open wounds, the beginning stages of frostbite. Soon, women were bandaged and set on their way, or kept in a closed-off area so they could be monitored. I looked at the tower and saw a light. *Someone is in my room.* Was it Ma'am? Was she preparing the loom for shipment to Alaric's fortress even now?

I fought back the scream from deep within my throat, exchanging it for sadness and pain. I knew what I must do, though once again I would be losing my past and my connection to my family. If we were to save the kingdom and protect these women, I must forfeit the one thing, save for my locket, that meant the world to me. I must give up my loom. The loom that had been at once my bane . . . *and* my salvation. Just then, snow began to fall . . . and fall . . . and fall.

Birsha rode his horse out into the meadow. He needed to clear his head after his meeting with his father. As he drove his horse at a good clip, the heat of the day burning down on his head and shoulders, he thought about his most recent meeting with Alaric.

"I've set Mother Nature, in all its most abhorrent forms, upon The Bookbinders."

Alaric had laughed, causing Birsha's chest to swell with anger. Didn't the man know that Beatrice was a family friend of the Bookbinders? Know that Birsha had spent one summer close by the manor as a child, had actually liked the people he'd met?

"You're going to set Tempestous on them?" Birsha had asked the previous night, over dinner, fury making his veins run hot.

"Of course not." His father had scowled. "That woman has been acting strange lately. I don't trust her. Her *or* her Council."

"Then who?"

Here, Alaric's eyes narrowed and a smirk played across his face. "This is a woman you have yet to meet. I ordered for her to be raised in the countryside."

Like me? Birsha longed to say, but thought better of it.

"She has been trained in every form of warcraft," Alaric gloated. "I urged my people to search far and wide to find a child with promising skills. Now she is grown and ready."

He lifted his forefinger to his lips, the nail honed to a fine point as sharp as any blade. One wrong word and his opponent would wear a permanent scar.

Birsha shook off the memory as he drove his horse deeper into the countryside. He rode like this for some time, when suddenly, he heard a cry from behind. He turned to find Beatrice riding alongside Tempestous, Chame Leon and Liz Herd nearby. Birsha pulled on the reins, bringing his black Fresian to a quick halt. The horse ducked its head and pawed at the ground. Birsha had named his sire Bucephalus after Alexander the Great's horse. According to legend, Alexander had been a good man, until he'd begun to drink and lost compassion for his men and his people. Birsha had taken that lesson to heart. A lesson he wished his father would have learned. But like Alexander, Alaric was obsessed with conquering his neighbors, an obsession that had been Alexander's downfall, in the end.

It was an unusually hot summer's day. Within moments, the foursome was upon him and he could see by their serious expressions that something was wrong. *Very* wrong.

Birsha pointed toward a nearby copse where they could find shade and shelter from the bristling heat. When they approached the river, where breezes played across the water and provided a respite from the sweltering sun, Birsha confronted them.

"What is it?" he demanded. "What has happened?"

Beatrice, who was always forthcoming with him, appeared frightened, as though fearful that what she was about to say would cause undue difficulty. But for whom?

"Spit it out!" Birsha said.

It was Chame Leon who first spoke. "We have some rather unsavory news."

Beatrice pulled tight to her rein, causing her horse to buck under the pressure of the bit. Birsha brought his horse up beside her, and loosened her grip. "What is it, Beatrice? Tell me. Whatever it is, we'll see our way through together."

Beatrice nodded, but he had seen her swallow hard as if to force back the words she was about to say.

"An underground has been formed."

"What sort of underground?" Birsha asked, his mouth going dry, suddenly.

"Of miss-creantss," Liz Herd said. "Devilsss."

When faced with bad news, Birsha tended to go still, as he had now, scarcely daring to breathe.

"I know that you think the Council are Devils," Chame Leon said, "but compared to the Diāmons, we're quite tame."

"Diāmons? What are they?"

"It iss ssimilar to the Latin word for Demonss."

Birsha grasped the pommel, his knuckles white. "Demons? What sort of Demons?"

Chame Leon quickly explained each of the monsters from the below-ground chamber and their capabilities.

"So, you can see that they mean to put the entire Jackal kingdom under their leadership, and they're ten times more powerful . . . and more frightening, than Alaric and the Jackals."

Birsha fell back in his saddle. His entire life he had been trained for just such an event, had learned the game of chess which taught one that a leader often faced more than one enemy, and often as not, the enemy would be one of their own. But this . . . *this* he hadn't anticipated.

He peered up toward the fortress, only one turret visible from where he sat atop his horse. Though he couldn't be certain, he thought he saw a dark figure perched there, dressed entirely in black. He could only guess at the man's identity.

His father. Alaric.

8

Winnifred hoped the ruse would work. She peered down
at the duplicate loom that now sat in the corner by the room
next to Brigid's bed. While Brigid had been busy tending to the
wounded, Winnifred had asked Lofgren, Jocelyn, and Gertrude
to help her carry the loom she'd managed to locate, up to
Brigid's room. She had replaced the very plain tapestry with
one she'd discovered from a nearby castle. It had been hard, but
she'd managed to string it onto the loom with Lofgren's help.
He, of all elven people, had a knack for anything involving his
mind, and what was a loom except a problem to be solved?

Relieved to have the replacement loom in clear view of
Ma'am, should she deem to remove it and send it to the fortress,
Winnifred turned and made her way to the door.

"Quick, we must each take a different exit, so none will
be the wiser, Right-O? And not a word!" Winnifred put a

single finger to her lips to ensure that her orders wouldn't be countermanded.

Ten minutes later, she stood in front of the wagon where the real loom was now stored. There it sat, the factual loom replacing the fictional one, inside the wagon that had brought it here. She covered it with canvas and tied it off, then climbed into the seat, alongside Lofgren, who would act as driver, the man they'd asked to guard the real loom sent on his way with the required shillings to earn his silence.

Once they rode toward their new place of residence, Winnifred scooted closer and rested her head on Lofgren's arm.

"What if something happens to the loom?" she asked, fear setting her heart aflame.

"I've asked two of our elves to keep an eye on it," Lofgren said. "Nothing will happen to it. I trust them with my life."

"But how can you be sure?" she asked, not normally the fretful type.

She puzzled her brow in worry at the pain she would cause Brigid, should her friend learn the truth. And yet what were the alternatives? If they hadn't made the trade, the loom would soon be on a wagon making its way northward toward the Jackals' lair. And, if Ma'am had her way, the loom would blow up when Alaric and his people were in the room. It would be disastrous for everyone, most of all Brigid. That loom tied her to her past. It had seen her through dark times. She cherished it the way one would cherish a favored son or a daughter. No, Winnifred couldn't allow Brigid's loom to be destroyed. Besides, she couldn't help feeling that without the loom, the entire Bookbinder Kingdom would be at grave risk. She shivered in the newly falling snow as the wheels crunched the snow and ice.

Snow and ice! In July?

Some great magic was clearly afoot. She tucked her frozen hands into the shawl she'd donned after the hail had fallen. No, she was right to have done what she did. She was saving the kingdom by protecting the loom. She was sure of it.

I knew what I had seen. Someone was in my room, but who? Ma'am? A thief? I apologized to Emma as I made my way from my knees to my feet. By the time I arrived at the manor, all I could see was a cart in the far distance. Did that person have my loom?

I raced up the stairs, Henry following in my wake. Even Phinney had taken to hopping from the Big Ben newel post, up the bannister and into my room, circling overhead and cree-ing. I slid to a stop in front of my beloved loom, but there it sat, as though nothing were amiss. On it was a most placid scene that didn't represent anything currently happening in the kingdom. I frowned.

"What do you make of it, Henry?" I said.

"Make of what? It's your loom, sitting exactly as it always has."

And yet something wasn't quite right, but I couldn't put my finger on it. In the past, it always seemed to have a presence about it, as though it were a living thing, not an inanimate object. Now, I couldn't . . . *feel* it. I knew Henry would think me crazy if I told him so, but my loom wasn't my loom. I just knew it. No matter that it was the same style, the same color.

But then I saw it. "Aha!" I pointed toward a wingnut on the right side of my loom. "The wingnut was broken on my loom, Henry. This is the wrong loom."

"You're imagining things, Brigid." Henry inspected it closely, nevertheless.

"I am not. I know my loom. I've lived with it all these years—"

As my volume increased, he held up his hands as though a prisoner asking for pardon. "Okay, okay. So what if it *is* another loom? What does that mean?"

"It means that someone has stolen my loom."

Henry paused, as though thinking. "Let's say you're right. This could be our ticket."

"Our ticket to what?" I asked, seriously wondering about Henry's sanity.

"Maybe the loom has somehow supplanted itself, to send this fake loom in its place so that it will be the one to perish rather than—"

"Do you think?" I said, cutting him off. For a moment, I danced with excitement. Then my mood just as quickly soured. "But then where's the real loom?"

My heart sank. Either someone had taken it or . . . My loom was magic, but to leave, on its own, only to be replaced by an imposter . . . ? Though I thought alot of my loom and its abilities, I couldn't fathom such a thought. No, someone must have taken it. Perhaps Ma'am. Perhaps she had done as planned and left me this in consolation.

"What will we do, Henry?" I cried, grasping his hand.

He merely shook his head. "I don't know, Brigid."

But *I* knew. We needed to make inquiries about the loom. Then we needed to do something about this wretched weather. I peered out my bedroom window that overlooked the garden. The Bookbinders had been blessed with a large garden chock full of vegetables in every stage of production. None could withstand this rapid change in weather. If we didn't get rid of the snow and ice pronto, our people would starve. A chill settled over me and I looked at the barren hearth, wishing for a fire when only yesterday I had sought relief from the heat.

"Quick!" I snapped my fingers, recalling what the gardeners would do when the cold came to the valley too early. "We need to smudge the orchards and vegetables."

We ran downstairs so fast that I nearly stumbled near the landing, but fortunately Henry caught me by the arm and righted me before I went sprawling on the floor like a veritable oaf.

"What's all the falderal?" Sir Bookbinder held his pipe in one hand and pointed it at us. It was an ivory Meerschaum's pipe that he had consigned as an exact replica of himself.

"No time!" I called over my shoulder as I sped toward the door. "We need smudge pots!"

Henry, bless him, shrugged an apology to his father, then raced after me. I had no sooner headed toward the maze, where the master gardener resided in an underground cavern, when I ran smack dab into Thomas, who had just exited the maze.

"We need smudge pots."

"I have a load of smudge pots coming."

We both spoke at once, laughing when we realized we were talking about the same thing.

"Not to worry," Thomas said. "The master gardener has things well in hand."

I nearly collapsed in relief. So at least we wouldn't starve.

"Furthermore," Thomas whispered, leaning in, "you are to tell no one . . ."

I frowned, wondering what on earth Thomas was blathering about. He looked around, then bent down so that both Henry and I acted as barricades should anyone be listening in.

"The master gardener has been worried about the possibility that the Jackals would attack our crops for some time, so he has made provisions."

"Provisions?"

I looked first at Thomas, then Henry, to see if he had an idea what Thomas was on about, but again, Henry simply shrugged and pursed his lips, the worry evident in the tightness of his jaws.

"The caverns have been turned into giant greenhouses. I don't know how he did it, but he has found a large light source and heating as well. The man is a genius, if you ask me. He's growing only those foods that will prevent starvation: potatoes, corn, beans, pumpkins. And he has thrown in some tomatoes and cabbage as well so that people will get the nutrients they need. That way, if something goes awry as it did just over a year ago, we'll be prepared this time.

Until now, I hadn't realized I was holding my breath, when suddenly I released it with a large expulsion of air, blowing the hair on my forehead.

"Then we're safe."

"For now," Thomas agreed. "But danger's lurking in the air.

The whole town is abuzz with it. We have to be vigilant, Brigid. We can never let our guard down, understood?"

I nodded, but fear edged the corner of my thoughts. What would come next? I shivered. Only time would tell.

Birsha looked at the huge glass orb that took up nearly one entire section of the hidden library set high above the only library he had known, until now. One in which he'd had yet to explore as it was hidden, in a sense. For if one were in the library below, one had only to look up to see tier upon tier of books that ascended ever higher toward the stained-glass dome that even now was being replaced, scaffolding in place for the brave craftsmen who dared to repair the dome. But Siegfried had unwittingly come upon a surprise when he had placed a three-story ladder up to inspect the repairs. For there, in the bowels of the library, was a room cordoned off to any who might chance upon it, but chance upon it he did.

Birsha peered out a small transom window. The fortress had been built nearly two centuries prior, long before the Europeans had settled the continent. The history of it was murky. Supposedly, the original people were descendants of Spaniards, which is perhaps where he'd inherited his dark features. And upon closer inspection, it would seem plausible as the Spanish Inquisition was in full blossom then. No doubt many were fleeing to better climes, and yet why bring so much of it with them if they were trying to escape persecution only to foist it upon others? Birsha had so many questions, and yet questions spelled disaster when secrets were so clearly prized in his society.

"Do you suppose Alaric knew about this room?" Birsha asked, keeping his voice low.

"I don't know," Siegfried replied, "but I was with him most of the time, and he was never near it when we were together. Nor did he allude to it."

"Then who built it?"

Siegfried merely shrugged, but before Birsha could speak further, the orb began to glow, a fog swirling from within. A voice boomed out, nearly knocking both Birsha and Siegfried backwards.

"Your ancestors built it," said a dark figure dressed all in black and wearing a red silk cape, red on the inside, black on the outside.

"Wh-who are you?" Birsha asked, not sure he wanted to know the answer.

"I was nicknamed Fearsome Foul, Faineant the Foul's father before . . ."

"Before?" Siegfried asked, his eyes wide.

"Before my people were killed and I was taken captive in this god-forsaken orb and made to live out my life, never aging, only existing."

Birsha's heart hammered in his chest as he stroked his goatee. It seemed as if this entire new world he'd been thrust into when his father died was one of mazes and false mirrors. He never knew which way to turn. Instead, he felt as though he was racing through a funhouse with no exit. Only trapdoors and surprise shocks that made him want to go screaming into the night.

As if to show them what he meant about the vial, the dark

visage evaporated into the swirling smoke and another image materialized. There, before them, was a man who appeared bent and old, but from a pouch inside his pocket, he pulled a vial that he released in slow measure.

"What is it?" Birsha said through the hush surrounding him.

In answer, Fearsome reappeared, his face glowing, as if from the pits of hell, fire blazing all around him.

"We don't know what was in the vial, or how our enemy obtained it, but it decimated our people, including me. That's when my son, Faineant, began his quest to attack anyone who was not of the kingdom. So you see," he said, lowering his voice to a dull roar, "when the Bookbinders built their manor and the cities and towns around it began to spring up, it could not be allowed."

Finally, Birsha understood his father's blinding ambition to remove the Bookbinders or to see them quelled under one banner, the Jackals'. Then a thought occurred to him.

"What does your orb do?"

"Do?" both Fearsome and Siegfried said in unison.

"I mean, can you speak only of the past, or are you able to look into the future, perhaps tell me what is happening in my own kingdom."

"*Your* kingdom?" Fearsome said with a surprise lilt to his voice and one lifted brow.

"Pardon. My father's kingdom," Birsha corrected himself.

"Aye," Fearsome said, narrowing his eyes. "I have eyes in the kingdom. What do you want to know?"

Birsha braced for what was to come. "I've heard there are

monsters in the kingdom. Not the Council," he added, in case Fearsome misunderstood.

"Ah! The monsters. The true puppeteers of the kingdom. I know them well. What do you want to learn about them?"

"Can you show me them?" Birsha asked, curiosity getting the better of him.

"I can try," Fearsome said, even as he began to fade.

Birsha bit his lower lip as a floating glass table filled with creatures that could only be described as freaks of nature sat around it, each more loathsome in appearance than the last. Seated among them was Liz Herd, Chame Leon and Tempestous. So, it was true that they had joined but were determined to escape the evil the monsters represented. And yet, the trio could be useful too, if kept where they were, for they could learn any and all plans of attack, should the foul creatures resort to it. For days now, Birsha had been mulling over what the trio had said about this underground of misfits. And yet he'd heard whispers of a newly formed resistance group. He couldn't help but wonder if Chame Leon was part of the Resistance. Perhaps Liz Herd too. Anymore, he didn't know who to trust, and yet his instincts told him to pay attention. To listen and learn. He had employed those same instincts in the life-and-death training sessions he'd received as a teen, ones that had often ended in someone's death. Those instincts had carried him far.

Fearsome reappeared out of the morass. "I can not stay long. My energy is fading. It takes weeks, if not months, to get it back," he said. As if to prove his point, his image flickered, and the orb made a sputtering sound. Then he was gone.

"Well, that was useful," Birsha said. And yet it did nothing to quell his inner turmoil.

9

As I sat on the manor rooftop, Henry at my side, I felt untethered without my loom, as though a silk balloon that had been released into the sky only to float away, never to be seen again except by someone from a distant land.

"Brigid, you have to stop mourning," Henry admonished. "If your loom is gone, it's gone for a reason. You must trust fate."

"*Fate?*" I felt as if he'd pricked me with a needle and sent me spiraling earthward. I couldn't say why, but the back of my throat grew heavy with unshed tears. "It was fate that tore my family from me. Fate that kept me locked away in an attic both summer and winter. Fate that took away everything I hold dear."

Henry paused for a long moment before speaking. "Yes, Brigid. All that is true. But fate brought you here, as well. It brought you your women warriors. And it brought you to me," he finished, his voice thick with emotion.

I hung my head, cowed. He was right. If not for all of those things I might never have met Henry. Might never have gained a friendship with such a vast group of women. Might never have been able to help save the slaves that had been denied their freedoms and, in many cases, their lives.

"You're right, Henry, I need to be more appreciative of what I have, most of all the people around me."

And yet some had betrayed me, like Beatrice. But had she? Had she really? Who was to say whether she knew the thread was tainted with some evil magic that had thrust our world into darkness? Perhaps, like me, she had thought it a kind gesture. A beautiful gift. That's all. I had to start thinking better of people, but how could I manage that when so much was hidden from me? So much imbued with double meaning? So much meant to deceive, like the foul winds of a year ago, filled with hateful words and innuendo, sent to us by the master magician, Alaric. For that's what he had become with his constant dabbling in sorcery.

I had been silent too long. Finally, Henry said, "Penny for your thoughts."

I huffed, the wind tugging at the tendrils of my dark hair. "I was just recalling the winds of a year ago."

"Ah! Those!" Henry said, only too aware of that horrible time. "At least we don't have *that* to deal with these days."

"Indeed," I said, taking his hand.

From our rooftop perch, we stared up at the sky, reveling in the peace, despite the cold that had obliterated much of the landscape. Fortunately, our crops had been spared with the smudge pots. For now, at least. We lay like that on the tiled roof for some time. I was about to tell Henry we needed to get back to work, to help prepare the women for what may come, but before I could do so, I heard an odd noise that sounded like a million bees buzzing.

"What is that, Henry?" I asked, bolting upright.

"I don't know," he said, as clueless as I.

We scrambled to our feet and climbed to the furthest peak of the manor only to discover some weird formation taking place in the sky. The swarm moved in and out like ocean waves, only they were morphing into shapes . . . rather frightening shapes that had my stomach tumbling. Henry clung to me lest I take a spill off the slate tiles. Then I saw it. Starlings by the thousands, if not millions. Their shapes drifted in and out of formation. First came Typhon, that most fearsome of beasts from Greek mythology, with one hundred dragon-like heads and a dragon-like tail. Then came the Gorgons, three women of the same mythology, whose hair was said to be like coiling, venomous snakes and whose eyes breathed fire. It was claimed that to look upon the Gorgon risked turning one into stone. Lastly came Charybdis, another monster of female origin, her body like that of a great whirlpool that sucked everything into its round, teeth-filled maw.

Just like that, the wind from the birds' wings indeed felt like a whirlpool and I realized we were all being sucked into it. Around the manor, I heard screams.

"Quick!" Henry yelled. "To the window. We need to get inside!"

There, mere feet away, stood the opened window. I

pressed with all my might, the eddy tossing me like a leaf in a windstorm. But as I reached for the transom, my foot slipped, and I slid down the slate tile, Henry grasping me just before I fell beyond his reach.

"Hold on!" he pleaded. Slowly, methodically, he worked his way up the roof, pulling me along.

I tried to find purchase with my feet, but no sooner would I make progress than I would slip backwards.

"Visualize!" Henry urged. "You are crawling up the roof. You are almost there. You are reaching out for the window. Now you pull yourself inside."

I did as he commanded, and oddly enough, it worked. Little by little, I overcame the pull of the wind, the flapping of the birds sounding louder now. Closer. I had just managed to get a hand on the window and drag myself inside, when I heard a whoosh and a cry. Then Henry was lost to me forever.

"The siege has begun, your highness," said Belial, Devil incarnate. He bowed slightly to the Queen of Mammals who headed the table.

She regarded him with distaste. "Of course it has. I ordered it. That fool, Alaric, believes that he is the one in charge, but I implanted the idea in his head. It has been easy to do. Since his stay inside the globe, I have been able to work all of my magic on him."

She sipped dragon fruit lemonade, made from trees that grew inside the greenhouse. Then, she waved her hand for him to be seated. He backed away slowly, still bent as if in acquiescence, his red irises snapping like a crackling fire. His goatee rested on his shirt, done in a rare black and red satin brocade, rounded out with a pair of black leggings and matching boots with red leather buttons.

All of the Diāmons were present: Jinn the shapeshifter, Samael, the Angel of Death, Astaroth, the Great Duke of Hell and of course Tempestous, Liz Herd, and Chame Leon. The last three were of the old guard, and yet she had known them nigh on seven years. The Queen of Mammals hoped they would cede all power to her, but she was wise in the ways of the world and had assigned lookouts, just in case they got any ideas to upset the order of things. *Her* order.

She turned toward a screen she had brought in specially for the occasion so that all could witness her handiwork. And although Alaric and his ilk were trapped in the web of place and time, The Queen of Mammals had made it her mission to travel through time and to bring back those most precious of objects from the future and beyond. It was this that kept her at the top of the pecking order. She smiled as she clapped her hands and enjoyed the thrill of their "oohs" and "aahs!" as the room went dark and the battle began to spool before them.

But they were soon silenced as the screams rang out from the citizens of Bookbinder manor as the starlings swept in, in numbers too vast to count. The sheer quantity of birds assured that people were toppled, the landscape destroyed. And the way the starlings moved about in formation, making frightening images like hand puppets on a wall—of reptiles and dragons . . . why, it made her laugh outright, which only strengthened the silence in the room. She had shocked even The Devil himself. It was then that she realized she had miscalculated their reaction to her words. By showcasing her handiwork, she had made enemies of some, she felt certain, but whom? She narrowed her eyes, scanning each creature, but if they meant to betray her, none showed it willingly. Still, she best be careful in the future. One must have the stomach for war. Especially an unjust war, such as hers.

Winnifred had no sooner returned to the manor, after depositing the loom someplace where no one would find it, when she spied a cloud forming on the horizon. A funny buzzing sounded in her head, but she couldn't tell whether it was internal or external. However, she soon had her answer because Lofgren tilted his head as he was wont to whenever something puzzled him. And then she saw it. The cloud was actually a flock of birds, but not just any flock, a whole hoard of flapping wings.

"What are they?" she whispered, as though to speak out loud might draw their attention and bring them toward her and Lofgren.

"Starlings." He took her hand and moved slowly at first, then picked up speed until he was dragging Winnifred behind him.

"What are they doing?" she shouted to be heard.

"It's called murmuration, where they join in vast numbers, but I've never seen this many. Ever. Quick!" he yelled.

Before she could respond, the starlings were upon them, turning the daytime to nighttime within seconds. Fortunately, just as the birds swooped in, Lofgren was able to pull her behind the manor, where they tucked their backs against the wall so the birds flew past them, the sound of flapping wings deafening. This went on for so long that Winnifred thought she might faint before it was through.

Above her, a piece of slate slid and fell to the ground in front of her feet. She looked up, and to her horror, Henry was hanging off the roof. Just as she let out a scream, he fell, his body twisting and writhing. He was about to hit the ground when another group of starlings swept in, their numbers so vast that Henry was cradled on their backs as they swooped in and upwards in a reverse arc.

"Help me!" Henry screamed. Then his words were swallowed up and he was gone.

Frantic, I rushed outside into the snow just as the last of the starlings had taken flight up and over the hornbeam maze. For one brief moment I spied Henry on the back of the birds, panic causing his eyes to go wide, his mouth to open in a silent scream that set me running while tossing aside any remaining birds that stood in my way of saving him.

Winnifred must have spotted me because she raced over from where she stood beneath the eaves and fell in step beside me as I fought my way through the thick swarm of black-feathered birds. Their beaks and claws tore at my hair, my face, my hands, but I grappled my way through as I attempted to make a path.

Please stay alive, I willed Henry, hoping against hope that he could somehow hear my message and hang on until rescue could come.

Lofgren was the first to locate the opening to the hornbeam maze, the last point at which I had located Henry. We raced through it, turning this way and that.

Where are you, Henry?

Fear clutched me in its grips as the birds had Henry while I slipped and slid through the maze. All sorts of scenarios ripped through my mind. What if the starlings soared higher into the sky and let loose of him? What then?

"Don't think it," Lofgren said.

I halted for just a second. "Wait, what?"

"He can read minds," Winnifred explained, in answer to my puzzled expression. "It's an elf thing. Come!" She took me by the hand, her hand frigid in this unseasonably cold weather.

Together, the three of us twisted and turned until I thought we must surely be lost, when out of the shrubbery I heard a faint moan.

"Henry?" I whispered to myself. "Henry!" I shouted. "We're coming for you."

But all I heard was continued moaning and a brief gasp, then silence.

Is he dead?

"Brigid!" Lofgren admonished, but this time his word rang inside my head, startling me. "We will find him. Be patient."

"Thank you," I said, never losing momentum.

I had just about given up on ever finding Henry, when suddenly, there he was, atop the hornbeam maze, his limbs flailing uselessly as he attempted to right himself and search for a way out of his predicament.

"Don't move!" I called. "We're here, Henry. We'll get you down."

He lay back, his eyes facing upward, relief evident in the sagging of his body.

"How will we get him?" I asked Lofgren. The hornbeam maze stood at least twelve feet tall, if an inch.

Lofgren tugged at the hair he had begun sporting on his chin since his return from the fortress. "Winnifred, I'm going to hoist you up on my shoulders. You grab Henry and slide him down. Brigid, you are going to break his fall. Everyone, take off your winter jackets and lay them in the snow!"

No one hesitated, determined to save Henry at all cost. I said a brief prayer as Lofgren hoisted Winnifred onto his shoulders. Henry's arms trembled as Winnifred tried to yank him down. He was able to slip his legs out from under him, so that they hung from the top of the hedge. The next step would be the real test. Could we get him down without hurting him any worse than he already had been?

"Henry, I'm right here below you." I extended my arms. "I'm going to break your fall."

"No," came the feeble reply. "You'll hurt yourself."

"I'm strong," I said, even though I didn't feel strong. But I would need to be if we were to get Henry out of here and back to the manor.

"Let go," Winnifred said.

"You can do it," Lofgren encouraged.

I heard a feeble, "Okay."

Then suddenly, Henry began to fall, gaining momentum

as he closed in on me, but I was able to grab one leg and slow his momentum so that the two of us fell backwards into the snow and pile of coats with a plop. For one moment, no one said anything. Then all four of us began laughing, Henry's laugh weaker than the rest. Then he groaned from the pain in his side.

"I don't think I can walk."

I looked around. The only thing we had were the jackets. Perhaps I could tie the arms together to make a sling, a travois like the one the Mohawks and Oneida had made during the last foray into the fortress.

To my surprise and delight, it worked, and two at a time, we pulled and dragged poor Henry through the snow for what seemed hours, our bodies out of breath by the time we reached the opening of the maze.

When we arrived at the clearing, a whole crowd was there to greet us. Henry's parents, first and foremost, many of the women, including Jocelyn and Gertrude, and Emma and Thomas, who had been through so much with us over the course of the past few years.

"Welcome home," Thomas said to Henry, to which all of us began talking at once.

10

Birsha listened to the pop-pop-pop of fireworks. Music played, while horns blasted from every end of the fortress to know that the Bookbinder Kingdom had been hit. Surely now, with summer turned to winter, and the ground covered in snow, all food stores in various stages of devastation, the Bookbinders would give up. Wave the white flag. And yet, for some strange reason, it filled him with a world-weary sadness that made him want to retire to his bedroom, to encase himself in darkness, to shut out the world.

"Are you okay?" Beatrice asked, placing a hand on his arm.

He wrapped her hand up in his and brought it to his mouth, kissing it. How had he come to be so lucky, to have found someone so like himself? Yes, she had his instincts when it came to power and place within society. But she lacked greed, the root of all evil. And like it or not, he lacked it too. His father would find it a weakness. She saw it as a strength, and he valued that in her.

"You've been awfully quiet today," Beatrice ventured. "Does that mean you don't believe what your father is doing is right?"

As he stood on the turret, he turned to her and took both of her hands in his. "The Bookbinders . . . were they good people?"

"Of course," she said without hesitation.

"I thought so, too."

He blinked and was surprised to discover tears. He hadn't teared up since a child, when he'd had them nearly beaten out of him. Then and there, he'd vowed never to show weakness. And yet, was it a weakness? Was it truly? So many things he had accepted at face value he now questioned. The irony was, Alaric had declared that dissent, in any form, was now outlawed. Even a whisper of objection to an unjust decree could have one arrested, tortured. Birsha had no doubt that he would suffer the same fate should he protest any of the rulings, and that's what frightened him. For even his *thoughts* would betray him, should they somehow make their way to his face. He had been careful to appear placid at all times, and especially in front of his father.

"What if I can't live with what's happening?" Birsha immediately regretted the words the moment they left his tongue.

Beatrice grabbed his shoulders and shook him. "Don't say that. Don't ever say that! We'll get through this together. We'll find a way."

"A way to what, Beatrice? To survive? Is that all there is to life, survival? When the mad hatters of the world have jumped off a cliff and taken everyone with them?"

"Mad hatters?"

He explained about mercury poisoning, how fur to make hats had at one time been treated in mercury which had given rise to what was known as "Mad Hatter" disease. It was as if all of the crazies had taken hold of the world's reins and had decided to take everyone off a cliff with them.

"I see." She folded into his arms, her head cradled on his chest as though listening to his heart beat.

He held her tight. For the first time in his entire life, he felt as if he were on a precipice. A thought had been brewing in his head for some time. A thought that gave him pause. To act on that thought could get them both killed, and yet he couldn't sit back and watch everything good in the world be destroyed, while the monsters of the world imprisoned and enslaved everyone else, ironically calling it justice. Their means were only becoming more punitive and cruel. He had to stop them.

"I know you're thinking about something." Beatrice pulled his arms from around her waist and peered up at him. "Want to tell me about it?"

He pursed his lips, clasped them tight to keep the words from spilling over onto his tongue. Finally, he could hold them back no longer. He just prayed that she was the woman he hoped she was when he met her.

"Beatrice—" He closed his eyes and inhaled the acrid smell of firework residue. He opened them, slowly taking her in. "I'm thinking of joining the Bookbinders. They deserve to live in peace."

"They're not perfect," Beatrice was quick to add. "There are the traditions, after all, and they are brutal."

"I know but . . ." Birsha swallowed hard. He had found something in the old library, something he had yet to discuss with her. Until now, he wasn't sure how to broach the subject.

"Come with me," he said, taking her hand.

"What? Where are we going?"

"You'll see."

Now, he prayed he was right in trusting Beatrice, that she was the woman she had proven herself to be up until now.

Slowly but surely, the noise of the crowd died down
and Henry's mother bent forward to help her son to a sitting
position in front of the hornbeam maze. Her eyes were moist
with tears—tears that were never allowed to be shed. Almost
instantly, she broke out in hives. She peered up at me with a
deep sense of anger and loathing that she couldn't even comfort
her son without being set upon by what I was quickly coming
to think of as the thought police . . . *the traditions*. In that
moment, something broke inside her. I could see it in her eyes,
in the firm set of her jaw.

"What can I do, Brigid?"

I knew then that she had snapped. That she no longer held
to the traditions. That she had joined the women's movement
and would fight alongside us, if need be. I reached out a hand
to her and felt a hum pulse between us, as though we had

physically bonded in some way. By the sheer joy and amazement in her expression, I could see that she felt it too.

"You can help me fight them," I said, our hands sparking between us.

She paused for no more than a few seconds, then nodded her head firmly. "Together."

I bent forward and she wrapped me in her arms and wept . . . for all the times she hadn't wept when she'd needed to. Welts blossomed across her face, her chest, her arms. But, at that moment, neither of us cared. We were going to fight the traditions. All of them. And we were going to win.

"Let's take you inside," I said, grasping Madame Bookbinder by the elbow. "Emma can give you an oatmeal scrub, while I take care of Henry."

She nodded, but I could see she had lost none of her determination as she marched toward the manor, Thomas and Lofgren pulling the travois with Henry on it. The women all returned to shoveling snow and tending to the injured and sick. I knew, in that moment, that we must find a way to retract the curse. I turned back one last time to survey the devastation the starlings had left behind. Although I dare not cry, not when so many needed me to be healthy and strong, the pit that lodged like a stone inside my stomach grew with each passing moment. For there, in a swath far and wide, stood destruction far worse than the one I'd first encountered when the jewel beetles had been set upon the manor and the lands around it. The gardens were gone. The barns that housed the livestock had fallen under the weight of the starlings. I heard cattle lowing, and the sounds of pigs and sheep, each bearing witness to the wreckage wrought upon them by those inside the northern fortress of the Jackals.

I called to Thomas, who stood before the side entrance to the manor. "Take care of Henry!" I shouted. "I have work to do."

He saw my meaning and nodded, his eyes hooded from fatigue and anger. I understood it. For I felt it, too. Now, to start anew. Then we would fight . . .

The minute Winnifred had Henry to safety, she and Lofgren returned to her home in Battersbog and began speaking to the loom in earnest, asking it questions, pleading with it to offer up answers to the many questions she had regarding the fortress in all its machinations, but it remained silent, as though deliberately snubbing her. But then, in the late afternoon, to her surprise, the loom went from dark to light. In the newly formed tapestry, the manor stood in stark relief, but shadows played across the entire manor, shadows of people.

"What does that mean?" Winnifred asked, but Lofgren only shrugged. "We have to get back there, you know."

"To the manor?"

"Of course. But the problem is, we don't know what the Jackals' next step will be, so we have no way to counter them, and the loom has been less than helpful in that regard."

Lofgren peered through the telescope Winnifred had made in order to see farther distances, but unfortunately, she'd only been able to design a telescope that would allow her to see close distances, not the distances she would need if she were to learn what was going on inside the fortress. The challenge had left her shoulders sagging in failure, but she couldn't give up. Scientists and inventors could *never* give up. After all, an invention or discovery could be just on the horizon if one searched long enough.

"Lofgren," she said.

"Hmm . . ." Lofgren responded, pointing the telescope in multiple directions.

"What if we lose? What if the Jackals win and we fall under their jurisdiction, what then?"

Lofgren set the telescope down and swept her up in his arms. If one didn't look too closely, one might mistake him for a human.

"If we lose, we will do what we must to survive, but until then," he said, lifting her jaw, "keep your chin up." Then he winked.

She sank into his arms. "I don't know what I would do without you, Lofgren."

"I don't know what you would do without me either," he said with a sly grin. "Now, I'll have the elves guard the loom. Your women are awaiting you."

A weight pressed down on Winnifred, though she knew he was right. She had been gone far too long, and at a time when her warriors desperately needed guidance. For a while now, Winnifred had thought that with Brigid's return, her services would no longer be required.

As if the wind had heard her and carried her message to Brigid, a note blew in on the wind, swirling downward in a funnel until it dropped succinctly at Winnifred's feet. She bent down to pick it up.

The note simply said, "Hurry!"

She thanked the wind, then grabbed what belongings she could and stuffed them into her knapsack. Once she had it firmly hoisted over her shoulder, she looked to Lofgren, who, as usual, was one step ahead of her. She gave him a short nod.

"Your carriage awaits, m'lady." He marched her outside to the waiting *barouche* with a bow and a swish of his hand.

"Oh, Lofgren." She climbed into the carriage and he climbed in after her. "What would I do without you?"

"Don't you know?" He turned to her, a serious expression on his face. "You don't have to. I have a good eight hundred years left in me. That should do the trick, don't you think?" Again, he winked.

The coachman gave a hearty "haw" and set the carriage in motion. Soon, Battersbog disappeared in the distance and the countryside enveloped her in its green and warm embrace, so like Lofgren, the man she had come to love.

For the past hour or more, I had been barking orders as we attempted to pull rooftops off of livestock as we had for two days now, the roof batted in from the weight of the starlings. One half of the tiles appeared completely normal, while the other half of the roof looked as if a giant had put his foot on it, caving it in. Some of the cows lowed while others bawled. Still others were eerily quiet, their sightless eyes staring up at some unseen spot on the ceiling. My heart rushed out to them, wishing them a speedy journey to the other side, where I knew their promise of an Eden-like afterlife would be waiting. But it also reminded me of our mortality. I had almost lost Henry the other day, and though I'd been able to hold back all emotion, seeing the lifeless cows made my eyes sting and my chest burn with emotion. To shed tears now would only cause me more grief, so I fought them with all my might. But as the day wore on, I feared I might lose that battle.

Finally, too exhausted to go on, I allowed the tears to flow and immediately moaned at the bruise swelling my lip. My head began to throb, no doubt another one of the "traditions" meant to keep us smiling. And quiet. And alone, isolated from the very people we needed in our lives if we were to help each other survive this hellhole. I sat back on my haunches, shivering from the snow and fatigue. No, I could not give into anger. To do so would be to give them total control of my destiny, and that I would never do. Instead, I chose to focus on what lay ahead. We would need every cow, every sheep, every chicken, every goat, if we were to survive, and survive we would or my name wasn't Brigid Anne Dunsmore.

"How many of the livestock are dead?" I asked Thomas, who had just arrived through the south entrance, the north entrance to the barn still blocked by falling debris.

"We've lost at least thirty cows. The sheep are all safe, all except one, because their pens were farthest from the collapse. As to the chickens, their pens are now open to the air, and a number have flown up in the trees or are picking through what remains of the gardens."

"That's not good."

Poor Thomas had cuts on his arms where he had been lying on his belly in the snow, trying to pry what animals he could from beneath their wooden graves. Sweat ran in rivulets down his brow, which was smudged with dirt and mud.

"Have you heard from Madame Bookbinder? Is Henry okay?"

"Ah, right." Thomas swiped at his filthy brow, his wet shirt torn and as dirty as his face. "I was supposed to relay this message to you. Henry is running a fever—"

I gasped, but before I could set off in a panic, Thomas held me off with two moist hands that made me shiver. "It's okay. Emma is tending to him. She sent for the local doctor who theorizes that his lungs may have become infected because he breathed in so much dirt and dust from the starlings. He's not sure. But if it were up to me, I would put my bet on Emma and her cures. That awful doctor wanted to put leeches on Henry. To bloodlet him." He shuddered, his face suddenly pale.

"You didn't let him!" I cried, attempting to pull away.

"No, Brigid." He spoke to me patiently, as though I were a child. "Emma tore into him. We'll be lucky if he ever returns to the manor after the way she treated him."

"The red hair," we said in unison, as though that explained it.

Then we laughed. Even she made jokes about her fiery temper that was said to be a trademark of redheads, though that could only be a wife's tale. Still, she had succumbed to the tale and though she was loyal to a fault, her anger was legendary when it came to "her people," as she liked to call us, as though she were the queen, and we her subjects.

"Thank you for telling me about Henry."

I looked down at my arm, then up at him. Wearily, he

released me and nodded toward the manor. "He's all yours. I'll stay behind to deal with the livestock."

I thanked him and was just about to leave when he said, "Brigid. Wait! There's something odd that you should know about before you leave."

He didn't have to say anything. I had noticed it too. After the starlings had left, I began seeing shadows. They were small at first, but before long they had grown. They seemed to be trailing us everywhere. And these were no ordinary shadows. Every time I turned, I thought I saw something out of the corner of my eye, as though a monster of some sort were following me. The same was true for everyone else I had come across.

"What do you think it is?" I asked.

Thomas merely shook his head. "I don't know. But whatever it is, I would bet it's up to no good."

I pressed my lips together, wishing for just a small break in the action so that I could compose myself, figure out what was going on and how to stop it. But I feared I would never get that break. Not now, not anytime soon. Whether any of us knew it, we were living under a shadow moon, though truth be told it was not the moon that captured us in its spell but the sun that was casting a heretofore unknown shadow over each and every one of us. What it meant, I had no idea. I just knew that it was another plague needing a cure. But how could we rid ourselves of the snow and shadows, when we didn't even know the purpose of it in the first place?

"We must stop them," Birsha cried, no longer in the thrall

of the Council.

And now they had to contend with these new creatures that were even more absurd than the council members in their appearance and actions. Frustrated, Birsha grabbed Beatrice's hand and nearly dragged her through the halls to the library. Once there, he started at the beginning of the alphabet, going right to left and bottom to top, a strange anomaly in alphabetization common to his people, according to Siegfried who had beat them there.

"What are you looking for?" Beatrice asked, the bow on her head askew and looking for all the world like a princess who had gone bonkers.

Birsha laughed, despite himself, but quickly hid the laughter behind his hand. Still, it crept out.

"Oh, for heaven's sake, Birsha." She turned to Siegfried. "Do you know what he's looking for?"

"A map," Siegfried said. "Of the underground. Beneath the fortress. Julius Sizemore, earl of Leicester, designed the fortress and its many underground caverns. An entire network of paths is said to lie beneath us, with secret doors inside rooms. But which rooms. That's the question."

Beatrice turned to Birsha, green eyes wide. "Is that true, Birsha?"

"It is, I'm afraid."

Beatrice shook her lovely curls. "But why not just ask Liz Herd and Chame Leon? Surely they would be more than happy to tell you. After all, they were the ones who told you about the cabal in the first place."

Birsha sighed. Clearly, she knew nothing. The pair had

already said too much. If they were caught speaking with Birsha further, they could be put to death. He tried to explain it to her as best he could.

"Oh, I see. Okay, then. Where do we find this map?" She peered around the room at the beautiful tomes, many done in goatskin bindings.

"The problem is," Siegfried explained, "we have known about the underground for years. Alaric searched for the map but failed to locate it in the library."

Beatrice threw out her hands. "Then why are we here?"

"I'll explain," Birsha said, taking her delicate fingers in his. "Alaric and Siegfried have searched the entire library, top to bottom. But they didn't know about the hidden room above. If not for the dome having broken open, we would never have found the room nor the odd ghost from the past inhabiting it. The rarest, most valuable books are up there. I was just doing a double check of the ones down here to make sure we didn't miss anything, which we haven't. So, if we have any hope of locating it, we must search up there next."

Beatrice's eyes moved skyward. "But that has to be at least eight floors up." When she spoke, her voice echoed through the cupola, her words bouncing back on them in a series of echoes.

"Surely you don't expect us to go up there?"

Birsha was not only serious, he had every intention of searching this final area in the hopes that he could find the map. But finding this map wasn't only to learn where the creatures might be staying, as Beatrice suspected. It was to be his escape route. His and Beatrice's. Because he knew that if he stayed here, he would be expected to do the unthinkable—to beat and starve and pillage his enemies. *And my own people.* And that, he could never do.

12

What Winnifred found when she and Lofgren returned to the manor could only be described as chaos. People raced back and forth, while the gardens were plundered of any nutrients by the birds who scavenged as they passed. And what the birds didn't eat, the insects were now finishing off, especially the jewel beetle, the shiny, multi-colored insect they had destroyed after their last foray into the manor and the surrounding areas. In her reading, she'd discovered thousands of varieties of said insect, this version an especially small one.

Winnifred stood over one especially fat little beetle, its body shining amid the sunlight that was beginning to melt the snow, much to everyone's relief. Still, it hovered over the remnants of a blueberry plant, sucking the juices dry, its body expanding rapidly. Just below its head was a small triangular shape that turned colors when the light hit it just so. Orange, red, blue, green. If the insect weren't so despised for its unique ability to destroy, she might actually find it beautiful. But the wee beastie burrowed into fences to make its nest, coming out in the sunshine to devour anything and everything in its wake. It seemed a particularly undiscriminating pest, for it went after flowers, leaves, berries, virtually anything it could fit into its suction-like mouth.

With her thumb, she squashed it and watched it burst like a ripe watermelon, spilling its blue contents onto her thumb.

"Remind me not to hold that hand!" Lofgren said, leaning over her with a look of complete and utter disgust.

She couldn't tell if he was joking, but seeing that he was, she laughed.

"Seriously, wash that hand," he said, his expression never faltering.

She walked over to the koi pond and bent down, rinsing her hand in its waters. A large orange and white koi, with irregular black markings neared the surface, its bulging eyes staring up at her, its round mouth moving in and out in a "wah-wah" fashion that made her giggle.

But when she looked up, she saw one of her warriors staring down at her with a hint of undisguised anger and she quickly jumped to her feet. "Gertrude!" Winnifred cried, happy to see her friend. But clearly she was not as happy to see Winnifred.

"Where have you been?" Gertrude hissed. "We have women down all over the place, and Henry is hurt. He's developed a fever," she added, her voice catching, her brown hair protruding at all angles.

"Oh, Gertrude, I'm so sorry." Winnifred scooped her

friend up in her arms and gave her a hug. "You know me, I get to inventing and time disappears. But to be fair, I was working on something that should help the women warriors in the long run."

Gertrude grew flustered, her face turning beet red whenever she showed anger. "I know. I shouldn't have snapped. It's just that we seem to move from one disaster to the next."

Winnifred took stock of her friend and fellow warrior. Apparently, Gertrude had done without the amenities of a shower and clean clothes during the preceding days, because she appeared disheveled, her clothing marred by bits of dirt and grime.

Winnifred recalled their last foray into the fortress where they had freed the slaves from their shackles. "We did save our people and Lofgren's from starvation and death," Winnifred reminded her friend.

"Yes, I know, but we seem to be back to where we were before all this started."

"Which is where, exactly?" Lofgren asked.

"On the defense. Just waiting for the next volley. It has the women on edge. It has *me* on edge," Gertrude admitted.

"I can see that." Winnifred put a finger to her chin and thought for a moment. "Let me speak to Brigid, formulate a plan. Then have the women meet us in the glade outside of the bird sanctuary tonight, before dusk."

With that, they said their farewells, and Winnifred and Lofgren set off for the manor to speak with Brigid and to see how Henry was faring.

It was far worse than I could have imagined. Poor Henry was laid out on my bed like a mackerel, his breathing as irregular as his heartbeat. My hands shook as I checked his pulse.

Please, God, spare him, I prayed. For despite the calluses I had developed on my heart these past weeks and months, there were no calluses when it came to Henry. I claimed him as my own to care for, to keep safe. I had made it my duty to look after him. I couldn't live with him gone. Tears wavered on my eyelashes, and though I fought to prevent them from falling, the onerous traditions caught wind of them and blinded me with a searing pain to the jaw. Still, I refused to give them the satisfaction of seeing me cry out, seeing me recoil. Instead, I stood steadfast as I held Henry's hand in mine, my jaw set in anger and frustration that I couldn't lash out at such evil without severe and utter punishment.

From the corner of my eye, I saw that Phinney had entered the room, my rare blue falcon who followed me everywhere, though he had taken a special fancy to Yesimeh, of late. She, who loved all things small, like herself. Yet now, as Henry hovered especially close to death, Phinney had begun standing vigil, squawking out every moan or twitch, as if to keep everyone apprised of Henry's health, and yet it only served to get on each of our nerves.

Just then, my falcon let out a particularly loud blat and I opened my mouth to scold him, but then I heard a commotion and turned to find Winnifred and Lofgren entering the room. I rushed to greet them, embracing them in a three-way hug.

"You came!" I breathed out in spent emotion.

"Of course we did," Winnifred said, "once we learned about . . . well, everything."

She splayed her hands out to encompass the entire kingdom, one would suspect, or at least I had.

"Oh, Winnifred," I said, trying, with fierce determination not to cry. But too late, a tear fell and a welt appeared on my eyelid so that I could see out of one eye only.

"Oh, Brigid."

Winnifred cradled me despite the fact that I knew she didn't go in for emotion, too much like her father, rest his soul.

"If I had known how bad it truly was, I would have come sooner. Will Henry . . . ?" Here she paused and gestured at the stirring form on the bed. He appeared thin and wan, a fever wracking his body, sweat dripping off his brow.

"I don't know," I whispered, willing myself again not to cry. Yet I'd had the thought no more than a second when I felt my lip begin to swell.

Winnifred watched in horror.

"What is causing all this?" Lofgren demanded, bending down to take a closer look.

"That's just it—" Winnifred turned to him, her eyes bright with an underlying fury. "We don't know. It's as if an unseen force knows every move we make. Often no one knows what caused the punishment, but we do know that emotions are never allowed. *Ever*."

"Is that why Brigid is so . . ." His voice trailed off as though hesitant to say more.

She nodded.

"And you, Brigid? Why are they constantly after you?"

"Brigid isn't from here," Winnifred explained.

"Punishments weren't meted out like this where I'm from," I explained. "Or perhaps I was just too young and unaware. I never learned to control my emotions." I wanted to add that I'd never learned to lie about my real feelings, but feared that, too, might elicit retribution so I kept quiet.

"They listen to our words," Winnifred said in hushed tones. "We must be careful of every single thought or deed. We're told it's for our own good."

"Hogwash!" I immediately threw a hand to my mouth but not before my forehead began to swell.

Lady Bookbinder came to the door, Phinney apparently having snuck out to retrieve her. "Here, here. What is all this?"

Her eyes went first to the bed, where her expression told of the devastation that played havoc with her heart at the possibility of losing her son. "And you, Brigid." Lady Bookbinder raced over and cupped my chin, peering at me this way and that. "Oh, Brigid, will you never learn?"

But how did one fight an enemy that couldn't be seen? Couldn't be heard?

"Well, we have no time to fix the swelling. You'll just have to deal with it for now, I'm afraid. We need to get Henry's fever down first. Then we'll work on you." She shouted down to the cellar maid. "Guinevere! Get me some ice!"

It seemed a long time before the young cellar maid came dashing up the stairs, the tie from her apron swinging in her haste. She'd had to retrieve a block of ice from the cellar, bring it to the kitchen to chip the block into a bowl, and then make the final ascent to our room upstairs. Clearly out of breath, she sat the bowl onto a bed stand, then gasped for air, a hand to her chest to still her overburdened heart.

I ran to where the bowl sat and wrapped the ice into a towel that I then placed under Henry's armpits. I repeated the process several times until he looked like a frozen snowman, his face puffy and his breathing beginning to slow, as though the fever was starting to abate, if only slightly.

I beseeched God to keep him safe. *Please, please, please, be okay.* Emma appeared at the door moments later with tea. Now, if we could only get it down him.

13

"Here!" Birsha set the book down on a table caked in dust, a mini explosion of airborne particles filling the air.

Beatrice sneezed into the back of her hand, while her eyes screwed up and her nose turned red. "Let me see!"

Siegfried crab-walked over to the pair, just as eager as the rest, it would seem, for he nearly toppled onto the book in his haste to cross the room in such an ill-suited manner.

As if the glass orb had heard their cries, fog began swirling inside it and Fearsome the Foul appeared, but his energy must not have returned, as he began fading in and out, like a face in a mirror marred by billowing steam.

Birsha opened the book with reverence. It was a volume on architecture, but not just any architecture. It was of the fortress in its infancy, when first built by two Spaniards who escaped from the wars and Inquisition rocking their country. At first, disappointment settled in Birsha's gut. For although the volume contained an accurate accounting of the fortress and all its nooks and crannies, he hadn't seen anything that would suggest that warrens ran beneath the fortress like a rat's maze filled with creatures, who even now scurried to overthrow his kingdom, or should he say *Alaric's* kingdom.

Birsha released a subdued laugh to think what a fool he'd been when he'd first heard of the creatures. When Chame Leon and Liz Herd had warned him of these underground dwellers, he'd felt a sense of glee that at last, freedom might once again rule the land. But that hope was dashed the moment it had seen daylight. To think that there might be worse than Alaric . . . *much* worse. He shook his head, at the unfathomable idea. Now, their only hope, his and Beatrice's, was to find the warrens, to destroy the hive, and then to seek escape beneath the dungeons that held prisoners in a perpetual state of destitution. Quite frankly, that thought kept him up at night.

"Look, see?" Beatrice pointed to a hand painted fold-out in the book. "You almost missed it. A map. It was hidden in the folds of the book. Apparently, the underground maze was added sometime later."

Birsha inspected the odd writing. It seemed almost Persian, but how could that be if the people who had built the fortress were Spaniards? He didn't know, and although he couldn't read the writing, he knew enough about the layout of the fortress to know that the hidden room lay just below the ballroom. But first he had to find the opening. That detail had *not* been laid out.

"What will we do now?" Beatrice asked, smudges of soot

and dust marring her cheek and forehead.

"We keep looking. Siegfried?"

Siegfried peered up from where he'd been hovering over the manuscript. "Yes, sire?"

"Where would you put the openings if you were hiding them?"

Siegfried paused for a moment, a funny expression causing his lip to rise at one end as though a thought had just occurred to him. An altogether brazen one.

"I think I may have an idea . . ." His eyes darted to the window.

"Do you care to tell us?" Birsha demanded.

Siegfried nodded and stood, crouching as he made his way toward the ladder. "After me," he said. Then he disappeared down it.

Birsha had nothing left to do but follow the man's lead. But where was his adjutant taking him? "Hmm . . . Come, Beatrice. Before we lose him."

I knew that the women must be getting restless by now, but I hadn't known how restless until Yesimeh came rushing up the stairs, breathless, dragging Hannah behind her, whom I'd barely seen since the mishap in the cave nearly two years back when a storm had nearly taken Hannah from us.

"Brigid, you really must come," Yesimeh urged.

I was slated to meet the women at the bird sanctuary at dusk, but that wasn't for at least two hours. Winnifred and I had decided that it was high time we went on the offensive again, but this time the stakes were higher. What with the Diāmons and their many sorceries, many of them straight from the very pits of hell itself. I blinked rapidly. What did we have to counter it? If anyone would know, it was Yesimeh.

"What's wrong?" I demanded, not yet ready to leave Henry's side at such a crucial moment in his recovery.

"Winnifred has gone mad. She's simply come undone."

Yesimeh's face was even paler than usual, if at all possible. I shook the cobwebs from my head. Had I heard her right? Winnifred, the most stable of people I had ever known?

"Someone took an ax to her time machine, to her quantum computer that she brought back from the future. Then they warned her that she would be next."

"Next for what?" I asked, none of this making any sense.

"I don't know, but it doesn't sound good." Her lip quivered, but give it to Yesimeh, she didn't cry, too afraid of the traditions to make a sound.

I looked at Henry who moaned in his sleep, his head tossing and turning with fever. If we couldn't get it down soon, we would lose him. But neither could we afford to lose Winnifred, my battleworthy sister. We needed her. Should anything happen to me, she stood next in line as successor. I closed my eyes, the decision blindingly difficult.

With a sigh, I snapped them open. "Okay, Yesimeh, tell her I'm on my way. I'll call Lady Bookbinder to watch over Henry."

Then, when she and Hannah had left, I bent down and rested a hand on Henry's forehead. I gave him a brief kiss on the mouth. In that moment, he stilled, as if knowing the touch was mine. "I love you, Henry Bookbinder," I whispered into his ear.

"Never forget that."

Then I called down to Lady Bookbinder, who came running in haste, the door flinging open in fear of bad news.

"I have to take care of an important matter." I paused, worry no doubt written in the newly formed creases on my forehead. "If there's any change . . . any change at all, call me."

She took my hand and nodded, empathy alighting the contours of her face. And with that, we parted ways, but not before I took one look back at the man I had come to love more than life itself, lying in the bed, broken.

Before I had even arrived at the back of the stables, which had been spared from the wrath of the starlings, I heard Winnifred shouting and tossing things, her fury formidable. And though bumps and bruises were sprouting from every part of her body, she couldn't be stopped.

"Why, why, why?" she screamed, falling to her knees.

Yesimeh and Hannah stood back so that I could see for myself the damage that had been done, and indeed it took my breath away. To have been spared the starlings, only to face this, must have been devastating for Winnifred, who now sat on her knees, rocking, tears dripping down her cheeks and onto the dirt floor.

I bent down and wrapped an arm around her shoulder, our foreheads touching. That seemed to calm her because she stopped moaning and merely rocked, the tears slowly subsiding.

"It's okay, sweetie," I said. "We'll face this together, yes?"

She sniffed and nodded, but I could see the defeat written in her expression. Never had I seen her so forlorn. Lofgren, who had been standing in the corner, seemed at a loss. He shrugged and shook his head as if to say he had tried. From what I knew of elvin culture, they didn't go in for emotion, except possibly laughter, so all of this was new to him.

"Don't worry," I told Lofgren. "Winnifred will be okay. She hasn't had time to process this yet."

I refused to say the things I had said in the past, that it would all be okay and that she could rebuild. She had done that—had put in hours, weeks and months to build machines and inventions to help us in our quest, so I knew what all of this meant to her.

When she finally settled down, she peered up at me, her head cocked. "Why did they do it, Brigid? Why?"

"For the same reason they do everything," I said, refusing to sugar coat my words. "Because they can. Because they're more powerful than us. Because it gives them the feeling of autonomy over everything and everyone. We mean nothing to them."

And even as I said it, I knew it was true. This was not about love, family, community, country. This was a power grab, pure and simple. And whoever controlled the masses, controlled the power. I thought back to ancient times and times not long gone. Caligula of Rome, who from 37 AD to 41 AD instituted a wave of terror upon his people, a sadist at heart who relished in sexual depravity. Then there was the genocidal Britain, Oliver Cromwell, who tore at the very heart of the Irish and Scottish Catholics. Whereas Ivan the Terrible, whose manic fits led him to take the life of his eldest son, gave terror a new name. Despots had ruled throughout history. But there had been brief periods of benevolence, led by men such as James the First of

England who had ruled with a steady hand. Or Augustus of Rome, who had kept peace with neighboring states. One had only to view the current Queen Victoria of England, whose rule had been marked by a blossoming of the sciences along with cultural reforms.

I could see that Winnifred was just as broken as Henry, in her own way, but I also knew that something broken could be glued back together again if we worked together as one. If we nourished the good in each other. Treated each other with respect.

I lifted her off the floor. "We're going to get through this," I told her, looking her squarely in the eyes. "I promise you, Winnifred. We will help you in any way we can. And Winnifred?"

She sucked in a quivering breath. "Yes?"

"You will always have us." I held her shoulders and stood there until she nodded. "Good."

I gave her a firm hug. Lofgren threw his head back in relief to see her finally calm. Then together we scooped her up in our embrace, all of us, and led her toward the aviary. It was time we had that talk with Conestra. And it couldn't come too soon, in my opinion.

"It's done."

The Queen of Mammals stared at all of those around the floating table, her eyes hooded. When her eyes landed on Chame Leon, he squirmed even as he forced a placid smile. She paused for only a moment, but long enough to set his heart racing. He dared not breathe until she'd turned the room to nighttime with a tiny switch, and set the overhead projector on to show the devastation of the Bookbinder Kingdom.

Chame Leon's mouth gaped in awe at the utter destruction. He turned to Liz Herd, who sat next to him, to witness her reaction and realized that she, too, was taken aback. After all, how could starlings have done that much damage, but their sheer numbers had made it so—crushed buildings, barns and homes, many set on fire when their oil lamps were overturned, the structures burnt to the ground. People and animals were scattered everywhere, many of them dead. But what caused his heart to still and Liz Herd to gasp was the sight of Henry Bookbinder, lying on a bed, near death.

"Is there something you would like to share with us?" the Queen of Mammals demanded, pinning Chame Leon and Liz Herd with a glare.

"N-no," Chame Leon assured her, putting up his hands. "I just hadn't realized the level of damage. Good. Very good." Again he forced a smile though his heart sank at the sight. True, Henry was the second in line, leaving Thomas as the inheritor of the realm, but that meant there would be no back-up should anything happen to Thomas.

The Queen of Mammals turned back to the screen to point out other devastation while laughing. As Chame Leon peered around at the Diāmons around him, he couldn't help but wonder how he had ended up here, though it was the mission given him. Still more shocking was the Queen of Mammals herself. For the umpteenth time, he wondered how a small, plain-looking woman such as herself could be filled with such rot and corruption, like a tree left standing though its interior was hollow.

He'd been so caught up in thought that he didn't realize what the Queen of Mammals was saying until he heard the words, "Now for Phase Two of the demise of the Bookbinder Kingdom."

She turned on the lights. All around him, the generals of the damned wore an unhealthy glow of pleasure. In that moment, Chame Leon knew he couldn't stay in this room much longer. To do so might spell his death. As if Liz Herd had thought the same thing, she glanced at him and blinked. To anyone else, it would have meant nothing, but he knew her well enough to know she was just as concerned as he was at this turn of events.

"I can't reveal any future plans. I'm sure you can understand that few must know them, as stealth is of the utmost importance. Suffice it to say that the Bookbinder kingdom will be no more. Any questions?"

No one dared speak, least of all Chame Leon who wanted nothing more than to leave this room and run as quickly and as far away as possible from these people, if they could be called that. For the first time since joining this group, he realized how different he looked among ordinary people. He peered at his reflection in the floating glass table. At his color that had faded so as to be almost indistinguishable from the table and the room. But he could just make out his outline. He blinked, fighting an emotion he'd never felt before. Actually, he had never experienced emotion at all, until now, his throat tight and raw with unshed tears. Perhaps he was softening, changing, becoming more human. But then he saw the most human of them all, The Queen of Mammals, and a shudder twisted his tail into a tight coil. If that's what it meant to be human, he wanted no part of it. No part at all.

14

"Where are you taking us?" Birsha demanded.

Though winded, despite the shape he had to be in as heir apparent, he raced down the narrow corridor within the inner fortress walls, holding tight to Beatrice's hand for fear he might lose her at this fast pace.

"You'll see," Siegfried said.

"Wait!" Birsha paused. "Isn't this my father's wing? Surely you can't mean for us to go in there?"

Terror gripped him. His father had made it clear that he must never enter these halls unless invited, and his father had never sought to do so, instead, insisting they meet elsewhere, whether for safety purposes or otherwise, he couldn't be sure. He just knew that the consequences would be severe, should he disobey.

But the terror soon faded as he peered around in wonder.

This portion of the building breathed opulence, between the gilt-framed portraits of past leaders, to chairs with gilded arms, legs, and backs, sumptuous tapestry inlays for the cushions. Even the rugs were of imported Aubergine in rich colors that reminded him of oxblood.

"Come!" Siegfried pulled a key from his waistcoat, placed it in the lock and turned it, bending his ear to listen to the click. He smiled when the lock popped, and the door fell open.

"No, no, no!" Birsha backed away, hands up. But Beatrice moved past him, eager to see what was inside.

Birsha couldn't say why, but as he entered the room tears blurred his vision to know that his father had lived in such a regal manner, while he had lived in a small hovel, low ceilings, tallow candles the only light. Here, no expense had been spared. This was no fortress. *This* was a palace. A gilded one at that. All along the walls were pastoral paintings framed in gold. The bed that filled one side of the room bore huge pineapple finials, the canopy that covered it done in the finest silk from the Orient.

Off to one side set a nineteenth-century French Baroque, Neo-Gothic secretaire with intricate carvings, a desk at which to write missives, to plot and plan, quilled pen in hand. If not for his worry about one of Alaric's guards entering the room, or worse, Alaric himself, Birsha might have explored more, but his heart was racing and his eyes kept darting to the door.

"Hurry! Where is this supposed entrance to the tunnels?"

Siegfried began tapping the books along the bookcase, but none of the walls moved. "I don't understand," he said. "I thought sure I had noticed cool air coming through here."

"You risked our lives for that? A breath of air?" Birsha

hissed.

Beatrice grabbed his arm. "Stop, Birsha. Give Siegfried a moment to think." She rushed over and began tapping the wall alongside the adjutant.

Panic seized Birsha as he heard the click of footsteps coming down the hallway. "Hurry!" he whispered in a rush.

"Help us!" Beatrice whispered back, fury guiding her words.

It took only a moment to gain her meaning and then he too was tapping walls, pulling on books, even a bust of Alaric himself. Just as he heard the click of the key in the lock, he pulled on the bust and the wall opened enough for all three to glide through. The door opened as the wall closed behind them with a soft whoosh. Birsha waited until his eyes adjusted, only to discover the three of them in a dark, dank space meant for creepy crawlies, not men.

He heard voices on the other side of the wall. Had Alaric seen them? Would he find them and have them hanged? Birsha found Beatrice's hand and grasped it. Suddenly he heard a strike and the smell of sulfur followed by a match lighting up their faces in a garish moue. Siegfried peered around until he found a torch on the wall and lit it.

Birsha blew out the breath he had been holding. "Where, for mercy's sake are we, Siegfried?" he hissed.

Siegfried's face appeared stark in the gloaming of the torch. "I do believe, my good friend, that we are beneath the fortress. But where, beneath it, I have no idea."

Before we could reach the aviary, Ma'am intercepted us and ushered us toward the manor. She was wearing men's knickers today, and boots that reached her knees. Her hair was thrown back in a bun with an ascot tied around her neck so that she reminded me of a young ingénue.

"The women are assembling, but we have time," Ma'am assured us.

"Time for what?" I asked, Lofgren and Winnifred still in tow.

"You'll see." Ma'am waggled her finger for us to follow her.

I frowned, but Lofgren merely shrugged. Winnifred, for her part, was still recovering from the shock of having the last of her inventions and discoveries destroyed. She would need something to preoccupy her until we could come up with a way for her to begin rebuilding all that she had invented over these past few years. Until then, she would never be right, just as *I* would never be right if I lost Henry, my compass, my true north.

To my surprise, once inside the manor, Ma'am began ascending the Big Ben staircase, Phinney chirping as he flew ahead of us, excited to have so much company. And even more to my shock, Ma'am entered my room and pointed at the loom.

"Which of you traded out the loom?" she demanded, one eyebrow cocked.

We all looked at each other. That's when I noticed Winnifred's cheeks flush a deep burgundy. Surely my eyes deceived me. "You?" I squeaked.

Winnifred dared not look me in the eye. At last she raised her head and nodded. Then she added in a rush, "I knew how much that loom meant to you, Brigid. I couldn't bear to see you lose it to someone of Alaric's kind." Her shoulders slumped in apology.

"Thank you," I said. Who but a true friend would think to protect me in such a way? Warmth flooded me at her thoughtfulness.

"Ah, just as I suspected," Ma'am said, pinning Winnifred with a look. "Well, not to worry, ladies . . . Lofgren. I have a plan." She gave a sharp whistle.

Seconds later, I heard a scrambling noise, followed by a thud and an "oof!" Then the door flew open. There stood Yesimeh appearing sheepish and toting a large tapestry made up of some odd weave.

"Are those . . . *feathers*?" I gasped.

"Yes, they are," Ma'am stated in that no-nonsense schoolmarm voice of hers. "And you'll see why. Yesimeh!" she ordered. "Will you do the honors?"

"Certainly." Yesimeh pushed up the round spectacles seated at the tip of her nose.

She heaved and moaned with such relish that I ran over to help her with the heavy tapestry. "What on earth is it?" I asked, eager to view the end product.

"See for yourself," Ma'am said as we finished unloading the loom's tapestry and replacing it with this one.

Though I stood back and gazed at it, none of it made sense.

"Oh, here." Ma'am walked up to it and bent down to adjust the knob at the side of my loom.

"Oh, my!" I gasped.

It was the most lovely tapestry I had ever seen. The feathers, when laid in such a way, appeared to show an army of Jackals bearing down on the Bookbinder Kingdom dressed in their finest.

"But I don't understand? You show them *attacking* us?" I tapped my lips with my index finger, trying but failing to understand her plan.

"Don't you see, Brigid?" She peered back and forth at her handiwork. "We give this loom in place of the other. It has no magical properties, but it will look as though it has magical properties. It will guide the Jackals by suggesting they should enter here."

She pointed at the road I had traveled the first day I arrived at the manor, where I had met my beloved Henry, who lay even now on a bed in this very wing, fighting for his life. I couldn't let him down. Somehow, I intended to keep him safe, to keep the kingdom safe. Maybe Ma'am had offered me the gift I had been seeking. A plan. Hopefully, a good plan.

"The landscape provides a natural pinch point, so that there's really no place to enter *but* here." She made an imaginary "X" with her hand.

"And the women warriors will lay in wait here." I pointed to two spots opposite each other, the road separating the two sets of warriors.

"Precisely," Ma'am agreed. "Not only that, but some of the women will meet them head on so they will believe they are playing on an open battlefield."

"And we have another contingent of women here." I pointed to a copse of trees just west of the manor house. "When the Jackals enter here, those women will come from behind—"

"And they will be completely surrounded," Winnifred said,

finishing for us.

"Exactly," Ma'am and I said in unison.

Lofgren, who had been silent until now, cocked his head in that funny way he did when he was thinking, his expression so like that of a puppy dog that I had to laugh.

"What is it, Lofgren?"

"You forgot the elves. They will be in the trees . . . here . . . and there." He pointed to two of the copses. "Now, we have them cornered in every direction," he said with a smile.

"Oh, you smart green man," I said, squeezing Winnifred's hand. "That one's a keeper."

For the first time since she'd discovered her inventions shattered beyond repair she seemed to brighten.

"That he is," she said.

Then we all laughed. But the laughter died in my throat when I heard Madame Bookbinder scream from an upstairs room. *Henry!*

"Quick!" I yelled, but Phinney was already ahead of me. The women and Lofgren brought up the rear as we raced up the stairs only to hear a loud crash and see Madame Bookbinder falling to the floor, the tray she carried in her hands and everything on it now scattered at the opening of the doorway.

Siegfried led the way up the steep incline from Alaric's room, but not before Birsha had heard the words, "Someone has betrayed me."

Alaric.

Birsha imagined his father marching throughout his inner

chambers, fury mounting in the ever-increasing pitch of his voice. Now, more than ever, Birsha knew he must step lightly if he was to survive this nightmare that had become his life. Though Birsha hadn't betrayed Alaric, the very fact that he was crawling through the walls of the fortress made the thin thread between life and death that much more real. As if Beatrice understood that too, she gripped his hand so tightly that his fingers ached.

When they were far enough removed from Alaric's quarters, Birsha whispered into the frigid air, "If we're beneath the walls of Alaric's room, why are we going up, not down?"

"I don't know," Siegfried said, the fear palpable in his words. "We can't be going up." He paused as though thinking. "As a child, I heard a rumor that whoever built the fortress built magic into it as well. That one had to be very careful when wandering its halls that one didn't buy into the illusion."

"Illusion?" Beatrice hissed, turning wide eyes on Birsha, who only shrugged.

"I'm only repeating what I was told." Siegfried paused, listening.

Birsha heard it too, a moan, but it was coming from the fork in the path, one portion going downwards, the other up.

"What is it?" Beatrice's breath came out in a cloud of steam.

Siegfried held his torch out to get a better look, then rubbed his forehead with his other hand. "It sounds like the dungeon. But the dungeon shouldn't be going downward."

"Which path do we take?" Birsha asked, the moans growing louder.

Just then, he heard a clink of metal and the sound of a door opening with a scrape.

"I don't know," Siegfried said, "but I think wherever we go, it should be away from that sound."

"Agreed," Birsha said, Beatrice chiming in concurrence.

"Then we continue up."

Siegfried pinned them with a look that set Birsha's nerves on end. As a child, he would have loved this game of hide and seek, but now he wanted no part of it. "Just get us out of here, Siegfried. That's all I ask of you."

15

I knelt down and put a hand to Madame Bookbinder's forehead. As I did, she stirred, her eyes fluttering open. She looked around, as though wondering what had happened.

"You fainted," I explained, taking her hand in mine. "Are you ill?"

"No," she said with a firm shake of her head.

Even as she spoke, her eyes looked past me, her facing going pale as if she'd seen a ghost. And I suppose it was a ghost of sorts, I realized as I turned my head to see what had frightened her so.

"Henry!" I cried, dropping Madame Bookbinder's hand and jumping to my feet. "It's you!"

I threw my arms around him. He was still dressed in the white linen gown Madame Bookbinder had asked the maid to dress him in when he'd first taken ill. He wobbled on unsteady feet, so much so that I took a step back and guided him by his elbow.

"I . . . my fever broke, I think." He peered around the room with dull eyes, then put a hand to his forehead.

Winnifred helped Madame Bookbinder up off the floor while Lofgren gathered the tray, a glass of milk having spilt across the doorway entrance.

"I was bringing Henry lunch," Henry's mother explained. "But when I opened the door, there he was, standing there like a wraith."

"There, there, Madame," Ma'am said. "No need to fret. We'll see Henry back to bed, won't we, Brigid?"

"Of course," I said, only too happy to comply.

With Henry well, that would be one more worry down. Now to save our people . . . no small task. I closed my eyes to regain my composure. When I opened them, I smiled at Henry, who seemed none too well, despite his assurances otherwise. I touched his forehead, and felt a moment of giddiness.

"He's right! His fever *has* broken." I wrapped him up in my arms only to hear him groan. "Oh, sorry," I said, releasing him.

"I don't mean to put a damper on the party." Ma'am walked over to stand by me. "But the women are waiting."

"What about Henry?" I asked, relieved to have him among the land of the living.

"Until we are finished, your mother can care for him, isn't that right?" She turned to Madame Bookbinder, who was slowly regaining color.

"Yes," Henry's mother said, rubbing her elbow that had caught the brunt of the fall. "I'll call the nurse to come look after him."

I couldn't say why, but I felt a twinge of jealousy to know that someone other than me would be looking after him, now that he was getting better.

"I'll be back as soon as I can," I told Henry.

For the first time in days, he offered a wan smile that brought a watery glint to my eyes to see him so helpless. Henry, who had been through so much with me. Who had fought beside me through thick and thin. I said a hurried goodbye, then we left.

Moments later, we were racing through the glen, Phinney flying ahead of us and squawking our late arrival. Already, women had amassed in the thousands. It gratified me to know that so many women had willingly put their lives on hold to help in our quest to save the kingdom. I owed them a debt of gratitude, one that could only be fulfilled by ridding us all of the onerous traditions, those most evil of punishments for every perceived infraction, too numerous to track.

Emma and the others had set up a wooden platform from which to speak, a bullhorn at the ready. I couldn't possibly talk to them all at once, so stationed around each grouping of women was someone to relay the message to those further back.

I climbed up on the dais and looked out at the war weary women who had followed me to the ends of the country and back, seldom complaining. Their eyes sparkled back at me—me with eyes the color of condensed glass. Suddenly, a hush filled the air, as if every one of them was straining to hear what I had to say.

"Fellow warriors."

I recognized so many friends in the crowd: Gertrude, who now wore jodhpurs, Jocelyn, who was the picture of wholesomeness in her military garb, Hannah, who had overcome nearly being swept away by a giant of a storm two years back, and Emma, whose women now wore red crosses to signify that they would handle the wounded. Dear sweet, tiny Yesimeh stood with a satchel over her shoulder, no doubt filled with military plans for the two of us to go over in the coming days. The one missing face in the crowd was Beatrice. She was with Birsha. I sighed, wondering how she was getting along, and surprised to realize I actually missed her.

"We have it on good authority that The Jackals are about to attack us again, and this time will be more formidable than the last."

A stir arose like the humming of bees, and as if they too had heard it, a swarm of bees came buzzing in to see what all the fuss was about. Fortunately, they found flowers in the nearby meadow that had somehow survived the cold, and settled onto them, buzzing in pleasure.

"We have a plan. Your company commanders will fill you in on each of your upcoming roles. Anyone who has a special gift—"

"Gift?" she heard one woman say.

"Talent. Any skills that are, let's just say—"

"Magic?" another woman close to the first one asked.

"Yes, I suppose you could say magic. Or ability. We need anyone with—"

One woman stepped forward, a rather thin waifish looking

girl with freckles on her nose, green eyes and a large braid down her back. Though I knew her by sight, I couldn't put my finger on her name, our army had grown so large, of late.

"I have the ability to . . ." She peered around the clearing, her face paling.

"Out with it," I said, pointing to her. No one will think any less or more of you, I promise. Anything we can do to help the cause would be much appreciated.

"I can fly," she said, then immediately stepped back into the crush of women, as though afraid of the others' reactions.

For a moment, no one spoke. The wind rushed by, bringing with it the scent of squashed plants that had yet to recover from the starlings and their foray into the kingdom.

"You can . . . *fly*?" I knew my face must have registered surprise, but who was I to judge? After all, hadn't a flying machine taken Brigid to a completely new century in the future? Hadn't Lofgren shown us that time was relative as he moved like the wind from place to place? And then there was Yesimeh's isinglass. Who would have thought the sticky glue could act like cement when paired with water.

Smatterings of laughter could be heard around the glen, but that soon died down and the gathering grew silent.

"Thank you, uh . . ."

"That's Claire," a stocky woman with a rough voice yelled out. "She's our resident crazy, but we love her." She gave the young woman a hearty squeeze so that Claire would like to keel over, had the stocky woman not held her upright.

"Yes, well, thank you, Claire. Any others?"

Suddenly the trees came alive, and from everywhere the

Mohawk and the Oneida appeared, their faces painted to reflect their warrior status. With them was Kahwihta, one of my dearest friends who had been through so much with me. I raced to greet her, throwing my arms around her. As always, she simply demurred, hugging my custom, not hers.

"We heard of your otsi'tén:'a."

When I looked at her with confusion, she merely said, "Birds."

"Ah, the starlings, yes." I dipped my head.

Kahwihta was dressed in a yellow tunic overdress and leggings, along with her traditional moccasins that she had beaded in a pretty pink and white pattern that reminded me of peonies.

"Our warriors are here to help." Kahwihta peered behind her.

"Where is your father?" I asked. He was usually the first to show his face.

"Father is becoming elderly," she said, somewhat apologetically. "He can no longer perform the functions he once did. But my husband has been asked to fill the role."

It's then that I saw a handsome man of thirty-odd years, black hair hanging down his back in a ponytail tied near the end. The sides of his head were clean-shaven, but he wore the top of his hair upright, which reminded me of porcupine quills, and it had been painted red to match the lines down his face. In his hands he cradled a baby, which he brought closer for me to see. Gingerly, he handed the baby to me so that I could get a good look, the baby's dark round eyes staring up at me in quiet interest. His little face was round and flat, and he had a head of sleek black hair like both father and mother.

"What is his name?" I asked.

"We call him Wahta."

"Wahta," I whispered into his ear. I held his tiny fist in my hand that felt like a giant's hand next to his. I had forgotten how sweet a baby could smell.

"He will be a great warrior someday."

"And your name?" I asked, turning to the father.

"Tyendinaga," he said, "but you may call me Ty."

"Ty it is." I had almost forgotten those around me until I turned back to see the crowd waiting patiently for us to finish our greetings.

I handed the baby off to her mother and finished speaking to the women. "We will prepare for battle!"

Those women who owned spears lifted them in the air in salute, others their rifles, and still others their bow and arrows. "To Dances the Loom!" they cried, remembering my native name. "Hut!"

It was as if a dam had broken and women flowed in all directions, a human river washing to the sea, each to their respective camps where they would go over their parts in the battle.

"Yesimeh!" I called, seeing her about to depart. "Could you bring an updated list of women with unique skills?" I asked.

She bobbed her head, her expression serious. "I'll get right on it, Brigid."

I liked that we held no titles, and instead used our names as we always had. It made our army seem more egalitarian somehow.

"Thanks, Yesimeh," I said.

Then I turned back to Kahwihta, who looked even more cherubic than I had remembered her with her narrow brown face, her hair tied back in a braid, and a beaded headband circumnavigating her forehead.

"Rumor has been flying." She seemed suddenly out of breath, as though she had run all this way here to tell me what awaited us. "Alaric's Jackals will be on the march any day now. There are at least thirty thousand men, all in uniform."

Up until now, the Jackals had used only magic on us. Why had they actually placed men into action this time?

As if she'd read my thoughts, Yesimeh said, "Alaric wants to capture you and Henry this time. He believes if he has you and the loom, he will be able to bring the kingdom to its knees. And Bri-gid," she added, in that rather unusual way she had of saying my name using clicks and clacks native to her tongue, "he has the backing of some horrible creatures. It is like our legend of Sky Woman's Daughter."

"Sky Woman?" A chill wind blew over me, encircling me so that I looked at her through the eye of the wind. Her hair blew outward, as mine blew inward, cocooned in this most oddest of storms designed just for me.

This daughter birthed two twins, one good—the Bookbinder kingdom—one bad—the Jackals. The twins grew. One created all that is evil in the world, the other created all that is good. The good son eventually banished the bad twin to the pits of what you would call hell. Yet, even from this place, he was able to send evil to disrupt the good twin's world. This is what Alaric has done. You must fight him with everything you have inside you.

Kahwihta handed the baby to Ty and took my hand in hers. "We, too, live and die by the evil and good loosed into this world. And Bri-gid," she said in that affected way of hers, "we see your heart." She tapped first her heart then mine. "We know it is good. We are sisters in this. We are one."

The swirling of my personal storm gained speed until all of a sudden it lifted with a swoosh and was born off on a breeze. I sighed with relief to see it gone, to see clearly once again, but most of all to know that I had so many people behind me in my quest to see normalcy returned. To see *decency* returned also. Without it, we would become Barbarians. We would become like The Jackals or the Vidunders that Lofgren's people so feared for their power to enslave, to starve, to brutalize.

As if Kahwihta knew my plans and understood them, she said, "Our people will be here, Bri-gid." She pointed to two sets of copses on either side of the Bookbinder manor. "We will be here, and there, at the how do you say—"

"Pinch points?" I filled in for her.

"Yes, pi-itch po-ints." Though she struggled with the words, we both understood her meaning. "You can count on us."

How had I been so lucky to have found such loyal friends? "Thank you," I said, pointing my chin in the direction of her people. "All of you."

Then, just as they had arrived, they disappeared into the trees and were gone. I needn't ask where they went. They had left to prepare, just as I must, now.

Ma'am sought me out, now that the Oneida and Mohawk had faded into the forest, a mere memory to remind me that they had been here only moments before. Something was in the air. I could smell it, as if the seasons had changed overnight. And although the snow had disappeared and summer had returned in full, the aroma was not of plant life growing big and strong, but rather of plant life dying, wilting on the vine. Between the rapid change in seasons, and the starlings doing damage to what remained, it was as though the very garden had been trammelled under thousands of feet and left to rot. I had only to pray that Thomas was right, that the Master Gardener had thought to grow in his many greenhouses what we could not.

"I know you have much to trouble you these days," Ma'am said, stating a fact that we both knew to be true. "But at least one thing has gone to plan."

"Oh?" I puzzled my brow. "And what's that?"

"I have it on good authority that one of the downstairs maids has just taken off with your loom."

I felt a quick check in my breast. "The fake one or the real one?"

"The fake one, of course," she said with a laugh.

For the first time, I noticed that Ma'am had a weak chin, and her eyes were slightly off-center, but she had a presence that commanded attention, and not just because she had run a household all those years.

"But surely once they realize there's only one tapestry, they'll recognize they've been duped."

"Oh ye of little faith," she said, quoting the scriptures.

"I've taken that into account. As I was about to tell you before we were so rudely interrupted earlier, there's a knob that can be turned eight different ways. Each turn of the knob creates a new scene. So you see, Brigid, we've made certain they'll believe the loom to be real."

"But how?" I asked.

Ma'am winked at me and whispered, "It's our little secret. But that's not the real reason I'm here."

"No?"

I absentmindedly peered into the distance, watching the women go about their practice, only this time in earnest. No doubt each of them was thinking about the future and what it would entail. Could we really hold off an army of Jackals, especially since they seemed to possess an unending array of magic, each one more virulent than the last?

"I'm worried about you, Brigid." Ma'am lay a hand on my shoulder.

"Me?" I frowned, not understanding in the least.

"You've hardly slept and you haven't eaten since I've been here. I fear that if you don't find time to rest, you may end up ill. Do take care of yourself. I can speak to Thomas and Emma . . . and Winnifred—"

"But Winnifred isn't herself!" I blurted out.

She marched me over to a log and sat me down under a beechnut tree, Phinney looking down at me with a bemused expression.

"Which is precisely why she needs to get back in the saddle, Brigid. Winnifred is a resilient girl, but she needs to keep busy. Why do you think she invents?"

I shrugged my shoulders. "Because that's who she is, I suppose."

"Precisely. She's a doer. Don't take that away from her."

I could see Ma'am's point, and in truth I was bone weary. The only thing that kept me from collapsing was that I never stopped moving.

"Are we agreed then?"

I nodded reluctantly.

"Off with you then." She nodded toward the manor.

Though I laughed and shook my head, I rose and did as instructed, but as I peered back, I saw the trace of a smile playing across her face. *Oh, Ma'am!*

16

"Where are we?" Birsha hissed.

"I don't know," Siegfried said as he fought at the cobwebs with his free hand, the other hand holding the lit torch.

From the look of things, they were inside a giant hollowed out tree trunk, if Birsha were to guess.

"Wait, there's a door." Beatrice turned the knob and the door flew open.

The three of them stood, peering out. Birsha stepped beside Beatrice and placed a hand on her shoulder.

"Where are we?" she asked.

"I'd say we're deep in the forest on the south side of the fortress," Siegfried said.

Beatrice marched out first, Birsha following suit. He'd no sooner left the trunk when he heard Siegfried say, "Uh-oh."

At first, Birsha didn't know what worried Siegfried so, but

then he saw it. Poison oak. They were smack dab in a thicket of it. As if at the very thought of it, welts blossomed across his cheeks and Birsha began scratching at his arms. Soon, they were all scratching with varying degrees of ferocity.

"We'd best get back to the fortress and put something on that," Siegfried said.

Just then, Birsha heard the crackling of footsteps. Woodsmen often hunted in these woods. If they weren't careful, they could all end up with a round of buckshot in their bums, a far worse fate than poison oak, though Birsha wasn't sure about that at the moment.

The sound ceased. No one breathed, least of all Birsha. Suddenly, it was as if the woods came alive, people dressed in camouflage coming toward them from all directions. Within seconds, they were surrounded and their hands tied behind their backs before they'd been able to give up so much as a struggle.

"Who are you?" Birsha demanded, to what he assumed was the leader of the bunch. The man shot out hand signals to the others, who then did whatever he commanded.

"The question, sir, is who are *you*?" The man's face was painted green and brown, his clothing mirroring the forest around him.

Birsha didn't know whether to tell him the truth. He weighed his options but realized time was running out when the man prodded him with the barrel of his muzzle loader rifle.

"The name's Birsha, son of Alaric, and you, sir are . . . ?"

Their captors buzzed with both shock and awe that they had captured someone of such high value, though what they hoped to gain, he had yet to decipher.

"My name is of no importance," the leader of the bunch said. "Why are you here, in the forest, hiding in the—"

"Tree?" Birsha finished for him. He peered over at Beatrice and Siegfried whose eyes registered fright in the gloaming of the shadows deep within the glade.

"Exactly." The man peered at his compatriots, each nodding in turn.

"That's for me to know and for you to—" But he never finished his sentence because the man landed a blow to his head and knocked him clean out.

Winnifred reveled in her reprised role as leader to the women as she shouted orders. Ever since she'd returned to Battersbog, where she lived with her mother and Lofgren, she'd lost her bearings. Winnifred peered over at him and released a flag. As if a single unit, women on horseback, five abreast, came charging, using the lances the Oneida and Mohawk had made for them, each with a long wooden shaft and feathers tied on with thin strips of leather. As one, they split the hay-bale humans they'd designed for practice in half. All the while the women screamed as they charged, the sound echoing off the canyon to the northwest. Lofgren ran fast as the wind behind each woman, pulling out the lances so the next wave could have a go.

"What do you think?" Winnifred turned to Lofgren, after each of the women had been given a turn.

Lofgren seemed to choose his words carefully. "Um . . . you do know that all of this could be for naught, that they might use magic instead."

Winnifred had worried about the same thing. How could they possibly counter the unknowable?

"That's where the loom comes in, I suppose," she said with a sigh.

"Yes, but the loom doesn't speak to you. It only speaks to Brigid," Lofgren reminded her.

As she turned to face him, she was struck by how much she now looked like his doppelganger, only in female form. It's as though she had gradually taken on his appearance, not just his light green color. She'd never thought to ask about this most peculiar of circumstances before she'd agreed to marry him. Never *knew* to ask. And yet when she peered in the looking glass each morning, she found herself pleased at their similarities.

"So, what are you saying, Lofgren?"

He took her hands in his. "We need to show Brigid the loom."

She shook her head as she watched the women fall one by one onto their backsides beneath the shade of the copse and begin to eat the food that Dele served them. She and her husband had decided to stay instead of escaping to Canada. And now that they no longer acted as trail captains, they had taken on the role of camp cooks, which suited everyone just fine as they were both great cooks.

"We can't risk someone seeing the real loom and reporting back to Alaric's people," Winnifred hissed.

"Unless . . ." Lofgren ventured a sly smile.

"Unless what?" Winnifred frowned.

"You'll see."

Winnifred rolled her eyes. Whenever Lofgren got something in his head, there was no use fighting it. "Gertrude!" she shouted. "Could you take over for the rest of the day?"

Gertrude gave a quick salute.

"Right-O. Then I suppose we're off!" And with that, they took their leave.

I awoke, still groggy from sleeping so long. "What time is it?"

I peered at the grand*mother* clock, a smaller version of the grand*father* clock. Mine was a silly thing that tilted and had arms, so that it looked for all the world like a mother scolding a child. Even its "foot" appeared as if it were tapping a rhythm. Time to rise and shine. I lifted my head up, but fell back with a moan.

"What day is it?"

I hadn't realized Phinney was in the room until I heard a squawk and saw her perched on the curtain rod. Squinting, I saw that a full day had passed and dawn had risen anew.

"Dawn!" I gushed.

When was the last time I'd witnessed the full glory of the sun in the morning? Not since that horrible day that I had so unceremoniously threaded the loom. *My loom!* My heart sank at the realization that I had yet to see it. So much had happened since I'd last learned that Winnifred had it that I hadn't had a chance to go see my loom, nor did I know where she'd hidden it. The loss of it brought tears to my eyes, which I quickly hid to avoid the backlash of the traditions. Somehow the loom had supplanted my family in my mind as though it had become what I missed most—a connection to all those I loved.

Love!

"Henry!"

I bolted upright and rushed to dress. I quickly donned my beige pants, white blouse and boots. When I peered in the mirror, I realized that I had dressed exactly like Ma'am. I had to say, I liked this new version of myself, as though by changing clothes, I had grown more confident and strong.

I ran a quick brush through my hair, then whistled for Phinney, who immediately landed on my shoulder, and out we went. But when I flung open Henry's door moments later, the room was empty. I turned in a circle, panic setting in.

"Henry? Henry!" I yelled, flying down the stairs, nearly tripping in my haste.

I barrelled to the bottom, running smack dab into Madame Bookbinder who had come out of her study to see what all the commotion was about.

"Here, here, Brigid. Compose yourself. What's all this yelling about?"

"Henry!" I said, panting.

But to my surprise, she only chuckled as who should walk through the door but a very wan, tired looking Henry. He coughed even as I launched myself into his arms. "Oh, Henry, you're alive!"

"Of course I'm alive, Brigid. Where did you think I would be?"

"I don't know," I said, the worry causing me to fight back fresh tears. "It's just that you weren't in your room . . . and I had fallen asleep so I couldn't protect you."

He wrapped me in a tight embrace and whispered into my swath of ebony hair. "You don't have to always be the one to protect me. I've got an entire family."

And that was the rub of it because he had one, I did not.

As if he understood what had me so raw, Henry turned to his mother, and said, "Brigid has a family in us too, doesn't she, Mother?"

Lady Bookbinder paused for only a moment. In that lapse, I could see her mind working, weighing the pros and cons of a woman who had led an army of women, who had unwittingly sewn threads into the loom that had caused the kingdom to go black. But also a woman who had saved her son, the brightest star in her sky.

"Of course you do," she finally said.

That broke the ice and suddenly we were all smiles as she ushered us into the dining room for a morning meal of eggs, bacon, and fresh melon. I wondered how she had conjured such a meal with the devastation that had befallen the manor grounds.

As if in explanation, she said, "So much was lost, but what could be saved must be eaten."

And yet I heard the trepidation in her voice. The uncertainty. So much rested on the Master Gardener and his crew now. Only they could help us out of this mess.

Birsha awakened to the sound of cattle lowing, of roosters crowing. Next to him lay Beatrice, her hair filled with bits of hay and straw, their bedding for the night, it would seem. He attempted to rub his eyes only to realize his hands were still secured behind his back. Worse yet, he could just make out welts over a good portion of his body, and something else. Someone had poured liquid over him. He sniffed at the herbal scent and guessed that it was an elixir for the curtain of poison ivy he and Beatrice had negotiated when exiting the underground maze.

"Oh, Feathers!" he hissed, awakening his sleeping wife. Though her hair was mussed, and her eyes swollen from the ivy, to him she looked like an angel.

She shook her head slightly and yawned, then tried to stretch her arms, only to discover, as he had, that they were tied behind her. She turned her back to him and whispered, "Help me out of these."

He set to work. However, try as he might, he couldn't get the bonds to release. Just then, he spied a wagon wheel lug wrench hanging on one wall of the barn. Opposite him, a man sat guarding them, only he had fallen asleep as the night wore on and was snoring. If only he could reach the wrench without waking the man, they might stand a chance of leaving this godforsaken place.

Carefully, he crept to where the wrench hung on a hobnail, got onto his knees, and with his teeth, secured the wrench, heart hammering so loudly that it sounded like a field drum in his chest. Still, the man remained sleeping.

Birsha paused for only a moment, then crept toward Beatrice and dropped the wrench unceremoniously onto her lap. She almost let out a gasp, but the fear he wore on his face must have stopped her, as she grimaced and said nothing, only mouthing a "Thank you."

For the next ten minutes, Birsha worked to free Beatrice, pausing only when he heard a rustle from the guard, whose mouth was parted and whose hands lay across a Colt Dragoon. Each time the man stirred, Birsha's hands shook but still he worked to free Beatrice from her bonds.

He was in a full sweat by the time the last of the ropes broke free. She rubbed her sore wrists and was about to help him when the guard let out a snort and his eyes fluttered open, but not before Beatrice had the foresight to grab her ropes and thrust her hands behind her back.

The guard yawned and picked up his pistol, then pointed it at Birsha and Beatrice. "So, you're awake, I see. Time for you to meet our leader but first . . ." He walked over to a hay bale. Atop it lay two blindfolds. "We can't have you recognizing those in charge, now can we?"

Birsha shot Beatrice a silent plea to stay quiet and play along. Fortunately, she was only too willing to comply. Now, they just had to find a way out of their current dilemma before Alaric caught word that they were missing.

Lofgren had driven the team of horses hard to make it all the way to Battersbog and back again in a single day.

"Do you think this will work?" Winnifred asked.

"It has to." Lofren whipped the reins, the hoofs of the galloping horses clipping the rocky soil beneath them.

More than once, Winnifred wished she'd had the machine

that had taken her to the future. Every time she saw its broken timber, its limbs scattered about the barn, she'd had to force back tears. Until the other day, she hadn't realized how much she'd viewed her inventions as an ode to a life she'd once lived, to a family she'd once had. Maybe that's why she identified so much with Brigid because each of them had faced loss in some form. And now, the women warriors had faced losses as well, uniting them in this most exclusive circle of grief and wont.

They pressed onward, Lofgren nearly tipping the wagon over in his haste, only to right it in the nick of time.

"There!" Winnifred called out.

She pointed toward the shack Lofgren had found to secure the loom near the manor. But now, as they peered at the copse of trees where the small cabin was hidden from view, Winnifred could see that someone had already beaten them to it, for through the trees she saw . . .

"Smoke signals! They're here! The Mohawk and Oneida are here!"

Lofgren had scarcely pulled on the brakes and yelled a loud "whoa!" before Winnifred bolted out of the carriage and ran over to hug Kahwhita, whose child clung to her back on a brightly colored, carved cradleboard. After a brief reunion, Winnifred told her friend about the loom.

"Bring it here." Kahwhita pointed to a large wigwam made from the neighboring fir saplings and covered in birch bark.

Normally, Kahwhita's clan would have lived in a longhouse, Winnifred knew, in large wood-frame buildings covered in elm bark, but here, most laid out mats that surrounded a fire and slept out in the open. Either that or in smaller wigwams, except for the chief, who slept in an especially large wigwam where he held tribal meetings.

Lofgren leapt down. Kahwhita spoke in her native tongue to one of the young men, who immediately set to work helping Lofgren carry the loom to the central wigwam. The chief appeared to be waiting for them, as if he'd known all along that Winnifred would arrive, the loom in tow.

But oddest of all, the loom began clacking in earnest the moment it was set before the chief, the heft and weave moving as if by an unseen hand. Winnifred's throat went dry.

"We need to get Brigid, now!"

Kahwhita turned to the man who had helped carry the loom in and said something in her native tongue that sent the man flying out of the teepee and into the forest, his feet scarcely brushing the ground. Now, all they could do was to watch and wait.

17

I hurried off, the moment I got word. *My loom is back!* I rushed through the clearing to the largest of the wigwams, a guard standing sentry. As if expecting me, I heard Kahwhita call to me through the open flap. Immediately, I bent down to enter.

Inside, I waited for my eyes to adjust to the darkness, thinking it odd that only days before all had been dark for months. The interior of the wigwam smelled of wood smoke and dust, but beneath it all lay a hint of dampness that chilled me, despite the warmth of the fire.

When my eyes finally adjusted, I saw my loom and knelt to search its contours as one would a lost child. Suddenly, it began to clack and the shuttle pierced the weft. "What is it?"

"I don't know." Winnifred stared at the loom that began clacking in earnest now.

I prayed my eyes had deceived me because all that I could

make out was a bubbling caldron of . . . lava? Maybe the loom was simply showing me Tempestous, that most colorful and odd member of the Council. Her dress often spewed ash and flame. Perhaps that's what the loom referred to. But then, as the loom clacked furiously, each weave adding a new detail, I could see that indeed, something was afoot, but this time I recognized it for what it was. Alaric had released the giant chessmen yet again.

So, we will be subject to the attack.

We had thwarted the Jackals and chessmen mere months ago when we had rescued the slaves trapped outside the Fortress where all manual labor took place. Now, the pair were headed our way, only this time an entire army of them. And the odd thing was, in the distance I saw the manor house, above it lenticular clouds, a series of clouds that reminded me of an Egyptian pyramid, the thin strips of blue between the clouds appearing like steps that led to the top, should one choose to go there.

"What does that mean?" I asked Winnifred and Kahwhita. But both shrugged just as confused as I.

For the rest of the day, as I set about preparing the women for the upcoming attack, I pondered the loom and what it meant. The pyramids, if memory served, housed the fallen pharaohs in Egypt. Did that mean that the manor was to become a tomb, its inhabitants the lost leaders of the free world? Just the thought made breathing difficult. More than once, Henry rubbed my back in a circular motion and reminded me to breathe.

"Look." Henry took me aside. I'd been running drills with

my women and planning magic of my own. "You can't lead effectively if you don't calm down."

He was right, of course, and yet that was easier said than done. "What do you suggest I do?" I gave another wave of the flag for the next group of women setting out on horseback, their guns aimed at fictitious warriors.

"Come with me." He crooked his finger and pointed in the direction of the copse where the Oneida and Mohawks had faded into the background.

I gave the job over to Gertrude, who accepted it gladly, then followed Henry. As I did, I saw what I hadn't earlier, too frightened to think clearly. The pinch point.

"Stop!" I said, yanking on Henry's shirttail. "There!"

"What?" He frowned, his lovely brown eyes narrowing, as if trying to see what I saw.

"Imagine this." I splayed my arms to encompass the large tree at the narrowing in the road opposite another tree that sat like a sentinel just east of the manor. "We tie a rope here, and one there. When they turn the corner—"

"They fall like dominoes!" Henry laughed, a sound I had desperately missed over these past few days as he recovered from breathing in all the dust and feathers from the starlings. He scooped me up in his arms and swung me around, but when I landed, he bent over, hands on knees, breathing heavily.

This time it was me rubbing his back until he had enough wind to breathe properly. "Now, what is it you wanted to show me?" I asked, once he'd caught his breath.

"Over there," he said, pointing with his chin.

"Who are you?" Birsha demanded, remembering only too well what had happened to him the last time he'd asked such a question. He touched the lump that had formed on his scalp.

He tried to look around at the small room with not a single window, but a hand on his neck shoved his head downward, putting an end to any such notion. Yet he'd had enough time to see that the man at the head of the small butcher-block table was an older gentleman wearing a vest and brown cotton work pants, the same man he'd seen the other night when he'd exited the underground maze.

"*I* will ask the questions," the man said. "What were you doing in the tunnels beneath the fortress?"

Birsha searched for options, but in the end, decided to tell the truth. "Beatrice and I escaped through a hidden door in Alaric's room."

He looked up in time to see the man throw his hands up in the air and fall back in his seat as though struck by Birsha's words.

"Why were you in your father's room?" The man leaned forward, a quill in his hand as if prepared to write down everything Birsha said.

"We were looking for something."

The man's eyes widened. "Looking for what?"

Birsha decided he'd said enough. He clamped his lips shut and merely shook his head. If these men were the people he thought they were . . . If they were fighting Alaric's tyranny, they wouldn't torture him. Now, he had to hope he was right.

Fortunately, for him, the man scratched at his neck, a measure of displeasure written in his expression.

"Okay, so you went to Alaric's room for an untold reason. Had you been there before?"

Birsha paused, then shook his head.

"Why not? You're his son, *non*?"

"Yes."

Birsha turned to hide the emotion playing at his lips. The truth of it hit him like a barrel from an apple cart. He had *never* stepped foot in his father's private quarters. He had never even been asked. Most of his life had been spent in exile in the countryside. And yet now, looking back on it, he felt grateful to his father for sparing him a life of duty. It had allowed him to be close to nature, to avoid the trappings of leadership. The Machiavellian way that he now lived.

"I consider myself fortunate, sir," he said, holding his hands together in front of him.

"And why is that?" the man asked, his quill dipped in ink and poised above a white sheet of paper.

"Because I was spared the trials of an heir. In effect, I lived freely for a time, although I did have my lessons, I suppose."

"You preferred it so?" The man frowned.

"Decidedly, yes. What I didn't know was freeing, in a way. It allowed me to believe in the goodness of mankind. I saw it, at the manor."

The man honed in on Birsha, his eyes wide with shock. "And what manor was that, pray tell?"

"The Bookbinder manor."

Pandemonium erupted between the man, who jumped to

his feet, the guard still holding Birsha, and the two people who entered at the sound of the leader's cry of surprise.

"What is it?" asked one of two men, the taller of the two standing guard at the door, the other one short and stocky.

The leader of the men held up a hand and waved the guards away, but the message was clear. *If I need you, I'll call.*

The man began pacing. "When were you at the Bookbinder manor?"

Birsha looked to Beatrice who nodded for him to continue. "As a child. I was brought there by my nanny." He paused, deciding how much more to say. "They treated me well . . . the Bookbinders."

The man with the vest let out a breath and sat. For several minutes, he merely shook his head as though trying to take this all in. Then he paused, his eyes narrowed, as though considering his next words.

"Can we trust you?"

Once again, Birsha turned to Beatrice who gave her assent. "You can. What do you need?"

"We need someone to guide us. To help us fight Alaric and his people. They've enslaved our men, women, and children, and they are about to do much worse. Can you help?"

It was Birsha's turn to exhale the breath he had been holding. It took him only a moment longer before he said, "I can."

"Then it's settled. We start today."

I couldn't take my eyes off of it. "What is it?"

Winnifred smiled up at me from where she knelt underneath the giant machine, tapping in a bolt with a metal clang and then cinching on a lock washer and a nut to keep the whole thing from coming apart. When she was done, she scooted out from under the contraption and Lofgren came around to give her a lift onto her feet. She swiped at her face, leaving a streak of grease across it, a bandana tied around her head to keep the sweat from dripping into her eyes.

"Do you like it?" She held her arm out like a showroom model displaying her latest wares for sale.

"I think so," I said, not at all sure.

"Look here." She pointed to what looked like a catapult of some sort, a series of straps holding it down. Inserted into the catapult was a boulder that once swung through the air in a giant arc, would rain down on the unsuspecting warrior. "We can use one large boulder, or a load of smaller rocks. Either way, it will serve to buy us time. And look!" she added, barely taking a breath. "I have the women recreating this again and again."

And true to her word, in the meadow dozens of women hammered and sawed, nailed and drilled. I knew for a fact that these women had never worked with hand tools. "How?"

"Lofgren comes from an entire clan of builder elves. I hope you don't mind, but we sent Phinney to collect them. We chose only those who live in the trees closest to us."

"You mean there are more of them?" I asked, Henry shrugging his shoulders beside me.

"Oh, many more," Lofgren assured us. "We have clans all over the forest. We don't reproduce quickly, but we have time on our side."

Thomas and Emma, who had been notably absent after my fall from grace, saw us and waved as they made their way toward us. Emma seemed perpetually in her white nurse's uniform with the large red cross. From the look of it, she hadn't seen much sleep, not with the damage done by the starling invasion. I took her hand when she neared, eager to learn how she'd fared these past days.

"Did you know about this?" I asked.

She nodded. "Actually, it was Winnifred who didn't know about it."

I puzzled my brow, confused.

"Lofgren surprised her. They've only started and already the elves were able to assemble much of this and to train the women in the rest."

"How?" I felt like a broken clock, repeating the same time over and over.

"Their superhuman speed," Thomas chimed in. "They're amazing!"

Thomas, who until recently had always been clean shaven and fastidious about his manner of dress and cleanliness, appeared rumpled, the hair on his chin halfway to a beard. Like Emma, his eyes appeared tired. Only now did I realize that while I had been finally able to rest, they had continued to work into the wee hours of dawn.

"This is amazing, Lofgren. You're a saint."

Then I turned to Emma and Thomas and said, "And you two need some rest."

They started to protest, but I would have none of it. "Go, sleep. Jocelyn can take over for you," I told Emma. "And Henry and I can fill in for you, Thomas."

They glanced at each other, weariness written into their expressions. "Okay," they finally agreed. "But call us if you need us."

I promised that I would. Once they were gone, I began counting the number of catapults being built and I came up with ten. Between that and my plan to stop the chessmen at the pass, we stood a good chance of besting them. But things don't always go according to plan, I knew. And I had a feeling, this time would be no exception.

18

Never had Birsha felt in such danger as he did now, as he navigated the underground passageways once more. The cold dank walls and the smell of mold and dust filled his nostrils. He fought back the urge to sneeze. This time they were taking a different route back through the underground fortress, one that would lead them to the lair of the "Creatures of the Night" as he had come to think of those most hideous of creatures that Master Clyde had told him about. *Master Clyde.* Thankfully, he had overheard the name of the man who had captured Birsha and Beatrice and had also heard that the man was head of The Underground.

Suddenly, they reached a bend in the passageway. Birsha heard the sound of voices rumbling from an interior room somewhere within the walls of the tunnel and grabbed Beatrice's hand to halt her. He leaned forward and listened but caught only every third word.

". . . found . . . keeps his . . . book."

"Good . . . search . . . 'morrow. Find . . . magick."

"What book?" Beatrice whispered.

Birsha shrugged and pressed his way along the wall of the tunnel, while motioning for Beatrice to be quiet. All morning, he had been suppressing one sneeze after another, yet suddenly one came on without warning, and before he could do anything to stop it, it burst forth in a gust of exhaled air that filled the chamber with the sound of a gunshot.

A shout of "Who goes there?" rang out from within the interior wall of the tunnel.

Just as he heard someone running toward him further down the tunnel, something hard dug into his back and the tunnel wall slid open, thrusting both him and Beatrice outdoors. The opening closed with a silent whoosh afterward. He peered around him as he sought escape only to discover that they were in the Kazakh's aviary. All around him birds of prey perched in their individual aviaries, looking down on him with golden or black eyes, each appearing angry, as though wearing a perpetual scowl. He turned on his heel and set out running, Beatrice in tow, and had scarcely made it around a series of aviaries when who should he run into, but the Kazakh himself.

"What are you doing here?" the Kazakh growled.

The man had always seemed imposing, yet here, in the Kazakh's own territory, he seemed especially formidable. For one, he was a giant of a man, built of sinew and muscle, not a spare ounce of fat to hint at a life of leisure. No, this was a working man. And as with his birds, Birsha felt the man's eyes drill into him. They, too, spiked golden rays of light as if judging their prey and finding the pair lacking somehow.

"We . . . we are lost." Beatrice's eyes widened as if professing her innocence of any wrongdoing. "Birsha and I weren't familiar with this section of the fortress. We saw the birds from a distance and just had to come see them for ourselves. They're quite beautiful, really."

To Birsha's surprise, he could see by her expression of awe that she wasn't feigning delight at seeing them up close, in all their glory. He held his breath, waiting for the Kazakh's reaction and exhaled in relief when the Kazakh's eyes lost some of their tension. It was as though she'd complimented his children, for he was soon smiling and showing them around the compound, explaining the many peculiarities of the birds. In all the time Birsha had known the Kazakh, he'd never heard him speak this much, believing him a man of few words.

When they had made a complete tour of the compound and had reached the exit, the Kazakh turned to Birsha, though his attention remained on Beatrice and her interest in the birds.

Quite cryptically, he said, "Should you need my help, or the help of my birds, you have only to ask, yes?"

Then, with a ceremonious bow from one royal to the other, a bow so slight as to scarcely be seen, he bid them ado. Within moments, they were swallowed up by the aviary and its birds.

"Did you hear that, Henry?" I asked, taking his hand.

"Indeed." He followed the sound with me in tow.

The chirps were lovely, soothing, as though hundreds of

people were chittering at once after a long day of toil, their murmurs content.

"What are they?" I whispered so as not to bother the birds. Though I couldn't see them, I could hear their chorus, their melody . . . so sweet was the sound.

He tilted his head and frowned. "If I'm not mistaken, those are starlings."

I gasped. The last time we had seen starlings, they had sailed down in such numbers that they swept Henry off his feet, not to mention eating everything in their wake, including the acres of vegetables meant for this year's harvest. We had been left with only what the Master Gardener could produce. Fortunately, I had great faith in him, because he had proven himself beyond reproach and if anyone could keep us alive, it would be him.

I turned my attention back to the birds. As I listened, I realized that these were but a small sampling of starlings, not the hoard that had wreaked havoc on the manor earlier.

"What do you think?" I asked Henry.

"About the birds?" When I nodded, he said, "They sound harmless enough."

"They do, don't they?" Had Alaric somehow magicked the birds? Here, they seemed quite sweet, as though a family of starlings sharing in after-dinner musings.

"Do you think we could harness them somehow?"

"Harness them to do what?" He turned to me, his eyebrows pulled together in a single line.

"I don't know. Maybe they could be used to tell a story to Alaric's people."

Henry shook his head, clearly not understanding what I meant.

"Okay, did you see the way they moved in and out of formation to paint a picture, if you will? What if I got Conestra to teach them how to tell a story, like in a picture book. We could use them to warn our people of impending danger faster than any horseman. We could also use them to gain sympathy for our cause—send them out over Alaric's fortress to tell his people the truth about what Alaric is doing in their name. How many people know that he enslaves his people and ours to create monstrosities of architecture, all for his own ego? That thousands of people are dying because of it?"

Henry shrugged. "Possibly only a handful, and those are all in Alaric's inner circle, I'm sure."

"Exactly!"

Grateful for his support, I leaned into him. During those months that the world had gone black, I had become such a pariah that I had begun to feel I could do nothing right, as though I were the evil person that so many had portrayed me as. I didn't know that person that they spoke about so blithely. Nor did I have any of the wiles or intrigue that they believed me to have. Instead, every word I uttered had been turned inside out, upside down, until I had no idea who I was anymore. The memory lingered and at times I couldn't shake it.

I sighed and felt Henry's comforting arms around me. Sometimes I felt like crawling in a hole and disappearing forever. But then I would never see the people who had come to mean so much to me.

"Henry?" I said.

"Yeah?"

"Do you love me?"

He turned to me and lifted my chin with his index finger so that I was looking directly into his lovely brown eyes. "How could you doubt it?"

It was my turn to shrug. "It's just that sometimes I think I'm not enough."

"Enough of what?" He tilted his head in confusion.

"I don't know. Good enough."

He took me by the shoulders and shook me, then pulled me into a bear hug. "You *are* good enough. It's the world you live in that's not. But Brigid," he said, resting his chin atop my head, "no matter what people say or think, you're a good person. You *are* enough, and even if men like Alaric don't know it, your women warriors know it. They believe in you."

"I hope so," I said with a watery laugh. Apparently the laughter had kept the traditions at bay because I felt no new welts or bruises, for now.

"Left, right, left!" Winnifred called. "Halt, turn." When all the women were lined up, she went over their instructions. "Gertrude, your women will be there." She pointed to the copse at the left. "And Jocelyn, your women will be on the right." She pointed to the copse nearest the foothills. Then she looked over to the Oneidas and Mohawks hidden by the trees, their warpaint creating such camouflage that even she had a hard time distinguishing them among the vast woodland. "And there—" She pointed to the ground. "Yesimeh!"

"Here, sir!" Yesimeh stepped forward and saluted.

"At your ease," Winnifred said with a smile. "Your women will come from behind and rush the Chessmen so that they trip on the rope we will place across the pinch point. If all goes well, they should fall like dominoes."

"Aye-aye, sir!" Yesimeh saluted once more, clicking her heels for good measure.

It was all Winnifred could do not to laugh at the serious little sprite. Who but Yesimeh would take her role as scout leader as earnestly as her dear friend and fellow warrior.

"Now, Emma?"

Everyone turned to search for Emma who was nowhere to be seen. After much murmuring and confusion, she popped her head out of a nearby tent. "Over here!" She waved a white flag. Everyone laughed.

"Save the white flag, Emma," Winnifred said. "We won't be waving that today."

"Here-here!" someone shouted among the ranks.

"Do you have your supplies at the ready?"

Emma nodded. "I've been collecting them from far and wide. The neighboring towns have been more than generous in helping us with supplies."

"Good!" Winnifred said.

Just then, she heard the fluttering of wings and her heart sank as she recognized more starlings. For a brief moment, the ranks of women ducked and scattered, but Brigid came running out, Henry at her side, and yelled, "No worries! Conestra will be training the birds to fly in formation."

"What sort of formation?" Winnifred asked.

"We're trying to get them to paint pictures with their murmurations," Brigid explained.

"Their what?" Jocelyn called.

"Their patterns. See?" Brigid pointed toward the sky and sure enough, the birds flowed in and out creating a unique pattern. "Conestra has spoken with the starlings—"

"Spoken with them?" Gertrude frowned, her eyes searching out the other women as if to see if they understood what Brigid was talking about.

"She speaks their language." To the surprised murmurs of disbelief, she whispered to Henry, "Help me out."

Henry held up his hands until everyone quieted down. "You see, Conestra has learned a series of bird languages. Twenty-three, to be exact, and she's learning new languages daily. She has spoken to the birds and they explained that the only reason they attacked was because Alaric had starved them and had his birds of prey chase them so that they couldn't land for food until they arrived at the manor. They were ravenous. Learning of our plight, they're only too ready to help us. In exchange, we'll supply them with food."

A wave of discontented chatter arose and settled on the wind. Finally, seeing that the women would mutiny at this news, Winnifred whistled for silence. Once they were all calm, she turned to Brigid.

"Explain yourself."

"See, the Master Gardener agreed to grow grain they can eat."

Then before anyone could protest after the huge loss of agriculture, Brigid held up her hands and waved for everyone to be seated. With much grumbling, they all sat down on the dry earth nestled beneath the canopy of trees.

"But he has also agreed to grow food for us. He has an entire contingent of men and women working on that daily. The food may not be perfect. Gone are the days when every piece of fruit or vegetable will be uniform, but it will sustain us, and for now, that's enough." She turned to take in all those around her.

A huge measure of relief washed over Winnifred now that the women understood what was at stake. Just as she was about to take over the reins of their conversation and launch into more on their preparation for the upcoming battle, Thomas galloped in on his horse, Emma running to greet him.

"As some of you know," he said, jumping down from his steed and still breathing hard while throwing an arm around Emma, "I've been away, but I have news."

A chorus of sound once again set the meadow abuzz at this announcement. Winnifred turned to Brigid to see if *she* knew what was afoot. Brigid merely shrugged and shook her head.

Thomas stared in all earnestness into Emma's eyes before making the announcement. "I should amend that to say I have *bad* news that will affect us all."

19

The fortress was alive with the news that someone had broken into Alaric's chambers. Birsha fought down the rising panic to think that they might be caught. And yet he had work to do before he could even think of leaving the palace walls. The Diāmons, as they were coming to be called, had said something about a book, and the only place Birsha could imagine a hidden book was in the library where the globe once again stood, placed there by Alaric when he'd been freed.

"Where do we look?" Beatrice's eyes grazed the dome covered in a tarp to keep out the elements until another could be built.

Birsha tugged at his braided goatee, his eyes scanning the shelves. "Look for a book on magic, I suppose."

"But didn't Siegfried say that almost all the books contained magic of one form or another? That's not much to go on."

"No, it isn't. And even if we could find the book, look what happened to Alaric when he opened the wrong one."

Beatrice's eyes went wide with alarm and she snapped her fingers. "That's it!"

"What's it?"

"The book that caused Alaric to become trapped in the globe. Didn't Alaric say something about it when he was in the globe?"

Birsha paused, trying to remember. His father had said many things when he was in the globe, and truth be told, Birsha froze up whenever Alaric spoke, as though some part of him went blank when around him. It had gone back to childhood, when he had been caught playing with an especially valuable trinket in the nursery as a child. Like any child, he had found a rocking horse that whinnied and pretended that he was a great knight. In the center of the room stood a crib, built like a stage with a short moveable stairway leading up to it. He had climbed down from his rocking horse and ambled up the stage. But before he did, he pulled down a mobile, shaped like a crown with five stars hanging from it. He placed it on his head. Then he reached into the crib and removed the royal red blanket. He used that as his cape. Lastly, he searched for a sword and found one high atop a shelf, one that appeared quite old, the hilt gilded. He had pushed the stairs over to the shelf and had climbed up to reach it. Now, having all the elements he needed to become a fine knight, he shoved the stairs back to the crib and mounted them until he stood in the middle of what looked like a round stage. There, he held his sword aloft and had just taken a solemn oath to protect the kingdom when in should walk Alaric. He'd torn the sword from his son's grasp.

"Where did you get this?" he demanded. "It's mine and you are not to touch it." Then he'd hauled Birsha out of the room, shouting for the boy's nanny to come get "the beast."

It shamed him even now, to know that he had cried that day like the child he was. The next day he had been sent away, back to his caretaker in the country.

The memory washed over him like waves upon a battered shoreline, imbuing him with melancholy after all these years. Beatrice seemed to sense his change in mood, and grasped his hand.

Misunderstanding what had made him so sad, she said, "Don't worry, we'll find the book."

But before he could respond, he heard footsteps headed their way down the outer hallway. "Quick!" he urged, looking to either side of him for shelter. Finding none, he turned to the globe. If they crouched down, the two of them just might fit. "Here!"

He pressed a lever and it opened. A small squeal escaped Beatrice's full red lips. They scampered in and pulled the top shut just as the door to the library opened.

"Shh!" a woman whispered from the other side of the globe. "It's got to be in here where I left it."

Birsha could hear a movement of books. "I don't understand. I left it right here."

A low rumble followed as another person spoke—a man's voice. "If it's not here, it must be there. Birsha lifted the top of the globe a hair, just enough to see the man's index finger pointing upwards. Slowly, Birsha pulled the top of the globe down.

"We'll have to come back, preferably at night, when everyone's asleep," the woman said.

With that, the door opened and closed with a soft whoosh.

Days had passed without news of the impending siege that Thomas had filled us in on, and Henry had been acting strangely. Everytime I searched for him I found him deep in conversation with one person or another, especially Conestra, our resident Master Birder. As for Conestra, she had begun training the starlings in earnest and as I watched their formations in the sky above me, hand over my eyes to protect them from the blinding sun, I saw the image that she had projected on them and laughed. It was of me and Henry, a royal wedding complete with gown and veil, the birds holding the veil aloft, Henry coming to greet me in full military regalia. Again I laughed at the absurdity of it all, the sheer banality. My women warriors and I dressed in battle gear these days. I hadn't worn a gown in nearly two years. I glanced around to see who had put her up to what could only be someone eager to see us wed.

Conestra appeared out of the shadows made by the copse of trees that surrounded the aviaries. "Why do you laugh?" She lifted her eyebrows, as though offended.

"I'm not laughing at you, Conestra. You're doing a great job. But if you haven't noticed, times have changed." Case in point, I nodded toward my female warriors, their uniforms quite stunning.

"Oh, I see."

She let loose a shrill whistle and spoke in what could only be determined as "starling speak." Soon, the starlings rearranged their movements so that I was now dressed in my uniform instead, though she refused to give up the veil, apparently, as the birds still flew behind my image, holding it aloft with their beaks.

The women, who had been practicing drills, stopped to watch the starlings. All across the practice field, women hooted and hollered and whistled their approval, one cheeky young woman yelling out to Henry, "When's the date?"

My cheeks burned with embarrassment to have Henry put on the spot as he was, but unbeknownst to me, he must have had it all planned as he knelt down in the grass and pulled a heart-shaped wedding ring box from his tunic and held it up to me. The starlings paused mid-flight to chitter their approval.

Heart thrumming in my chest, I opened the box, and gasped at the lovely London blue topaz engagement ring mounted on rose gold with fourteen small sapphires surrounding it. Entwined were ornate golden curlicues that laced around them like delicate honeysuckle vines.

"Brigid Anne Dunsmore, would you do me the honor of becoming my wife?" Henry's eyes held mine.

My throat thickened with emotion and I couldn't speak. Why had I not noticed it before? When had he gone from being the boy I had met at the turret, low those many years ago, to this man, a real and truly grownup person? I ran my hand across his forehead and down his cheek.

"Yes," I whispered.

I didn't care that tears welled up in my eyes. Perhaps the

traditions saw fit to leave me be for this one special moment as I felt neither welt nor bruise, cut nor itch. Instead, I simply felt elated, my heart soaring with love for the man who had seen fit to be by my side these last few years.

"Yes," I repeated more loudly now.

The grounds erupted with applause and more cries of joy and happiness. Some even took to circle dancing, taking each other's hands as they skipped and threaded the circle to the clapping of others watching.

The starlings flew up in the sky as if in a fireworks display, rifles sounding the joyous news. Soon, everyone around us was taking turns pumping our hands, Henry's parents there to join in the festivities. Everyone was there except my family. I felt the necklace that graced my neck, wondering if somehow they knew of my changing fate. Would they wish me well? Did they even remember me? I doused the hot tears that coursed down my cheeks. This time the traditions found me as a series of rashes raced down my neck and back, tempering my joy.

Madame Bookbinder must have noticed the change, as she came up to me, her green eyes filled with sympathy. "Time for calamine lotion, I see."

I smiled a silly smile, not even caring that I must look like a velvet red pincushion. Henry gave me one quick kiss. Then I was swept through the throng of people toward the first-aid station where Emma awaited me, calamine lotion in hand.

"Oh, Brigid." She shook her head, then ducked into the tent with its large red cross, pulling me with her.

Fortunately, whoever stalked the hallways had headed a different direction, giving Birsha time to scour the library shelves. "We have one afternoon to find the book and we don't even know what we're looking for."

"Well, one thing's for certain" –Beatrice's eyes peered upwards– "we won't find it here."

"You think it's in the dome recess?" Birsha's eyes grazed the ladder that led skyward.

"You heard it for yourself, the woman said it wasn't on any shelf at this level. That's the only place we haven't looked."

Birsha hated the idea of climbing to the *intrados* again, the upper room just beneath the cupola. He'd always had a fear of heights, though he fought it with alacrity.

"Very well, I suppose if anyone might help us, it would be Fearsome Foul, my great-grandfather."

And yet, he could tell by Beatrice's fearful blue eyes that she was just as reticent as Birsha himself to reconnect with the man in the orb in the loft above. Birsha offered her a nod of reassurance, then guided her toward the stairs, where together they ascended to the hidden room above. Surely, by now, Fearsome's powers had returned.

As Birsha entered the secret library, hidden even from Alaric, Birsha assumed, he saw a mist in the orb begin to swirl and within moments, Fearsome's blazing onyx eyes were upon them, his voice transmitting as if from the bowels of hell, it was so low and booming.

"What have we here?" Fearsome rubbed his hands together in anticipation.

"We need your help." Birsha fell onto his knees so he could

face the man directly. "The Diāmons are in search of a book–a book of magick, if I am not mistaken. They seek to find it, for what dastardly deed, I know not."

Fearsome tugged at his chin, his brows furrowed as if deep in thought. Slowly, he narrowed his eyes and nodded. Then his hand projected outward toward a large tome high atop the farthest bookshelf and lightning flashed outward, its energy seeking the book and pulling it toward him, as if agile fingers in search of its prey. Its binding appeared Medieval as it floated in the air, its outer cover made of tawed goatskin, a process that involved aluminum salts combined with flour, egg yolk, salt and other material. The codex was made of vellum, a parchment constructed from stretched calf skin. It landed at Birsha's feet, and as it did, a howling wind swept through nearly blinding Birsha. The book fluttered open, its pages filled with a golden glow as though a spectral had taken possession of it and was now turning its pages in rapid succession. The sound of each page was deafening, until at last it slowed its frantic pursuit as it landed on a single page.

Birsha stared at it, his eyes seeking out Beatrice's. Her mouth fell open and he could see by the rapid pace of her breathing that she was nearly as stunned as he.

"Be careful," she whispered. "You don't want it to do to you what it did to Alaric."

Birsha nodded, his eyes returning to the manuscript. What he saw was both lovely and frightening, all at a glance. It had surely been inscribed by a monk, for who but a monk could have known how to read, much less put pen to paper in those dark times? And yet whoever had written it had been anything but spiritual, as the page was done in cobalt blue, with golden and black ink incising the terrifying images. It showed a world ruled by creatures of the night.

Creatures like the Diāmons.

And yet as he peered at the demons roaming its pages, he felt the pull of it, as though it contained some magnetic charm that dragged its reader to it. Dazed, he touched his fingertips to the drawings only to pull back in alarm at the heat the pages generated. He let out a shriek of surprise. Beatrice clasped his hand in hers and rubbed his fingertips gently to soothe the pain the book had caused.

"I should have warned you." Fearsome's deep voice reverberated through the room as if it too were a living thing that swirled about the room like the wind that preceded it. "This book contains black magic. It is to be avoided at all costs."

"But how can I keep it from the Diāmons? They will return tonight to look for it." Birsha recoiled at the catch in his words, as though his voice had returned to puberty and was playing tricks on him as it had then.

"Magic runs many ways, does it not?"

Birsha gathered Beatrice's hands in his, not sure of the man's meaning.

"If something can be magicked to do one thing, it can just as well be magicked *not* to do something."

Birsha felt as if the man were speaking in riddles. "I don't understand."

Fearsome laughed, his laughter rumbling the floor that Birsha was seated upon, causing him to grasp for better footing. "I can make it disappear . . . for now. Would you like that?"

"We would like that very much," Beatrice interjected.

"Well, then. It shall be done." With that, the man bobbed his head once and blinked, and the manuscript disappeared with a loud poof into a cloud of smoke.

"What happened to it?" Birsha peered around him, expecting to find it somewhere.

"This is no concern of yours. Now go!" the man shouted. Then the orb began once again to swirl in a mist. Soon, Fearsome disappeared, in the same way he had first arrived.

Breaching no opposition, Birsha turned to Beatrice and grabbed her hand. "Hurry! Let's get out of here, while we can."

20

Winnifred burst into my room as I sat in front of my ornate gilded mirror, preparing for the day, pink polkadots spotting my face. "They're on the move!"

Phinney, who was standing on the bedpost staring down at me, flapped his wings, feathers floating downward and covering me in their snow as I stood so quickly that I nearly knocked my chair onto the floor.

"What do you mean? Who? Alaric?"

"Come see for yourself." She grabbed me by the hand and began yanking me before I could even finish covering up the remaining rash with calamine lotion.

On my way out, I called for Henry, who opened his door down the hall, still half dressed. I explained my dilemma.

"Go on without me," he said. "I just have to get my pants on, then I'll meet up with you." He closed the door but then tore it open again. "Where are you going?"

I shrugged and turned to Winnifred who was still out of breath from running all the way to my room.

"To Conestra's. The loom!" she said by way of explanation.

"Ah! Right." He quickly closed the door and we ran all the way down the stairs, the Big Ben newel clock opening its sleepy eyes and yawning.

"What have we here?" He raised an eyebrow.

Big Ben's eyes had a way of expressing his emotion, and right now, that emotion seemed to be churlishness at having been awakened at dawn. Usually, the early birds had the decency to walk on slippered feet and eat their breakfast in silence, but I didn't have the luxury of that. Not today.

Winnifred had at first planned to have the elves watch the loom, but instead strategically placed it with Conestra, for two reasons that I knew of. One, few would think to look there. And two, the birds of prey would protect the loom with their lives in exchange for the fish and small prey we provided them.

"No time to talk!" I patted Big Ben's head, covered in a red-striped nightcap that someone had placed there to prevent him from getting cold at night. "We're on a mission. Hush-hush!" I laughed to which he merely yawned and closed his eyes, his bushy eyebrows lowered to show his displeasure while he worked his lips as if to settle himself back to sleep.

Moments later, with half the household awakened and in disarray, we flung open the front door and raced out through the grass, sheep grazing as we passed. By the time we reached the aviary, Conestra was waiting for us and hurried us inside, where the loom lay waiting.

"Here." Conestra pointed. "See for yourself."

I turned and gasped at the sight, for hidden within the weave, an army of chessmen was lined up in formation as though awaiting a giant hand to guide their movements, and behind were the Jackals in uniform. But what surprised me most was that they were using conventional means to come after us. I tapped my chin with my fingertip. Something didn't seem right.

"Do you notice something odd about this picture?" I turned to face both women.

Conestra, who as always appeared lovely in a gown of feathers that could turn at will, changing both color and design in an instant. To my question, the pastoral scene that had been in and of itself breathtaking, switched to storm clouds rippling over a field of wheat, which was in short supply these days following the starling invasion. Now we must find a way to not only feed the citizens of our village, but the birds as well, if they were to provide a service for us, though in its infancy.

Winnifred shook her head. Just then, Henry came bursting through the door and nearly angled into me and bowled me over. "What is it?"

But he had only to look at the loom to understand what we were up against. "Oh."

His eyes went to mine. In response, my ice-blue eyes sparked, their fiery blue embers glancing about the room as if in search of a way out, which in truth mirrored my own desire. To find a way out of this mess should the Jackals invade, which it appeared they intended to.

Henry turned to me. "What will we do?"

"I don't know, but again I ask, do any of you know what's

missing in this equation?"

They looked at each other as if hoping to find an answer, but none of them seemed to get my point.

"Don't you think it's odd that Alaric's men aren't using magic, when magic has proven so useful?"

Winnifred was the first to speak. "Right-O." She followed it up with a huge sigh.

"Why do you think that is?" Conestra formed the question we were all wondering.

I scratched my head, thinking.

"Perhaps they plan to use both." All eyes turned to Henry.

That would make them considerably more formidable, which meant we would need to be on our toes even more so than usual. For several minutes, we all stood in silence, each maintaining our own private thoughts.

Finally, I said the words I felt certain we were all thinking. "Well, we'd best get on it." Then to the loom I added, "And keep us posted on any new developments."

For one strange moment, the shuttle moved back and forth in rapid succession. To my surprise, it had written "Right-O" into the weave.

"Winnifred?"

She shrugged in apology. "I thought I would try to teach it a few words while it was in my possession." And with that, she gave it a gentle pat to which I could have almost sworn that it sighed.

Birsha paced the ramparts, the cool northern breeze passing

over him and leaving him chilled despite the season. All around him, warriors raced in all directions. The Chessmen were on the move, every step they took creating a minor tremor that rocked the ground and had everyone grabbing for the nearest solid object.

So, Alaric had declared war. The thought made his stomach churn despite the fact that he had yet to risk eating anything on a day such as this. Plus, rumor of a traitor in their midst had everyone peering over their shoulders wondering who would be declared the offender. Birsha knew only too well that a scapegoat made for an easy target.

He turned at the sound of feet headed his way. "Oh, Siegfried. I'm so glad you're here."

Siegfried, who believed in a strict dress code, appeared tired and disheveled this morning, adding further proof to Birsha's fear that not only was something afoot, but that the consequences could be catastrophic.

"What news do you have?"

Siegfried clutched the top of the ramparts as though grasping for a lifeline. "It's terrible. Worse than I feared, actually. The book is missing and it's rumored the Diāmons are furious and will stop at nothing to get it back. And Alaric—" Here, he covered his face.

"What? What about Alaric, tell me?" Birsha blinked rapidly to hide his turmoil.

Siegfried dropped his hands to his sides, but Birsha could see that the man was trembling. "He . . . he thinks that I was the one in his room. That perhaps I've sold the book of magick to the highest bidder. He is having me watched. I shouldn't even be here!" he hissed.

Birsha laid a hand on the adjutant's arm. "Listen to me, Siegfried. You *must* stay calm, act naturally or they *will* have reason to suspect you."

"But don't you see?" Siegfried hissed. "The truth doesn't matter, only what they believe to be the truth. And as long as they have someone to blame, their bloodlust will be satisfied. I can't take that risk."

Birsha's heart sank. "What do you plan to do?"

Siegfried once again grasped the top of the rampart for support. "I must leave. Today."

"Where will you go?" Birsha gazed out over the land where entire units of men prepared for the battle ahead, each brandishing a weapon or packing food and tents for the weeks and months ahead.

"I don't know, but I've spoken to the Underground—"

"Don't!" Birsha cried, reaching for the man's hand. "It will mean instant death if they find you. I will help protect you."

"But how? How can you protect me?"

"By telling the truth."

The moment the words left Birsha's mouth, he knew it was the only way. Now he just had to hope and pray that Alaric would understand that what he was doing wasn't meant to subvert him.

"What do you mean it was you who was in my room?" Alaric demanded, his reverse widow's peak more pronounced than before and his face sallow from days of little sleep.

"I was looking for a book, the book that forced you into the globe and held you prisoner."

Alaric had just returned from the war room, his black cape reminding Birsha of the skin of a black adder. Birsha forced himself not to shudder.

"But why? For what purpose? To reimprison me?" Alaric demanded.

"The Wrestling of Dragon and Tiger" tea Alaric had delivered to the primary drawing room where he spent most of his mornings was now growing cold. Birsha knew that though the name sounded fantastical, it was nothing more than black tea and brandy served in a dainty glass cup with gilded handles, glass roses on both handle and cup. A butterfly graced the side, bent to taste the cup's sweet nectar. Alaric's coat of arms topped the small spoon that dipped inside it.

"Of course not." Birsha plopped down onto the plush velvet seat opposite his father. "To protect you."

"Protect me, from what?" Alaric set his spoon down next to his glass teacup.

"The Diāmons—the creatures who wish to rule the kingdom."

"I don't understand." Alaric leaned forward, his braided goatee swinging in a disjointed rhythm. "Who are these Diāmons of which you speak?"

Birsha explained. "Creatures, dangerous ones at that. They want to see you succeed in your quest to overtake the Bookbinders. Then once that's accomplished, they have only you to fight. Don't you see that you are walking into their trap?"

Alaric fell back into his seat. He peered at Birsha through

hooded eyes. "Maybe I was too hasty in judging you, son. You may be a Faineant after all."

21

Something had changed in the days since we'd learned that the Jackals and their Chessmen were on the move. We had all become more purposeful. Everywhere people bustled. Spies sent out to gather information returned with the news that the Jackals were on the march, the Chessmen bringing up the rear. No doubt Alaric and his army had a plan, but what, we had yet to fathom. Nevertheless, we were scurrying about when Yesimeh, who I hadn't seen in forever, poked her head into my tent as I prepared for the morning briefing. It would now take place in the center of the aviary, the prey birds in attendance as well, as if they too were preparing for war.

"Yesimeh!" I scurried to my feet, eager to greet my friend. She had grown thinner in the past days, and more sallow. I wondered at the change. "What is it?"

She paused before answering, as though uncertain how to

proceed, which was so unlike her. Finally, she pointed with her chin to the camp chair that I kept next to my folding table used for any number of missives.

"May I sit?"

"Of course." I helped her to the chair, fearing she might fold like that table should I release her to her own devices.

"Oh, Brigid!" She buried her face in her hands. "I don't know how to tell you."

"Tell me . . . tell me what?" By now my heart was beating like a side drum, a faint buzz fluttering inside my chest.

"I did something stupid."

I knelt down. A terrible foreboding caused my breath to quicken. "What? What did you do?"

"I thought this person was my friend. I was speaking to her about our—"

"You told her, didn't you?"

She nodded, her blue eyes pooled with tears. "I didn't know she would disappear—that she was from the fortress."

All my fears were confirmed. I sat there, numb. And yet I knew Yesimeh would never do anything purposely to hurt us, and I knew how much it had cost her to come here and tell me this.

"Did you tell this person everything?"

The tears that had pooled now fell freely down her face. "I'm so sorry."

"So, the enemy knows our plans."

She nodded, but the Yesimeh I knew had flown away, her spirit gone. And though I felt as though the wind had been knocked out of me, I decided to tell her what someone had once told me to hopefully ease her pain.

I lifted her chin. "Sometimes bad things happen for good reasons. Do you understand?"

She searched my eyes with such a look of devastation that I snapped her up in my arms and hugged her tight. Suddenly, instead of fear gripping me, I saw a plan forming, a different plan that would take into account this newfound knowledge. Now, the Jackals would come expecting to find us. Only we wouldn't be here. We would be miles away, in another spot I knew only too well. Battersbog. And if I had my way, this time it wouldn't be our city on fire, but theirs.

The Diāmons had taken on a dark aura that filled the room with fog so that it was hard to see across the table. Chame Leon shivered from the cold that now permeated the room with a moist dampness that made his skin crawl. He couldn't wait to leave the room, and yet he had work to do. Important work. Still, every day that he remained seated at the glass floating table was one day closer to death. He felt the guillotine closing in on him as surely as if it hung over him now, waiting for the executioner to give the order. He forced himself to stay calm, to act naturally despite the rapid beating of his heart.

The Queen of Mammals paced the room, her very ordinary looking clothing and demeanor making it that much more appalling to know that inside such a creature lived the heart of a monster. Her gray-green eyes paused on his, and for a moment, she didn't blink, simply stared. Chame Leon's heart stilled in his chest and his color began to fade so that he all but disappeared from her view. Her head twisted right then left, but seeing nothing, she moved on. Yet, for that one brief second, he'd seen inside her soul, had seen the wheels churning in those cold storm-filled eyes, and he knew his time here was numbered. If he left, would Liz Herd go too? But if they no longer attended the meetings, The Queen of Mammals would know they were traitors to her own traitorous cause.

The Queen lifted a gnarled pointer stick and pointed it at the words that hung magically in the air in front of the room. Then to the map. "We have sent those Jackals favorable to our cause into the field along with the others. We have been informed that a counterattack is imminent. That they are aware of our plans and have plotted a counter strike here, and here, and here. Though the map was merely a hologram, each time she touched it with her stick, Chame Leon heard a tap as though she had touched a real map.

"We will send in a small contingency first, then swoop in this way, and this way so there is no escape. Any questions?"

Liz Herd raised her hand. "Excuse me, but is it my understanding that you're able to *direct* the incursion?"

A cry rang out among the Diāmons, those most evil of creatures, as if they too had been wondering the same thing.

"Let's just say that we have many among us who are most happy to lead the forces into battle."

She offered Liz Herd a self-satisfied grin that sent a chill through Chame Leon's already cold blood. He needed to find a warm place soon or he would freeze to death in a room such as this one.

"Any other questions?" She peered left to right. "Then you

are dismissed."

Chame Leon saw relief in Liz Herd's eyes, a relief that matched his own. As soon as they managed to escape the room and climb the steps into the room above, Chame Leon dragged her to the nearest heating vent, where they stood and warmed themselves until they were again able to move. Until then, all he could do was to make plans for their future, for him and Liz Herd, should she agree.

"Brigid, come with me now!"

I had gathered around the Oneida and Mohawk's campsite, Kahwhita at my side, when Henry had rushed in as though a foul wind were at his back, propelling him forward. I stood and hurried to a spot beneath an overhang of trees set in bracken, where we could speak in private.

"I'm speaking with the chief about the best way to move an army of women through the countryside without being seen!" If anyone could navigate these forests, it would be my native friends.

Henry clutched my hands. "What do you mean, move?"

I told him about Yesimeh's earlier visit to which he whistled and plopped down on a fallen log. He pulled off the wool cap he was wearing and rubbed at his scalp.

"You mean for all of us to move?"

I glanced over at the fire, in the dim light of early evening. The Chief's eyes danced with the reflection of the flames. So much to do, but so little time, while too many unknowns played inside my head. I winced. What if we didn't arrive in Battersbog soon enough? What if we were spotted by their spies? Worse yet, what if one of our own was among that number? I couldn't let my imagination run away with me or I would crumple into ashes like the very logs that even now spit embers into the sky that floated on the wind and were carried away.

It dawned on me that I had forgotten why Henry had come. I peered up at him. "What is it? Why are you here?"

"Come. You need to see this for yourself."

How many times had I heard those words? I wondered, as both a weary and morbid curiosity vied for refuge within my very tired brain. I stood up and called to Kahwhita.

"I'll be back!"

She merely nodded as she tended to her infant. Then I followed Henry, whose hair blew in the breeze, the lines around his eyes showing age as they hadn't a year earlier. He all but dragged me to the clearing in the center of the aviary. At first, I didn't register what it was that had him so upset.

But then he said, "Don't you see it?"

"See what?" I sighed, trying not to show my fatigue and frustration.

"That!" He pointed to the aviaries.

I peered up just as Conestra entered the clearing. Her eyes were swollen and her feathered dress had turned black, as if in mourning.

The words, "What has happened?" barely left my mouth when I saw what I had missed upon entering the clearing and gasped. Slowly, I spun around in a circle. "Where have they gone?"

"Someone took them!" Conestra covered her eyes, her

shoulders trembling.

And it was true. Each of the cages had been opened and the winged creatures had all been released.

"Who would have done something so horrible, Brigid?" She wiped the tears with her sleeve.

Who indeed?

Though Birsha had done everything in his power to dissuade his father from sending out troops to wrest power from the Bookbinders, Alaric had deemed his goals too important to set aside. Now, as Birsha gazed out at the rear battalions of Jackals in their burgundy coats and gray pants, their boots black as the coal from the coal mines just west of the fortress, he felt a frisson of alarm to see this last troop of warriors prepare to march. Siegfried, whom he rarely saw anymore since Alaric's return to power, surprised him with a visit along the rampart walls.

"Beatrice said I might find you here." Siegfried nodded toward the soldiers below.

The rumble of the chessmen struck up a new note of disquiet that nearly unsettled Birsha's morning meal, and without thinking, he rubbed his stomach of the increasing pain that he had experienced of late.

"You might have the doctor take a look at that." Siegfried frowned down at Birsha's middle.

"Aye." Birsha sighed. Beatrice had been telling him as much but he abhorred the thought of going to see a doctor with all their leeches and bloodletting and other ignominious diagnoses too hideous to name. "I think I shall keep my own council for now, thank you very much!"

"It's your stomach."

Birsha growled just beneath his breath. He didn't like being told what to do. At least he had that in common with his father. And truth be told, he missed Siegfried. Of all the people in his kingdom—or at least it *was* his kingdom until Alaraic returned—Siegfried had been the one true friend he could turn to with a question, or simply a word of friendship.

"I know," Siegfried said, as if reading his mind, "I miss our daily talks as well. Alaric, well he is all about decorum, power. I knew this when I took the job, but I grow weary of it sometimes, always walking on eggshells."

Birsha closed his eyes, feeling the sting of tears he would never shed. To hear it said from another man gave credence to his own emotions, the ones he had carried with him like a carrion beetle on the back of a fallen stag.

"So what now?" Birsha spoke the words he knew they must be both feeling, to see the Jackals gear up for yet another upcoming war.

"We dig in," Siegfried said, "hunker down."

"And that's enough?" Birsha turned on him, a surprise anger burbling up inside him and spilling out of his mouth.

"No, it's never enough, but what do you suggest we do under the current circumstances?"

Birsha shifted his attention to the faraway mountains, to the beauty that anchored this land in a swath of green as far as the eye could see. Even as a child, this spot—a spot he had deemed special for its spectacular view—had filled him with awe for nature and all its bounty. Each time he saw it destroyed by mines and roads, or simply people's lack of care for the land and its many treasures, a piece of him died along with the land.

"We fight." Birsha knew the moment the words left his mouth that they were right.

"Fight?" Siegfried rubbed the temples of his brow as though working out the soreness lodged there. "For what?"

"For this . . ." Birsha reached out his arm, palm up, and made a sweep with his hand. "For life. For our children."

"So then you are in agreement with Alaric?" Siegfried's back went rigid, as though a marionette on a wooden dowel, waiting for the puppetmaster to pull on his strings.

"Of course not. I didn't mean for Alaric. For the Bookbinders."

Siegfried gasped and peered around him, as though looking to be sure that no eyes or ears were hiding amidst the ramparts. "You can't be serious, Birsha. It would be treason. You could be killed."

Birsha sighed and cupped his chin in his hands, the nausea returning along with the searing pain. "You're right, of course. But the Bookbinders don't deserve this. They have done nothing to us except to fight to free their enslaved people. You or I would do the same."

"I know," Siegfried whispered under his breath. His eyes appeared haunted and his face gaunt and pale.

"This feud can't go on, and if anyone should succeed, I would like to be on the side of human kindness, wouldn't you agree?"

Siegfried paused as though frozen, despite the warmth of

the early morning sun. Finally, he gave one short nod. Then, before Birsha could say anything more to persuade him to listen, he turned on his heel and hurried down the rampart and to the stone stairs below.

Birsha once again gave his attention to what was happening below. He had to hope and pray that Siegfried would remain a true friend, that he would keep Birsha's musings to himself. And yet he knew he couldn't go on this way. Something needed to give before he lost what truly mattered most. *My integrity.*

His eyes drifted to the tower where he and Beatrice resided. Now, he had more reason than before to prove himself as a man. No longer would it be just Beatrice who counted on him. She was with child. A child that would bear his name. Just the thought of it filled him with a love so deep that he could scarcely name it. With that knowledge came a fierce desire to protect what was his. And one thing he knew for certain. He would never send his child away as Alaric had him. He would keep his child with him, always. Now he just had to hope that was possible.

22

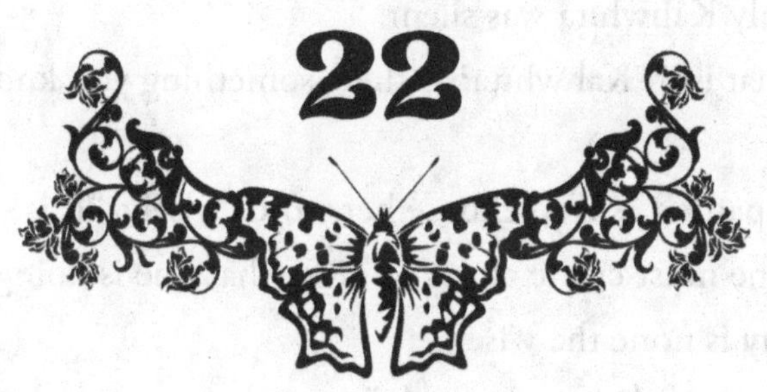

I set everyone I could think of to the task of finding the birds. Nearly four hours later, and with the sun down nearly an hour prior, I knew that we could do no more today. Or at all. We needed to be in Battersbog to head Alaric's army off at the pass, and we couldn't do that if we hung around here much longer. Each of the camp leaders circled the fire, as we spoke in hushed tones.

"We can't wait." Gertrude stoked the coals, sending a shower of sparks over the skewer of roasting turkey meat. "I say we leave at dawn."

"I agree," I said, my eyes doing the talking.

Every woman nodded her head in compliance.

Jocelyn leaned in, the shadows backlit by the fire creating a macabre mask across her face. "The women are on edge. Something's different about this incursion."

"I agree." Henry, who had been standing just outside of the shadows walked forward, the remaining fire lighting his frontside so that he appeared cleaved in two. He reached out a hand, and I took it with gratitude. "Perhaps it's the brazen manner in which they plan to attack that has me so uneasy."

A murmur arose around the campfire as everyone spoke at once. Only Kahwhita was silent.

"What is it, Kahwhita? Is there something you know? Tell us."

She paused as if to choose her words wisely. "It is said that in war, one must create chaos to hide what one is doing. Thus the enemy is none the wiser."

"You mean bait and switch."

Kahwhita frowned. "I do not know what that means, but I believe they are hiding their true intentions."

Once again the campfire was abuzz, everyone talking at once. Finally, I quieted them down with a downward motion of my hands. "So, what do you suggest?"

"I suggest that we hide in the forest as planned, only in Battersbog. That we call together everyone with special powers. Then we use those powers in a surprise offensive."

"So, you are saying we don't go on the defense." I smiled for the first time that day. "We go on the offense."

"Exactly!" She bowed slightly and slid back into the shadows, no doubt to go in search of her baby, a wet nurse assigned to her while she'd slipped away into our camp.

We all looked at each other to see who was on board with her suggestion. One by one, the women nodded. "Henry?"

"I concur."

"All right, then. It's settled. We set out tomorrow." Then under my breath I whispered, "Sorry, Conestra."

We were on the road by dawn, each of us anxious to be gone. Even the horses seemed to realize that the atmosphere had changed around camp because they began stamping before the sun had risen, snorting their impatience to be off. Only Kahwhita seemed more sullen than usual.

"What's wrong?" I asked when I had her alone.

She walked beside my horse, her baby on her back, small bubbles at the infant's lips as she burbled like a babbling brook. My heart melted to see her so, the two a picture of love and motherhood.

Kahwhita paused to allow the warriors to go around them. Again, the image of water filled me with love and longing. Someday, that might be me and Henry, a child made of our flesh, a symbol of the love that we had for each other.

"Call it what you will—an omen, a fear—but I feel that this time will be different, that what we have to offer won't be enough." She peered around her before leaning in. "I hope I am wrong, Bri-gid, but I fear I am right."

Her twin onyx eyes held mine, sorrow written into them that seemed to swallow me up with their sadness. I peered over at my loom, hidden beneath the folds of the tarp in the wagon. Elijah and Dele promised to guard it with their lives. The loom had been strangely quiet, as though it too was afraid of the future and didn't want me to see it for fear of my reaction. My mind wallowed in the what-ifs, each scenario worse than the last, but I couldn't allow myself to be swept away by the unknowns. I had to stay focused, if we were to survive what might soon come our way.

"If what you say is true, what do you suggest? There must be something we can do."

For the longest time Kahwhita paused, her eyes blinking rapidly. "If anyone can help, it is our Skywoman of legend and her two grandsons, Flint and Maple Sapling. Maple sapling is the giver of life, whereas Flint is the harbinger of death. We may need both in the end."

"I don't understand." My horse stamped his impatience. I knew I couldn't hold him much longer, the pull of the other horses and humans around him too strong.

"You will." Kahwhita unconsciously grabbed her infant's outstretched hand and kissed it. "When the time is right, my people will help you, but know this—you think it is a physical war they will bring, but you are wrong."

"Wrong?" I didn't like the sound of that. As if my horse felt it too, he flinched, his withers shaking off what might have been a fly, but felt like an omen instead. A portent of what was to come.

"This is a spiritual war. Your physical abilities will not save you this time."

All sound seemed to disappear as if I were in a giant wind tunnel, whirling through space and time. From a muffled distance, I heard her say, "You must trust in the spirits, Bri-gid." When she spoke my name, it was as if it were two separate words. "You must call on them when the time is right. Remember her name, Skywoman."

I sounded out the word. I would remember. But the tide of

humanity was too great and it swept me away in its flotsam. The last I saw of Kahwhita, she was disappearing into the forest, as though she had never been there, simply gone.

"You there, halt! What do you want?"

Birsha turned slowly and saw the other man pale and step back as though an invisible hand had shoved him in the chest.

"Who are you?" The man's eyes narrowed.

"The point is, I know who you are, Master Clyde?"

Birsha had clearly hit his intended target because Master Clyde's eyes darted to the small dwelling in the middle of the forest. At that precise moment, a woman popped out through the front door, a basket in her hand from which to collect eggs or herbs, or some such thing. Her eyes lifted and she paused, just long enough for Birsha to register the fear that dwelt inside them.

"Your wife perhaps, Master Clyde?" Birsha cocked a brow.

"*Non!*" A man called from the edge of the clearing in a decidedly French accent. "Eleanor, *ne bouge pas.*"

Though rusty, Birsha's French had been fluent at one time and he deciphered the man's words. *Don't move!*

"Pierre!" she cried.

Just then, two children, one a girl and the other a strapping young man appeared at the door and looked above her outstretched hands.

"Jean, take Celestine inside," Pierre yelled.

The boy did as told, bidding a hasty retreat, but the girl only acquiesced after much prodding.

"Leave our children out of this, Birsha," Pierre said as he hastened to his wife's side. He placed a protective arm around her, one hand near his waist, ready to brandish a weapon, no doubt.

Birsha threw his hands out before anyone got any ideas of escalating what was already a tense situation.

"Why are you here?" Master Clyde demanded.

Birsha turned to the swarthier of the two men, the other man taller and thinner, his body used to hard work and little food. Where to start? "The truth is—"

But before he could finish his sentence, Beatrice popped out of the surrounding gorse, small twigs in her hair, her clothing filled with nettles.

"What are you doing here?" Birsha growled. This was becoming a veritable circus.

"I followed you. I knew where you were going, and the truth is, I didn't trust you to muck it up."

Birsha winced at her assessment of him.

Beatrice turned toward the assemblage, directing her words toward Eleanor. "As my husband was trying to say, we need your help."

"Our help? How?"

"We need your aid in making our way south undetected. We want to speak with the Bookbinders. We fear the growing conflict will only make things worse, *much* worse. And we can't afford any more fighting. People keep dying. On both sides."

"Because of your husband's father," Eleanor reminded Beatrice.

Beatrice's eyes went to Birsha who struggled under the

weight of the accusation, his loyalties torn. He could never be like his father, who believed in slavery wholeheartedly, and yet if not for his father, he wouldn't be here now, in a position to change things. Or die trying. So much was at stake. And more often than not, he was uncertain of the wandering allegiances. The Diāmons had made that more than clear to him. As to the Council, they were an unknown quantity. Who to trust? He decided to put his faith in Master Clyde.

"We know you have a hidden route."

"No!" Pierre hissed to Master Clyde. "Don't tell them. It's a trap."

Master Clyde stood motionless, his eyes never leaving Birsha who blanched under their disdain.

"Please." Beatrice held up her hands in supplication. "We really do need your help. We have to stop this massacre."

"Why should I believe you?" Master Clyde drew his chin up in challenge.

Beatrice looked back at Birsha as if to ask his permission. He nodded his encouragement.

"Because they're my people." She paused, her tongue seeking refuge against her upper lip. "And because I am with child."

23

The entire way to Battersbog a heaviness weighed me down. The others felt it too as evidenced by the silent movements, the hushed whispers. Few would ever guess that an entire army of women was making its way through the forest. It was as if even the forest floor, leaves and all, had lost their ability to produce sound. Sadness engulfed me as though I alone lived inside a cloud of foreboding. Henry, bless his heart, had gone off to rally the others while I brought up the rear, for a change, wishing to linger before facing the inevitable. What did Kahwhita mean when she said this was a spiritual war?

We had been riding our horses for over an hour when I finally saw the outskirts of Battersbog, the place where we had bivouacked last year, the city that had caught fire, set upon by Tempestous in one of her fits of rage. Despite the passage of time, many of the burned-out buildings were still visible, even at this distance. Temporary housing had been set up here and there, and new buildings were being erected, some in the final stages of completion. I wondered about Winnifred. I hitched up on my saddle to see if I could locate her, but she must be near the front, no doubt eager to be home.

We had just come out into a clearing, when to my surprise, I saw the starlings, the ones that Conestra had been training. "What on earth are they doing here?" I whispered.

As if all of the women had seen them at once, a murmur of surprise rose like a wave and soon the women were laughing, a sound I hadn't heard in quite a while. But stranger than that, Phinney seemed to be leading the charge. What on earth was Phinney up to?

I spurred my horse, weaving my way forward through the throng of women, who were either on foot or on horseback, until I was directly under the swarm. Leave it to Phinney to be drilling the starlings as if she'd formed an army of her own.

"Phinney!" I cried. "Get down here at once."

Phinney seemed to shrug, then barreled downward in a slow spiral until I thought she might dive right into me, but she pulled up at the last minute and circled around, opened her wings wide to soften the landing, and fluttered down slowly, her talons grabbing onto my pommel. Fortunately, Red, my horse, was used to Phinney by now and only danced a little before settling in. Phinney stood erect, as though awaiting orders. I had to laugh, silly bird.

"What are you up to Phinneus P. Falcon?" I asked.

She blinked an eye, but I swear I saw a glint in the one left open.

"Are you training the starlings?"

She blinked her eye again. I wanted to say "one for yes, two for no" but thought that might be going a bit too far. Surely, Phinney couldn't train starlings, could she?

"Phinny," I began as the women gathered around me, "show me what you can do."

At that, she ruffled her feathers and moved her feet, then bent low before jettisoning into the sky, her eyes trained on the birds which had taken to a series of trees by the clearing and were talking freely amongst themselves. As she made a pass by their tree, she let out a high-pitched cree. As if one, the birds took flight and began moving ever skyward. Soon, they were dipping and swerving.

"Phinney!" I called. "Can they form pictures other than the ones you've shown me already?"

She let out another cree, as if to ask what kind. "I don't know." I glanced around, hands up, unsure what to ask. Winnifred saw me and came dashing over on foot.

"Ask Phinney if she can get them to draw a picture of the fortress!"

I called as loudly as I could. Phinney went straight into action, dipping and diving, but what surprised me most, and had all the other women crying out in awe, was that other birds, the birds from Conestra's aviary flew in from out of the forest and began to herd the birds until at last, the starlings made almost a perfect image of Alaric's fortress.

I sat back on my pommel and heaved a sigh, the creak of the leather as familiar to me as my beloved falcon by now. *Well, well, well.* I would have never known Phinney had it in her. She had single-handedly gathered together the birds to get them in shape on a much tighter timeline than Conestra could have ever managed by herself.

When the birds were finished, the entire gathering of women hooted and hollered and congratulated Phinney and the other birds. They had done what we could not. Now we truly had a warning system in place.

We finished up here, then continued our movement toward the large clearing near Winnifred's home. Unfortunately, her barn had gone up in flames last year, but by the time we arrived at her place, we saw that the homestead was still standing, and dear sweet Winnifred had somehow managed to put up another barn, with the help of the elves, who were nothing if not good carpenters. And this time, the barn no longer leaned. Plus it had embellishments strewn here and there, all elfin in feature. Little upturns at the corners, pictures of mushrooms and treehouses on the outside cladding. I do have to say, it was one of the most unique barns I had ever seen.

"Lofgren made this for you?" I asked, as Winnifred proudly showed off her new workspace.

"And look," she said, nearly yanking me off my horse.

I slid down, my feet touching the ground. Green grass was once again growing beneath my feet, the ash having supplied nutrients to the soil so at least some good had come out of all this. She practically dragged me in to see what she and Lofgren had accomplished. And true to form, inside was a veritable treasure trove of shelves with varying stages of experiments atop them. She had even managed to take what was left of the quantum computer and try to recreate it, though truthfully, it looked nothing like it had before, and yet I had to give her kudos for trying.

"I'm even working on my time machine." She marched me over to a spot in the corner that held something similar to her previous time machine, only this too had embellishments, the kind that only a master elfin craftsman could make. The wheel that ran the machine had beautiful mountain scenes carved into it. Overhead was a bird. I bent closer and saw that it had been painted blue.

"Phinney?" I squeaked.

Winnifred nodded. "And look here," she added, the excitement evident in her voice.

"Our women?"

"An army of them." She dipped her chin in satisfaction. "And here's the manor."

I had to turn my head sideways to see, but just as she'd said, there it was, the intricate carving warming my heart. With reverence, I ran my hand over the entire circumference of the wheel. Then I turned to her and paused, a thought exuding from my overloaded mind.

She frowned. "What is it? What's the matter?"

"Do you miss being in charge, Winnifred?"

For one brief moment, she blinked rapidly as I hit the proverbial nail on the head.

I slapped my forehead. Why hadn't I given this consideration? Just as I had felt lost after returning to the manor with nothing to fill my days after our previous foray into enemy territory, she had felt the same, only I hadn't realized it until now.

"Well, we'll have to do something about that." I winked at her and was pleased to see her blush a deep crimson. "I'll tell you what. Why don't you take half of the women, and I'll take the other half, then we'll coordinate our plans. Deal?"

As if she'd been thinking about this for some time, she said, "I would like Gertrude."

"Then I will take Jocelyn and Emma."

"That leaves Yesimeh," she said with a smile. She peered at me through thick glasses, her short bob bouncing up and down as though it too was excited by the news.

"Perfect. Then we're set."

We shook on it. Just then Lofgren popped his head into the barn. "What do you think?" he asked as he bounced up and down on his toes.

"I think you're amazing, Lofgren. And you have a pretty smart cookie for a wife."

Winnifred giggled at that. Lofgren weaved his arm through hers and held her tight. In that moment, with the light angling through the window and the sun casting rays that highlighted what the pair had accomplished, I felt very lucky indeed to have two such smart and capable friends. Now, we had only to survive tomorrow.

Birsha packed what few belongings he could safely keep tucked away for the journey, but there was one thing he wanted before he left with Beatrice at his side. *The book.* The grimoire that was vellum bound with artist renderings of all manner of spells and incantations. For although he detested such things, and it went against his religion, he couldn't help but think that what might be done through the wickedness of the Diāmons, might be undone with the help of this book. Still, before he headed to the hidden library where Fearsome Foul had hid it so that none but he could find it, Birsha met with the priest in the clergy house that sat just north of the maze garden which was now empty of the Chessmen, who had all left with the Jackals. The place seemed especially barren, with them gone, and he found he liked it that way. It was as though a breath of fresh air had taken its place so that he held his face up to the breeze and breathed in its clean scent filled with the odors of summer and all things good. As a child, he had relished the outdoors. Never had he been tucked away, as was expected of him now, as the predecessor of the restored ""king", which Alaric had begun calling himself of late, as though the heavens had manifested the position just for him.

"Pshaw!" Birsha murmured just as the priest was exiting the clergy house.

The building held an aura, hidden as it was behind hedges in varying shapes—oblong, rounded, or sprawling—its chimney stack made of brick, like the building itself. Steps led up to it, if one were so inclined.

"Did you say something?" the priest asked.

He stopped as though he sensed something amiss. And indeed something *was* amiss, so much so that Birsha needed to speak to him now. Birsha peered around to be certain no one observed the two talking amongst themselves. When he was sure the coast was clear, he leaned in and said, "Is there somewhere more . . . *private*. I need to speak to you."

The priest glanced quickly around him, then touched Birsha's sleeve ever so slightly and said, "Come this way, Your Grace."

Birsha nearly laughed, as though he had been ordained a bishop in a single day, and yet he was anything but a bishop. Or a priest, for that matter. No, what he meant to ask was an unholy request, but he must do it to stop the Diāmons, if possible.

The priest wound his way through the side yard and to the private walled gardens out back used only for the priests during their daily meditations. At last they arrived at an arbor of jasmine tucked deep into the recesses of the garden. The smell was both heady and sublime. Birsha might have enjoyed it more, had he not had such an earnest request to ask the poor priest.

The priest bade him to sit. Birsha plopped down onto the ornate carved stone bench, Nile rushes carved into its arms, two finials topping them, and a giant cross traversing the middle. It seemed somewhat sacrilegious to be asking something so ignoble of a man of the cloth, but it could not be helped.

"Dear Priest, I have come to ask . . . no, *beg* of you to place your protection around me and my loved ones."

The priest, a scraggly man with bushy black eyebrows so opposite to the thin strands of white hair on his head, raised one of those eyebrows now. "I say, I hadn't expected this. May I ask why?"

How to explain in a way that wouldn't offend. Birsha turned toward the priest, whose vestments were now the same loathsome colors of the realm, burgundy and gold.

"You see, I am going on a mission," Birsha tried to explain without going into further detail. "And I will need the aid of a book. A very horrible book. A grimoire."

The priest gasped and his face turned red, but no redder than his bulbous nose which made him appear a drunk, and as if the thought had just occurred to Birsha, he thought he could detect the lingering remnants of stale wine.

Birsha threw his hands up before the man could turn him down cold. "I assure you, it is to be used for the utmost good, to counter an evil spell only."

"Oh, I see." The priest turned his one good eye on Birsha, the other one wandering slightly, as though directionless. "For good, you say."

"Aye, Father."

"Hmm." The priest coughed to clear his raspy throat. "Yes, well, perhaps God will not frown on you if you are doing good."

"Of course."

"Stand," the priest ordered.

And yet as Birsha did so, the priest seemed incapable of following his lead so that Birsha had to reach out a hand to help the poor man up.

The priest coughed into his fist, and his eyes grew steady as he peered up at Birsha who towered above the man.

He moved his hand up and down, and said something in Latin. Then he kissed his white and gold embroidered stole. "I have given you and yours my blessing."

"Thank you," Birsha said, bowing slightly.

"Now go!" The priest waved a hand in the air in the general direction of the maze garden.

Birsha bowed yet again and did as commanded, but as he left, he could hear the priest muttering something under his breath that sounded surprisingly like, "Grimoires. Pah! Heathens all."

Heathen indeed!

24

Word came the following day that the Jackals were on the march. Though they were still at least two weeks away, something in my gut told me that this was a ruse of some sort. That this wasn't the way Alaric operated. Nor the Council, though of late rumors had reached us that a far greater threat lived beneath the castle walls. Had they been there two years ago, when we had searched the warrens for the dungeon, where we had saved Thomas and Emma from certain death? I shuddered to think. Still, I felt certain that something was out there just waiting for the right moment to strike. We would need all the magic we could possess. That's why I called the meeting together and why the leaders of each of the groups sat gathered in Winnifred's barn. Winnifred had offered us each a stool and she dragged her work table into the middle of the room so we could "talk turkey," as she so blithefully stated with that undercurrent of a grin.

"So, we need magic," I began. "Any magic. I'm afraid our old tricks won't be up to the job. What do we have?"

All of us looked at each other, Thomas shrugging, Emma merely mimicking Thomas's movements.

"Gertrude? Jocelyn?" I turned to the two sisters who were as different as night and day.

"You used the only thing I had back at the fortress two years back."

"The snake?"

Jocelyn nodded.

"How about you, Yesimeh?" I knew Lofgren had speed as his special ability, and that might still be of use in the coming battle, and I, of course, had the loom which we had decided to take with us this time on the condition that it be guarded by only the most trusted women.

Yesimeh squeaked a tiny "I'm sorry," but offered nothing more.

"Okay," I said on a sigh, "then I will need you to begin searching high and low for someone, *anyone*, who uses magic, but only white magic, understood?"

Yesimeh's eyes transformed into two giant saucers as though I had asked for her firstborn. "You know I would never use—" She peered around then lowered her voice to a whisper so that we must all lean in. "—use *dark* magic." She shivered as though taking a sudden chill and rubbed her hands together to warm them, despite the balmy weather outside, as it was the time of year when most of us spent our leisure time outdoors, in years past, but those days were long gone.

"Of course not, Yesimeh," I assured her. "And I would never ask it of you."

"Good!" she said with a harumph.

For the first time since I had known Yesimeh, she reminded me of a mini-version of Winnifred, and had in fact been spending more time with her, both of them rather brainy, though I meant that in a good way. For here, women could be smart. They didn't have to smile and dip their heads in coquettish mimicry of simpletons. Here they could be intelligent and brave. In short, they could be who they were meant to be rather than who they were told to be, and that brought joy to my heart in unfathomable ways to know that these women no longer had to subvert their abilities to the greater good of men.

"Okay, let's adjourn for now, but I want each of you to put your feelers out for anyone with special abilities. We have two weeks tops before the Jackals will be in our vicinity, and if they use magic, we could see battle sooner. So I implore you—" Here, I turned an eye to each and every person in the room. "Do not let me down. Don't let the *women* down," I amended at the last moment. For we were a team, and as a team, we owed it to each other to stick together. Our very lives depended on it.

Birsha dressed early, before the light of dawn. Beatrice awakened and stretched, her eyes widening as she realized what he was doing. She jumped out of the enormous oak Renaissance bed that had been gifted to Alaric from an English nobleman. In its finials were carved two knights who stood guard over the pair while they were sleeping. Though small in stature, the knights took their job seriously and were apt to warn them of danger, though Beatrice found them intrusive. As a result, she dressed in complete darkness to avoid their stoic gaze. Now, Birsha feared the knights might give away their departure. If only he could silence them in some way, but how? He peered over at Beatrice and nodded toward the pair whose backs were to them, their fronts facing the door and therefore the hallway.

She placed a finger to her chin as if thinking, and then, coming to a decision, she tiptoed to the chest where she kept all of her things. For several minutes, she dug through their belongings. To Birsha's disappointment, she merely pulled out the clothing she would wear for the day, though he saw she meant to disguise herself as a male guard. Birsha shook his head, glad that he had married such a resourceful woman. She quickly dressed, bringing only the essentials that they planned to carry with them. The rest would be provided by Master Clyde who would supply most of their provisions.

But before she shut the chest, she reached in and grabbed one last item wrapped in plain burlap. Birsha frowned. She peeled back the top layer, and in the center of the burlap was a vial filled with a dark brown liquid. Birsha recognized it instantly. Laudanum. That should keep the pair of knights quiet until Birsha and Beatrice could slip past the gates.

Beatrice loaded the liquid onto the burlap and dripped it onto the knights' tongues, each one's voices muffled by the thick burlap. Soon, they were fast asleep.

"Hurry!" Birsha grasped her hand, then was careful to open the door quietly. He held his finger to his lips lest she speak and cause someone to stir.

On stealthy feet, they tiptoed through the door and down the hallway, their footsteps more hurried now as they neared the exit. Birsha didn't breathe until they had traversed the labyrinth of hallways and were out the main door of the inner portion of the fortress. Together, they rushed hurriedly toward the meeting place agreed upon by Master Clyde, but as they neared the edge of the fortress, Birsha told Beatrice to wait for him.

"I have something to do, but I will be back shortly. Don't move, do you hear me?"

She opened her mouth to protest, but he merely put a finger to his lips to silence her. He gave her one quick kiss, then on stealthy feet hurried toward the library. He prayed that Alaric was out doing something or other, rather than perusing the library. Fortunately, it was early enough that Birsha doubted he would be about, other than to eat his morning breakfast of eggs on toast with the treacle he was so fond of.

Birsha's heart was pounding by the time he reached the library. He listened for footsteps before entering and ran straight to the mahogany book ladder that would take him to the hidden rotunda above.

When he arrived at the top, he shimmied onto the floor of the hidden room and coughed to let Fearsome know that he was present so as not to surprise him. From the crystal ball, he heard a luxurious yawn and saw two arms stretched into the air. Fearsome was still wearing his smoking jacket and silk pajamas and his coal black hair appeared ruffled from sleep. His eyes were watery and bloodshot, no doubt from an evening sipping cognac, the bottle still visible through the round ball and placed squarely on a Georgian table that would no doubt fetch a hefty sum these days.

"What do you want?" Fearsome demanded without preamble.

"The book—the grimoire," Birsha said, getting straight to the point.

"Ha!" Fearsome growled. "I thought you wanted it gone, disappeared, poof!" He snapped his fingers to reveal swirling smoke inside the ball.

"Yes, I did, but I've learned that it can be used to *undo* what has been done, and I have a strong suspicion that I may need it."

"Oh you do, do you? And why is that?"

"Because Alaric has set the Jackals upon the Bookbinder Kingdom, at the easternmost tip of the Kregs."

Fearsome laughed, but the sound held no mirth. Instead it came out as a low rumble that shook the walls.

Birsha pressed the air with his hands in an attempt to get the other man to keep down the noise. The last thing Birsha wanted was for his exploits to be made known to Alaric.

"So, Alaric is doing what I could not, eh? Unite the kingdom under one rule."

"*His* rule," Birsha reminded him.

"Ah, and you think him foolish because of his quick temper, aye?"

"And his treatment of the enslaved," Birsha added before it could be taken back.

Fearsome stared at him in silence, his look both frightening and appraising, all in one glance. Finally, he broke the silence by saying, "You have audacity, I can say that for you. Most people wouldn't stand up to such a man as your father. That makes you either quite brave or quite foolish, it remains to be seen.

Birsha's stomach roiled as though a war were taking place within it, but if he was to ever show his courage, it must be now. He lifted himself up, his head touching the ceiling.

"I want that book, Fearsome. We need to right our wrongs."

"You feel strongly, do you?"

"I do."

The man narrowed his eyes as he stroked his chin whiskers, his eyes never once leaving Birsha, who felt like a bug on a pin.

"You'll need protection before I give the grimoire to you."

"I already have it." To prove it, he turned, an iridescent blue mist turning with him, like bioluminescent algae he'd once seen when out trekking next to the ocean.

One of Fearsome's eyebrows shot up in surprise. "So, you have thought of everything, have you?"

"I have," Birsha said, humbled by the man's remarks.

"Then you shall have your book."

With that, Fearsome shot out his hand, his fingers long and dagger-like. A series of lightning bolts flashed from his fingertips and his eyes turned a cobalt blue as he sought the hidden grimoire and pulled it toward him. As it had before, the grimoire flipped open, page upon page, until it landed on one particularly beautiful and deadly page, its meaning unclear to Birsha.

Birsha held it in his hands, despite the heat that it emanated. On the page, a glowing swirl of stars circled round and round, causing a great wind to stir up dust in the room, stinging Birsha's eyes until he could stand it no more. He quickly shut the book with a loud "Whap!"

His hands trembled and his body shook, but he was safe and alive. Still, he wondered about the book's meaning.

Suddenly, Fearsome's eyes grew blood red and his voice was so low as to scarcely hear it. "Someone is coming. You have but moments to escape with your life. Go now!" Fearsome hissed.

Birsha didn't need to be told again. He fairly slid down the book ladder and rushed to the large wooden door. Sure enough, as he opened it, he could hear footsteps around the corner. He tucked the book into his coat jacket and raced to the opposite hallway and around the bend before the person belonging to those footsteps could see him. His heart was beating double time by the time he met up with Beatrice who appeared frantic by his absence.

"Where were you?" she whispered, glancing both ways before speaking.

"No matter, I am here now." He placed a hand on her shoulder as they hurried down the alleyway.

Like Beatrice, Birsha had been careful to wear a disguise that would hide his reverse widow's peak and his braided goatee, clear giveaways as to his heritage. No, he had thought of everything . . . Everything *except* the Kazakh who was just now leaving his aviary of predatory birds.

"Aye, Son of Alaric, great-grandson of Faineant the Foul. Going somewhere, are you?"

Birsha's stomach swirled in turmoil and his heart quaked. All that he had feared was coming to pass in this one meeting of Alaric's most standard foe. A man who was unafraid to use his birds to pluck out the very eyes of his enemies. Birsha glanced over at Beatrice and saw that she had paled to the shade of white linen, the very linen that covered his bed at night.

Beatrice let loose a loud sigh that gave away the desultory manner in which they were leaving the fortress. Skulking, as it were, though the warren of streets.

The Kazakh's throat rumbled in delight to see them so exposed. A twinkle lit up his dark brown eyes, like marbles, they were.

"Come with me," he said, curling his finger for them to follow him.

Birsha gulped back his fear as he clutched Beatrice's hand. He'd thought the saying about one's life flashing before one's eyes prior to death just that . . . a saying. But now he realized it to be true as his mind spooled through all the things he'd done as a child, all the actions that had led him to this place and time. So this was it. This was how it would end. Strangely, he felt calm. He no longer fought what he'd believed to be inevitable from the moment he'd taken office. His death. His and Beatrice's.

But to his surprise, the Kazakh whisked them through the aviary at a dazzling speed. Until now, Birsha had thought the man with his trademark fox fur coat and hat, and his boots trimmed in yak fur, too cumbersome to move quickly. He inevitably had something to learn of the man.

"I don't mean to be rude, but we're in a hurry."

"I can see that," the Kazakh said. "But first, I have a gift."

"A gift?" Birsha exchanged a hurried glance with Beatrice, her expression just as confused as his own.

"Yes, for your—how should I say it . . . trip, perhaps?"

Birsha paused for only a moment before deciding to trust the man. After all, what choice did he have?

"Yes, for our trip. It's a secret, you know."

"It always is," the Kazakh said with a low rumble of laughter that sounded more like a growl.

From an inner chamber, he brought out one of his finest falcons.

"Why are you giving us this?" Birsha asked, confused by the man's odd behavior.

"Because you may have need of him. Should you get into trouble, send him to me and I shall help save you."

Birsha stilled, the moment stretching out before him. "But why? Why are you helping us?"

The old man laughed. "You don't remember, do you?"

"Remember what?" Beatrice said before Birsha could respond.

Suddenly, the man's eyes softened and Birsha read something in them he hadn't before.

"When you were a small boy, I found you alone in a courtyard, crying."

Birsha felt the inklings of a memory just off the horizon. Of a man, who had knelt down to him and wrapped him in his coat. Of him showing him one of his smallest birds, so small in fact that the man could have easily crushed it in his hand. But he hadn't. He had held it out to Birsha and allowed him to set it on his finger. The bird had stayed with him through those lonely days in the fortress, when his father was too busy to see him.

"Do you recall what I told you then?"

Birsha scoured his brain but couldn't come up with an answer.

"I told you that no matter where you were, or who you were with, I would watch over you like a son. Protect you against all enemies. And I have kept my promise, though you never knew it."

"You have saved my life—in the past?" Birsha felt the welling of tears, but forced them down where they belonged, no longer the boy of six who could freely shed them.

"Many times," the Kazakh said. "And I will save you many times more, until my life has ended."

"But why?" Birsha asked. "Why would you help a little boy who could have meant nothing to you?"

The Kazakh smiled. "Ah, but there you are wrong. You meant everything to me."

The skin on Birsha's arms and neck prickled. "Again, I say why? Why did I mean so much to you?"

A sadness filled the man's eyes and Birsha saw something he hadn't seen before. Longing. A longing so deep, a yearning so wide that it made Birsha gasp.

"You loved my mother."

A tear glistened in the old man's eyes. "That I did, my son. That I did. Now, let me take you out the back way where your carriage awaits."

It hadn't taken long before Yesimeh reappeared, two days later. We had settled in Winnifred's barn once again, our tents scattered around it for miles. Kahwhita worried about the location.

"You do not use the forest for shelter?" she asked one morning as she fed her sweet baby, Wahta, and rocked her.

The smile on her face said it all. She was smitten. And why wouldn't she be? I wondered if I would ever give birth to such a beautiful child as this. Or perhaps I was destined to live the life of a warrior, but surely even *they* bore children.

I considered her question. To her, it made sense that we hide in the shadow of the fir and oak, and yet from everything I had known about the Council of Jackals, they tended to use other, more magical, means by which to find us, to attack.

"I wish that the forest could keep us safe," I said quite frankly. "But with Alaric and his men, there is nowhere safe." I shrugged apologetically, because what else could I do.

She merely nodded. Like most of her people, they tended to be laconic except when something had them excited. I thought of her now, as Yesimeh came running toward me with three women in tow, each as different as the ocean to the mountain spring. One was no more than ten, if a day. Her light brown hair ran in rivulets down her back, and her keen green eyes held an intensity that belied her age. The other was a stocky woman who wore her apron as though she had been kneading dough when she had been ferreted away by Yesimeh. Her short brown hair gave her a rather utilitarian look. The third was an elderly woman bent low at the waist, with a cane almost as gnarled as her. The more I looked at this rather motley bunch, the more my heart sank. How could three women such as these help me against an entire army of Jackals and their sort?

"Come, sit," I said wearily.

They sat on the stumps that surrounded one of our many fire pits where we cooked our meals each day. For several moments, we all sat staring at each other until finally, I broke the silence.

"So, are these the women with . . . gifts?" I tried to sound cheerful, but the words spilled out in a warren of disbelief.

"They are." Yesimeh dipped her head toward the women.

"And what gifts do they possess?" I asked, certain they would be silly, each and every one of them.

"First off," Yesimeh said, "this here is Hannah's aunt's daughter, Edith.

I whooshed out a sigh of relief. Hannah was a stalwart companion and a seasoned warrior. If she had agreed to the meeting, then I held out hope for Edith.

"What can she do?" I asked, smiling at the girl in encouragement.

"Tell her," Yesimeh said.

"I can stop the stars from falling."

I blinked, and blinked again. What on earth was the girl talking about? What kind of stars? Falling stars? Comets? And what did that have to do with us? I buried my face in my hands to give me time to restore my composure. Finally, I lifted my head and said, "Thank you, Edith. That will be all."

"And you?" I turned to the stocky woman with the apron.

"Ja, back in the old country, the women from our family were all shieldmaidens," she said in a very Norwegian dialect. "We carry a shield that has supernatural powers to repel the enemy."

Now we were getting somewhere. I breathed a sigh of relief.

"And how about you?" I said to the elderly woman.

"I make craters out of the earth," she said in a scraggly voice, "with my walking stick." She held it up for me to see. And indeed it was as she said, and yet it was the most intricately carved walking stick I had ever seen. On its head was a lion, while down the length of its staff were all of the major animals of the kingdom, as though she could simply call upon them to do her bidding should she ask.

"Craters?" I looked to Yesimeh for an explanation.

But all she said was "Poof!" and made a huge circle with her hands like a giant explosion. As she did, all the air whooshed out of me. So I had a woman who prevented stars from falling, a shieldmaiden, and an old woman who made craters with her cane. I rubbed my face with my hands. Hopefully, somewhere in all this, I could use their help. Until then, I felt only the weight that had settled on my chest like a large boulder. It was clear the wait was getting to me and I needed some time to think . . . to breathe.

"Thanks," I said to Yesimeh. "Could you keep all of the women handy? If they have families nearby, could you relocate them closer so that we can call on them at a moment's notice?" In the meantime, I would ask my loom what this all meant. Surely, the loom would know why these women had been brought to me so that I could prepare for the upcoming battle.

As the foursome walked away, the old woman peered back at me with a twinkle in her eye, as though she held a secret that I would only learn when the time came for the secret to be revealed, and I had a feeling that meant when we were in the midst of battle.

Though no words passed between us, I nodded to acknowledge that I understood, and she nodded in return. Then she turned, and I was surprised to see that she no longer stood hunched over, but instead erect. Strong. In that moment I could feel her courage transfer to me and I whispered a quick "thank you" before I turned to go in search of my loom.

25

The Queen of Mammals was in the stables grooming the Mongolian horse in her collection called a *"takhi"*, which translated to the word "spirit". The dun-colored horse was quite stocky, with a mane that stood erect and a dark stripe that ran down its back. She had seen the Kazakh speak to it in low tones and heard the animal respond, as though he too was contributing to the conversation. As she ran the bristle brush down the horse's side to remove the dirt and debris, she recalled the rumors. She'd heard it whispered that the Kazakh had been raised with both takhis and birds of prey from birth. He'd been saddled to the takhi's back as a toddler and taught to ride as a small child, Mongols being the best horsemen in all of Europe and beyond. With the aid of the takhi, Mongolians had at one time ruled most of the Asian continent, from China to Russia, and much of Persia. After seeing the Kazakh ride, The Queen of

Mammals had no doubt this was true.

"What secrets do you hold, eh, takhi?" she asked as she stoked the horse's back with the boar brush. "The Kazakh knows something, I can feel it in my bones."

"Are you looking for me?"

The Queen of Mammals dropped her brush onto the ground where a powder puff of dust claimed the air at her feet. "Oh, you shouldn't sneak up on a person like that!" she admonished the Kazakh.

"A person? That is what you think you are?" He chuckled.

"What do you mean by *that*?" she demanded, her hackles rising at the insinuation.

"I would have thought you one of *them*." He nodded toward the fortress.

For one brief moment, her heart stilled. Did he know? About the Diāmons? Surely not, a man who never traversed below ground, and yet sometimes she would see him bent to the dirt, his ear pressed to the earth as though he could read the living breathing soul of it, the odd man.

"One of them?" she asked, determined not to give away her hand.

"The soulless ones."

This time his laugh came out a growl that caused her very marrow to run cold. Surely he didn't know. How could he? And yet that blessed aviary was close to where they kept their weekly meetings below ground.

"You flatter yourself," she said, her teeth grinding together in a show of anger. "You know nothing of me or my business, and if you did, you wouldn't be long for this world!"

His laugh was low and loud this time as he bent over, bellowing in mirth that she could be so foolish as to threaten him. Her face flushed with a heat unlike anything she had ever experienced before. She wanted to tell him to watch himself, and yet maybe it was she who should be cautious in the coming days, because the Kazakh was anything if not ruthless. She had heard the tales. And yet in each of the tellings, his actions had seemed just, in light of what had preceded them. Still, she had no wish to tangle with him.

"Here!" she said, handing him the brush. "I can see that you wish to be alone with your . . . *charge*."

She hadn't meant the word to escape so venom-filled, but it was too late to eat her words. Instead, she shoved the brush into his hands and stormed off. Yet even as she did, she could hear him talking to the beast and the beast responding, as if the two spoke the same language. And for the life of her, she couldn't help but think he was telling the animal about her. And that the takhi agreed. But agreed to what? That was the question that shadowed her as she fled toward the bowels of the earth.

Winnifred regarded Brigid as she passed. For days now, she had seemed preoccupied, which was so unlike her. If anything, she could be bubbly and effervescent. Something was eating at her. Winnifred decided to follow her, and sure enough, Brigid headed straight for the loom, which she had brought with her for the first time since they had started this adventure. That, too, seemed out of character for Brigid.

Winnifred hid in the shadows, only coming out when she

was sure her friend wasn't looking. She followed her to the tent where one of the women stood guard, a spear in one hand, an Enfield rifle at the ready should anyone attempt to breach the interior.

For several seconds, Winnifred waited as Brigid entered. Then she strode up to Hannah, the current guard on duty, and placed a finger to her lips to urge the woman's silence. Hannah, who had been a close friend and confidante in the previous campaign tilted her head slightly, but did as requested. They had been through too much together to question each other now.

Winnifred tiptoed to the window where she saw Brigid, bent down to the loom, talking to it as though it were a long-lost friend rather than an inanimate object. A hum filled the air as though it sensed a portentous moment. Then, after a brief pause where the loom turned an inky void, a cloud began to whirl inside the tapestry and before Winnifred had time to ponder its meaning, a loud pop startled her and stars whooshed out, knocking Brigid on her backside as they scattered all throughout the room in a swirl of motion that was both magical and ominous. Winnifred rushed to the door and flung it open. Before she could stop them, the stars sailed outward and flew to the sky, disappearing among the clouds. Around the tent, every man, woman and child stopped to gape.

"What was *that*?" Winnifred breathed.

Brigid, who had been huddled where she'd landed until all the stars had passed, rose on unsteady feet. Winnifred went to her, and grabbed her hand to steady her. As if in unison, the pair turned to inspect the loom. On it, every man, woman and child in Battersbog lay dead, like a carpet of flowers that had yet to bloom.

"What does it mean?" Winnifred gasped.

"I don't know," Brigid murmured. "But one thing I do know, we've been warned. And the future is fluid. It can change, if enough people move to stop it. And we must."

They both peered out the open doorway that was now filled with the residents of Battersbog peering in, their expressions just as horrified as both Winnifred's and Brigid's. We had only to look at them to know what was at stake.

"Right-O!" Winnifred said. "Then we had better start preparing."

Surely, I could do something to halt the wholesale slaughter of my people. I left in search of Henry to tell him what had happened and found him staring intently at some trembling spot in the forest underbrush.

"What is it?" I peered over his shoulder, still frightened after what I had witnessed on the loom.

I didn't have long to wait for my answer because at that moment, one of the sprites, who I hadn't seen since our last foray into Battersbog and beyond, popped his head out and looked around as if to be sure the coast was clear. Then he whistled to his friends who came from all directions, each of them chittering away in their gibberish language, the noise becoming so loud that I had to stamp my foot for silence. Slowly, the din died down. Though I still had yet to learn their language, I had picked up a few key words and one of them I recognized when the first sprite began talking. And the word

I heard was monster. Another sprite began to pantomime, stomping around the ground with fingers that looked like large fangs protruding from the sprite's mouth. And finally, something that sounded like "Charge!" followed by a pretend bugle.

Henry and I exchanged looks. What I assumed they were saying is that a monster was on the loose, but how far away was anyone's guess. Furthermore, how had they heard? I tried to ask them these simple questions, but it only further agitated them so that they all began talking at once.

"Oh, for heaven's sake!"

I scolded them, wishing I had learned their language as Winnifred had, but I had never been very good at languages. Oh, I had picked up a word or two here and there, but usually just enough to ask for directions to the library, my favorite place outside of nature.

I was just about to lose my temper when they suddenly silenced in a reverent hush, their expressions that of fear. When I turned, I saw that it was the old lady with the cane. *Who is she?* She reminded me of someone out of a fairytale, her white hair shocked in every direction so that it looked like bent wire. For some reason she held sway over the tiny sprites who had jammed in tighter, as though recognizing safety in numbers.

"Good!" she said, as though she had telepathically silenced the poor sprites. "Now! We need to talk."

I looked around, until I realized that she meant me. I pointed at my chest and she nodded once, quite firmly, I might add. Though I couldn't say why—possibly it was the fact that the sprites had all stepped back a few steps—but my mouth suddenly went dry and my breathing grew labored.

"Yes?" My voice came out a squeak. I cleared my throat and tried again. "You wish to speak to me?"

"In private!" She stepped aside, as though urging me toward the path that led to the river.

To my surprise, when I glanced over at the sprites, they wore a look of extreme empathy and, for once, I felt like they were on my side. Before leaving for the river, I turned to Henry, who only shrugged, and yet he stayed rooted to the spot as well.

Thanks a lot! I thought churlishly, but I knew I was on my own with this one, and just as well. If she was as frightening as everyone seemed to think, it was best that we met alone. No use risking anyone else's life. As I passed her, I prayed she was truly on our side because she would make a formidable foe.

Once on the path, she led me to the portion of the river where I first met the sprites. And though this was to be a private conversation I noticed that they, too, had filtered through the forest and were now hiding just at the periphery of my vision.

I turned to the old woman, who identified herself as Lawanda. "By the way, I see you sprites," she chided in a schoolmarm's voice. "If you're going to listen in on conversations that are not yours, at least have the decency to show yourselves."

One by one they appeared on leaves, sailing down the river, or on rocks, pretending they were fishing, though what for, I could only imagine.

"You, too, Henry." She snapped her fingers

Henry sheepishly appeared from behind a tree. "Henry?" I said, surprised at his cunning.

"Well, I couldn't leave you alone with . . ."

I wasn't sure how he'd plan to end that statement, but whatever he'd meant had been burned from his memory because he stood there in awkward silence, wearing a decidedly scarlet complexion.

"Now that we are all assembled" —Lawanda eyed each and every one of us— "I suppose you might as well know what it is I have to say."

Henry walked over to me and grasped my fingers in support, which I was more than grateful for.

"There's something you need to know about our gifts."

"Oh?" I said, loosening my collar with my index finger. "And what is that?"

She paused as if to reveal an important secret, her eyes narrowing, yet instead of appearing more frightening, as I had suspected, her face actually softened, as though she too had been young once, the world an unwelcoming place at times.

"You're given exactly what you need, at the time you need it. That's why I have appeared in your life now, as well as the others." She pierced me with a look. "I saw the disdain you had for them—"

I started to protest, but she held up her hands. "They wouldn't have appeared now, if you didn't need them, so hold them close. *Very* close."

Her words chilled me to the marrow because in my heart of hearts I believed she knew something—something that even now held me . . . no *all of us,* in its sights. The sprites had hinted at it. And I already knew that the army of Jackals was at hand—that they had left the fort and were on their way here to Battersbog, where, with any luck, we would halt them before they arrived at the manor. But I also knew this couldn't be the sum of it, because they had never used their forces in this manner without the aid of magic. And after my foray into the fortress, I knew all too well from my time in their library that they had learned magic and had books from which to draw.

"Okay," I said at last. "I'll speak to Winnifred, make sure all three of the women's families are stationed here with them until . . ." I allowed the rest of my words to trail off, fearing what might come next. But how could a ten-year old keep the stars from falling? I simply couldn't fathom it.

"See that you do!" Lawanda turned as if to leave, but then stopped. "And Brigid," she said, her tone softening for the first time since I'd met her. "Keep Henry close. Mark my words. You will need him in the coming days."

I squeezed Henry's hand, my eyes misting over. What had she meant by that? I feared the meaning, as there were already too many questions with not enough answers, or the right ones, at least.

Then I watched as she used her walking stick to secure her footing on the forest floor where all sorts of ferns and bracken were wont to snag a person, if they weren't careful. And I had been snagged too many times, in too many ways, to ignore her warning. For it was a warning, and I best be on my guard from here on out. As she toddled off, even the sprites seemed sullen. Whatever was out there, waiting for us, it meant to find us here. All of us. And I must be prepared.

26

Birsha's nerves were on fire and his breathing as jangled as his body as he stood inside the barn, Beatrice at his side. At least he had been able to send the Kazakh's falcon ahead to a place where they would meet up, later, that way he could send word back if things got dicey. He had yet to deal with his father.

What if Alaric got word that they were leaving? That they were headed for the Bookbinder Manor? The pair's lives would be forfeit. Worse yet, what if the Bookbinder's wouldn't accept Beatrice and the former leader of their most hated foe? He would be a man without a country, without a kingdom. That thought sent chills racing through him so that he thought he might be sick right then and there.

Beatrice braced herself for both of them, her arm encircling his waist as they waited for Master Clyde to take them on the first part of the journey. Supposedly, there were those who would take them further into the kingdom, should they continue on, which they would. But Birsha had one trick up his sleeve, one ace in the hole that he hadn't even told Beatrice. The thing that might save them all, or cause them to perish.

No, he refused to think about that now. He had to stay strong, to hope for the best. As the seconds mounted and sweat formed on his brow, he circled back to his father. This morning, at breakfast, Alaric had taken him aside and, hands on shoulders, asked him if he was feeling well.

"Of course," he'd squeaked.

He'd prayed that his father hadn't read the lie in his eyes. He didn't know if he was doing the right thing. Part of him longed to stay, to stand shoulder to shoulder with his father, and yet to do so would betray Beatrice and her people. To betray the slaves who'd nearly lost their lives from harsh working conditions, lack of food, but most of all from cold, the silent killer. How could one possibly condone that? Especially when the slaves had done nothing wrong. And even those who had, surely their punishments couldn't be so harsh that they paid with their very lives. Few deserved such cruelty.

No, he was doing the right thing. The moments of waiting tore at his nerves, wearing them thin. He was about to do the very thing Master Clyde had asked him not to do, to go outside where he might be seen and possibly pegged as a traitor. That's when the door to the barn finally opened and Master Clyde slipped in. With him, he carried two packs. He loaded Beatrice and Birsha each with a pack, then blindfolded them.

"Sorry, but you cannot know where you are being taken. For your safety as well as ours."

Birsha nodded, understanding only too clearly what was at stake, relieved to finally be starting the journey that would take him far from the evil that this court had become. And yet he was bringing a small piece of it with him. He tapped the book hidden deep within the inner lining of his coat pocket, the one that Fearsome had made to disappear. It stirred, as though a living thing and he could have sworn that it made a low rumbling noise, but no one else seemed to have heard it as they continued onward. Now, he just had to hope that Fearsome was right, that what could be done could be undone and that magick could be reversed, used for good rather than evil. Yet, what if he was wrong? That thought sent a wave of nausea running through him.

"Okay then," Master Clyde said. "Off to the tunnels."

And with that, they descended cautiously into the warrens that would lead them to who knows where.

The first sign of trouble occurred when things came up missing. First it was a quiver of arrows. Then it was a horse, later a gun, all things that would protect us when the onslaught came. Soon, the entire camp was abuzz with the news as nearly every person present found something missing. Before long, I found myself surrounded by women fuming and hurling one accusation after another until finally I was forced to shout to be heard.

"You, Jocelyn," I said, pointing at her, "what do you know?"

"I woke up this morning and my armor was gone. I always

keep it on my fold-up chair so that it's ready when I wake, but today it was nowhere to be found."

"And my boots that I sit next to the inside of the tent turned up missing," Gertrude added.

Soon, everyone was speaking in unison until Winnifred let out a whistle that quieted them all down. Then, from the back of the clearing I heard a rustling and someone murmuring. I watched as Lawanda began her trek down the aisle that was now forming. This time, besides the walking stick, she had a dog at her side, an Australian shepherd, if my knowledge of breeding was at all correct. It whirled around her at such a frantic pace that I feared she might fall, but the pup seemed to know just where she would step and always managed to be out of the way when her foot found purchase. Finally, she arrived to stand in front of me. She held her head erect, shoulders back, as though she was ready to take whatever punishment I deemed to mete out, but punishment for what?

"Have you word about the missing articles?"

Before the old woman could answer, Henry and Thomas threaded their way through the women as they sought their way forward, clearly out of breath.

"Brigid? What's happened? What's wrong?" Henry demanded.

I quickly explained to him about all the missing items. Henry frowned, while Thomas looked the poor woman up and down as though she were an especially interesting centipede that he'd discovered as a child. Lawanda poked him with her walking stick.

"Ow! What'd ya do that for?" Thomas squealed. Then he

tested his arm where a small red welt was forming.

"For being rude to an old lady," she said quite tersely. "Now, do what you will, but I'll take my lumps."

"What lumps?" Winnifred said.

"And for what?" I narrowed my eyes, an awareness dawning that she had something to do with the missing items, but what? Furthermore, why?

"Well," she began in that gritty voice of hers, "for takin' your stuff like I did, but I had my reasons, mind you."

"And what reasons were those?" I demanded.

Suddenly a stir erupted near the rear of the gathering, until a volcano of noise drowned out anything I might have said. Shouts and curses rang out and I feared what my women would do next should I fail to quell the clamor immediately.

Fortunately, Winnifred was on it, because she cried out with a megaphone unlike any other I had ever heard. It produced a tidal wave of sound that flowed out in waves and stunned everyone into silence.

"What is that?" I whispered out of the side of my mouth.

"It's a *megalosonus*." Winnifred offered me a sheepish smile. "I invented it."

Would wonders never cease. "Thank you," I whispered back.

"Now, step aside and let those at the back join me here at the front."

I waved a hand, and soon the seas parted to reveal a large contingent of men, women, and children. They made their way forward, the youngest a girl no more than six, if a day. To my surprise and delight, the little girl, with her yellow bonnet and

sunny blonde hair, curtsied in her gunny sack apron dress, a
bright flower made of yarn tied around one of the buttons that
held her apron dress together above the creamy white petticoat.
She finished the look off with bright red boots, though where
she'd found something quite so extravagant compared to the rest
of her attire was yet to be explained.

"And who are you?" I asked, bending down to greet her.

"Jenny," she said in a voice that tinkled like a set of
windchimes. "And this is for you, ma'am."

She removed the flower from the button with much angst,
then handed it to me with a smile so sweet as to melt my heart.
"From my family."

Then she stepped back and curtsied once more. I placed
a hand across my mouth so she wouldn't see me giggle at such
earnest formality. Then her mother stepped forward.

"I hope you'll let us explain," she said, as one after another
brought the stolen items forward and laid them in a pile at
my feet. Soon the pile became a veritable mountain of our
belongings.

The crowd gasped, and I have to admit that I did as well.
Why had they stolen our things? I turned to Henry, but he
was none the wiser. That's when Lawanda once again stepped
forward, this time in an almost officious way, chin up as though
daring me to protest.

"What's the meaning of this?" I asked the old woman.

"It had to be done!" She gave her chin a single wag, as
though that said it all, then stepped back.

"You're not getting off that easily," I growled, angry that she
expected me to just acquiesce to her misguided will.

"I understand, but as I said, it was necessary."

"Why? Why was it necessary?" I began to pace back and forth, until I came to a halt mere inches away from her. I could smell the garlic on her breath, rumored to keep away evil spirits by those who believed in such things. I did not.

She bent forward until I feared her intentions, and in a voice so low that I could scarcely hear it, she said, "Your women warriors were in need of a protection spell."

She spoke as though I was daft, and I suppose I was at that moment. Perhaps I'd been too hasty in calling together some of these so-called women with gifts, but I had seen what some could do. I just hadn't counted on there being charlatans among them. But now I could see I'd made a mistake.

"You're not to touch our things without our permission," I hissed. "From now on, you are to stay clear of here."

Yet even as I spoke, I detected an unexplained shimmer emanating from the many articles of warfare. But when I turned, the shimmer would dissipate. I rolled my fingers at my side, unsure whether I should trust the woman. And yet Yesimeh wouldn't have brought her here if she wasn't sure of the old woman's gifts, would she? No, perhaps I was being overly critical. Still . . .

"I'll accept what you say . . . for now. Just don't touch anything without our permission in the future, understood?"

She paused, as though coming to a decision, then shook her head once and the team of people from the village departed, leaving us to sort out this horrid mess at a critical juncture in our lives and the lives of those at the manor. I drew in a deep breath, then turned to Henry and Thomas and the others.

"Well, we'd best get our belongings back to their rightful owners."

Fortunately, Winnifred had seen fit that every woman in the group marked their clothing, for obvious reasons, so we were able to return the clothing bit by bit over the course of the day. But we were well into nightfall before the last of the clothing and weapons had been returned to their rightful owners with much grumbling. Yet as darkness fell, all of those pieces with the protection spell seemed to shimmer so that the meadow lit up with a ghostly quality, as though haunts were even now marching back and forth around the campfire. A chill settled into my very bones because I could feel it. The old woman had indeed put a protection spell on our belongings. But it wasn't just that. It's as if that protection spell had somehow entered each of us through our articles of clothing. I could feel it residing within my chest. A calmness that I hadn't noticed before, as if to prepare me and the rest of the women for what lay ahead.

27

"They're gone, Your Majesty," Siegfried said when Alaric called him to his room.

Siegfried could never get over the sight of such opulence for one so ordinary as Alaric, though indeed, he wore his stature as though a bigger man, a finer man. Only Siegfried knew the truth about the Foul family. They had come from peasants, centuries back, and had only attained stature through an odd fluke of fate. One of the Foul family had come upon a lost child in the forest, one of King Edrain's children back when the Edrain family had ruled much of the land. In repayment for saving the child, the Fouls had been given a title and a large portion of land. Slowly, they had worked their way into the King's graces, all the while setting up a plan to overtake the kingdom and rid it of its heirs, which they soon did.

Now, still in his crenelated black suit, Alaric reminded

Siegfried of a black adder, ready to strike. And in fact the very silence that filled the room didn't bode well.

"Sir! Say something."

"So, my son is gone, tail between his legs to the Bookbinder Kingdom."

His words were so laced with venom that Siegfried shivered beneath his robes, thankful that such clothing hid all manner of discontent.

"It would look that way." Siegfried's eyes scanned the room for any and all exits in case his superior decided to punish him for his son's escape.

Alaric plopped down into an ornate, oversized chair, the state seal sewn into the weave where he sat. His fingers gripped the two knobs carved to imitate Jackals' heads, his knuckles turning white. It only served to showcase the large rings that adorned his fingers. The one that stood out most was a Rococo-style baroque ring with a blood red ruby at its center. The face of a Jackal peered through as though a bug encased in amber, its fangs dripping a darker red. Even that caused Siegfried to shiver as though evil magic had placed some poor unfortunate inside the ring, forever lost to time.

"Well, well," Alaric said in a rather oily voice. "So, it's true then."

Alaric eyed Siegfried slowly.

"Have you ever had children?" Alaric asked, even though he knew he did not.

"No, sir." Siegfried decided to play Alaric's game, but what that might be he had yet to learn. In the meantime, every second spent in the man's presence felt like a lifetime.

"Yes, of course not," he said with a laugh. "You are a eunuch, for all intents and purposes."

And yet no humor filled his eyes, only a deep-seated anger that caused Siegfried's throat to suddenly feel parched.

"No, sir, I am not!" Siegfried lifted his chin, hoping he hadn't made an incalculable error by challenging the senior leader. "I just choose to be by your side, to help in your daily life at the fortress."

Alaric pulled at his braided chin hair as he appraised Siegfried. "Yes, of course. I'm being insensitive to turn my anger on you, Siegfried. You've been such a good and loyal servant."

And that was the rub of it, though Siegfried would never tell Alaric so. Birsha had treated Siegfried ever more like a man than Alaric had done. Had seen into his heart and soul, using his station only rarely to reprimand Siegfried. And though he would never admit it, not even in thought, for those too could be seen as suspect if the right magic were to be employed, he simply liked Birsha better. An inner core of morality made him a finer leader than Alaric, in Siegfried's mind, and made far fewer enemies, as a result. Except for the Diāmons. They were altogether different in the way they viewed the world.

Alaric stood and moved toward the window that opened out so that one could view the beautiful countryside as well as the large field where the mock battles were normally played in exchange for the real ones to come.

"Come, Siegfried, let us observe the remaining soldiers before they leave for the Bookbinder Kingdom, shall we?"

And with that, they watched as the last of the riders left for parts unknown. Siegfried felt a sense of destiny stir within his chest, though what that destiny might portend remained to be seen. Yet in his mind he whispered to Birsha and Beatrice.

Good luck, my friends. And stay safe.

Then the wind picked up, blowing dust and debris into both Siegfried and Alaric's eyes, until finally they were forced to retreat behind the fortress walls.

I could feel it, in my chest, as though a great horde was even now on the horizon and ready to do battle. I gritted my teeth in consternation.

"It does no good to worry, Brigid," Henry said.

He came to stand beside me as I stared off into the distance, willing myself to see what I could not. Surely the Jackals were out there, somewhere, if only I could divine it. Both the starlings and the loom had yet to provide confirmation, merely watching and waiting, but for what?

"What did you think of LaWanda and her protection spell?" he asked. "Do you think she spoke the truth?"

Though Henry had proposed to me just weeks ago, we hadn't spoken about it since, as though to speak of it might somehow jinx it, break the spell of possibilities. And yet it stood between us like a silent thread. I often wondered if we shouldn't just elope as Winnifred had, that to do so would prevent all the what-ifs that might sink our plans.

"I feel it, Henry," I said of the protection spell. "It's as though something has taken up residence inside of me."

"I feel it too. The women as well. They've become much calmer, more certain, less worried."

"I know." I watched the women move about, chopping wood, preparing food, practicing their bowmanship and shooting skills atop horses and on foot. They seemed unstoppable, as if they'd gained a renewed sense of purpose.

"What will you do now?"

Henry turned to me and took my hands in his. It had been so long since we'd had alone time where we could just be the two of us, a couple. I longed to take him in my arms, to cradle him in the heart-shaped roots of the tree that he had cradled me in on so many occasions when the light had been extinguished in our kingdom. Funny that. I had seen the darkness as all bad when it had happened, but there had been peace too. And moments made just for me and Henry.

"I miss you, Brigid," Henry said, as though reading my thoughts. "I miss us!"

My thoughts exactly.

"Do you think we'll ever have time alone, me and you? Just the two of us."

"I hope so," I said on a sigh. And yet I knew that the likelihood of that happening anytime soon was rare if not impossible.

We were about to lean in for a kiss when a rider came dashing through the meadow, jumping from her steed before the animal even had time to come to a full halt.

"What is it?" I demanded. "What's happened?"

The woman struggled to catch her breath as she inhaled short pants of air. "Birsha. Beatrice," she said between gulps. "They've abdicated. They're on their way here."

"Here?" My thoughts pulsed waves of excitement and

despair, in equal measure. "You're sure?"

"Dead sure," the woman said. "And Brigid?" she continued, our army decrying all forms of hierarchy.

"Yes?" Trepidation filled my heart.

"Alaric is none too pleased. He's blaming the Bookbinders. But more than that, he's blaming you and Henry."

28

"Where are we?" Birsha growled as the courier removed his head covering.

"Not for you to know, sir."

The man busied himself with a pair of horses. He wore a cowl so that little of his face was visible, just a beard and mustache. But Birsha could tell by the way he handled the two horses that the man was well versed in horsemanship. When he was done cinching the saddle, the hooded figure handed the reins to Birsha, then prepared the smaller horse for Beatrice, who stood in silence at his side. What she was thinking, he didn't know, but he had a suspicion she was eager to return to her homeland, to those she loved.

"When you leave here, stay to the route on your right. All directions will be posted. Green means take the left trail, red the right. If you miss a turn, no telling where you'll end up, so you'll want to be watchful. If you find your targets, then you should arrive just to the south of Battersbog in three day's time, if you hurry. God's speed."

"You're not coming with us?" Beatrice spoke for the first time since their head coverings had been removed.

Birsha read the panic in her voice and took her hand, giving it a gentle squeeze. "We'll be alright," he reassured her.

She gave a single nod, but he could see by the set of her jaw that she was worried.

"You ready?" the courier said, dipping his head to indicate the horses.

Even though Beatrice was an expert horsewoman, Birsha helped her up. Then in one quick stride, he climbed aboard his quarterhorse, the one that would take him to lands beyond. The animal gave one quick nod of its head as though eager to be on the trail.

"Thank you," he told the courier. "All of you."

The man dipped his head, then was gone—simply disappeared into the forest as though he'd never been there. Birsha gazed over at Beatrice and gave her the signal. Now to begin their trek. He just hoped they wouldn't get lost in the process.

"Gone! What do you mean it's gone?" the Queen of Mammals turned on Liz Herd and Chame Leon. "I ordered you to get it for me!"

"I know but it has been removed from the library," Chame Leon said, glancing at Liz Herd to see her reaction to the woman. Fortunately for him, Liz Herd had a backbone and didn't cower as the other Diāmons were doing now in the tight quarters of the underground chamber.

"Who would have removed it?" the Queen of Mammals hissed.

She paced up and down the underground room with its floating glass table. As she did, those nearby scattered. Even the Diāmons feared her wrath when she was in a mood such as this.

Chame Leon held his counsel, fearing that the woman would find out soon enough and all those around her would pay.

"Madame," the Prince of Darkness said, bowing slightly. "It disappeared at the exact time Birsha and his wife Beatrice escaped into regions unknown."

The Queen of the Mammals turned with a fury Chame Leon had never seen before on the vile looking man.

"Birsha and Beatrice *gone*? Why is this the first I'm hearing of this?" she demanded, her normally placid face blood red with fury.

"Their absence was just discovered. I received word from a trusted palace spy, your Goodness."

For several moments, the Queen of Mammals didn't move, her face becoming ashen, her eyes large. But what frightened Chame Leon most was the way her body seemed coiled to attack if one were within striking distance. He grasped Liz Herd's hand and took a step back, and well that he did, because the woman's hand burst forward and she slapped the Prince, her handprint a stain upon his face. His eyes narrowed to slits and smoke billowed around him. The Queen of Mammals recognized her mistake too late to rectify it. Before she could make amends, he turned fiery eyes on her, a growl emanating low in his throat. Then the Prince shouted an incantation and, just like that, she went up in a ball of flames and she was no more.

Chame Leon grasped Liz Herd's hand firmly as he took another step back, and another until he was close enough to the door that they could escape before the man turned his fury on them. Together, they ran down the hallway, searching door after door until they found one that opened. He wasn't even sure where they had landed until he heard a voice from one of the Council. It came from behind a screen.

"They've fled," the female voice said. "There's no longer an heir should something happen to Alaric."

"I know," said a male voice. "We must put pressure on Alaric to launch his attack now, today. Before he can change his mind."

"But why?" the woman asked.

Chame Leon held a finger to his lips as he and Liz Herd crawled out of the opening beneath a red and gold Aubergine rug. They moved quickly toward a door, yards away.

As they were about to open it, the man behind the screen said, "Because he must be kept busy so that the Diāmons can strike."

"You're with that sorry bunch?" the woman demanded.

That's when Chame Leon detected a clicking sound. *Cricket!* He saw a flash of brilliant color display behind the screen and another, the first one red, the next one bright yellow. *Fishmonger!* So, they were involved too, or at least Fishmonger.

"Better to be with those in power and strength, don't you

think?" Fishmonger said in an oily voice that made Chame Leon's flesh crawl.

Just as he reached for the door, it made a creaking sound.

"Halt! Who goes there?"

But Chame Leon didn't wait to find out what Fishmonger would do if he found them spying on the pair. He yanked the door hard and fled down the corridor, never stopping until they were in an entirely different wing of the building and inside his own personal chambers. Only then did he begin breathing properly.

"Why blame us?" I demanded as we walked over to a more secluded part of the forest where we could speak in private.

And yet it didn't take a scientist to see that we had been the face of our people, Henry and I. *We* attended the ball. *We* escaped the palace, leaving Beatrice behind.

"Alaric seems to think you influenced Birsha somehow through Beatrice," the courier said. She was a lithe woman, willowy and thin. And she wore jodhpurs, a nod to the British Crown and their colonization of India, though the idea of colonization of a people had a sorrowful ring to it. "He has set his army upon you and they're getting close."

As if to confirm it, the starlings began to hover above us, swirling at first, round and round until I thought I might pass out from dizziness. Then, as if given a command, they swooped to the right of us, while others swooped to the left, meeting in the middle where an image began to form . . . of troops of Jackals trudging through the mountains, their canons at the ready. Behind them were the Chessmen, who had to file one by one to keep from taking out huge trees, though they still managed to clip quite a few.

I put a hand to my forehead to block out the sun. "Where are Birsha and Beatrice in all of this? I don't see them."

The courier peered upwards and saw what I saw. Yet instead of it making her gasp, she went deathly silent.

"We don't know where they are. We believe they've taken a different route from that of the Jackals and Chessmen, for security reasons, as you might well imagine."

I thought of Beatrice and Birsha. So many questions. Would they be absorbed into the Bookbinder Kingdom, and could they be trusted? After all, Beatrice had been the one to give me the threads that I had sewn into the fabric of my loom, which sowed chaos when the sun had descended, seemingly forever. Until I had figured out a way to reverse the damage, that is.

"Thank you for your warning," I told the courier. "My women will repay you for your service."

"No need," the woman said to my surprise. "The Jackals killed my father. That's reason enough for my service. I want to make sure they don't do it to anyone else's family member." She clicked her heels together, and within moments, she was back on her horse and headed north.

"Thank you," I whispered into the air, daylight slowly turning to dusk.

We would need to prepare the campfires for dinner. The job had been taken over by a core of women. Bit by bit, women were being divided according to their talents. But most of all their desires. That was the one thing I wanted for my army. *Choices.* Some women liked to hunt. Some women liked to cook. Some preferred to lead, and that was as it should be, so long as they did it well and with as little recrimination as possible.

Henry, who had stood by my side in silence this whole time, read me like a book, one that he had read cover to cover, apparently. "Come," he said, gesturing to me. "No use going hungry before a big campaign. Let's eat. Then in the morning, we'll send out a scout to see how close the Jackals are."

I nodded, feeling numb.

He reached for my hand, but I said, "Wait! I'll meet up with you in a minute. There's something I want to check."

He just stood there staring long after I had departed. I needed to speak with my loom. If I'd received confirmation that the army was well within reach of the kingdom, why had I heard nothing from my loom? Yet even before I arrived at the tent where it was being guarded, I heard clacking and saw the tent lighting up with sparks like it had on that first night when I had awakened to the loom weaving its magical web like an orb weaver. Chills ran down my arms as I ducked my head to enter. For there it was, in all its glory, moving with the speed of a thousand hands, the pedal pumping as if some wayward spirit were even now pressing their feet to the pedals. Tears formed in my eyes, as it was a sight to behold. *So beautiful!* The weave was a blue-black with a myriad of stars twinkling, some sending shooting stars through the night sky, the moon in its orbit. Below it were the campfires, the women in their tents, backlit by lanterns aglow amid the darkness, their lights like a beacon against the night.

I knelt down on my knees, watching in wonder. How peaceful, tranquil. I reached out a hand to touch it, to connect with a memory that I saw almost nightly, and yet here it seemed so much more lovely in its entirety. It was as if this was the way it should be. Peace. Why did we not have more of it?

Then something began to change, the heavens began to swirl, the stars dancing in the night to a rhythm only they could see. My heart pumped in my chest. I could see it now. Something was wrong, as if the sky had been taken over by an evil magician that was even now twirling a magic wand and making it roil like a bubbling cauldron. The sound of the heavens in tumult grew louder and louder until I let out a scream and fell on my backside, the loom choosing that moment to go entirely black, as though it couldn't go any further without creating real damage to itself and those around it.

For several seconds I sat there, scarcely breathing. Finally, Winnifred, who must have seen me wander into the tent, popped her head in and said, "Is everything alright?"

All I could do was shake my head and point.

"What is it? What's wrong?"

"I . . . I don't know," I said, shaken. "The loom . . . it went wild. I'm scared, Winnifred."

"Right-O." Winnifred came to kneel beside me. "Let's get you out of here and put together a plan. Don't you think that's a good idea, Brigid?"

She spoke to me like a child, and I suppose I was acting like one at that moment. But what did it mean? The heavens, the turmoil? My hands couldn't stop trembling, nor my body. I allowed Winnifred to usher me out of the tent and scarcely heard her as she told the guard to monitor the loom closely.

"I'll get a couple more of the women to help you guard it," she said, cradling me like a mother, though she'd had little experience in that regard.

"Thank you," the guard said. Yet she appeared as shaken as I by this most peculiar event that had just taken place.

I knew I didn't have much longer to get my ducks in a row. Whatever was meant to take place, was meant to happen soon. And I best be prepared.

29

Birsha had been up all night, Beatrice fast asleep behind him on the saddle. A pack-bearing horse was attached by rope to Birsha's saddle when, suddenly, he heard Beatrice stir.

"Where are we?" she said, rubbing her eyes and yawning.

"I don't know," Birsha replied.

For hours now they had come across one trail after another, and so far he'd been able to follow the signs set out for him. And yet he knew there might come a time that he missed one, and if he did, God help them. But he tucked that worry away, for now. Better to focus on the task at hand. It was nearing nightfall, and they'd best find a campsite. He waited until he found a clearing in the forest, a glade that looked as if someone—or rather a *lot* of someones—had slept there.

"You don't suppose we're on the same trail as the Jackals!" Beatrice exclaimed.

Birsha brought his horse to a halt and jumped off. He inspected the markings, the hackles on the nape of his neck rising as he warranted what had caused the grass to become so trodden. Indeed, they *were* following the Jackals.

"I thought the courier said we were to take a different path." Beatrice threw her leg over and slid down off Birsha's horse.

"He did."

"You don't suppose we missed one of the markers, do you?"

Birsha shook his head. "Not possible. I've been following them right along. Perhaps we're meant to diverge, at some point."

"That must be it."

Still, Birsha read the misgiving in her voice, the same misgiving he was feeling in his gut. And yet he knew he hadn't missed a sign. He was diligent in his scouting, a skill taught to him as a child onward.

"How long ago do you think they were here?"

The fire pits they'd made revealed the charred remains of the wood fires. "I would guess two days prior."

Beatrice came to stand beside him as though needing his warmth. Birsha shouldered her against him, throwing an arm around her waist. "Not to worry. We'll sort this out. In the meantime, let's put together shelter before the night sets in."

He removed their tent and bedrolls from the two horses while Beatrice retrieved the stones from the previous fires and made quick work of a fire pit of her own.

"How did you ever get so resourceful?" he said, surprised by his wife's ease into life on the road.

"You forget, I was once a warrior along with Brigid and Henry. We did this nightly."

Birsha frowned as he watched her set about her work.

"What's wrong?" she demanded, her chores forgotten for the moment.

"It's just that there's so much I don't know about you, so much of your life hidden until now."

She merely harrumphed. "You want to know about my life, husband?"

He nodded, uncertain whether he wanted to hear it all.

"Okay then." She bent down and used a flint to start the fire with the tiniest bit of lichen, which she then blew onto the twigs beneath the larger logs. "I'm not very proud of who I was in my former life. I could be harsh—"

"You?" His eyebrows flew up in surprise.

"It's true. I suppose I had envisioned a grander life and I tried too hard. It was because I didn't feel adequate, but that's all gone. I'm different now, thanks to you."

The admission shocked him and he stood in silence, unsure how to respond. How ironic that in many ways, he had felt the same, always living in the shadow of his father. Never quite measuring up, at least in his mind. No wonder he had found a kindred spirit in her.

"Well, I would say we're both different now, don't you think? We just have to hope that the Bookbinders can believe that of us."

"Aye."

The flames took hold and the wood began to burn just as night fell. Somewhere in the distance, an owl hooted.

"We have only pemmican, dried meat and a few roots left. I'll get water from the stream and make what we can of the meal."

"You're a good woman, Beatrice."

For a moment, she paused, the light from the fire giving a shine to her curly black hair. Then she bent her face, as though afraid to look at him lest she give away the emotion playing behind her watery brown eyes. How different she was from Brigid, like fire and ice, their eyes. But now, with the cold settling in, he was grateful for their heat.

"I'm worried about Brigid," Winnifred told Lofgren as they settled around the fire. Dele was busy finishing up with the evening meal, Elijah's honey rich alto reminding her that he was ready to sit a spell.

Lofgren, who seemed to display extraordinary wisdom gleaned over a lifetime of eight hundred years, sat on his haunches and poked at the fire with his stick, sending sparks rising to the heavens as if in prayer.

"Hmm?" he said, waiting for her to continue.

"This latest prophecy of the loom really has her worried."

"Did she tell you what it predicted?"

Winnifred shook her head so hard her glasses nearly flew off her head. "I wish she had, especially if it affects us all."

"Maybe she doesn't want to worry the women."

In her heart, Winnifred knew this was true, but as a woman of science she felt it best to be as prepared as possible, and she told him so.

"But what if this is something you *can't* prepare for?" Lofgren, who was poking at the fire, paused to look up at her with those soulful green eyes of his.

"What do you mean?" The thought had never occurred to her that a problem might arise that she couldn't fix.

"I mean, what if it's magic that we've never seen before, that we can't prepare for, what then?"

She stood and stomped her foot, her scientific mind simply refusing to fathom it. After all, if she didn't know what was wrong, how could she set about resolving it?

"Not everything is within your power to fix," Lofgren reminded her.

His even temper only made her madder that he couldn't see reason, logic. She was about to tell him so when she suddenly began laughing.

"What? Why are you laughing?" He cocked his head in that puppy dog way she'd come to love.

She wiped her eyes, the laughter slowly dying along with the fire. "Here I was thinking you were being illogical, and yet you're possibly *the* most logical person I know. Still," she said, lowering her voice, "I plan to find out what Brigid's hiding."

"And how do you plan to do that?"

She waggled her eyebrows. "I plan to ask the person she confides in most."

"Ah," he said with a chuckle, "so you are going straight to the source." He winked.

She knew he was only teasing her, but her logic was simple. Most of all, smart. The one person who knew Brigid better than herself was Henry. But the thing she liked most about him, when he didn't know what to do with Brigid, he was only too happy to share.

"Um, Dele." Winnifred wiggled her finger to beckon the former slave. "Could I speak to you for a moment?"

"Whatcha need, Miss Winnifred?" she asked, still used to Southern expectations.

"Do you have any more of that pecan pie you made earlier?"

"I got me a slice or two. Why? You and Mr. Lofgren wantin' some?"

"No, actually I had someone else in mind."

Dele followed her gaze to where Henry was standing. "Oh! I see!" She chortled as she returned to the makeshift kitchen she and the others had put together for such a large group of people. She came back moments later with a slice of pie on a tin plate. "You use that wisely now, ya hear?"

"Oh I will," Winnifred assured her. "I will!"

Alaric couldn't help but seethe as he tore apart each room of the enormous castle in search of his son and Beatrice.

"They've got to be here!" he shouted to the four walls of the ballroom. But the only sound was his echoed voice making mockery of him.

He thrust a finger in Siegfried's face and waggled it until it tapped the poor man on the nose, then he jumped back in surprise.

"Have you asked everyone, Siegfried? Could they have been kidnapped?"

He paled at the thought. Surely no one dared do such a thing in his kingdom. Though he'd hardly made mention of it to anyone outside his inner circle, he'd made sure to keep a stringent eye on the heir and his wife. So, if the rumors were true and they *had* escaped to the Bookbinder Kingdom, it meant that someone from within his inner circle had betrayed him. The very idea sent him into a paroxysm of fury that had sweat rolling down his very red cheeks and spittle flying from his mouth.

Something seized him and he went silent, as he always did when hitting upon an idea. He turned so fast that he ran into Siegfried and nearly knocked the man out cold.

"You're like a dog, Siegfried, always under foot."

If he hadn't been so angry, he might have chosen his words more carefully because the damage he'd done to their relationship, if it could be called that, had clearly taken its toll. For Siegfried, the most vocal of all his inner circle, was suddenly silent, his lips pursed so that they were barely visible amidst the anger that rode just beneath the surface of an otherwise placid face.

"Don't take me so seriously, Siegfried. You know me. I don't do well with betrayal."

But the other man wouldn't budge. Give him time. That was Alaric's motto. Keep moving forward to the next conquest, but he hadn't factored in Birsha and Beatrice absconding into the night. No, there had to be more to it than what he could see on the face of things. He strode out of the massive ballroom doors and into the hallway lined with marble busts, all of them family members or in some way related to the kingdom. This one with a receding chin. That one, overly large—no doubt a gourmet. That one with a narrow jawline and aquiline features, much like his own, and sporting a goatee.

"Siegfried."

"Yes, Your Liege."

Siegfried must be mad at him if he'd called him that. Alaric would have laughed if he hadn't realized how serious the fracture was to their friendship.

"See to it that you scour the kingdom. Oh, and Siegfried—"

"Hmm?" Siegfried seemed lost in thought, his eyes glazed over, his hand unwittingly going to the overly large ring the adjutant wore, a gift from Alaric himself in exchange for his loyalty.

"Do see what the Kazakh is up to, eh? He has made himself awfully scarce in the past few days, and that doesn't bode well, wouldn't you say?"

Alaric narrowed his eyes and worked his jaw as he searched for telltale signs that Siegfried knew something, but if he did, Alaric was unable to detect it. Either the man was good at cards, or he had none worth sharing. Which was it? He tapped the long nail of his pinky finger against his front teeth, pondering the answer. One way or another, he would find out who was behind his son's disappearance and who knew. Whoever it was, they would pay. He ground his teeth together. Make no mistake about it, they *would* pay.

30

I could feel it in the air, as though a cold wind had suddenly blown in, and with it, a storm. My hair was pulled back from my face and I leaned in and pressed forward against it. The women also took note of the gale and apparently came to the same conclusion I had.

This is not natural.

A flurry of activity followed as everyone jumped into action. The Mohawks and Oneida disappeared as one into the forest, as though they had never been there, while the women took their positions on each side of the road, their colors blending perfectly with the setting.

As for Phinney, she and the starlings had risen high into the air and were now getting into formation. I narrowed my eyes, straining to see what it was they were trying to tell me. As if sensing my confusion, Phinney and the others began to circle and circle ever faster, then swept down toward the ground so that any others foolish enough to still be standing in the middle of the glade bent low to keep from being swept away by the birds. What on earth were Phinney and the starlings up to? I wondered, my heart a staccato rhythm inside my chest.

"Do you suppose a tornado is coming?"

Henry grabbed me by the arm and we ran while bent so as to prevent the starlings from pulling us up into the circular cloud that indeed did remind me of a tornado, and yet there was something different about it. Something I couldn't quite put my finger on. It was as if the cyclone resembled the bottomless pit of a well, entirely black, only now I saw something else. Something winking through the inky void as though stars. We ran bent over until we reached the copse where we ducked inside a hollow of a tree. But instead of a fierce attack, like the one we were expecting, a face appeared from inside the circle, one so hideous as to knock me back on my haunches. For a few brief seconds, I cowered like the chicken I was, eyes closed, face tucked into the crook of Henry's arm.

I opened one eye into a slit, and slowly opened the other one, but what I witnessed didn't relieve the fear that quaked through me like a squall. Instead, it sent my fear spiraling to a whole new level that left me in a ball of sweat and hammering at my heart, for the face was none other than a demon so evil that it left me breathless.

"Brigid Bookbinder!" the demon yelled. "We have waited a long time to meet. Now, your fate is ours. When next you see us, your kingdom will be no more and you will be ours. Make no mistake about it. You will be our treasure, our captive that we trot out to showcase our power and intent. To let everyone know what will happen to them if they do not submit. Be forewarned!" he bellowed.

When he spoke, the whole earth shook beneath us. I hung on for dear life as did the others. What did he mean that I would be his treasure, his captive? I didn't know, but I had a feeling I would soon find out.

Winnifred spotted Brigid on the other side of the glade and raced to her, Lofgren moving in warp speed and arriving ahead of her. She would have laughed had the situation not been so dire.

"What was that?" Brigid sat panting, her face as white as a snowdrop in springtime.

"That, I fear, was a Whirlpool Galaxy, its tail connecting with our own, a cosmic phenomenon that I learned about when I traveled to the future. But how the demon's face became a part of it, I have no idea. I only know that you're not safe here. We have to find a way to protect you until we can figure out some means of thwarting the demon and his kind."

Brigid thanked Winnifred, clearly shaken by what she'd witnessed. "But how? We understand only a small portion of their magic. How can I possibly protect myself? Or the kingdom, for that matter?"

One by one, people from around the glade poked their heads out. To Winnifred's intense surprise, they had all faded into the background, behind rocks and bushes, in trees. One enterprising young woman lifted her head from inside the pond, where she had squatted down until the danger passed. She sucked in a whoosh of air and crawled out onto the bank, her body sprawled spread-eagled on the grass.

"I . . . I . . . thought I was going to perish."

"Gertrude, is that you?" Brigid raced over to her and turned her on her side, then tapped her on the back to get her breathing again. Gertrude dribbled dirty pond water from her mouth.

"Poor Gertrude." Winnifred shook her head. "Right-O then, we must come up with a way to halt any further incursions, but how? The Jackals clearly have no intention of fighting fair."

"Fair!" The voice was from Emma, Thomas by her side. "Since when have they ever fought fair? They would have us pushing up pomegranate flowers, the symbol of death from Greek mythology, if left to their own devices."

"Here, here," Thomas agreed.

Dele and Elijah hunkered forward, their children folded into the skirts of their mother. "We'll help in any way we can, ma'am." Elijah removed his hat as if in deference to the desperate need for calm.

Winnifred wondered how those at the manor were coping, wondered if they had seen the Whirlpool Galaxy spin its starry tendrils through the dusky sky. "Brigid, I don't want you to worry, so Lofgren and I are going to get right on the problem, aren't we, Lofgren?"

Lofgren nodded, but his puzzled expression made it clear that he had no idea how.

"You're a builder, Lofgren. Let's build. Your people and

ours, together."

Lofgren's eyes darted about as though searching for the exit. "What would you have us build?"

Winnifred crossed her arms and raised her chin. "Why, we'll build our own fort, and this one will have all sorts of hidden chambers, won't it Brigid?"

Brigid appeared mildly surprised if not stunned.

"To play Devil's advocate," Thomas said, "couldn't they attack it from above? They clearly have magic on their side, magic that we can't possibly account for."

"Look, everyone, we can't sit idly by and do nothing. Any number of things could happen to us and have, but at least we don't need to make it easy for them."

Brigid brightened, her icy blue eyes flashing whenever she had an idea. "What if we make this fortress like a giant snail's shell with thousands of chambers, both underground and above ground so that no matter where the Jackals strike, we can be somewhere else. We could make it so convoluted that only we know how to traverse it. And, Lofgren, you and your people can move at warp speed. How long before you could have it built?"

Lofgren tapped his chin with his index finger. "Two weeks, if we can find the right materials."

"We could make our fortress out of straw and mud, then reinforce it with dung." Winnifred turned to the group who had gathered in the hundreds by this point. "Who's in?"

A chorus of shouts rose up as one.

"Right-O then. That's settled. We'd best get to work? Brigid?"

"Let's do it," she said, her expression more confident now.

"Okay, then. Let's gather up straw!"

Two weeks had passed since the death of the Queen of Mammals, that most elusive of creatures whose face bore the illusion of a normal human but whose heart was black as coal. Chame Leon stared at the gathering around the table, the faces staring back at him each more hideous than the previous. Every day grew more perilous. To stay risked discovery, but to leave risked . . . *everything*.

Chame Leon peered over at Liz Herd whose silence was so absolute that he thought he'd just imagined she could speak. But she reached a hand beneath the table and grasped his. For one brief second, he closed his eyes, wishing those around him were gone. Vanished. Poof! But when he opened his eyes, he saw that they were all still there, and now they were staring at him. He tried to make himself appear larger, and it must have worked, because they turned their attention to the plans ahead.

"We will strike here, and here." Samael, the Angel of Death, used a glass stick to point at the map of the Bookbinder Kingdom.

"What of Alaric?" Astaroth held his forefinger to his pointed chin, his eyes as fiery as hell itself, hence his moniker, The Great Duke of Hell.

Samael laughed, as if he thought Alaric of no consequence. None at all. "The man is blinded by his own ambition. He plans a very ordinary attack."

A cackle of laughter arose around the table, settling like a toxic mist above them in the low-ceilinged room.

"Very straight forward, I'm afraid," Samael continued, then pointed to his companion to the right, a rhino-headed crustacean. "On the other hand, Raksha, here has called upon the very heavens above to target—"

Samael's stick landed upon an image that suddenly appeared on the screen of a young, dark-haired woman with the most arresting blue eyes that reminded one of the shards of an iceberg that glinted from the sun. Chame Leon released a slow sigh. He would know those eyes anywhere. *Brigid.* So that was the true target. Not only to destroy the Bookbinder Kingdom, but to display her like a trophy of war. Parade her through the kingdom to show its people the power that the Jackals held over all their enemies, especially one so different from them as to be almost another species. Chame Leon could read it in Brigid's eyes. There lay a certain kindness in them, or was it empathy? Perhaps those eyes were merely weighted by justice and fairness, something sorely lacking in Alaric's kingdom.

Yes, that was it precisely, Chame Leon decided. Unlike those around him, Brigid had a conscience. The realization stunned him to the core that there could be someone left in this world of monsters who actually cared.

31

We had turned into a huge construction machine over the past week, everyone in the entire kingdom taking time away from their own pursuits to work on the labyrinth we were so intent on building. And yet, how was it humanly possible to build a fortress to protect us, even with the help of the elves, who had arrived in record time and were working at warp speed?

"Heave! Ho!" the sprites yelled in unison as though urging us on.

We set spies out to retrieve information and learned that the Jackals and Chessmen were within three days of arrival. That knowledge was daunting. Everywhere I went, blurs of color whizzed by me, the elves speed making me dizzy. Whereas I did a normal day's work by comparison, they did the work of a hundred or more men.

I wiped my brow, covered in dust. Despite the danger

of what lay ahead, I couldn't help but feel pride in these people who had worked well beyond what seemed humanly possible. Already, circular mounds erupted from the earth in every direction reminding me of a shell I had once seen at the ocean. True to their word, Lofgren and his men had designed a warren of underground passageways, some leading to nothing, others splitting off into a dozen directions so as to confuse the uninitiated. But what surprised me most was how beautiful the separate rooms of the fortress were, those near completion that is, for they appeared semi-translucent, as though they radiated light from within. To my surprise, whoever was behind the walls couldn't be seen, as though invisible to the naked eye. I had yet to learn how the elves had managed it.

"Calen!" I called to the master builder who had been around for several centuries and had even seen the Wall of Hadrian built. "How close are we to completion?"

Calen, a gruff elf with whiskers that ran to nearly his belly button, sucked on his pipe, one eye half closed as if to help him think. He blew out a puff of cherry tobacco. He used the translator megaphone to answer. "Three days, maybe four. That's with all men and women helping."

He must have seen my crestfallen face because he quickly added, "There, there now, miss. It will be okay."

I blew out a sigh, my throat tight. "We have three days, at best."

He tapped out tobacco onto the ground and blew through the stem of the pipe to assure that it was clean. "Then we need more hands."

My shoulders sagged with fatigue and resignation. "We

don't have more hands."

To my surprise, a little girl standing nearby said, "My name's Cedra, and I can help."

"Me, too!" said one of the boys with her.

Cedra smiled sweetly. "I could ask all my friends to work."

"You would do that?" I didn't know why I was so surprised that ones so young were willing to aid in the effort.

The girl nodded, and with that she took off running, shouting the whole way. Within the hour, hundreds upon hundreds of small hands flew to work carrying building supplies, taking buckets of dirt away and pouring them into a pile that was then mixed with straw for more of the walls' bases to support those most translucent of materials that made up the snail shells.

"What are the above-ground rooms made of?" I asked Lofgren as I dug a trench for yet another portion of the fort.

He paused to catch his breath. "What do you think it is?" he asked slyly.

Just then, I saw a snail pass, leaving a slimy trail behind him. "You're not serious."

"Of course. When we add ground snail shells to isinglass, it makes an almost cement-like material that is amazingly strong. Watch this!"

He walked over to where I kept my bow and arrow and picked it up, notched the bow, and "zing" the arrow went flying with a whir. Yet when it hit the material, it bounced back and fell to the ground without leaving so much as a dent in the new building material."

"Oh, my gosh. Does that stuff have a name?"

He frowned, as though thinking. "I shall name it Lofwin."
He laughed and off he went to put up more "Lofwin."

It didn't take a genius to realize that he'd named it after
himself and Winnifred. For some reason, it felt comforting to
know that their name would be etched into the lexicon of our
lives forever with this new invention.

I continued digging along with everyone else. Though I
had numerous duties and was continually being called away for
one thing or another, we needed all hands on deck, as the saying
went and everyone, even the children, seemed to recognize that
we must be vigilant. I just prayed we wouldn't be so exhausted
by the time the Jackals arrived that we wouldn't be able to fight
them.

I had no sooner put my shovel into the ground and hit a
rock with a loud ping then it came to me. An idea. We needed
time and I had just the idea how we could buy some.

"Winnifred!" I shouted.

"Yes, ma'am, I mean Brigid?" The woman was indefatigable,
her bright smile brimming with optimism.

"Could you take over the work site? I need to go make
some inquiries."

"Right-O!" She put her hands on her hips, clearly awaiting
a reason.

Unfortunately, I had no time for that. I needed to get to
the aviary quickly. I whistled for Phinney, who came bounding
down out of the tree.

"I need your help, girl," I said, to which she merrily chirped
as though I had offered her a year's supply of suet. "We have
work to do, you and I."

Now I had to hope that my plan wouldn't backfire, and that my beloved Phinney would be safe after what I was about to ask her to do.

Alaric always had a fear of heights, and now was no exception as Siegfried helped him up the ladder to the second loft. For years now, he had known that Fearsome Foul was locked away in what looked like a giant glass globe, but his equal hatred for heights and for Fearsome had outweighed any need to test his limits. Instead, he steered clear of his ancestor who had grown especially surly over time, having no one to speak to in his godforsaken corner of the palace.

As Alaric entered the loft, he fell on his hands and knees, as though pushed, and indeed Siegfried had pushed him to keep him from backing down at the last second.

"Let me be, Siegfried," Alaric growled as he crawled unceremoniously on his hands and knees toward the glass globe. He heard a yawn from within and the black, swirling clouds slowly cleared to display an image of his grandfather, a man whom Alaric had summarily despised as cruel and ambitious, traits that Alaric had inherited, to his everlasting chagrin.

"Still groveling, I see." Fearsome chuckled, as though especially pleased with himself today.

"I merely dropped something." Alaric stood, but flushed at the way he must look, staggering on the wooden floor, his feet slipping and sliding as if the floor were made of ice, rather than wood.

"Searching for a book perhaps?" Fearsome howled with

laughter.

"I . . . I . . . that was my book. You shouldn't have taken it."

Fearsome held up his hands to show that there was nothing in them. Then he peered side to side. "What? You think I can perform magic?"

Actually, Alaric was quite certain of it. Just as Alaric himself had performed magic over the years, the knowledge passed down to him by each generation and found within the confines of these books, should one know how to search for it.

"Yes, I do, but I haven't come for the book or to watch you do magic."

"No? What then?" the old man demanded.

Though, truthfully, he didn't appear old at all to Alaric. That was the secret of the crystal ball. One stayed young forever inside it—or at least not old.

"I have come to ask you to show me where my men are . . . the Jackals. To see what they are doing."

"You mean you've come here to ask me to tell you the future, am I right?" the man's voice boomed.

Like the child he'd once been, Alaric trembled. "Maybe?"

Fearsome scowled. "Then say so, man! What do you want to know?"

Alaric wilted in the heat and dust. "What the future holds. Will I be successful in my campaign?"

Fearsome began pacing. "And what do I get out of this, huh?"

Alaric shrugged. "Why, to know that you have helped your grandson, I suppose."

Fearsome's voice boomed. It shook the rafters and caused

Alaric to be dislodged from his moorings, only to land squarely on his backside two feet away. Siegfried helped him to his feet, then wiped off the dust and grime like a schoolmarm looking after one of her students.

"Get back!" Alaric hissed, eager to regain his decorum, what was left of it, that is. "What is it then?" Alaric decided to pull no punches. "What is your price?"

"Freedom!"

"Freedom?" Alaric squeaked. "But that's im . . . impossible, right, Siegfried?"

Siegfried, bless him, seemed to understand what was at stake and said, "Oh, right, sir."

"You were freed from your prison inside the globe, were you not?" Fearsome stared toward the ceiling that was yet to be finished, despite the threats and cajoling Alaric had done to get the men moving faster in its repair.

"I . . . well, that was different."

"How so?" Fearsome pierced Alaric with his inky black eyes.

"You need to offer something in exchange," Siegfried whispered in Alaric's ear.

"Like what?" Alaric whispered back.

"Speak up! Are you two men or mice?"

As if he'd heard his name called, a mouse came out of a small hole drilled into the wall, let out a squeak, its whiskers trembling. Then seeing the three men, he let out a high-pitched squeal, turned around and raced inside the hole, only his tail left visible.

For the first time since they'd entered Fearsome's domain,

the man smiled. "Well, at least one of us has common sense." He turned back to Alaric and Siegfried. "Okay, if you won't release me, find a way to make my life a little more bearable. Have someone bring me food each day. You can pass it through the glass, so long as neither of us touches it at the same time. You could do that, could you not, for your dear grand-pa-pa?"

Alaric had never heard Fearsome referred to in this way and would have laughed, had he not feared the consequences. "Alright, I'll see what I can do."

"Good!" Fearsome rubbed his hands together in glee. "Then so be it!"

Clouds of black swirling mist hid Fearsome in its folds, replaced by a bird's-eye view of the Jackals and the Chessmen. They were on the march when something small came into view. Something at a great distance, followed by something else. A teeming mass that flew in and out on itself like a tidal wave from an ocean.

"What is it?" Alaric breathed.

"I don't know, sir," Siegfried said.

They huddled together like two men at sea with a wave prepared to breach the bow of their tiny craft. And just like that, a tidal wave of shimmering black-and-bluish-green wings drowned out all else, the sound deafening, so much so that Alaric and Siegfried fell to the floor, hands over their ears. Alaric screamed into the inky void around him.

For one brief moment, the birds actually entered the room and hovered overhead, their wings flapping and feathers flying, the stench of them at such a close distance overpowering.

"What does it mean?" Alaric cried when at last the birds

had departed, the sound of their wings echoing in his ears.

"It means," Fearsome said, one eyebrow raised, "that you, dear man, have problems. But you'll have much worse problems than mere birds, if you're not careful."

"W-what do you mean?" Alaric hadn't stuttered since he was a child and was loath to realize that he was doing it now.

"I mean, you have a whole bevy of usurpers, malingerers, creatures of the night beneath your fortress."

At the words "creatures of the night," Fearsome's voice took on such a low, malevolent tone that Alaric felt as though a skeletal hand had crawled down his back and sent shivers racing along his spine.

"They plan to take over your throne, don't you know?"

Alaric stood perfectly still, a statue of his own making. *So, my son was right. Why had he not listened to him? Tucked him under his wing instead of tossing him to the winds.*

"Where is my son, Fearsome? Tell me." When the man wasn't forthcoming, Alaric steeled himself. "I command it!"

For once, Fearsome didn't make light, rather he looked as though he, too, recognized the mistake he'd made in not supporting his family. "Your son," he said, his tone softened by their shared understanding, "has taken his wife, and if I am not mistaken, they are lodged somewhere on the trail, far, far from here. They plan to give themselves over to the Bookbinders, that is if the Jackals don't find them first."

Alaric felt as if the wind had been knocked out of him. He sat back on his haunches, devastated to learn the consequences of the seeds he had sown. He had all but pushed his son away from an early age. Moreover, he'd kept him far from the kingdom. Had convinced himself that he was doing it for the boy's own good. Then he had ejected the one person from the boy's life who actually loved him. His mother.

As if sensing his mood, a soft wind blew in, sweeping up the dust, tugging at the tendrils of his hair. Tears sprinkled against his eyelashes. Why had he not paid more attention to the boy when it would have made a difference? Cared? But he'd had a kingdom to run, worries far greater than Birsha could ever imagine. When he'd been younger and more ambitious that had been enough. But now . . . now he felt bereft.

He turned to Siegfried. "Help me down, good man. I'm tired."

Together they crawled toward the ladder that would take them to the bottom floor of the library. Just as Alaric was about to extend a foot onto the second rung, Fearsome said, "Wait! Maybe I can help. Come back tomorrow and perhaps I will have an idea that will aid us both . . . and your son."

Alaric had never heard the man so conciliatory. "Thank you . . . grandfather."

But Fearsome merely nodded and disappeared in a cloud of black smoke.

32

Birsha stood atop the highest peak, then took out his spyglass and placed it to his eye. He adjusted the lens until it cleared just so. And yet, as he gazed at the swarming mass below him, he couldn't be sure what he was seeing.

"Take a look at this, Beatrice," he said, then handed her the spyglass. "What do you suppose is happening?"

Beatrice pursed her lips as she squinted into the round tube then cocked her head slightly, as though trying to make sense of what she saw. She drew the spyglass down slowly, her head still atilt.

"I can't say, really, but it reminds me of a swarm of bees, and yet it would take millions of bees to form such a large formation. More like birds, I would imagine, but I've rarely seen birds in that large a number. The only ones I've ever known to create swarms are starlings . . ."

But as she spoke, her mouth formed a wide "O".

"What is it, Beatrice? Tell me?"

Beatrice gulped, as though in need of water. "The aviary . . . they have birds. Starlings."

"What aviary, where?"

"The Bookbinders. We have a master birder, Conestra. She has a talent far greater than most."

"Like the Kazakh?" Birsha couldn't help but think of the man who had loved his mother. The man who had taken him under his wing as a child, one of the few in the kingdom who had even noticed him.

"Precisely."

"But what purpose would they have here?" He placed the spyglass up to his eye once more and willed himself to see what lay behind the birds' odd behavior.

Then he saw it! There, beneath the birds he caught just the edge of the Jackals' military campaign as they moved into the valley. And only seconds passed before he realized what the birds were up to.

"Oh my stars, Beatrice, look!" He handed her the glass and watched as her eyes widened suddenly and her face grew ashen.

"They are . . . they are . . ."

"I know," Birsha shouted in glee. "Isn't it wonderful?"

Below, he could see the birds flying in formation, and what they had created would send even the most die-hard warrior running for cover because they had swarmed into a mass of a multi-headed monster and somehow let out a roar with their wings as they dove into the middle of the warriors' formation, sending them scattering in every direction.

"They did it!" Beatrice cried. "They've thwarted the Jackals!"

Together they danced a jig of glee to know that the Bookbinders were safe, for now. But Birsha knew the warriors well enough to know that this was only a temporary setback and that soon they would be again on the move. And then there would be no stopping them. No stopping them ever.

Yesimeh ran up to me, out of breath, her look, one of excitement. "I . . . I . . ." She blinked rapidly, her chest heaving with the effort it had taken her to race all the way over from . . . where, precisely?

"Take a breath, Yesimeh," I urged.

The mousey little girl who I had come to know and view like a sister had grown in stature, if not in height, among her many peers. She had shown herself to be a shrewd planner who kept the tribe humming along smoothly with few bumps along the way and mostly mine. I would be forever grateful to her for her kindness and loyalty.

"The . . . the loom."

By now anyone close by had gathered around to see what Yesimeh was going on about, knowledge, after all, being the salvation to our endeavors.

"What is it?" Emma asked, as Thomas came to stand beside her. As always, he kept a hand firmly planted on Emma's shoulder as if to show her his support in all matters, big or small.

"Come see!"

As if one, the entire group moved in the direction of my

tent until I had to beg off by saying, "Just Yesimeh and I. You, too, Emma and Thomas."

Henry, who had been working in the stables held a hand to his eyes to block out the sun, lifted his head, the breeze catching his hair and lifting it slightly, displaying a glistening auburn that made me gasp for the want of him. Yet, as always, it was not to be. A war was at hand, and as before, it came first before even the simplest of things. Still, we found moments to steal away, to remind each other why we'd fallen in love in the first place. He hurried over and together we rushed to the tent where I could hear the clacking of my beloved loom.

No sooner had we entered the tent, then the clacking stopped. For a moment, I wasn't sure what I was seeing. A cloud, perhaps, but an angry black one. People appeared to be fleeing, scattering in all directions as the cloud descended. Then it finally hit me. Phinney had been successful in her campaign. She and the starlings had thwarted the Jackals, for now. But for how long? Long enough for us to prepare properly? To get our new fort finished so that we would have a place to hide and, hopefully, strike once they entered the warrenlike maze? I knew only that we must hurry. This was the break I had been seeking. As such, I practically dashed out of the door of my tent, not waiting for the others to catch up.

"Everyone!" I yelled. "Gather round."

Slowly, those nearest put their tools down. To imagine that we could build a fort in such a short period of time would have been daunting to even the most ardent believers. But truth be told, the place was beginning to look like something special. Something unique, like nothing else I had ever seen, for indeed it *did* look like a snail shell, or dare I say an entire cluster of snail shells. And now there would be time for more, with any luck. The caverns underneath were a different matter. That had taken all hands from as far and wide as we could get. Bless their hearts, carpenters and blacksmiths, stablemen and liverymen, had all put their shoulders against the grindstone to help us succeed. Too many saw what the Jackals had done to their people, saw how emaciated they had been upon their return, how weak. And none dared believe that it couldn't happen to them, given half the chance. No, everyone had united as one, under one banner, the Bookbinder banner, thanks to Winnifred's flag that she had designed. I snapped my fingers. "Winnifred!"

I rushed to find her, only to discover her handing out supplies well up the rise, with Lofgren and his people scurrying back and forth in lightning quick speed, their bodies a blur amid the green backdrop of the forest.

"Winnifred!" I cried.

"What is it? What's happened?" she demanded, never giving pause in her duties as she spoke to me.

"Phinney! She stopped the coming horde. The Jackals are turning."

Though she nodded, I could see the wheels turning behind those bright brown eyes that had reminded me of an owl upon our first meeting. And I could swear that like the owl, she was a wise one, our Winnifred. And smart too.

Jocelyn and Gertrude, who had been passing by, paused to see what the commotion was about. I told them about our good luck.

"Still, we haven't much time," Winnifred reminded us.

"This is only a temporary solution. We must keep moving. Lofgren!" she yelled. He flashed over to her in an instant. "Phinney has stopped the Jackals. This will buy us more time. How is the underground maze coming?"

"Better than expected. We've had one cave-in, but other than that, we keep getting new recruits daily to take up the slack when our men and women weary."

"Right-O," she said, clearly pleased. She pulled out a pencil that she kept tucked behind her ear and drew out new plans. "We need to be sure that everyone can hide inside the maze. In an attack, we must have trap doors from which to spring."

The woman was a fount of knowledge, having studied the history of warfare, a study that few women were privy to. I thanked my lucky stars that we had her.

"Okay, everyone!" I yelled. "Back to work. We must get this finished before the wet season, and more importantly, before the Jackals arrive."

Just then, Hannah appeared. It had been some time since I had seen her, with all the thousands of new recruits that took up my time. But I was happy to see her now, and I scooped her up into a warm embrace.

"Brigid," she said, glancing around. "May I speak to you in private?"

I read the seriousness of her expression and cocked my head, but said, "Sure. We can talk outside my tent." There, I kept several foldable chairs for just such impromptu discussions. I excused the guard, for the time being, so we could speak in private. Once we were properly situated, I said, "Okay, what is it you wanted to talk to me about."

"There's a rumor going around."

"A rumor? What kind of rumor?"

I looked into her guileless eyes. She, of all of us, had changed little. She was still meek and mild. I could picture her with an adoring husband and a brood of chicks beneath her skirt, a mother hen to all.

"It's said that Birsha and Beatrice have abdicated."

She could have blown me over with a feather, I was so surprised. "What? How? No," I said, shaking my head, "start from the beginning."

"You'll be surprised to learn that it wasn't Beatrice's idea. It was Birsha's. His father has returned to life and there's no place for him in the kingdom. He saw the writing on the wall, and get this . . ." She paused and looked around. "He met Henry as a child. Even came here to the Bookbinder Kingdom one summer with his nanny. Undercover, of course. But here's the thing . . ."

Again she paused, and I swear my heart stopped beating for a moment as I leaned in to hear more.

"The Bookbinders were kind to him. They treated him well and he has fond memories of them. And once he learned that his father had made slaves of those from the Bookbinder Kingdom, and that he was starving them and working them to death, he could no longer turn a blind eye as long as Alaric was in power."

I sat back, stunned. It was as though my mind had taken a mini-vacation and left me a blank slate. But then I rallied. "So, they're on their way here?"

My voice sounded funny even to my own ears. Perhaps it was the weeks of dust and grime that we all breathed in our haste to see the fortress built. More likely, it was the shock of what she'd said that made it so.

"They're on their way." She paused to place a hand on mine. "And Brigid, they're hoping you'll take them in once they arrive."

33

For years, Alaric had known of the secret passage that led to the dungeons, but he had been loath to search the depths of his kingdom with all the creepy crawly things that might entail. So now that he stood with his lamp at the opened doorway to his room, Siegfried at his side, he couldn't help but feel the cool brush of death wafting from it, the smell of it as well, as though to enter the tunnel meant one might never come out alive. It was this that had him halting at a single footstep, afraid to go further.

"You first," he told Siegfried.

"Me?" Siegfried squeaked. "Why me? You were the one who wanted to go down here."

"No time for semantics, good man, just do as I say!" For a moment, Alaric had forgotten to be quiet. When he heard his echo down the dark, dank corridor reverberate back at him, he paused: *Good man. Good man. Good man.*

It was as though the gods of the underworld were speaking directly to him, but about someone else. *Who* was a good man? And then it came to him. His son was a good man. So perhaps he'd done something right after all. Somehow, this pleased him, as though his struggle here in the world hadn't been for nothing.

They took another few steps into the bowels of the fortress when Alaric paused. "Siegfried, you know my son better than me. Do you think he's happy?"

Siegfried cocked his head, as though thinking. "Not happy, sir. It's hard to be happy when one is juggling an entire kingdom and its people. But if you're asking me if he's turned out well, I would say he has turned out spectacularly, despite the overwhelming burden of what has been handed him."

"But is that enough, Siegfried?"

Alaric knew that he sounded desperate. Some might think him cruel, and perhaps he was, but he had loved his son, wanted the best for him, even if he didn't have the time he would have liked to spend with the boy. And somewhere deep down, he had thought it for the best that his son was in the countryside, spared of all the double dealings of the kingdom. Being a ruler was a hard life. One that had begun to show on Alaric's face and the hunch of his shoulders.

Siegfried turned on Alaric and said, "Sometimes we have no choice in the matter, sir. We're given the cards we hold, and we must play them no matter the hand."

And yet the sorrow in the man's eyes confirmed Alaric's suspicion that it was a hard life for Birsha, as it had been for him. No one was immune to the vagaries of the kingdom and its machinations. They were all trapped in some way. Locked in tight, the key tossed aside. Oh, how he would love to reclaim the key to his life and that of his son—of *all* his progeny.

"Thank you, Siegfried. I needed those words. They will bring me comfort in the days when I am alone with my thoughts."

"You're welcome, sir," Siegfried said. "Shall we plow ahead?"

Alaric squared his shoulders. "I believe we shall, Siegfried. I believe we shall."

I couldn't stop thinking about Beatrice and Birsha as I set to work in the labyrinth below the three wentletraps, as we'd come to call our structure because of its similarity to the cream-colored sea snail. The name had harkened from the Dutch word for spiral staircase, and indeed it did look as though one could climb the many spirals that stood one atop the other.

Once inside the wentletrap, we'd filled the main cavity with food supplies, along with water filtered from a massive canister above ground, gravity moving it through a pipe. In another room we stored our weapons, and in yet another room we had what we called the "war room," though I rarely used the term, preferring to call it our planning room. "War" suggested that there was no alternative to it. And yet negotiation and compromise worked so much better. When had people forgotten how to do it? Had forgotten how to be human?

Yesimeh set up a huge chalkboard in the center of one wall, a large table in the middle of the room with chairs all around. How different it was from the state-of-the-art table I had seen beneath the fortress. That one had hovered midair and was clear as glass, only the holograph place settings revealing who sat there. Odd creatures of the night. Who were those people? *Or should I say monsters?* A chill trickled down my spine at the memory of their misshapen faces, the evil that lurked within them.

Yesimeh scratched her head and peered around, as though missing something.

"What is it?" I asked.

"I don't know. Ah!" She snapped her fingers. "A map!"

"Let me get mine." I had a wall mounted map of the surrounding areas from which to plot our next course. I kept it rolled up in the tent. Besides, it would give me reason to go above ground, which I desperately craved at that moment. To see sunlight. To revel in the warm feel of it against my skin. I wasn't made for underground living, I decided as I marched past her to the sliding door.

"While you're up there, could you ask the loom how long we have before the Jackals arrive?"

I slapped my forehead. Why hadn't I thought to ask it before this? And yet my loom was nothing like a crystal ball where one could simply ask it a question and it would cough up the answer. More like it had a mind of its own. My loom decided what it would give up and when, but I could at least try coaxing it to give me an answer.

"I'll do my best!" I cried merrily, then tottered out the door.

But try as I might, I still tended to get lost in the underground warren of rooms, so unlike the ones beneath the fortress. Those ones moved west to east, or east to west, depending upon your path. They also went up stairways and down them, though it was often difficult to tell whether you were going up or down. Instead, the stairs were like a kaleidoscope of indecision, an illusion that had caught me unaware the first time I had traversed them. Now, they suddenly seemed tame by our fortresses standards where hallways circled back on themselves, worked in figure eights, or simply went nowhere.

"Now where am I?" I muttered to myself. Panic settled in the small of my chest, and for one brief moment, I thought I might have an attack that sent me screaming through the bowels of the wentletrap like a crazed person.

Yet then I heard someone talking. I recognized the voice, but from where? That's what I couldn't decide. I was about to ask the speaker if they could help me find the exit when I heard the words, "I'm mapping the place as they build it."

"Alaric should pay a pretty penny for that, *n'est ce pas?*"

A Frenchman! That could only mean a trapper, and the last trapper I had known turned out to be a traitor. My heart stuttered aloud in my chest as I quietly moved in the opposite direction. It was imperative that I commit to memory the location of the voices I had heard if we were to catch them at their game. But then again, maybe we could simply station guards at each exit. The culprits would have to come up for air sometime, and when they did, we would lock them up.

I didn't breathe fully until I finally found the exit. Fortunately, I ran smack dab into Henry who, along with Thomas, was headed inside to check out the air ducts.

"Brigid! What is it?" Henry took me by the arms and

sat me down on a nearby bench. "You look as if you've seen a ghost."

Thomas appeared just as worried, the lock of black hair that seemed to always hang over one eye unable to hide his concern.

"The . . . the trapper and another man!" I said, as I tried to catch my breath. "They're down below. He's mapping the place . . . for the Jackals. For Alaric."

"Jumping Jehosafats!" Henry took a seat next to me.

"I'll put guards on each exit."

Thomas didn't wait for a response. All I saw was a blur of him and his long legs sprinting across the clearing as he yelled to the group of male and female guards that we kept at hand at all times. The group moved off quickly to each of the exits, their arms at the ready.

"Yesimeh is down there, Henry!" I breathed. "What if they take her hostage?"

"Chances are, they don't want to alert anyone to their presence. But out of precaution, we should send word for all to return above ground. That will delay any work below ground, but we can continue to build more wentletraps. We just have to make sure they don't connect to the original three until we have our culprits."

I nodded my head, his advice sound. "I had better go get Yesimeh."

"No," Henry nearly shouted, pulling me to him. "We'll send someone less valuable down below."

"Less valuable?" I pulled away to gaze into his beautiful green eyes. "No one is less valuable."

"I didn't mean it like that. It's just that if anyone were to be taken hostage, Brigid, it would be you. You're the one they want."

As much as I would have liked to deny what he said, I knew it to be true. I was what they called a high-level target because I had been the one to lead an army of women. Women who had given up everything to be by my side. Women who had homes and families that they cared about. Who had a life before this. But too many had been plucked from their homes, conscripted into forced labor, starved and beaten or had watched their loved ones be taken into Alaric's labor camps. I *could not* allow that to happen.

"Okay, but we must see to it that all are safe."

"Don't worry. Thomas will take care of it. You'll see. He may never have wanted the burden of the kingdom, but he'll support us in anything we do."

"I know," I said.

I loved him and Emma. They were like the sister and brother I had lost all those years ago. I often thought of them at night when I couldn't sleep. My parents too. What had become of them? Were they even alive? I didn't know. And the not knowing was a constant ache that kept me up at night. But I could do nothing about it now. I had a war to fight. People to save. Traditions to wrangle so that when we truly did gain our freedom, we would gain freedom from the punishments as well. The ones that held us hostage to a system that no longer worked. One based on punishment rather than reward. That saw people as incessantly evil rather than good. It sometimes felt as though those in charge of the punishments were looking for the bad in us rather than the good. I often wondered if they ever recognized all the wonderful things we'd done. How hard we worked. How much we cared. I might never know, and that saddened me.

"Brigid," Henry said, his hand on my cheek. "You're a good person. You know that right?"

How is it that Henry could always read me so well? That's what I loved about him. I nestled into the warmth of his embrace. I missed these moments. They had been too few of late. We kissed briefly, the smell of cinnamon on his lips. I relished our time together, but then I remembered why I had come above ground in the first place.

"Henry! I need to speak to my loom."

He looked at me with a puzzled expression, then shrugged, used to my outbursts.

"Quick!" I grabbed his hand and we were off to learn how much time we had left. With any luck, that is.

But I had barely begun to wind my way through the mass of women warriors when I saw something flying faroff in the distance. As it came closer, I could see that it was Phinney and her swarm of starlings. Until now, I hadn't thought birds could show excitement, but as every bird chirped at once, I soon learned that indeed they could. Furthermore, by the time I reached my tent, Phinney swooped down and landed on my shoulder with a loud cree of delight at her foray into enemy territory and her resounding success at scattering the Jackals.

"You seem awfully proud of yourself," I said with a sly grin.

But Phinney merely ruffled her feathers as if in agreement and scooted closer, as though missing me as much as I had her. "Good bird! Well done."

Henry laughed as she let out another cree of delight at my praise. Now, for the loom. If the clock was ticking, we needed to know for how long.

Birsha knew there wasn't much time. The Jackals would soon be on the move again, and then there would be no stopping them. He checked the stirrups of his horse to be certain that it would hold, then lifted Beatrice up by the boot onto the saddle despite her protests.

"Really, Birsha. I've been riding for years," she said, clearly miffed.

And yet Birsha continued on, per protocol. No lady of Beatrice's standing should have to ride unattended, and now was no exception. Once she was safely in her saddle, he gathered the reins of his horse and mounted it. His horse, like his father's, was of Fresian descent. The warhorse originated from the Netherlands and had been bred for strength and endurance, its silky black mane and body visible at a distance as though kissed by the sun. Then again, it could just as easily hide amongst the shadows, none the wiser that a horse such as this existed on the northernmost continent of the Americas.

Birsha clucked his tongue and pulled on the reins. They would need to circumnavigate the area to avoid the Jackals and the Chessmen, who had scattered following the attack of the birds. Any one of them could have traveled this way, leaving the pair exposed and in danger.

"We go west." Birsha spoke in a hushed tone as he nodded toward the southwest.

Beatrice's eyes widened as though understanding their need to avoid any possible meeting with the Jackals. They rode like this for hours, until they grew weary and hungry, no closer to the kingdom than they had been when they set out that morning. Too much time had been lost trying to avoid the Jackals. Beatrice made quick work of a hurried meal, while Birsha gathered their flasks to wash down the rough and ready staples that must sustain them until they could find other food and shelter.

Only now did Birsha realize how complacent he had become when he saw one of the pawns march out of the woods, appearing frightened and alone. Birsha knew he must tread lightly. Did the Jackals know of his disappearance? Had his father been alerted? He couldn't take any chances.

He held up his Sharps rifle and yelled, "Halt, who goes there?"

"It is I, Your Liege." The white pawn bowed as best he could, his little round head catching on a low-lying branch. He rubbed his bald pate and frowned.

"Oh, aye." Then Birsha whispered to Beatrice. "He doesn't know we escaped. Let me speak to him."

Her face paled, but she merely nodded.

"May I ask what you are doing here?"

The pawn blinked. Pawns, by nature, were harmless. The most they could do was to move forward in a wave, giving those behind them time to draw a sword or mount an offense.

"I am lost. A five-headed monster attacked us." The pawn's voice rose an octave and his face reddened to have shown his fear in such a direct manner.

"Aye, I saw it."

"You did?"

The pawn drew near. His eyes were large, like that of a baby seal. There was something quite loveable about its appearance, as though it were a child, rather than the front ranks of an army of Chessmen. Birsha supposed the pawn was conscripted into service like many others.

The pawn looked hungrily at their food.

"Would you like a bite?" Birsha asked.

The pawn shook his head so furiously that he had trouble sitting it upright on his shoulders and had to use his hands to steady it. Birsha offered the pawn a seat.

"So, do you have a name?"

The pawn nodded. "The name's Noble, Your Lord and Lady."

"Noble." Birsha ran the name around on his tongue. "And do you like being a pawn?"

The pawn once again flushed a royal red, clearly embarrassed by the question and unsure how to answer, for pawns were unable to lie. It was against their very nature, Birsha knew.

"I . . . I . . . miss my family," he said, and bowed his head as though preparing to be struck.

"Aye, how long has it been since you've seen them?"

The pawn lifted his head slightly. "Years," he said at last.

"Years." Birsha understood this sort of loss, having spent years away from his family as well. "Well, we will be your family for now, until we can get you back home. How would you like that?"

"Oh, I would like it very much." The pawn clapped his hands in glee.

"But maybe you can help us first." Birsha took Beatrice's hand in his and gazed into her eyes. Then he turned to the pawn. "Do you know the Jackal's plan of attack, Noble?"

Nobel shrugged. "I did overhear that they were going to go in under the cover of darkness, and that they have someone on the inside who is helping them."

Alarm bells rang in Birsha's head and he could see by Beatrice's ashen face that she had experienced a similar fright to know that someone was helping them from the inside. "Do you know who these insiders are?"

The pawn peered around him, but in the end decided to divulge what he knew, given that this was the Prince and Princess of the kingdom. "I heard the word trapper. That's all I know."

Beatrice grasped Birsha's arm. "You don't suppose that was the trapper who betrayed us long ago, do you?"

"It stands to reason," Birsha said. "But there's only one way to find out."

The pawn began snacking on the sandwich Beatrice had given him and appeared in fine fettle, now that he had the first remnants of food in his stomach.

"But that's the least of the Bookbinder Kingdom's worries," the pawn said with a shrug. Then he chomped down another large bite of the sandwich, his manners appalling. "Seems to me, it's the creatures they should be worried about."

"Creatures?" Birsha and Beatrice said in unison.

"Oh, yes. Quite frightful, they are." He set his sandwich on the log and brought his hands to his face like talons, grimacing all the while. He let loose a horrid roar to symbolize the ferociousness of said beast. Afterward, he immediately picked up the sandwich and continued eating.

"Do you know what these creatures have planned?" Beatrice's voice quivered as she spoke, her black hair framing an opalescent face.

The pawn paused before his next bite, a sorry expression clouding his features to have to speak when he would have preferred to eat his sandwich. His hand went to the sky while making swirling motions, and then he reached down as though plucking something or *someone* and yanking it up into the sky. Then he shook his head sadly.

"Then she is no more." His eyes grew watery.

"Who is no more?" Birsha demanded.

"Why, Brigid, of course."

34

I had barely set foot in my tent when I saw that the loom had gone black, just as it had when I had unwittingly threaded Birsha's grandmother's weave into it. For a moment, my heart stilled and I couldn't speak.

"What is it?" Henry whispered.

I shook my head, my mind dizzy with worry. First the trapper, now this? What next? It felt as though the world was conspiring against us when all we wanted was to live life, to put down roots, raise our children and bask in the glory of a sunrise and a sunset. I knelt down before my loom.

"What happened? Are we doomed?" I asked of it.

Silence.

My throat was thick with emotion. What did it mean? Why had my loom gone black? I searched around for an answer but came up empty.

Just then I heard the faintest of clacks as if from a far-off engine firing up. And another, and another. Soon, the black turned to swirling clouds that wound ever faster, around and around. Not like a tornado. No. This was different somehow. It seemed to encompass the whole of the universe in it, including the stars. So frightened was I that I forgot how to breathe until it made one loud bang and stopped just as I gasped for air and threw myself at Henry.

"What is it?" I asked, scarcely looking at the loom lest it let loose another loud bang.

"I don't know." But Henry's eyes were like saucers and I could feel the drumbeat of his heart inside his chest.

"Dare I ask it how much time we have until this . . . whatever it is, occurs?"

"There's no harm in trying," Henry said. And yet his voice, normally so strong, sounded suddenly weak to my ears.

"Loom," I said, turning to face it, "how long have we left before this" —I didn't know what to call it— ". . . *event* occurs?"

I heard a clack, and another, and another. At the end of the clacks were the numbers . . . 1, 1, 1, 1, 1, 1, 1.

Seven days!

One week to finish the wentletraps. One week to get all of our women underground to safety. Despite the speed at which the elves worked, we had only three wentletraps finished. How could we possibly get everything done by then to forestall the Jackals as we prepared a counterattack? And would we even be successful, considering the amount of people we had to store underground before the attack began?

"What will we do, Henry?"

He snapped me up into his arms. "I don't know, but whatever we do, we must do it quickly."

I thanked the loom then we ran as fast as we could to where the elves had decided to begin work on the far side of the meadow. Somehow, we would have to connect the two sets of wentletraps. But that was the least of my worries. I quickly found Winnifred and Lofgren.

"We have one week," I said.

It was clear they had heard the news of the trapper already as guards were stationed everywhere. Women in uniform held rifles at intervals. In the years of war, the women had grown strong, their bodies lean and muscular. I had only to look in the mirror to know mine had as well.

Lofgren stepped forward. "I've contacted relatives of mine, the woodland elves. They are within a day's time from here. That should double our time."

Still, that would give us six to nine wentletraps more. Not nearly enough for an army our size.

"Don't worry," Winnifred said, her owl eyes blinking faster than usual. "We're in the process of building a massive underground tunnel that will connect with the other one, once we can flush out the invaders."

She fairly spit out those last few words, her anger evident in the fierce set of her jaw.

"Yes, but how will we get that many women down a shaft with the enemy at hand?" I countered.

Lofgren, who could ill afford time to speak with me, said, "We're building a massive underground room with tunnels leading into the hidden recesses of the forest. The gradient of the tunnels will surface among the Mohawks and Oneida, who will lead the charge should the women be discovered, giving them time to get into position. The other tunnel will lead to the caves.

So much to do and so little time. I thanked Winnifred for her quick thinking. Still, the sheer size of the project overwhelmed me and my heart stuttered in my chest to picture it. Now, I must find Phinney and the starlings. Like it or not, I would need to use them once again to supply an air attack. Should we manage to thwart the Jackals from all sides, even the sky, then perhaps we stood a chance of surviving this. But how long could we go on like this, merely fighting each day for survival? We needed a lasting peace, and that could only come with a defeated army of Jackals and the ouster of the creatures that inhabited the underground caverns of the fortress.

A sharp breeze lifted my hair, bits of sand stinging my eyes. Suddenly, Alaric no longer seemed so daunting a man. Only now did I realize that he was a mere cog of a man in a machine much larger than himself and his warriors.

And how does one fight that?

Alaric raced back through the tunnels with Siegfried by his side. The creatures he had witnessed were indelibly etched inside his brain, their strange visages too frightening to put to words. No, best to forget he ever saw them. He opened the door to his room and thrust himself forward, relieved to have returned in one piece. So, his son was right, Fearsome too. He had lost control of his kingdom and hadn't even recognized it.

"Quickly! We must speak with Fearsome. I only hope he'll

know what to do about these interlopers."

"Yes, Your Royalty." Siegfried paused only a moment to open the door to the hallway, the library tucked inside the northeast wing.

Ten minutes later, they arrived at the gargantuan door that lent an air of privilege and fanfare to a room that was by all regards a denizen of an age of wealth and standing. For only the most distinguished of men could afford such a library as his. It contained literature from around the world and in many languages, too many for Alaric to ever learn much less master. Still, he kept them as tribute to his station in life.

Now, as he entered the room, the drum of the door ringing hollowly upon closure, he smelled the rich tones of bound leather. Rum. And just a hint of vanilla, brought on by the breakdown of lignin in the wood-based paper within each book, the lignin a close relative to vanilla itself. For one brief moment, he closed his eyes and allowed himself to revel in the aroma. When he opened his eyes, Siegfried peered back at him, a puzzled expression written on his brow.

"The library is a sanctuary, my good man."

Alaric failed to add that it was the place he had hid out from his grandfather, Fearsome, when at court. Or that he had played hide-and-seek in here as a child. He'd even listened in on many a conversation from his hiding places within the room. That's how he had known to enter the globe that day when he had unwittingly entombed himself within its walls. It was where he'd heard his juiciest gossip. From there he'd learned that his father kept slaves. That he'd sent adventurers to the farthest reaches of Africa and beyond in search of rare orchids that now took up space within the greenhouses.

Or learned that his mother was dying.

Something had died along with her that day. Perhaps it had been his innocence. For she had been kind beyond measure. Had always looked out for his welfare and happiness. Perhaps that's why he had withheld so much from his son, including love, so that he would never experience the pain of loss that Alaric had suffered back then.

"Sir?" Siegfried interrupted. "Are you alright?"

Alaric's hands shook, but he hid them within the folds of his wide, satin sleeves, modeled after those of the mandarins in China, another place his grandfather had sent explorers. There they'd learned of all things scientific. Had opened up a new world filled with ideas too numerous to explore. Movable type, paper, even the very gunpowder that Alaric now used to secure his kingdom far into the future. They had believed in divination and cleromancy, as well, a belief that random numbers could predict the future. Hence the expression, the roll of the dice. Alaric had called in his own seer, on occasion, to taste the future, to grasp it within his sites. But fate was a fickle lover. It gave what it wanted, and no more.

"Do you think Fearsome can really help us?" Siegfried pried, his eyes angling upward.

"Only one way to find out, my dear man. Help me up."

Siegfried bent down and lent a shoulder from which to step up to the first rung, then pushed Alaric from behind as they moved up the wooden ladder, oiled and darkened with age. At last they reached the top. Fearsome must have heard him, for a great yawn rang out from the smoke-clouded orb and soon the mist disappeared, replaced by a rather surly man with a rather longish goatee. It was a trait that all of Alaric's male relatives bore. But unlike Alaric, Fearsome's goatee was not oiled and braided, but rather left untouched and listed to one side as though a ship that had lost its ballast.

"What news have you?" Alaric said, without further ado.

"News?"

Alaric ground his teeth together, his molars mere nubs from what they used to be. "You said you had a plan. You said to come back tomorrow. Well? I'm here. What is your plan, or were you merely spouting off?"

Alaric could see that he'd hit a nerve as the cloud returned and had become a fiery red, flickers of flames beneath it.

"PLAN?! Of course I have a plan?"

Fearsome's voice resonated like the fiery belch of a volcano, and like the aftermath of a quake from the volcano, the ground shook beneath Alaric's feet so that he had to grab onto Siegfried to keep from tumbling to the ground.

"See here," Fearsome said, his voice so low that it nearly purred, "my spies are closely watching your den of thieves that you keep below your fortress."

Alaric had seen their faces in the floating tables. Like gargoyles they were, each more hideous than the former.

"You have spies?" Alaric squeaked, then quickly cleared his throat lest he seem meek.

"You have yours," Fearsome said, his chin tilting toward Siegfried, "and I have mine."

Alaric had never imagined that Fearsome could wield such power in the confines of his prison, and yet Alaric had from inside the globe. He'd even managed to innervate the Chessmen to action against Brigid and her warriors. At that, he laughed. Until he recalled that she had bested him then, just as she was besting him now. Why, just this morning a carrier pigeon returned with the news that a great beast, who came down from the sky, had scattered the Jackals and the Chessmen alike, sending them in multiple directions. It would take at least a week to restore order so that they could arrive on the Bookbinder doorstep to attack them in their sleep, the gods willing.

Fearsome continued. "Those beasts plan for you to win the battle so that they can attack *you* while the Jackals are away."

Alaric quaked at the predicament he found himself in. Why of course they would. He was left helpless while his men were away.

"That's why your men must return, immediately. I've already sent word and they are heading north as we speak."

"You did this without asking me first?" Alaric raced over to the orb. Had he a riding crop, he would have pounded the man upside his head, but alas, he was without a weapon, save for his dirk that he kept at all times inside his boot.

"I spared your life, Grandson! If not for me your days would be numbered."

Alaric breathed in, his nostrils flaring.

"He is right, I fear." Siegfried tapped Alaric apologetically on the shoulder. "These are desperate times. And they are desperate beasts filled with cunning and greed. You must listen to your grandfather."

Alaric acquiesced with some reluctance, not used to being

in a position of such little power.

"You would have me leave the Bookbinder Kingdom to its own devices, comfortable in the knowledge that they are safe?"

Fearsome laughed, the tenor booming through the upstairs library. "Of course not. We shall use magic similar to what they used on you."

"Huh?" Alaric's bushy eyebrows came together and he narrowed his eyes. "What do you propose then, Grandfather?"

"Leave it to me. Just know that the stars will be yours, dear Grandson. And with it, the cream of the Bookbinder crop."

Fearsome let out a belly laugh that shook the building. Alaric braced himself against the bookshelves, so like those of the greatest libraries in all of Europe. He didn't know what his grandfather had planned. But what he did know was that over the years, Fearsome had earned the reputation of his name. Whatever he set in motion, it would rock the very foundations of the known world, and for that Alaric couldn't help but smile.

35

I could feel it in the air, the smell of it different somehow, acrid, as though it contained a hint of ammonia. My tender nerves made sleep difficult. Though we had made great progress over the course of the week, time was running out. The howl of the wind only confirmed it, as if ridiculing me, mocking me. *Warning me.*

"How soon before the underground is finished?" I turned to Winnifred and Lofgren who had commandeered the construction of the now enormous building that lay strung out like a golden caterpillar upon the earth, its tail twisting this way and that. It shimmered in the midday sun, turning different colors depending on the light. It was like nothing I had ever seen before and I stood before it, my mouth agape.

"It won't be finished for at least a week." Winnifred shrugged apologetically.

"Hmm, I see."

The trapper and his friend had escaped, but Thomas and Henry had gone to apprehend them. How had they got past the guards, eluded each and every one of us? Perhaps they had created their own secret entrance. That thought sent a shiver tracing through me, despite the noonday sun.

Just then, Phinney, who had set out on another spy mission with a handful of the starlings, returned on wings bent low as she honed in on us and flew to a nearby branch, the floor of her mouth moving rapidly in what Conestra termed a "gular flutter," similar to a dog panting from exertion or excess heat. That could mean only one thing. She had flown on the wings of a current to get here and had taken little rest in her haste to tell me something, but what? She made a series of high-pitched crees.

"I don't understand," I said.

She tracked back and forth upon the limb of a mountain laurel, but I was still no closer to reading her signs. Suddenly, she let loose a loud cree and the starlings flew in formation, their murmuration like that of synchronized swimmers as though a single living organism rather than an entire flock.

I peered up, as did Winnifred and Lofgren. There, in what I could only term a sky acrobat, the starlings painted a picture of fleeing Jackals and Chessmen. *The Jackals are gone? No more worries?* I felt as though I should jump for joy, so why then did I sense only disaster?

When my eyes fell earthward, I caught Winnifred's gaze and noticed her inspecting my reaction. She, too, wrestled with some unnamed fear.

"It's a trick." Winnie peered at me with owl eyes. "I can feel it. We can't let up now, Right-O? Lofgren? What say you?"

Lofgren checked his vest for his pocket watch as though it somehow held the answer. He peered at it for no more than a second. "I agree. Something's not right."

Phinney turned her back on me as though miffed that I didn't believe her.

"It's not you, Phinney. I'm sure you saw what you saw, but there's got to be more to it than just that. They wouldn't have left permanently without a reason." I wondered what my loom thought of all this. Maybe she would have a say about Phinney's news.

"Okay, gang, time to talk to my loom," I said.

Many of the women had stopped what they were doing to listen in on our conversation and to watch the birds flying in their afternoon ballet.

"It all seems too easy," said Jocelyn.

"Maybe they've given up?" Gertrude countered.

Dele and Elijah spoke as one. "Nuh-uh. It be like a slave owner givin' up his slave. Don't happen much, I reckon."

I had to concur. What was in it for Alaric to retreat? More than ever, I wished Henry and Thomas would return. Their departure left my mind unsettled, and yet we simply couldn't allow the trapper to give Alaric the map to our new underground fortress. I thanked everyone for their input and set out toward my tent when I heard the sound of footsteps behind me.

"Wait up! I'm coming with you." Winnie groused, still mad at the loom from the last time it had turned black and popped, nearly scaring us both to death.

We walked in unison, while Lofgren stayed behind to tend the construction details. "You two make a fine couple," I said, noting the pink in Winnifred's cheeks.

"Thanks!" Winnie beamed.

She appeared happier than I had ever seen her, their two bright minds a twin reflection of each other. It encouraged me to see that marriage hadn't forced her to act small, to hide her talents behind a bushel basket. Instead, she'd been afforded full rein of her abilities so that between them, they multiplied their abilities as though one truly powerful mind rather than two smaller ones. It gave me hope. I imagined my life with Henry. Already, we finished each other's sentences like an old married couple who'd known each other for decades.

Winnifred stopped me with a hand to my arm. As though she could read my thoughts, she said, "Brigid, why don't you marry Henry?"

"What do you mean? We're engaged."

"I know but—"

"But what?" I asked, unsure what she was getting at.

"It's just that you're so good together."

I bit my lip as I stewed on what she'd said. We planned to marry. *After* the war. At least that was the goal, but I often wondered if maybe we were fooling ourselves, that the war might never end and we might never marry. That I might never know the pleasure of hearing a child call me mother, or experience the joy of having someone by my side as a life partner.

I must admit, I would love to be a mother. I think I would be good at it. I shrugged, unsure.

"You're right, Brigid, you *would* make a great mother. And we *don't* know if or when this war will be over."

A cascade of fear washed over me. "Wait . . . what . . .? Did you just read my thoughts?"

Winnifred blinked rapidly and cocked her head to one side. "I suppose I did," she said with a giggle. "Oh my gosh! I can mind meld just like Lofgren."

"What do you *mean* like Lofgren?" I took her hands in mine. "*Can* you read minds?"

Winnifred shrugged, then nodded. "I think so."

I let go of her hands and let out a whoop. I don't know why I was so excited, but for some reason the thought that the pair could read minds seemed somehow . . . magical!

"Okay, explain it to me," I said as we began to walk toward my tent again, the leaves swirling around us.

"All elves can read minds."

My expression must have shown my shock at the notion, but she pressed on.

"When I married, I inherited certain rights."

"Like what?" I nodded to the guard, and dipped my head to enter the tent.

"Well, I can live as long as Lofgren. Eight hundred years and counting."

"Wait, what?"

She plopped down at the foot of my bed. "And, until now, I didn't know I could mind meld with anyone except Lofgren, but there you have it."

I melted to the floor of my tent alongside her,

flabbergasted. "I'll have to be careful what I think in the future!"

"No worries, Brigid. I promise I won't intrude on your thoughts unless they're directed at me."

"Thank goodness for that!" I cried, then immediately regretted it when I saw her cheeks redden.

"Right-O," she said. "So, let's speak to your loom and find out what's going on with the Jackals."

I told my loom of my fears and asked her what all this meant. At first, nothing happened. Then she began to clack slowly, but soon she picked up speed so that she sounded like a runaway locomotive, steam nearly rising from the weft, she was in such high gear. When she was finished, I saw that indeed the Jackals and the Chessmen were fleeing.

"So, it's true?" I said when she was finished. "We're safe? No more worries?"

The loom immediately went black and, as before, the swirling began. In it were a thousand stars, maybe more. The darkness was so black that it appeared almost blue. And yet I could see the stars swirl, slowly at first, then faster and faster until the skies let out a roar that forced me to throw my hands to my ears to prevent the sound from damaging them. The whole room swirled with it, my clothing flying around me in a dance gone mad, while Winnifred hung onto the bed frame to keep from being swept away in the wind's currents. Suddenly, the wind died down, the silence deafening. I slowly uncovered my ears and Winnie let go of the bed frame, both of us shaken.

"What's happening?" I said to Winnie when everything returned to normal.

But Winnie only stared, her mouth agape, her eyes two

wide saucers filled with horror.

"What is it, Winnie? What's the matter?"

Winnie held her hands out as though testing the air around me for substance. "Where are you, Brigid?" Her voice quivered as did her hands. "I can't see you. You're not there. It's as though the air around you has turned to liquid silver."

"No, Winnie. I'm right here." I waved my hands to get her attention, but she peered through me, as if I wasn't there, as if I was already . . . *gone!*

Henry didn't return until late in the day, both he and Thomas, dusty and dirty, fatigue written in the drooping of their eyelids and the deflated set of their shoulders. Everyone rushed to them at once.

"Did you find them—the trapper and his accomplice?" Yesimeh blurted out, the women present all chiming in until I whistled to get their attention.

"Let the men speak," I said.

Fortunately, I had returned to the living, but both Winnie and I believed it an omen, my brief disappearance. Winnie had promised to keep an eye on me from now on, certain that I had been cursed in some way and that without her help, I would indeed disappear.

"The trapper escaped. We tried to track him and the other man, but we lost them in the river. They must have had a boat waiting and are long gone."

Gone. That was the second time in the day that I had heard that announcement. Winnie and I exchanged hurried glances, but Henry noticed and I knew he would ask me about it later.

Emma, who I hadn't seen in some time, her hours now spent in her medical tent preparing for the upcoming assault, came running when she learned that Thomas had returned. He leaned down from his horse and hugged her, then lifted her onto his saddle.

Henry turned to me. "We may not have found the trapper, but we did find something of interest. Or should I say some*one* of interest . . . actually, *two* people and a . . . pawn."

"Pawn?"

But before I could complete my thought, I heard a commotion. From the back of the glade, the sea of women parted and two other horses drew forth with two very surprising figures atop it along with one very odd creature, one of the Chessmen, a pawn.

"Beatrice?" I breathed the words, both a prayer and a curse, because her threads had thrust the kingdom into darkness. "And Birsha? This is your surprise, Henry?"

He nodded.

For one brief moment, I felt as if I might faint. Winnie grasped me by the arm and held me tight as Beatrice slipped down off her horse and came to stand in front of me.

"We escaped."

Never had I seen her so weary, so forlorn . . . and yet so hopeful. I tested her eyes to see if she knew the evil that resided within those threads she'd given me when I departed the fortress earlier in the year, but it was clear by the depths of her sorrow that she hadn't. That she had been just as duped by their beauty. Perhaps Birsha as well.

With that, I took her into my arms, and she sagged into

them as though grateful for a kindness she didn't deserve. But when I pushed her away to see her eyes once more, I read something else in them. She had changed. Had grown. No longer the petulant blue-eyed vixen she'd once been, who sought to create havoc wherever she went, she now revealed a humbleness as though brought low by circumstances beyond her control. I had vowed to give her only two chances, but now I saw that I would give her three. I just had to hope I was right in doing so.

Chame Leon stared at the pie on the windowsill, the hollow in his stomach making every nerve ending tense. He looked both ways, then turned to Liz Herd and whispered, "Wait here! If I'm caught, run. Head due east. You should make it to Bookbinder territory within two days."

"I'm not leaving you behind," she hissed, her eyes unblinking.

"Nonsense! Save yourself."

Before she could say another word, he leapt out into the open expanse nearest the kitchen sill and sprinted toward the cooling, meaty confection. Mincemeat, by the smell of it. It would provide the nourishment they would need if they were to make it all the way to the nearby kingdom.

Chame Leon snatched the pie in his hand and ran hunched over, lest he be seen through the window. But just as he neared the gorse where Liz Herd lay hidden, he heard a shout.

"Stop! Thief!"

They each grabbed a piece and shoveled it into their

mouths as they ran, higgledy-piggledy through the underbrush. From behind, they heard more shouting and the sound of boots stomping through the house, but they were already to the nearby river where they had found a boat tied to a dock.

Liz Herd flounced inside, the boat rocking back and forth as Chame Leon untied it from its moor and began pushing. He leaped in at the last minute and frantically rowed for all his might. A shot rang out, but by that time they neared a bend and soared the rapids that sped them downwards in the general direction they were headed. Only when they felt safe to do so, did they turn their attention back to the lamb pie with fresh suet, currents, raisins, and one Bramley apple.

"Just like my dear ma-ma used to make," Chame Leon said as he licked at the brandy and nutmeg filler on his fingers.

For a while, the pair ate in silence, only the babble of the river to while away the hours. Chame Leon patted his distended stomach after eating well over half the pie himself, Liz Herd eating the rest. They had gone so long without food that to save any back seemed improbable if not impossible. Now, Chame Leon regretted his gluttony.

"Thank you," Liz Herd said, her eyes on him.

"For what?" he asked.

"For bringing me with you. For being a good man. The Councccil . . ." She let the words linger between them.

"I know. It was becoming treacherous."

"Then when the Queen of the Mammalsss took over…"

Chame Leon knew exactly what she meant. Everything had changed. It was so hard to understand, that one so normal in appearance could hide such a black heart. The evil she amassed at her floating table still made him shudder. To be so cold, so calculating. Her end had been just, and yet she had unleashed something that couldn't be put back in its cage.

"Do you think the Bookbindersss will accept usss? We are not like them."

Chame Leon peered down at his scaly skin and at Liz Herd. For the entire trek here, he had thought of nothing else. What if they didn't accept them? Sent them back, or worse, put them in prison? The worry tore at his heart and filled his nighttime with dread.

"We will cross that bridge when we come to it, eh?"

"Aye," she agreed.

Now, all they could do is wait. And hope.

36

Fearsome had interceded and now the book was Alaric's. He held the ancient tome in his hand, the words within to be spoken at midnight of a full moon. An owl hooted in a nearby branch, the scent of pine made heavy by the moisture in the air. The chill of the evening bled away any warmth, while high above the kingdom, beside him on the parapet stood his adjutant, Siegfried.

"It is time, sir. If you are to speak the words, you must say them now."

Alaric drew himself up inside his cloak and nodded in acknowledgement. He opened the book to the vellum page marked with a ribbon. On it, hand paintings were scrawled of mythical beasts, the paints made up of minerals ground with pestles and combined with wood gum or egg white to bind the minerals in a technique known as tempura. The words that centered the paintings glowed richly in the night. With a cleansing breath, Alaric opened his mouth to speak the ancient words that would forevermore alter his destiny.

> *Starlight, the universe bring,*
> *Wrack and ruin*
> *To everything.*
> *Within the night sky,*
> *Fireflies dance,*
> *Bring me the one,*
> *Whose heart sings.*
> *Her goodness shall,*
> *Be evermore mine,*
> *On this the night of nights,*
> *Do I pledge my soul*
> *To the one who delivers*
> *My heart's desire.*

As he spoke, the night sky began to swirl, leaves and dust flying high against the parapet and stinging his eyes. And still he droned on.

> *Be ye not slow,*
> *Oh heart of mine,*
> *Reach out and pluck*
> *The night sky.*
> *Locked in amber,*
> *You shall be.*
> *And I, well I*
> *Am your eternity.*

He howled with laughter until he could howl no more, and still the stars twirled and the wind swept through the valley, taking with it anything not tacked down. The echoing howl of wolves rang out from the distant hillside. A blue-green light flowed up from the pages of the ancient book of Alchemy. The light pirouetted outward as if a thousand dancers dancing to a tune only they could hear. They spread out into the nighttime. Such beauty for the havoc they would bring. His heart could bear no more as he now stood in silence, entranced by the curls of light dancing away, far beyond his kingdom. Soon they would make their way to the Bookbinder Kingdom, and Brigid would be his. Now all he had to do was to stand back and wait. Yet he heard a rumble from below, as though the earth had awakened to swallow him whole.

"What is this?" he demanded, but Siegfried only shook his head.

The tremor came from the very same location where the creatures of the night resided. Surely, they dared not show themselves, not now, when Alaric was so close to achieving everything he had ever wanted.

"Come, Siegfried. Take the book!"

The book suddenly warmed his hands as though heated from within. Alaric, quickly handed it to his adjutant, who yanked his hand back at the fiery touch with a screech of pain. The book fell out of his hand. As it descended, the pages flipped rapidly, creating a wind all their own. The descent slowed and stopped altogether as the book touched down on the stone platform, a growl rising from inside its pages along with a figure.

Alaric jumped back and reddened at the childlike squeal

that emanated from his mouth while Siegfried crept slowly away to put distance between him and the book. The figure that appeared had horns and a face contorted in a perpetual scream. Smoke billowed from the creature's mouth as if from the fires of hell. How? How had Alaric been so stupid? Had he sold his soul to the Devil, his desire so great for revenge, and yet revenge for what? He didn't even know anymore. Hatred of the Bookbinders, like an errant gene, had been passed down from one generation to the other until no one knew the source of the rancor. A driving obsession that might now get him killed. He shuddered even as the earth shook. Below him, underground, he heard the footsteps of an army on the move, an army of cretins.

"Help me!" Alaric cried.

But there would be no help, for none was to be had. Not now. Maybe never. And yet he had to stop the evil he had set into motion, find a way to quell the army he had unleashed by setting free the words confined within the pages of this dark tome.

Years ago, he had overheard one of the Council talking about the ancient tomes and had heard that the only way to reverse the spell was to read it in reverse. Slowly, he began reading the words backwards, louder and louder, until at last, a shriek rang out and the Devil's figure was sucked into the pages and the book slammed closed, a cloud of dust the only reminder that it had ever been opened.

Until this very moment, Alaric hadn't realized that he'd backed into the stone parapet and hugged the stones as though willing himself to disappear inside them. For one brief second, his eyes caught Siegfried's and they both let out a sigh and bent holding their knees, the rumbling gone. For now.

"Saints be praised," Siegfried said.

But Alaric could only nod. Yet there was still the matter of the tome. His legs shaking from beneath him, Alaric walked over and picked up the book. Then, with a running start, he heaved it over the side of the fortress and watched as it fluttered to the ground below. Only when it landed with a distant plop did he realize his horrible mistake....

I ordered that Beatrice, Birsha and the Pawn be put up until we could decide what to do with them. Now, as Henry and I sat around the fire warming our hands, I leaned into him and listened to his heartbeat. It counted out the beats of my thoughts as they swirled inside my head.

"Alright, Brigid. Something's bothering you. What is it?"

He lifted my chin to gaze into the shards of glass that made up the layers of my eyes, their icy blue depths no longer strange to him. With the knuckles of his right hand, he caressed my cheek, then he kissed me on the forehead and drew me into him, the smell of leather and sweat comforting.

"Whatever it is that's been eating at you all night," he began, "you can tell me."

I gazed up at him. We had come so far, he and I. From mere children to adults with adult worries.

"The war, Henry."

"What of it?"

The fire crackled and popped, spitting embers into the night air. Even now, might those embers draw the enemy to us?

Might they signal an opportunity for a raid? And yet how long could we survive in the darkness, in the cold?

"What if this war never ends? If we never marry. If we die before it . . ."

Henry placed two fingers over my lips to silence me. "Don't say it. Don't even think it!"

"But it could happen. And I would never have a child . . . to remember you by, or you I, don't you see? And I'm aging by the day—"

He laughed and drew me in tighter. "We're all aging. It's a part of life, just as death is a part of life. It's something we must accept as the price of living."

"I suppose." I fell into him, defeated. My shoulders sagged with the weight of my worries.

"Let me get this straight," he said, stirring at the embers with a stick he'd found in the woods. "You're afraid we won't marry, won't have a child. That we risk death before we share a memory together through this being that is of our blood, our loins. Is that what you think?"

When he put it that way, I felt silly, and yet was it really? The fire ticked a countdown as if it knew what I knew. That life was never promised. Never guaranteed.

"Alright then." Henry stood and reached out a hand.

"Alright what?"

"Let's get married."

I bit my lip, my head tilted in an attempt to detect any mirth in a man so prone to it. But there was none. Instead, his eyes narrowed steadily on mine and he dragged me to him.

"Where are we going?" I demanded.

"You'll see."

For the next ten minutes, we wended our way through one cluster of women after another until we found the tent that housed the minister—a woman, oddly enough, as women generally weren't allowed such roles. However, in our army, the need arose and so we had sent out notice until we found such a person to give the rites to those who didn't make it home, and there were many such casualties. Sorrow filled my heart with pain at the memory of those losses, and yet now, the female minister brought only joy, which was apt, given that her name was Joy . . . Joy Hofsted. We knocked on the door to her makeshift tent, which was larger than many of the others.

"Come in!" she called.

We found her seated at a table, going over her notes for the Sunday service for those women who wanted to attend. Hunched over her text, she peered up at us through thick lenses, her lithe frame like that of a willow, always bent, even when standing.

"I want you to marry us." Henry stood somehow taller than normal.

"You'll need two witnesses to the event."

I could think of no better witnesses than Emma and Thomas, Henry's brother and my friend, both stalwart companions in this world we had inherited. I quickly dispatched one of the women to collect them. Five minutes later, we heard a rustle at the door, and the two popped in, surprise evident in the confused expressions they both wore.

"Did I hear right?" Thomas smacked Henry summarily on the back. "You're getting married, brother?"

Henry merely nodded, but he appeared paler somehow, as though shock had set in at what he was about to do.

"What will our parents say? Surely, they should be contacted." Thomas pressed on, oblivious to the discomfort it was causing both Henry and me.

Henry squirmed under his brother's protestations. "There's no time!" he shot back.

"*Time*? What difference will a few days make?" Emma inserted. "Can't it wait until we can plan a proper wedding? The women will want to celebrate. To be there for both of you." She turned to me, her hand making a sweep of my appearance. "You don't even have a proper gown."

Confusion reigned and I no longer knew which way to turn. Wait and perhaps never marry, or rush into something that would upset Henry's parents and the women warriors. Plus, I had always imagined my family present, but that dream might never be. My throat tightened as though put in one of Winnifred's vises.

"Maybe we should wait, Henry. Perhaps we're being hasty."

Henry turned to me with a ferocity that made me blanch. "Brigid Anne Dunsmore, we've waited through two wars. We've watched those around us marry." He gestured toward Thomas and Emma as a case in point. "Why wait any longer? Do you, or do you not, want to marry me?"

"Well, yes of course—"

"Fine." Then he turned to Emma and Thomas. "Either you two are our best man and woman, or we will find someone else," Henry hissed.

I blinked back my surprise. Henry, possibly the most mild

mannered man I had ever known, was showing a side of himself I had never seen before.

"Do you love Brigid?" Joy asked.

I had almost forgotten about her with all the drama surrounding our marriage.

"Of course I love her. What kind of a question is that?"

Joy dipped her head in response then turned to me. "And do you love Henry?"

"I do."

"Then may I now pronounce you husband and wife."

Henry and I looked at each other and blinked, our surprise complete.

"Do you have a ring?"

Henry scanned the room with his eyes as though a moth alighting on one flower after another but finding nothing of value. "I don't."

I shrugged and opened my hands to show that they were empty.

"Here!" Joy set down the Bible she had been holding. "Let me think."

She tapped her front teeth with her fingernail, then coming upon an idea she quickly rummaged through drawers at her bedside until she came up with something in a small black box.

"This was my grandmother's. I saved her ring for my own wedding, but I'm married to the church and this poor thing has languished by my bedside for ages. If you would be so honored."

"Honored?" I breathed.

The ring was breathtaking, unlike anything I had ever seen. A blue sapphire, to match my eyes, with tiny blue diamonds that reminded me of stars. All set in a platinum band with two small hearts to each side of the larger sapphire.

She placed it in Henry's hands. As he peered at me, his eyes filled with a love so deep that it mirrored my own, I am sure. My hands shook as he placed it on my finger. From this day forward, we would be one. I would no longer be alone, always wondering where I belonged, where I fit into this jigsaw puzzle called life.

"I love you, Brigid Anne Dunsmore," he said as he cinched it in place.

"And I you, Henry Bookbinder." I paused, frowning. "But I have no ring for you!" My eyes filled with tears.

Thomas pinched his earlobe, an odd habit he had when thinking. Then he looked down at his own hand that had not one, but two rings on it, one a wedding band, the other a smaller band that fit on his pinkie finger.

"Your fingers are smaller than mine, brother. This is granddad's ring. I'm certain he would want you to have it."

He pulled it from his finger and handed it to me. I laid it on my palm and inspected it through watery eyes. On the gold band set a Celtic cross with Celtic knots wending their way down each side of the band. It was breathtaking. Thomas encouraged me with a nod of his head.

"With this ring I do thee wed, Henry Bookbinder."

Despite their earlier misgivings, Emma let out a squeal and Thomas clapped Henry on the back.

Joy beamed. "You may kiss the bride."

For several minutes, we leaned in, the smell of him sweet and fresh, an aroma I would treasure just as I did him. When we came up for air, a cry erupted from outside as though a thousand women stood at my doorstep, listening in. The sound was so deafening that both Henry and I covered our ears. Henry opened the door onto a crowd so large that I cringed to think how we would make our way through it. First and foremost at the door stood Winnifred and Lofgren as well as Jocelyn and Gertrude and Yesimeh, all stalwart companions. In her hands, Yesimeh held the prettiest bouquet of flowers.

"How?" I asked, my voice giving way.

"We overheard the guard tell Thomas and Emma that you were to be married. You don't think we'd let you get away without a proper sendoff, do you?"

Yesimeh handed me the bouquet of lilies and baby's breath. I took the bouquet and inhaled the flowers' fragrance. Everything about this day felt suddenly divine. As though the stars had all aligned for this special moment.

"Now we have a surprise for you, but Henry will have to wait for a bit if he's to have his honeymoon."

Before I could protest, the women swarmed me and propelled me toward a tent they had set up, though for what purpose, I could only guess. Henry merely shrugged as they dragged me away, while Thomas said, "This calls for a toast, brother!"

The last I saw of Henry, Thomas was steering him toward his tent where I knew he kept a bottle of whiskey and vermouth.

"Farewell, Henry," I whispered.

Then I allowed myself to be hauled to Emma's tent, where lo and behold, just as the women had promised, they had a surprise waiting for me.

37

As I stood inside the tent, I shivered in the lace nightgown the women secured for me, though where they had found it on such short notice remained a mystery. The women made the tent up with rich quilts and candles that lent a warm glow to the interior of the room. On the floor, they laid furs to cushion our feet. They scented my hair and primped over it, weaving small white daisies throughout. Then they spread the juice of a garnet cherry across my lips to give them a red tint, not to mention a delicious taste. Lastly, they replaced the necklace that secured my family within its depths. I held it to my chest, memories too precious to dare open it now lest I give way to the emotions stirring within me.

At last, they gave me one final inspection, and apparently decided I would do. Then one by one they came and embraced me, Emma the last to do so.

"Don't be afraid," Emma said, her eyes capturing mine. "Henry is a good man. A kind man, like his brother." She smiled, her smile contagious.

"I know," I said.

Then why could I not stop shivering? For years, I had imagined this moment when Henry and I would finally be one. When he would be mine for always, and me his. And yet, now that it was here, every fiber of my being shook from the unknown.

Just then, I heard a knock and Henry's form appeared in silhouette against the canvas tent.

"Good luck," Emma whispered, then winked.

I watched as she turned and allowed Henry entrance even as she ducked outside. My breath stilled at the sight of him, and I saw that he did the same. For several seconds, we said nothing, merely staring at each other as though strangers rather than battle-weary warriors.

Finally, Henry broke the silence. "You look beautiful."

Never before had I felt beautiful, or even pretty. I had been too busy trying to survive. If anything, I felt old before my time, and yet today it was as if I'd entered Winnifred's time machine and gone back in time, back before the world had worn me down with all of its trials. Its many tribulations.

Henry moved slowly, as if to do otherwise might find me bolting for the door. Eyes filled with love, he reached up and pushed a curly tendril of hair behind my ear, then ran a finger down my face. His touch sent shivers of a different kind pulsing through me. I closed my eyes, determined to savor these moments in time. Precious moments unlike any I had experienced before. His finger reached down my breastplate, sending a trill of excitement shooting through me. I gasped. Then it was as if all those times we had squirreled away any intimacy broke open, unleashed in a torrent of emotion. He eased me onto the bed, the lace gown thrown open with a mere flick of his fingers.

For the next half hour, I learned what it was to be a wife and a lover. With each new breath I longed for more, and yet we had to come up for air sometime. When we were finally silent, our bodies covered in the dew of first love, we gazed at each other, explored the contours of our faces, our bodies that were now one.

"I love you, Henry Bookbinder," I whispered into his ear.

"And I you," Henry responded, his voice sleepy from a night of lovemaking.

For some reason, I needed this time to take in every piece of him, to know him as I never knew him before. It was as if I understood, even then, that it would be for the last time. The realization sent a tremor of fear darting through me, but I kept it from him, never daring to risk these special moments together filled with love. Here, in his arms, I was home. Never before had I felt at home. Anywhere. The thought that I might lose it so soon filled me with a pit of despair, but I fought it down. Instead, I held him tighter, hoping against hope that I was wrong. That tomorrow night I would still be here with him in my arms.

When he finally slept, I whispered, "I love you, Henry. Never forget me."

Because I will never forget you.

The new day started out like any other, only this time I lay in the arms of the man I loved. I studied the contours of Henry's face, his strong chin with just the beginnings of a beard. His almond-shaped eyes blinked as if in dream. For some time, I stared at him, wishing to commit every feature of his face to memory.

Suddenly, his eyes blinked open and he cocked his head to peer down at me in question. How could I tell him that today would be different? I felt it in my very bones. An unsettled feeling that had begun the moment I had awakened. It left me breathless and afraid. The future held a question mark for me, though I wished it otherwise. I drank in the scent of him, the sheer manliness. He who had given me so much, a sense of belonging I had never possessed before. A belief in myself that gave me wings to fly. And now I would soon be departing, though I didn't know why, or even if . . . I just knew. Like the loom, I seemed to possess powers I hadn't before, as if my very love for this man and these women warriors had given me a sixth sense that could predict the future. Oh, not the details, precisely. But a gut instinct that made me alert to even the slightest change in the earth's temperature.

The air coming through the tent flap spoke of early morning, the smell of firs leaving a tang in the air that I could almost taste. My mind slowed everything to a crawl as if to hold onto these most precious moments with the man I loved. But like all good things, I knew it must come to an end and that I must face the day ahead, no matter the cost.

"Ready to get up, sleepyhead?"

Henry's voice was husky upon awakening, his mouth eagerly seeking mine. I felt greedy with the want of it, with the want of *him*. But life had a way of blowing a person off-course like the whorls of a dandelion *pappus,* the ring of fine hairs that acted like miniature parachutes. As a child, I had wished upon them, one of my wishes being that I would one day find a man such as Henry. And here I was, only to seek the wind with hair too fine to hold me to the earth . . . to Henry.

"Let's stay in bed all day," I said on a whim.

"We can't," he replied with a frown. And yet the tilt off his head made it clear that he had read the desperation in my plea.

"Nevermind." I shrugged, and yet my legs felt heavy as I stood and dressed for the day ahead.

Already, the women warriors were up and about, the sounds of community awash with the snorts of horses, the barks of dogs, and the movement of women prepping for . . . what? I still didn't know. Even the construction laborers were fast at work. Normally, I would never have stayed in bed this long, but the women had offered me grace and this small measure of leisure. However, I knew it couldn't last forever. My fate awaited me outdoors. I stared at the flap as though it held the answer. But first I turned one last time to Henry.

"What?" he asked, sensing my tension.

"I'm afraid."

His eyebrows pinched together. "Of what?"

How could I lay all my fears out before him? Weight him down with the heaviness that filled my heart on a day that should have seen me dancing through the streets, happy to share my feelings for the man who had stolen my heart and made me feel whole for the first time in my life.

"I don't know, Henry. That's the thing. I just *feel* it."

"Feel what? You're not making any sense."

Language had no words for what I was about to say, but I was determined to try.

"I dreamt something. The sky . . . it was spinning." I growled, frustrated that my words had tumbled head over heels and landed in a heap at our feet. "Nevermind. I'm being silly."

Henry pulled me into the crook of his arm, where I belonged. I drank in the scent of him, the warmth. Reluctantly we parted, but only after a kiss so long and so loving that my heart stilled for one blissful moment. I would remember this moment forever.

Then we opened the door.

From the moment we entered the glade, the timbre changed. Already, the tension hung heavy in the air, the women's movements more purposeful, as if they felt it too, this disquiet, this dissonance. Even the air smelled off, as though laden with ammonia and charged with some unnamed static that made the hairs on my arms stand on end. Birds, who normally chirped and bobbed from tree to tree, now sat huddled together screeching as though a bird of prey was at hand, the sound raucous to my ears. And indeed, I peered up, but saw nothing. Whatever lurked beyond our vision, it wasn't yet ready to show itself.

"We'd best be prepared," I told Henry.

"Yeah, but for what?" He reached for my hand as if to tether me to the earth and to him.

As we stood there watching the hubbub of women running to and fro, I reached out for Winnifred who raced to provide Lofgren with a tool for the wentletrap.

"What is it? What's happened?" I demanded.

"We don't know." She waved the spokeshave at Lofgren, a tool used for shaving wood. He arrived at warp speed, only to fly away at the same speed. "But something's up, Brigid. The loom is going nuts. I don't know what it's doing, but we best get inside the wentletrap."

My breath caught at her words. The wentletrap wasn't ready. At best, it would hold a third of the women, leaving two-thirds outside, in the open.

"Where's Yesimeh?" I shouted, the chaos contagious.

"Over there!" Winnifred yelled. "Got to go!" Then she disappeared into the melee.

"Come on, Henry!" I called over my shoulder.

Once again, he grasped my hand so as not to lose me among the vast swath of women warriors. I bypassed Gertrude, whose horse snorted nervously as she urged it toward the area where Jocelyn stood speaking to her troops of women.

"Yesimeh!" I called, waving my hand to be seen.

Yesimeh, who was short by any standard, stood on tiptoes and waved a hand in return. "Over here!"

We weaved in and out until we found her at a table, maps strewn here and there. Before I could speak to her of my fears, she said what I had been thinking.

"The women aren't all going to fit in the wentletrap. According to Phinney, the birds are showing signs of distress in this region here." She drew a circle that encompassed the area where they sat and the areas surrounding it. "The birds from this point on are calm, so whatever is happening, is happening here. Therefore, the top leadership should be inside the wentletrap for safekeeping. The women that we can't fit in, should be over here."

"What about the Mohawks and the Oneida?" I asked.

Yesimeh shook her head. "They refuse to go inside. They will stay here." She pointed to the spot in the woods just beyond the encircled area. "With the women on this side and the Oneida and Mohawks on the other side—"

"It will create a pinch point," I finished for her.

"Exactly!" she echoed.

"And then the rest of us could come from the tunnels inside the wentletrap."

Henry agreed wholeheartedly with a nod of his head.

Yesimeh put her hand in the middle of our little circle. I placed my hand over hers and Henry covered both hands. "One for all and all for one," we cried in unison.

I suddenly felt lighter, as though a load had been lifted off me. So, we had a plan, but who were we fighting and how would it present itself? The army and Chessmen had all returned to the northwestern fortress, according to Phinney, who hovered overhead, moving back and forth between clans of starlings to try to calm them.

I watched her fly as I headed to high ground so I could let everyone know our plan. No sooner had I clambered atop an especially large mound of soil that had been dug out of the earth to make way for the wentletrap when the women began to stop and point. Winnifred, who was again racing back and forth, ran to get the megaphone and brought it to me as my army gathered around me.

"Something's afoot!" I yelled to which I noticed murmurs of agreement and the nod of heads. "It's time. There's not enough room inside the wentletrap, so we're going to draw straws to see who enters it." I mouthed an apology to Yesimeh for not taking her suggestion to allow the higher ups to go inside first. I understood her reasoning, but if we were to be a people's army, the rules must be fair for everyone. Be that as it may, I could see by the dark set of her eyes that I had offended her and that I would need to make amends, but for now, we needed the women's futures settled.

I called all the leaders of our army together where we drew straws. To my chagrin, I drew the longest straw and Gertrude the shortest.

"If Gertrude stays outside, I stay," Jocelyn declared, hands on hips.

It still amazed me how far these two women had come since I first met them in their fine dresses, their manner uppity. Now they both wore our crenelated uniforms and boots, their bodies lean from years of toil and sacrifice.

"Are your women okay with that decision?" I asked.

The women from her troop came forward. Though shaken, they all agreed.

"Then it's settled." I pulled out a map and pointed to where the women would hide in the copse to the left. Kahwhita, who I'd seen near the edge of the glade threaded her way forward.

"We will be here, Bri-gid." She pointed to a spot on the map where they would be well hidden among the firs and maple.

"Good!" Then I turned to the remainder of the gathering. "The rest of you, gather your things and begin filing into the wentletrap within the hour. Winnifred will show you where you'll be."

Winnifred, who had stayed to listen to the decisions, nodded her head. "Right-O! I'm on it. Be back as quickly as you can," she shouted to the remaining women warriors. "On the double!"

As the women scattered, I knew I'd chosen well for the previous campaign. She had been the right person for the job. The realization filled me with relief because, though I wished it otherwise, I felt the pull of something as if a string were attached to me, and I was the marionette. That thought saddened me because I'd had a marionette once, brought home to me by my father. A Spaniard, if I recalled correctly, with a floppy mustache that he'd found on one of his travels. The memory filled me with both joy and sadness. My family wasn't here to see all the changes that had taken place in my life. The love and the loss. As before, I wondered if I would ever see them again, or perhaps, even now, they were lost to me forever. I touched the locket at my neck, the hologram. It flipped open, and to my surprise it held not my family, but Henry.

How? Furthermore, why?

I had no time to ponder this new mystery as I rushed forward, urging the women to hurry. It's then I realized that Henry was no longer at my side. Something or someone had called him away, no doubt to help iron out some new wrinkle in our daily lives. For a moment, I stood there, my eyes searching the myriad women bumping into each other in their haste to escape some unnamed woe.

Well, I had best get our own things ready for the journey ahead. I raced to my tent to collect my things. Then I would head for Henry's tent, the one he had lived in before we were married. Which tent would we live in now? But then that old feeling returned, the gnawing in the pit of my stomach. As I bent down to enter my tent, I paused, my mouth forming a wide O and my throat tightening with emotion. The answer had been waiting all along, inside my tent. The answer that foretold the future. The one I'd hoped was only my imagination.

38

Alaric ran through the corridor and raced up the ladder to the hidden library in the dome. There, awaiting his arrival, sat Fearsome, a man who Alaric had so feared as a child that he had hidden whenever he entered a room. But now the two men were equals. Both had their lives snatched from them, locked away inside an orb. As such, they'd had time to think, to mull over their lives, to realize what they had done right, what they had done wrong. But now . . . now, Alaric's world was spinning.

"Help me, Fearsome!" He tried not to grovel even as his entire body quaked.

Siegfried, who trailed after him and was only now scaling the ladder, popped his head through the opening. "There you are!" he cried, as though speaking to an errant child. "You're safe. No one saw you come this way."

Alaric fell to his knees. "Thank heavens." His voice came

out raspy after all the running.

"What have we here, Grandson?" Fearsome appeared inside the smoky cloud of his orb. "Why are you so frightened?"

Where to start?

"The Diāmons! They materialized from their underground chambers and they are hideous! They are out for me, but the Jackals haven't yet arrived to save me, nor the Chessmen."

Fearsome's face grew dark, and he pooled his hands together, fingertips tapping an angry rhythm. "I see. I always suspected they would seize power someday, given the chance. And you have offered it to them like a ripe peach."

Alaric's chest seized and he wheezed in response. He pressed his hand against his sternum to fight off the rising tide of panic. "What have I done?"

Fearsome growled. "Nothing that can't be undone. Look, it's too late to worry about spilled books."

"How could you possibly know that I dropped the book?"

Alaric's hand fluttered to fend off the terror that one act instilled in him. Because of that misstep, he had allowed the Diāmons to be unleashed into his world. He closed his eyes against the memory. The book cascading over the balcony, its leaves releasing a howl, and then a scream so hideous that he had fallen backwards against the tower. But the ghouls that had dislodged from the bowels of the tome saw him scampering for safety, their images so hideous as to be inhuman. By comparison, the Council seemed somehow . . . *normal.*

Fearsome snapped his fingers in an attempt to end Alaric's misery. "How soon before the Jackals and Chessmen arrive?"

"A day, perhaps two, but—"

"Listen to me. This is what you'll do." Fearsome paced the small space, rubbing his beard as though a talisman to provide him wisdom for what lay ahead. "You shall stay here, wait them out." He paused his pacing to point to a book entitled, *Spells and Sorcery*. "In the meantime, get me that book and I will perform a spell on you."

"What kind of spell?"

Alaric never quite trusted Fearsome, but at this moment, he had no choice. He marched over to the book and lifted it off the shelf, blowing dust off of its contours. It brought about a fit of coughing in him that quieted only when the dust settled. But even so, the thrum of its inner workings bled through the covering and into his fingertips so that he felt as if a million bees had taken residence in his hands. Determined to hand the book off as quickly as possible, he rushed to where Fearsome waited and tried to press it through the orb. At first, it repelled any attempt to force it through the glass. At last, it finally relented and allowed the book to be absorbed into the glass enclosure.

Fearsome immediately glommed onto it, his mind turning the pages rather than his hands. *A neat trick that.* Apparently, Siegfried thought so too as he shared a surprised glance with Alaric.

"Ah!"

Fearsome pressed his hand onto one particularly onerous smelling page that sent plumes of offal wafting through the room. Alaric gagged, and Siegfried held a handkerchief to his nose that he'd retrieved from inside his sleeve, but still his eyes watered as did Alaric's.

"It says here that I may make you invisible with this spell, but you must repeat everything I say, do you understand?"

"I do," Alaric said through clenched teeth and tears running down his cheeks. "Just hurry!"

"Alright then, here we go."

"*Fortunicus optimus.*"

"*Fortunicus optimus.*"

"*Alaricus prime.*"

"*Alaricus prime.*"

"*Invisibilis fac nos.*"

"*Invisibilis fac nos.*"

"*Fiat voluntas tua.*"

"*Fiat voluntas tua.*"

"*Thy will be done.*"

"*Thy will be done.*"

Alaric peered down at himself, or what used to be his body and marveled. Then he turned to Siegfried who had disappeared as well. Even Fearsome no longer appeared inside the clear glass globe. Alaric had little time to process it, for at that moment a commotion of footsteps and voices made its way down the hallway. He walked over to the opening and peered below just as the door to the library blew open and in walked the most hideous of all the creatures, a demon with the face of a mole rat, its eyes alight in an unearthly glow that radiated outward, its claw held out as if to eviscerate its foe.

Frightened, he pulled his head back only to realize he was invisible. Cautiously, he peered below again and saw a face peering back up at him. This time it was a crustacean with the head of a rhino, wearing all black. He caught his breath, scarcely daring to breathe. But for one brief second, it was as

if the man looked through him to the dome, then turned back
to his friends who roamed the library for something, but what?
Whatever it was, they hadn't found it, because they stormed
out the door, their boots furiously tapping the marble below on
their way to the inner chambers. *Alaric's* chambers!

It had begun. I'd read of wars, of the havoc they wrecked
and yet this one seemed especially onerous. We all felt it.
Smelled it in the acidic air. Soon, I threaded my way through
women running to meet the deadline, only to be stopped at the
entrance to line up and wait for their turn into the wentletrap.
The panic evident in their fearful expressions sent a wave of
some unnamed emotion racing through me. Even the starlings
had begun to hammer a steady rhythm and were now fluttering
in the air in waves that changed direction at will. Occasionally, a
faint outline of some demon or other appeared long enough to
cause a stir among the women that had them nearly stampeding
into the wentletrap.

I raced to where the line had formed. "Keep the line
moving!" I yelled to those processing the women through. "You,
from this point back, follow me."

The women turned to each other, their murmurs indicating
their surprise as they reluctantly removed themselves from
the line to follow my lead. I hurried around the rear of the
wentletrap to where a series of trap doors lay hidden beneath
the sod that we had laid to hide the exits. Through a clever
design, the doors would open only when someone pressed on
a hidden lever tucked into the folds of the wentletrap. One by

one, I pressed the levers along the edge and the women ducked into the sloped chambers that led to a massive inner room where women were now grouping. To one side, stored in an auxiliary chamber, sat a series of tables with food and drink. Bunk beds lay end to end so that the women would have a place to sleep while they awaited their orders. The line seemed to go on forever. Soon, the room was filled with women talking, pacing, eating.

Now that the women were safe, I raced off to be sure that Gertrude and Jocelyn's plans to keep the rest of the women at bay until the all-clear proved feasible. Just as I had suspected, the pair had things well in hand. The women's tents were nearly all set up and they were in the process of digging a foxhole that ran the length of their quarters so that they would be less of a target, should it be needed.

Jocelyn saw me and rushed over, her rifle slung across her back and a knife slung on her waistband for easy reach. "Everything's good here, Brigid. We'll look after Beatrice and Birsha, and the Pawn."

I glanced over to see that she was right. The trio had settled into camp life with the rest of them.

"They can stay with us here, but Brigid," Jocelyn said, tapping me on the shoulder, "Henry's looking for you. He seemed pretty frantic."

We had hours left before nightfall, and if the loom had predicted what lay ahead correctly, that's when the attack would begin. And yet I knew it wouldn't be an ordinary raid. No, this would be sorcery, pure and simple. Black magic. I knew no comparable sorcery for what this magic might bring. That thought had my heart racing and my mind whirring.

I grasped Jocelyn's arm. "Where's Henry?"

"He headed for your tent. He has something to tell you."

"Did he say what?"

Jocelyn bit her lip and shook her head, but her green eyes widened, surely a sign that whatever he had to say, it couldn't be good.

"Thanks, Jocelyn. Stay safe."

"You, too."

We hugged briefly, then I flung myself in motion, the hubbub of the camp unlike anything I had witnessed before. I rushed across the road so quickly that I startled a six-mule team and its driver. Their freight filled with supplies nearly upended right there onto the dust-filled road.

I was out of breath by the time I reached Henry who grabbed me by the arms. "Why didn't you tell me?" He shook me, then pulled me to him, his face ashen as he raked his fingers through my hair.

"Tell you what?"

"You know very well what. The loom!"

He pushed me back and in that moment, I saw tears well in his eyes while he explored mine, as if searching for an explanation. So, he knew. My heart stilled and I didn't move.

"What did you see, Henry?" My voice shook, but it couldn't be helped.

"You know very well what I saw. It was you. You were lifted . . . into the sky."

A whoosh of air escaped me and I plopped down right there on the bare earth, my eyes drifting skyward to the clouds that had gathered over the past hour. The billowing gray clouds appeared ominous, like nothing I had seen before. A weird sizzle and pop spewed from them, followed by a hiss.

"I didn't know, Henry. You have to believe me. I knew *something* was wrong . . . *very* wrong, but I wasn't sure what. I just knew some kind of storm was to occur."

"A tornado?" He bent down next to me, clasping my hands in his.

"No," I whispered. "It's not of this world."

"Then what?" He pinched my hands together as if in joint prayer. "*What?*" he demanded when I didn't answer.

"I don't know, Henry. It's some sorcery. I've felt it . . . all day. And last night."

He paused as though he'd heard wrong. "Last night?"

I moved aside to keep from being stepped on by an anxious warrior who wore a duffle bag on her back as she headed for the Wentletrap that appeared abandoned now. The afternoon was waning, and I knew by the position of the sun that nightfall would be upon us in no more than two hours. Two hours to say our goodbyes. Two hours to make peace with the horrible hand dealt us.

"You can't give up, Brigid. You said so yourself that the outcome of the loom could be changed with correct planning."

I *had* said that, and I'd believed it . . . until now. Something had shifted. This was a sorcery too big for any of us, much less me, who had none of my own magic, save for the loom.

"I love you, Henry." I examined his face, his eyes, the set of his mouth, committing it all to memory. For one too brief moment, we kissed, savoring the taste of each other.

When we came up for air, Henry said, "I'm not giving up on you, Brigid. On us. Come!" He stood and grabbed my hand, his will alone pulling me forward.

"But how can we stop it?" I cried as he dragged me through the empty clearing.

"The wentletrap!" He shouted to be heard over the wind that had picked up, spewing leaves and branches every which way across the compound. "You'll be safe there. We'll battle this curse, you and I. We won't go down without a fight!"

"Thank you, Henry," I whispered into the wind. But I knew his test of will wouldn't be enough. Nothing would be. This time, all I could do was pray.

39

It was too late. They weren't going to make it to the Bookbinders in time.

"We'd best hunker down," Chame Leon told Liz Herd.

He spotted a narrow chasm in which to burrow their way in. The weather was changing, nightfall close at hand. Some great magic had been released. He'd seen it too many times over a lifetime not to realize that whatever happened, they would all be changed by it.

"So it beginsss," Liz Herd said, sorrow filling the contours of her face.

"I'm afraid so," he agreed. "But at least we have each other. M'lady?"

He ushered her into the sanctuary that would become their home for the foreseeable future. A mere slit in the earth's crust. But it would do. Because they had each other.

Alaric peered through the transom window at the actions below. Diāmons filled the corners of his kingdom. Everywhere they stood, the flowers withered on their stalks. Roses wilted and penstemon drooped, their bell-shaped petals dropping one by one. Even the grass beneath their feet browned as though the soles of their boots contained vinegar and soap. He growled, tired of his cage-like prison in the attic. What sort of man hid in the dome of his library while his kingdom fell?

"I'm going out there," Alaric growled.

"To do what, sir?"

Siegfried, who had been perusing a particularly odious grimoire, its pages wafting plumes of foul air, let out a moue of disgust and slammed the book closed. Particles of floating dust appeared golden from the light cascading through the window.

"I already snuck out to retrieve food from the pantries. The cooks have all fled to the countryside to be free of the Diāmons."

"I know, but I can't be seen sniveling in the upper chambers while my fortress burns." Alaric drove a fist into his palm.

"Technically," Fearsome said, yawning, "your fortress isn't burning, and what do you propose to do once you're free? The Jackals still haven't returned, nor the Chessmen."

Alaric stared out the window to where the Chessmen once stood on black and white squares to await their turn at life. Now, the board set empty except for two black crows who strutted among the bi-colored squares as if playing a game only they knew. How he wished his warriors would return. And what of the book, the incantation he had invoked to return Brigid to him? Once here, he planned to hold her hostage until the entire Bookbinder Kingdom fell to its knees in fealty. He sneezed and wiped at his nose with his sleeve.

Oh, he had no doubt the Bookbinders would fight for Brigid, Henry the greatest champion of all. Henry, who stood to run the kingdom when his turn came to lead. Better to head him off at the pass.

"I can stand it no more."

Before the pair could protest, Alaric climbed down the ladder and listened for footsteps outside the library door. Hearing none, he opened the door and shut it behind him as quietly as possible, then raced down the corridor in stockinged feet. Thank goodness no one could see him. He would be the laughing stock of the kingdom to be seen so.

His heart skipped a beat when around the corner he nearly ran into one of the Diāmons. At the last minute, he stepped aside and stood next to the wall of the corridor, his breathing labored from both fear and stealth. Wasting no time, he rushed through the fortress hallways until he reached his room. But when he opened it, he stood back, stunned. Someone had pawed through his belongings. Everywhere drawers lay empty, their contents dumped onto the Aubergine carpets. Even the covers on his bed were pulled back, pillows tossed to the floor, the dirt from his potted plants strewn here and there, a myriad of footsteps leaving traces of the Diāmons who had made them.

For one brief moment, Alaric couldn't move. But then he drew himself up and marched over to the balcony doors in a fury and flung them open, not caring who might be watching.

What he witnessed left a pang of sadness in his chest. For the zoo, that lay due east, had been flung open, and even now animals of every size and stripe roamed freely through the roadways, all the homes and shops boarded up tight against the marauders. Zebras and elephants, hippos and elands. He crouched back when a long-necked giraffe inspected the balcony with him on it. The loud trumpet of a bull elephant led the charge, hoofbeats tapping the cobblestone below. An utter menagerie of oddities in a once ordered kingdom.

"Oh dear God!" He hadn't realized that he had spoken aloud until he heard a voice cry out.

"Hey! Is someone up there?" A young man dressed in mauve tights and a skirted coat peered up at him. "I know you're hiding, but you best not be inside the king's quarters. He'll have your backside if he catches you."

Alaric, who had been holding his breath until now, stifled a laugh. The cheeky man. He would have to reward him once he wrested control from the Diāmons. For now, he must lay low.

But first, before returning to the library, he decided to take one last gander out onto the turret walls. What he saw once he arrived there gave him the smallest gesture of hope. For there, far in the distance, he recognized the outline of something that looked like ants threading their way to the kingdom. But they weren't ants. They were Jackals and the Chessmen. Relief flooded him in waves. Now if he could somehow warn them of what lay ahead and prepare an assault to rid the kingdom of the Diāmons once and for all…

Siegfried! The man had spies everywhere. He had no sooner thought it and turned when he ran straight into a Diāmon with a thud.

"Halt! Who goes there?" the monster shouted. But Alaric was already running on slippered feet, never stopping until he arrived at the library.

As I made my way through the bowels of the wentletrap, the air felt charged, as though an electric storm had passed through, lighting the warriors with its power. Everyone spoke at once, the room in chaos that echoed my own chaotic feelings. The constant movement and sheer noise seemed to bubble inside me until I boiled over with the one word, "Stop!"

It was as if I were the conductor, the warriors, the band, and I had commanded them to halt with a wave of my baton because silence reigned as each and every person looked one to the other to determine what had caused me to snap.

"Stop!" I cried again, the words softer now.

Winnifred came rushing to my side, her brown hair disheveled, her eyes even more owlish than usual behind her round glasses. "What is it? What's happened?"

How could I burden her with all my worries, my fears? I blinked rapidly to gain a control I didn't feel. "I'm okay now," I said. "I just need to speak to the women."

Winnifred hurried to grab a chair so I could use it as my dais. Then she and Lofgren urged the women to give me space. How much should I say? After all, I didn't know what my fate might be, but I knew something was about to happen soon. I couldn't delay any longer. I peered at Henry with watery eyes and saw that he was in the dark like the others.

I climbed up onto my makeshift podium. "Ladies?" I bit back my tears. "I want you to know how much you have all meant to me this past year. To acknowledge your hard work and caring. If it weren't for you, the slaves would never have been released and many of them would have died."

A bevy of murmurs stirred the still air then silenced as the women waited for more.

"We still have much work to do, I'm afraid."

Here, I placed my hand over my heart, the universal signal that we were all in this together. A flood of emotion stirred within me to see the women do likewise.

"I love all of you like a family. As many of you know, my family has been thrown to the four winds." A lump formed at the base of my throat and I fought to keep from letting it show in my voice. "So I've counted on you to fill the void."

The room erupted with a flurry of nods and agreement. Many looked at me in pity, but it wasn't pity I needed right now. I needed their attention.

"I will be gone soon."

Before I could finish, the chaos returned. I threw up my hands to quell the tide of emotion.

"It can't be helped," I added quickly. "Life is about to change for me, my fate sealed." Before they could protest I stopped them by saying, "But I will return!"

Henry pressed my hand and peered up at me, his eyebrows a ledge of misgiving. "What are you talking about, Brigid? You're safe here, with me."

He didn't understand. I would never be safe so long as what was out there needed me for some goal that I had yet to glean.

The tears that I held back now fell freely down my cheeks.

"You're wrong, Henry. I'm not safe. And kismet awaits."

I turned toward the women lest I break down and fail to say what I had planned. "Winnifred, you're in charge now. Watch after our warriors. I trust you to lead them as you see fit. But I ask for one thing."

"Anything," she said, her eyes blinking rapidly behind her thick lenses.

"We must change the traditions, make new ones, kinder ones, ones that serve *us*."

As if the traditions had heard and were offended, I felt one welt, then another and another, my body taking blow upon blow until I looked like a ripe watermelon, but I continued, determined to have my say this one final time.

"We can do it. We can make change. You and I…together."

Before the last word left my mouth a cheer erupted and women clung to each other, threw up their fists in resistance and shouted their glee, as surely the traditions couldn't hurt all of us at once.

Just then I heard a shout from one corner of the room. It was Yesimieh who yelled, "Wait! I hear something fluttering at the door."

Dusk was upon us, the silken moon beginning to rise in the skylight above us. Everyone stopped to listen. I lent my ear to that of those around me. There it was! A fluttering sound, just as she had predicted. What on earth could it be?

Then I heard a rumble in the far-off sky, and another and another, each one louder than the previous one.

Phinney! Where is Phinney?

My heart took flight in my chest. "Phinney! Has anyone seen her?"

Women throughout the cavernous room shook their heads, just as concerned as me. Then it came to me. The fluttering! It was pounding the door…with wings.

"Phinney!" I called, jumping down from my make-shift stage. "I'm coming!"

I raced to the door, Henry hot on my heels.

"Don't go out there," he urged, holding me back with his arms.

"Let me go!" I cried. "I have to save her."

"I'll only let you go if you stay inside. It's too late, the storm is here. Phinney's smart. She'll find a way to survive."

But I wasn't listening. As soon as he released me, I bolted for the door and opened it, the sky above aswirl in stars that angled toward me in a boiling cauldron of movement. There, beleaguered and battered was my beloved blue falcon, Phinney. On a gust of wind, she blew in over my head, just as I snatched one of her feathers and was sucked beyond the lintel, Henry reaching to save me. Thomas, who had been lingering at the edges of the crowd, grabbed a hold of Henry's coat, a dozen other hands grasping him and holding him back against the wind. The woman who told me that she could keep the sky from falling pressed her way forward and began an incantation. For one brief moment, Henry held me by the hand, but then the storm was too great and the two of us were sucked backwards and up even as the woman kept up an atonal chant that reminded me of the Mongolian throat singers. Her magic swirled around us, but in the end it was only strong enough to save Henry, who began to descend, even as I began to rise. At last, our fingers parted and the look of devastation that lined his face became a jagged wound to my heart. Like a ragdoll, I reached out with my hands and feet, but the swirling torrent pulled me ever higher into the sky, a coldness unlike anything I had experienced before enveloping me in its mist. And then, Henry was gone.

As I ascended, the light from the wentletrap grew smaller and smaller until, finally, the door to it closed, and Henry was no more.

"I love you, Henry," I whispered.

For a time, I lay in the womb of the chasm that held the universe and all that was in it. Suspended there, my mind seemed to slow. Once upon a time, Kahwhita told me a tale about the line between sun and moon, heaven and earth. She said that evil people disappeared into the Cosmos, whereas those who had lived a decent life reunited with the forests and prairies where the ancestors resided. I saw them now. Faces from the past, and faces I did not know.

But it was not my turn to die, I saw, as I shivered among the stars, in awe at the utter beauty of the universe, while quivering at the fear of what lay ahead.

For several moments, I hung like this, suspended between the two worlds, neither one ready to claim me. Then I heard the words of a woman, Skywoman from Kahwhita's myth, I felt certain. But I could see now that Skywoman was actually the woman I had met months back who had told me she could fly. At the time I had pegged her as crazy. Now, I could see that I was wrong.

"It is not your time, my beloved." Her voice held the power of the universe and once again a lump formed in my throat to know that the end could be so breathtaking, so beautiful.

You are loved.

The words came from inside myself and for the first time in my life, I felt peace.

I am loved.

I would need those words as succor in the coming days, months, and possibly years ahead.

Then the world went black and I felt myself returning, as though a babe being expelled from the womb, only this time it was from a new womb. Some other woman's in some other time and place.

I felt a whoosh of air, then emptied out into the hollow of the earth, stars all around me.

"Where am I?" I demanded to no one.

Inside, I heard the words, "You are here, and you are mine."

The pit of my stomach gnawed with an unnamed worry. Panicked now, I pressed my hands against the sphere that held me in its grasp. Suddenly, I heard a click and a lever popped open along with the globe.

The library!

I was in the fortress library, but what was that noise all around me? To my surprise, I held tight to one of Phinney's feathers. Kahwhita would say it was a sign. A good luck omen. To me, it was a lifeline.

With haste, I made my way out of the globe and tiptoed over to the transom from where the noises were sounding below. I peered out over the landscape, but shock gripped me to see such chaos. For there, scattered throughout the kingdom were animals, too many to name, and Jackals, followed by the Chessmen, whose movements rocked the very earth beneath them, causing me to skitter to the floor and slide.

"What in the—" I crawled back over to the window where there, below me, I saw something so strange, so awful that it made the hairs on my arms stand on end as if the electrical storm had indeed found its way inside me.

"At last, the prodigal son has returned home."

I turned, but no one was there.

"Now you will see what it means to be a prisoner of *my* kingdom."

Alaric! I knew that voice.

I fell on my bottom, defeated at last, just as the loom had predicted.

If I squinted hard, I could just make out a shimmer shaped like a figure of a man. A very evil man. "So, Alaric? What do you want from me?"

He laughed. "Why, your kingdom, of course."

I quailed at such a simple statement even as my skin prickled with an unnamed fear. But then I felt it, as though a seed inside me. I lay a hand on my belly.

"It is here, inside you," a woman's voice said.

I searched the room for the woman, the same one I had heard amongst the stars. Who was she? For me, the mere fact that she believed she could fly was an auger to a failing mind, so much so that I had forgotten to ask her name.

"*What* is inside me?" I whispered.

"Eh? Speak up!" Alaric shouted.

But I dare not answer. He couldn't know what I was only beginning to suspect.

"Henry is with you," the woman continued. "In there."

I pointed at my stomach. And then I knew. Henry's seed lay inside me, awaiting the day that we would be united as a family. I closed my eyes and thanked the heavens even as I knew I would protect my girl-child with my life. For although I had no way of knowing whether the child would be boy or girl, in my heart of hearts I knew this infant inside my womb was a she and I would name her Amora . . . Love. An ode to her father, Henry, who I would love to my dying day.

About the Author

Author **Carol L. Craig** is an author, editor, and gardener at heart. She has edited for numerous award-winning authors. You can find her on Facebook, Instagram, LinkedIn, X, and TikTok. She has published six books besides **Restoring The Loom**:

In the Fantasy Tapestry Series:
Dancing the Loom
Threading the Loom
Restoring the Loom

Southern Historical Novels:
The Vast In Between
The Great Unraveling

The Mending Warrior Series that blends suspense and romance:
A Thousand Bits of Wonderful
A Walk in the Dark
Look for my upcoming novel: The Heart of the Storm

She has been a guest speaker for Women Writing the West in Tucson, Arizona, has given one-on-one editing sessions at the Willamette Writers Conference. She has helped new writers get their start. And, she has spent many happy hours with friends at Colonyhouse, a writer's retreat in Oregon.

While at home in Oregon, she enjoys writing, reading,

gardening and editing as well as coffee klatches with her husband and dog, Parker.

Be Sure To Sign Up For Her Newsletter At

www.editinggallery.com to read articles from writers, editors, artists, filmmakers, book cover designers, interior book cover designs, professional bloggers, as well as those in marketing.

You Can Find Carol At

www.editinggallery.com

facebook.com/EditingGallery1

Instagram: @clcraig7

ACKNOWLEDGEMENTS

So many people help writers in any number of ways. Ever the former University of Oregon librarian, Laine Stambaugh has kept me growing as a writer with her handouts and Writers Digest Magazines. She's also a great fantasy author so be sure to check out the first two novels in her series: *Raven Wakes the Dawn* and *Raven in the Runes*. She also has a new book coming out: *The Sea Raven*. Thanks also to Elaine Stec with her cheerleading and her ongoing friendship.

Authors whose work I edit help me to become both a better editor and author. Matt Pearson has an awesome suspense series that I hope to see published soon. His tagline? *What if James Bond were a Christian?* And his wife Aly has a great children's book, *Bob the Wonder Horse*. Then there's Julie Demos, who wrote a time travel novel set in ancient Greece. Her prose is absolutely beautiful! I can't fail to mention Evan Howard whose dedication to the craft never fails to amaze me.

Always my support and the man who keeps me on task is my husband Les. Without him, I could have never published these novels. (Thanks, Henry!) And to the other two loves of my life, my daughter, Sara, and granddaughter, Kaylee. They keep me smiling! And finally, to all my gardening friends who send me photos of their lovely gardens. Want to win this author's heart? Just send me pictures of your garden. It doesn't hurt if there's a pond in there and some birds to go with.

Threading the Loom
By Carol Craig

In this reading group guide for Restoring the Loom, *I have included an introduction, questions for discussion, concepts for enhancing your reading experience, and a Q & A with the author, Carol Craig. Hopefully, the questions will help spur new ideas for your reading group so that your book club will enjoy more in-depth discussions. We also hope that the ideas that flow will provide a more meaningful and enriching experience. Enjoy!*

Introduction

Brigid Anne Dunsmore and her band of warriors have fought the Jackals and the Chessmen. Now she faces her worst enemy yet, the Diamōns, a group of dangerously frightening creatures. But first she must restore the magic loom that set in motion the tragedy that has befallen her people when the loom goes dark, and with it the kingdom. She has only a short time to prepare her people for the siege ahead. But can she restore her good name and build an underground fortress in time to prevent calamity from striking in this third novel of the Tapestry Series?

In this third book in the series, Brigid Anne Dunsmore must undo the mistake she unwittingly wrought in sewing new threads into the loom, threads that unbeknownst to her were cursed with black magic. Scorned by those around her, she must once again prove her worthiness to her new family and friends. Only then will she be forgiven. But those who know her best, know her heart, know that she would never do anything to hurt her community nor the women she has fought with and for.

Restoring the Loom is a story of love, friendship, and sisterhood in a time of deep strife. It reminds us what it means to be human, under the worst of circumstances.

Discussion Questions and Topics

1. In the previous book, we discussed some of the metaphors of the loom and what it represents. Besides the computer, what other parts of history and society are reflected in this book?

2. What ties does the loom have to slavery and child labor at the turn of the century when children were forced to work long hours at dangerous jobs beneath the looms in the woolen mills? What laws were enacted to protect children and workers?

3. Is there anything comparable in today's society to those times in the past when people were enslaved or forced into labor? (Hint: think about child trafficking in our own country and others, or countries that draw in workers from other countries then take their passports and refuse to allow them to leave. Or workers in our own country brought in from

other places to work the fields, who put in long hours under hazardous conditions.)

4. The need for cotton led to a system of slavery within our country. How have things changed for the better since the abolition of slavery? How have they remained the same? What systems still exist that prevent fair and equal treatment of some minorities? (Hint: red-lining and gentrification, or practices that prevent certain minorities from obtaining jobs or fair housing.)

5. What makes one person take up the mantle when it comes to injustice and not another? Does something in that person's background make it more likely for that to happen?

6. What strains does war have on relationships? Does it make them stronger, or tear at the bonds? How can society serve to strengthen those bonds in times of great strife? How can we as individuals do the same?

7. How are *society's* bonds strained during times of war? What were the differences between WWII and Vietnam, in that regard? Or between Afghanistan and Iraq, for that matter?

8. What can we do as a people to make life better for veterans and for families of veterans, including for the children whose parent often leaves for war and returns as a changed person?

9. Does Brigid redeem herself by the end of Restoring the

Loom?

10. If you could make one change to create a better world, what would it be and why?

Boost Your Book Club Experience

1. What creative ways could you use to make the world more magical for your children, or nieces or nephews? To help make them more resilient in tough times?

2. What could you do with your children to strengthen family bonds? Could you sew costumes together, build a treehouse or fort like the women and elves in the series?

3. As always, nature plays an important role in *The Tapestry Series*. Consider bringing a net, a magnifying glass, and a carrying case out into the field to identify plant species and insects. Or take a set of binoculars out and identify birds or animals—anything that will engage your family in a way that strengthens family bonds and engages your child in nature.

4. Write your own fantasy novel with your child and let them draw pictures. These days, if you have the money you can actually have them made into a real book that they can have as a keepsake. Or just do it the old-fashioned way using paper, crayons, and staples.

A Conversation with Carol Craig

Why did you choose the title *Restoring the Loom* for the third book in the series?

This book is about redemption and restoration. In Threading the Loom, Brigid made a terrible mistake, though inadvertent. She was given thread that she thought would enhance the loom's abilities only to learn that she was sadly mistaken. Life is often like this. Our intentions are good, even honorable, but may be viewed in a different light by other people. All we can do is to hope that our good intentions are viewed as thus, and try to do what we feel is right.

Despite everything that Brigid does to try to create a decent world where her people will be safe and happy, she often finds herself treading water. Have you ever experienced this in your own life?

I think we have all experienced this. We try our best to be good human beings, to make a positive impact on the world. But our agenda is not everyone's agenda and in a world where you have the Alarics and the Diāmons, as it were—whatever that means to you—you risk attack or failure. But like Brigid, I try to remain positive, to hope that we one day make this place a better world where people help each other instead of hurt each other. Where we lift each other up instead of pull each other down. This is where I see an especially important role for women whose strengths are often minimized and yet who are equally important and have qualities necessary, now more than ever, in an increasingly polarized world.

How is Fantasy different from other genres and how does that inform this novel?

Fantasy allows me to take heavy subjects, such as politics and religion, and remove them from the everyday arena. To remove the lens of this party or that party, this affiliation or that affiliation, and to instead see what happens when we can view things from a more holistic approach. See that right and wrong are not absolute and that there are many shades of gray when talking about such in-depth subjects as politics and religion, crime and punishment. As Americans, we tend to put a patriotic spin on things, never delving into the darker aspects of what it means to be an American, what it means to be a good citizen in the world today or what role we play in creating havoc among other nations for our own gain. It also delves into what nations will do to keep their citizens moving in the direction they want them to go, either through propaganda or through more coercive means, i.e. "the traditions."

After years of novels that reflect these very same issues, like Dostoyevsky's *Crime and Punishment*, Tolstoy's *War and Peace* or George Orwell's *1984*, we are still forced to navigate these same subjects, only they have been amplified because of "the loom," computers and technology. The problems this next generation faces are now on steroids. Part of me believes we need to go back to a more simplistic time, if there ever was such a thing. Where we live a more clean, sustainable life, which I guess is why I love the Tiny House movement so much because it offers up the idea that we don't need to pollute, to use up too much of a carbon footprint, to pit the haves vs. the have nots. It focuses on family and community, and more quality time spent living vs. surviving. I don't know the answer. I just know that if enough people don't begin questioning the way we live, things will never change and we will continue to fight to have more and more and more, while spiritually having less and less and less. That dialogue needs to be part of the national lexicon.

Will Brigid's character change once she has a child?

Life is never the same once children are involved because now we have an obligation to this person we brought into the world and the world we hand that child. We have to look at our own lives and ask, "Is this the world we want our children to grow up in, with fewer freedoms, less free speech or none at all, and where privacy is a thing of the past?"

In Mark Zuckerberg's 2019 Facebook F8 Conference, he said there is no such thing as privacy. But he also said, "I believe we should be working toward a world where people can speak privately, freely knowing that their information will be seen only by the people they want to see it and won't stick around forever."

Where do you think AI fits into all this?

It's too soon to say, but pundits are comparing it to the Industrial Revolution in terms of how it will change society and our individual lives. The frightening thing is, *we don't know!* Just like with the computer, it can make our lives better or worse, depending on the outcome. Computers allow us to have information at our fingertips, but it also allows disinformation. It allows us to connect with people all over the world in a way we couldn't before which can bring us together, but also separates us with a constant barrage of tribalist viewpoints designed to keep us apart and create an "us versus them" mentality.

These are some of the pros and cons I see with AI:

They allow us the ability to create right at our fingertips, but are they stealing material to do so, and if so, who will lose out as a result? Many artists have found jobs in the tech industry. How will that affect them?

One con is that AI can show anyone, anywhere, doing anything, at any time, so truth, which has been in short supply lately anyway, will now reach a new low. After all, if a person can be shown doing or saying something they've never done or said, it can affect any number of things from jobs, to homelife, to the judicial system. *Think about that.* That's a scary proposition and something we must all take into account as we dip our toe into this new wondrous and dangerous world.

What are you working on now?

I am writing a sequel to *A Thousand Bits of Wonderful and A Walk in the Dark* from my *Mending Warriors Mysteries*. Its title is *Heart of the Storm* and it has Native American elements. It also has a murder mystery (of course), and delves into the underbelly of what happens to wild horses on public land when the horses are forced to compete with livestock and the desire for "unspoiled" land. Like all of the books in the series, this one also deals with the trauma vets face when they return from war-torn areas like Iraq or Afghanistan or Syria, only this time it's about a female vet and the unique challenges a woman faces in the military.

Do you think the world can change in time to save the planet?

Only if we work as one. Only if we're committed to making that change and if we're all pulling together to make it happen. We can't continue to deforest the earth, to cleave large wounds into the ground in order to obtain rare metals, resulting in a toxic mix of waste that floods our rivers and streams. We can't continue to destroy large populations of wildlife that inhabit our earth because it's more convenient for humans without them. Right now, we destroy 10 million hectares of forest per year, roughly the size of Portugal. Some estimates suggest that we are losing 137 species of plants, animals and insects per year due to habitat loss. While further estimates suggest that it's more like a whopping 50,000 species per year! Let me repeat that. *50,000!* The size of our homes went from an average of 983 square feet in the 1950s to an average of 2355 square feet now, meaning a much larger footprint and the destruction of land that once housed wildlife as well as flora and fauna. When is enough enough? How much do we have to have in order to feel good enough? Why can't we be satisfied with less so that we have time for more? More time with our families. More time with our communities. More time spent in nature or doing the things we love? Those are the questions we need to ask ourselves as we

head boldly into this new century. I'm hoping that young people will take up the mantle. It's up to them now to save our world .
. .

9 781736 222782